'Tricia Stringer is a bestselling autho[r]... storytelling. She's back, and better tha[n ever]... about the journeys we take, professio[nal...] *on Track* is a double treat, combining two of my favourite things: train journeys and excellent storytelling…Pure (train) escapism but with guts and heart – and an ending that will make you smile.'

—*Better Reading*

'*Back on Track* is an engaging tale of troubled relationships, ageism, family drama and hope…Another warm-hearted and engaging read by Stringer.'

—*Canberra Weekly*

'…another great story of family and friends with Tricia, [who is] a master at producing authentic and real people and places that take you right to the centre of the community.'

—*Great Reads and Tea Leaves* on *Keeping up Appearances*

'Popular author Tricia Stringer returns with another engaging tale of friendship, family drama and changing times…[she] once again demonstrates why she is one of the best chroniclers of small town Australia.'

—*Canberra Weekly* on *Keeping up Appearances*

'"Masterful" gets used a lot in reviews, but Tricia Stringer really is. With *Birds of a Feather*, she firmly takes her place as one of Australia's most accomplished writers.'

—*Better Reading*

'Warm, sincere and thoughtful, *Birds of a Feather* is an engaging contemporary novel sure to delight readers, new and old.'

—*Book'd Out*

'A good, warm-hearted read with relatable and empathetic characters.'

—*Canberra Weekly* on *Birds of a Feather*

'A book you can't put down ... Stringer's skill is in weaving the experiences of different generations of women together, with sensitivity and familiarity, gently showing how context can shape women's decisions ... A moving, feel-good, warm read about strong, loving women ... the exact book we all need right now.'

—*Mamamia* on *The Family Inheritance*

'... a polished family saga ... all delivered with intelligence, wit and emotion in equal measures ... Perfection!'

—*Better Reading* on *The Family Inheritance*

'Tricia Stringer is an intuitive and tender-hearted storyteller who displays a real ability to interrogate issues that affect families and individuals. *The Family Inheritance* is another gratifying read from Tricia Stringer.'

—*Mrs B's Book Reviews*

'This book is the equivalent of a hot bath or a box of chocolates, it's comforting and an absolute pleasure to immerse yourself in ... If you enjoy well-written family sagas, look no further. *The Model Wife* is perfect.'

—*Better Reading*

'Tricia Stringer's *The Model Wife* is a beautiful multi-dimensional family saga.'

—*Beauty and Lace*

'[A] heartfelt saga.'

—*Herald Sun* on *The Model Wife*

'*The Model Wife* is a beautiful story with familiar challenges and a strength of a family who are connected via their life experiences together.'

—*Chapter Ichi*

'A well-written, engaging story of the everyday challenges of life and love … a wise, warm, and wonderful story.'

—*Book'd Out* on *The Model Wife*

'Delivers a gentle satisfaction that makes it a great choice for a lazy Sunday afternoon read.'

—*Books + Publishing* on *Table for Eight*

'A witty, warm and wise story of how embracing the new with an open heart can transform your life.'

—*Herald Sun* on *Table for Eight*

'… a moving, feel-good read … a warm and uplifting novel of second chances and love old and new in a story of unlikely dining companions thrown together on a glamorous cruise.'

—*Sunday Mail* on *Table for Eight*

'A wonderful story of friendships, heartbreak and second chances that may change your life.'

—*Beauty and Lace* on *Table for Eight*

'Stringer's inviting new novel is sprinkled with moments of self reflection, relationship building, friendships and love.'

—*Mrs B's Book Reviews* on *Table for Eight*

'Tricia has no trouble juggling a large cast and ensuring we get to know and connect with them … captivated me start to finish; if it wasn't the wishing myself on board for a relaxing and pampered break from reality, it was connecting with the characters and hoping they managed to find what they were looking for. Definitely a book I didn't want to put down!'
—*Beauty and Lace* on *Table for Eight*

'A heart-warming novel that celebrates friendships old and new, reminding us that it's never too late to try again … If you enjoy stories that explore connections between people and pay tribute to the endurance of love and friendship, you will love Stringer's new novel. *Table For Eight* is a beautiful book … If you're looking for a getaway but don't quite have the time or funds, look no further – this book is your next holiday. Pull up a deck chair and enjoy.'
—*Better Reading* on *Table for Eight*

about the author

Tricia Stringer is a bestselling and multiple award-winning author. Her books include *Back on Track*, *Keeping up Appearances*, *Birds of a Feather*, *The Family Inheritance*, *The Model Wife*, *Table for Eight*, seven rural romances and a historical saga set in the unforgiving landscape of nineteenth-century Flinders Ranges.

Tricia grew up on a farm in country South Australia and has spent most of her life in rural communities, as owner of a post office and bookshop, as a teacher and librarian, and now as a full-time writer. She lives on the traditional lands of the Narungga people, in the beautiful Copper Coast region, with her husband Daryl, travelling and exploring Australia's diverse communities and landscapes, and sharing her passion for the country and its people through her authentic stories and their vivid characters.

For further information and to sign up for her quarterly newsletter go to triciastringer.com or connect with Tricia on Facebook or Instagram @triciastringerauthor

Also by Tricia Stringer

Table for Eight
The Model Wife
The Family Inheritance
Birds of a Feather
Keeping up Appearances
Back on Track

Queen of the Road
Right as Rain
Riverboat Point
Between the Vines
A Chance of Stormy Weather
Come Rain or Shine
Something in the Wine

The Flinders Ranges Series
Heart of the Country
Dust on the Horizon
Jewel in the North

head *for the hills*

TRICIA STRINGER

HEAD FOR THE HILLS
© 2024 by Tricia Stringer
ISBN 9781867247746

First published on Gadigal Country in Australia in 2024
by HQ Fiction, an imprint of HQBooks (ABN 47 001 180 918),
a subsidiary of HarperCollins Publishers Australia Pty Limited (ABN 36 009 913 517).

HarperCollins acknowledges the Traditional Custodians of the lands upon which we live and work, and pays respect to Elders past and present.

The right of Tricia Stringer to be identified as the author of this work has been asserted by her in accordance with the *Copyright Amendment (Moral Rights) Act 2000*.

This work is copyright. Apart from any use as permitted under the *Copyright Act 1968*, no part may be reproduced, copied, scanned, stored in a retrieval system, recorded, or transmitted, in any form or by any means, without the prior written permission of the publisher. Without limiting the author's and publisher's exclusive rights, any unauthorised use of this publication to train generative artificial intelligence (AI) technologies is expressly prohibited.

This is a work of fiction. Names, characters, places, and incidents are either the product of the author's imagination or are used fictitiously, and any resemblance to actual persons, living or dead, business establishments, events, or locales is entirely coincidental.

A catalogue record for this book is available from the National Library of Australia
www.librariesaustralia.nla.gov.au

Printed and bound in Australia by McPherson's Printing Group

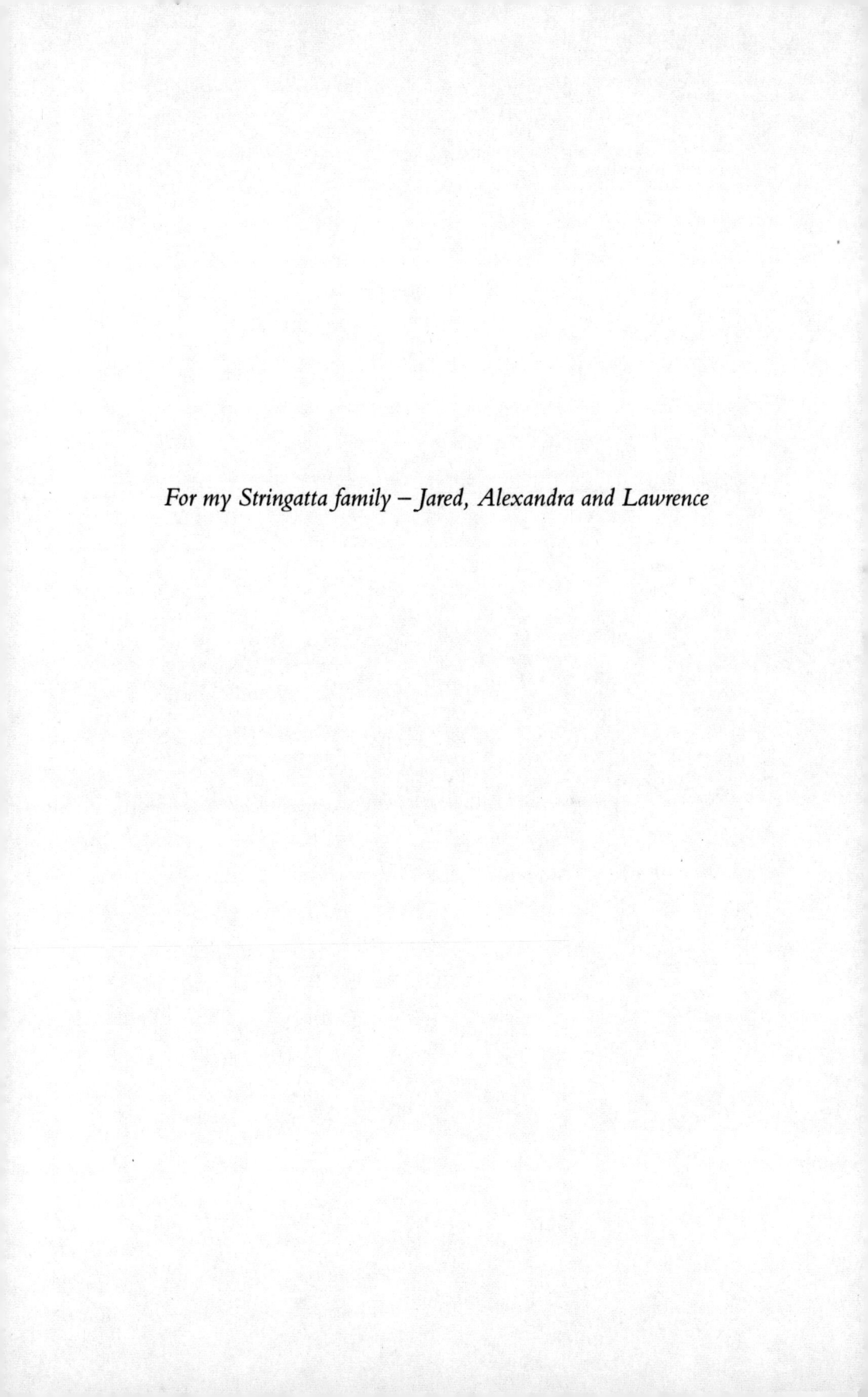

For my Stringatta family – Jared, Alexandra and Lawrence

one

It was the coldest of days – one of those Adelaide Hills winter mornings when the damp infiltrated from the outside and the chill permeated deep inside your bones. It hadn't stopped the good people of Jesserton from gathering in the Lutheran church for the funeral of Gunter Brost. The service had been short, after which his two sons had stood at the door as people had departed and stiffly thanked them for their attendance. Then they'd climbed into their smart hire car and driven away.

Margot Pedrick and her husband, Dennis, had lived next door to Gunter since they'd married and had built their home on the rolling hills beside his property. Margot had been prepared for his sons' lack of courtesy. They'd lost touch with the community they'd grown up in. Once they'd left, she'd asked those still braving the cold and lingering outside the church back to her home. It was almost lunchtime and she'd made two big pots of soup and purchased lots of crusty bread. There were slabs of cake and plates of biscuits to go with tea or coffee and of course there were gluten-free biscuits, eggless cake and a vegan slice.

"Great spread as always, Margot." Martin Threadgold joined her. He was a tall man but hunched in a way that made his jacket appear to be slipping from his shoulders. Margot badly wanted to brush away the large cake crumb that had caught in his beard.

"I'm glad I could do something for our dear neighbour," she said.

"Gunter's sons couldn't wait to leave."

"It's a pity they weren't a close family."

"I heard they emptied his cottage into a skip, locked the door and plan to never return."

She'd heard that rumour too. "That's not quite true—"

"And the *For Sale* sign has gone up already."

Margot frowned. "When did—"

"Poor Gunter's not even in the ground and they can't wait to get their hands on his assets."

"What *For Sale* sign?" Gunter's driveway was at the end of the no through road that ran past the Pedricks' front gate. "I haven't seen one."

"There's one on the other side of his property that faces one of our holiday rentals. Lot more traffic that way. I reckon it must have gone up while we were paying our respects in the church. Those sons of his couldn't even wait for the dust to settle."

Martin's wife, Anne, joined them, and to Margot's relief brushed at the crumbs in Martin's beard then began to discuss the large turnout they'd had at the church, and who'd been missing and why.

"It was wonderful of the mayor to come," Anne said.

Martin snorted. "Esther Jelinski never misses an opportunity to be seen."

"She was acknowledging Gunter's contribution to our community." Anne shook her head at her husband. "She knows how much he'll be missed. And at least she's keeping Gunter's lawyer-man company."

Margot glanced at Esther, who was indeed engaged in deep conversation with Elvin Wagner, a tall man in a very expensive suit who her sister had introduced to her as Gunter's executor.

Others joined them and Margot eased away. She wanted to tell her husband about the *For Sale* sign but as she moved around a group of people she saw that Dennis was ensconced at the bar. He'd put some wine aside for those who preferred it and was now propped there with several blokes, each with a glass of red in their hands.

Margot veered off and plucked a plate of gluten-free biscuits and one of cake from the table. They'd talk as soon as everyone had left. As sad as it was that Gunter was gone, this was the opportunity she and Dennis had been waiting for.

She moved among her guests offering food or a comfortable chair if they required one, content in her role as host. At times like this she was glad she'd insisted on a large entertaining space when they'd extended and enclosed the back verandah. It was perfect for this occasion and the many other gatherings that had taken place in it since their children had been teenagers.

She cast her gaze over the outdoor kitchen with big windows and doors that could be wide open or closed like they were now, dressed with elegant drapes looped back to let in what light there was on such a dull day. The furniture was casual but comfortable and her guests were being kept warm by stylish gas heaters. The whole room was topped off with soft furnishings in autumn tones, a small variety of glossy indoor plants, and an extra assortment of chairs brought from the rest of the house for today.

"This cake is so moist, Margot. You're such a good cook." Another of Gunter's long-time friends, Thelma Schmidt, helped herself to a slice from the plate and wandered towards the Threadgolds.

Margot took a moment to enjoy the small warm glow her compliment had brought. From the corner of her eye she spied her older sister, Roslyn, standing alone in front of the window. Roslyn and Gunter had been long-time friends and, although she'd not said as much, Margot knew she'd taken his death hard. Roslyn had her back to the room facing towards Gunter's property. It suddenly struck Margot that her sister might know a bit more about what was going on with the sale. She swapped her almost-empty plates for a bowl of choc chip biscuits — they were Roslyn's favourites — and set off with a fizz of optimism.

Roslyn stared from the window at the grey day, rolling her shoulders against the shiver that shuddered down her spine. Dear Gunter was gone. It had been sudden, unexpected, a shock, and she felt a sadness that ran deep like a chill in her bones. Surprisingly it was worse than when her own husband had died almost ten years ago to the day. Richard's had been a slow demise from cancer. His death had been a release that had buried her in guilt as well as loss. With Gunter's death she simply mourned the departure of a good friend but somehow it ached more. They'd known each other longer than Roslyn had known her husband. Gunter's friendship had come freely, no expectations or strings attached. Until now.

She'd been surprised when his sons had turned up at her place before the funeral and stunned when they'd informed her Gunter had included her in his will. Not just as a beneficiary of a small token to mark a friendship — although the row of flying ceramic ducks that had hung on his wall were now hers, handed over awkwardly, loosely wrapped in old newspaper — but as paid caretaker of his property until it sold and settled. And of bigger significance: the caretaker's position was not a weekly stipend but would be paid in the future in the form of a percentage of the sale price of the property.

Roslyn had been speechless. Gunter's place was worth a fortune. The two sons had shrugged their expensively suited shoulders when she'd finally found her voice and asked a few stumbling questions. They'd muttered that their father's executor would be in touch and had backed out of her house and set off for the funeral. They hadn't spoken again. Elvin had taken her discreetly aside after the service and had made a time for them to meet. It seems Gunter's generosity had other strings attached. She didn't know whether to be excited or concerned. Once more a strange shiver wriggled down her spine.

"It's chilly here by the glass, Roslyn." Margot's bright voice cut into her thoughts and then a warm hand grasped hers. "You're freezing." Her sister tutted. "Let me get you a cup of tea."

"I can make my own."

"I know you can but let me. We're all a bit sad and it's good to have a purpose."

Margot guided her closer to one of the fancy gas heaters and put a bowl of biscuits on a low table before moving off to get the tea. In giving herself a purpose, she'd denied Roslyn, but Margot wouldn't think of that. Several people had left since Roslyn had lost herself in her thoughts at the window. She was glad the numbers were thinning; she hated making small talk at gatherings like this. She'd make her own excuses to leave soon.

"Here you are." Margot handed her a cup. "Have a biscuit."

"No thanks."

"But they're your favourite, chocolate chip."

Roslyn took one to keep the peace.

Margot glanced around. "I think everyone should be happy."

"As much as they can be at a funeral."

"I meant with my catering," Margot huffed. "People need nurturing after a funeral. Once I heard there was not even a cup of tea and a biscuit planned I thought I'd do something. Those sons of Gunter's weren't much use."

"They've lived interstate since they finished uni. I suppose we're all strangers to them these days."

"Even to their own father."

"They kept in touch, rang him every week."

"I didn't think he ever heard from them. He rarely mentioned them to me."

Roslyn gave an indifferent shrug.

"Well, I'm glad I could do it on Gunter's behalf anyway," Margot said.

Roslyn wouldn't have invited half the town to her house. She had to concede it was a noble gesture from Margot. "He would have appreciated your kindness."

"He was a lovely man."

"He was." Once more the gnaw of sorrow ached in Roslyn's chest.

"You two were very close."

"He got on well with you and Dennis too."

"Yes, but he and Richard were great mates and since you've retired you've spent more time with Gunter. His sons should have acknowledged you at least."

"They did."

"When?"

"On their way to the funeral. They've asked me...or at least I think Gunter left instructions that they ask me to keep an eye on the place."

"They've emptied the cottage."

"Only of perishables, personal paperwork and any rubbish. The rest goes to charity. And I've only been asked to keep a general eye. It's not good once a place is empty." Roslyn spoke vaguely both because she didn't know the ins and out of what was expected and she didn't want Margot asking more questions before she did. "Gunter still has a contract for his grapes with Hillvale Winery, as far as I know."

"Surely that executor man would know. What was his name?"

"Elvin Wagner."

"Martin says there's a *For Sale* sign on Gunter's place."

"Already?"

"Yes. I thought they'd have to wait for probate to be granted before they could sell."

"You can make the contract subject to probate."

Margot's eyebrows shot up.

"At least so I believe," Roslyn added quickly. "But I'm surprised there's a sign up so fast."

"You didn't know about it?"

"Why would I?" Roslyn snapped. She didn't want Margot to know she would benefit from the sale yet.

"You and Gunter were good friends."

"I may have received a message via his sons but I don't have any form of communication with him from wherever he is now."

"Don't be smart, Roslyn. Gunter lived alone. I just thought he may have let you know what his instructions would be if he… when he died."

"He did not."

"Or that Elvin fellow. Surely there's a will."

They both glanced towards Elvin and Esther, who were still deep in conversation.

"I'm not family."

"Fine, fine." Margot's placating tone was annoying. "It's just that we offered to buy the place a few years back when he was thinking of putting it on the market."

"I know." He'd planned to sell before the pandemic and it had caused such a ruckus when he changed his mind when the world shut down. Dennis, and Margot even more so, had been disappointed not to have the chance to buy the land. Roslyn assumed that's why it had been worrying Gunter again lately. He hadn't been unwell but had talked again about selling and perhaps he'd updated his will. He wouldn't have wanted to upset Margot and Dennis again. Roslyn had listened to his concerns over many a vineyard inspection or a cup of tea or glass of wine depending on the time of day. She hadn't imagined this was about to happen though. Gunter had only been seventy-seven and had seemed in robust health but a stroke had taken him so swiftly that there'd been no chance for goodbyes. And now she was caught up in the sale.

"We'd better find out which agent is listing it."

"Same people as before…" Roslyn cursed under her breath as Margot's look sharpened. "At least that's what I'd be guessing."

"Dennis and I will discuss it tonight."

"I expect it'll be expressions of interest."

"Why?"

Once more Roslyn cursed herself for her stupidity. It was best Margot found out the details from the agent rather than from her. "It will all take time, probate et cetera…" she said vaguely.

"Oh yes. I remember poor Dad's paperwork took months and he didn't even have anything very complicated. Although I don't expect Gunter does either."

Roslyn took a big gulp of tea, which was thankfully almost cold. She hoped Elvin would be back in touch soon with the details about Gunter's final wishes so she knew exactly what was expected of her.

two

Three months later

All of the businesses on the main street of Jesserton were shut except for the garden shop and The General Providore. Both proprietors were out the front of their shops, one adjusting a wonky stack of pots and the other bringing in the Open sign.

It was early on a Sunday afternoon, and a glorious spring day full of promise and warmth. The main street was long and wide, and day trippers had been out in droves, their sun roofs open, or completely removed in the case of a few sporty numbers. Motorbikes with pillion passengers; vintage cars, their occupants in the jaunty caps and wide-brimmed hats of yesteryear; four-wheel drives packed with families glad to escape the city for a few hours – all of them enjoying a weekend drive in the Adelaide Hills.

Margot paused to glance up the street. As always Jesserton was as pretty as a picture, with paved footpaths and lawned verges touting a leafy green tree exactly in the middle of each plot. Some lawns were tended better than others and even had the addition of aggies or daisies in neat clumps, and some trees had been replaced where disease or decline had claimed the predecessor but there was a sense of neatness and quaintness. Houses, mostly old villas and cottages, sat behind fences of wrought iron, stone, picket or more modern aluminium. It was mid-November and there was the odd extra splash of colour with red bows, green wreaths and colourful baubles where some had begun adding Christmas decorations to their fences and homes – all discreet yet festive. Margot had recently overseen the setting up of a carefully crafted Christmas tree made from recycled wine barrel staves in her shop. One of the casual staff had helped decorate it with dainty red baubles and Margot had personally placed the wooden star entwined with tiny lights at the top.

At the low end of the street where she stood outside the food and local produce store Margot and her co-owner and friend Kath had proudly named The General Providore, there was also a garden shop and a post office. And opposite was a butcher, a small run-down supermarket, a hair and nail salon, and a hall.

Greg from the garden shop waved to Margot as she shut the Providore's sandwich board with a snap and leaned it against a verandah post. Then he wandered over as she stacked her outside chairs.

"It's been busy enough," he said. "Are you closing early?"

"Yes." Margot eyeballed the leather-clad couple taking their time over an oat milk cappuccino and a soy latte at one of the outdoor tables. "It's family dinner night at my place so I'm in a bit of a hurry."

"Anything else I can help with?"

"No thanks, Greg. Lani's cleaned inside so I sent her home early. We've been busy but it's gone quiet now." She lowered her voice and leaned closer. "No-one since these two."

She was relieved to see the couple rise from their chairs and pick up their helmets. The Providore was open till three on Sundays, according to the sign in the window. It was only a little after two but she planned to close as soon as they left.

"Thelma was in earlier," Greg said. "Evidently Teakles have sold the supermarket."

They both looked across to the forlorn little shop over the road.

"Yes, Thelma came in here too. But how many times have we heard that rumour?" Margot said. "It's sad to say it but they've let the place deteriorate. I think they'll eventually have to just close the doors and walk away."

Greg nodded sagely. "Sounds like Gunter's place has finally sold too."

Margot's heart skipped a beat. Thelma had also mentioned that. Margot and Dennis had put in their best offer two weeks ago, a week before the final date for expressions of interest. "It's still speculation as to who's bought it."

"Maybe the winery that's purchasing his grapes got it?"

"No-one knows who's put in an offer." Margot nibbled at the corner of her nail. She and Dennis had decided to keep silent about their bid. Even their family didn't know. It had been the longest few months keeping it to themselves. Margot had badly wanted to tell Emily. The plan was their daughter and family would move into Gunter's cottage after some much-needed renovations. Keeping it from Roslyn had been the hardest of all. Normally she'd confide such a momentous decision but not this time. There'd been such a fuss a few years ago when Gunter had changed his mind about selling. Margot had told everyone they were bidding and the great ideas they had for the place. It had been both devastating and embarrassing when it had come to nothing. This time Dennis had insisted they keep quiet in case it didn't happen but Margot felt sure the place would be theirs. She couldn't bear to imagine the alternative.

The agent had said she didn't have to inform those parties who hadn't been successful so they'd likely only hear if they'd got it, but Dennis had assured Margot he'd pulled out all stops to make sure their offer was a good one, well above the market value.

"You sure Roslyn doesn't know anything?" Greg said.

"Why on earth would she?"

"She's been looking after the place and acting as go-between for Gunter's sons. She might have heard something."

"Yes, but the expressions of interest would be confidential." Margot spoke with an authority she didn't truly feel. Did Roslyn know more than she let on about Gunter's affairs? Was it possible that Margot wasn't the only one keeping secrets?

"He always got a good price for his grapes," Greg said.

Another reason Margot and Dennis would like the property. "He has some of the oldest pinot noir and chardonnay vines in the Hills. They're sought-after varieties that always do well. Gunter cared for those vines like they were his children."

Greg snorted. "They were better company than his real children."

"Yes, well, since he died Roslyn's taken her role as caretaker seriously. She meets with the viticulturist from Hillvale Winery every couple of weeks."

"She was in earlier."

"Was she?" Margot wondered why her sister hadn't called in at the Providore.

"Organic fertiliser and some basil. Evidently she lost her last plant in that recent burst of heat."

Margot smiled. She and Roslyn had lived in Jesserton most of their lives, as had Greg. There was little any of them didn't know about each other's activities, down to whatever they purchased at the local shops. It truly was amazing that the bidders for Gunter's property remained unknown. For one giddy instant she imagined the offer she and Dennis had made was the only one.

The rumble of the motorbike drew her attention back to the moment. It revved then roared away from the kerb and up the street, carrying off the last of her customers.

"I'll get this cleared and be off. See you next week." Margot strode to the empty table. She couldn't wait to get home. It was extremely possible that she and Dennis would soon be the owners of Gunter's property.

The vacated kerb space was swiftly filled by a station wagon. A young woman got out, peered at the shop and moved around her car.

"Sorry, we're closed," Margot said. Up close the woman was barely more than a girl with tatty, loose clothing. Her hair was streaked with purple and looked like it would benefit from a decent wash and cut.

"I only want a coffee and maybe a ready-made sandwich."

Margot would have smiled and offered an apology but the girl's tone was defiant rather than a polite request.

"The coffee machine's off and the food's cleaned out." Margot had packed all the leftovers up ready for the volunteer from Tea on Sunday to collect. The local churches provided a meal for those in need in the nearby town of Sheffield and the Prov always donated. She could have offered her something but the girl's attitude didn't deserve courtesy. People who attended the free community meal would be far more grateful. "I'm closing up for the day."

She turned away and behind her she heard the girl mutter something that sounded like "bitch". Margot spun back, but a sleek black car pulling into the space behind the station wagon distracted her. The passenger window lowered and the slightly dishevelled face of the local mayor peered out at her.

"I'm glad I caught you," Esther said. "I'll come in." Before Margot could respond the window slid up and the driver's door opened. "I was hoping you'd have something I could grab to eat on my way to the next event."

"Of course." Margot didn't know Esther well, only because she was the mayor and their paths had crossed at meetings or events. She was a strikingly good-looking woman who did everything with an air of confidence. Right now that confidence was striding past Margot towards the shop door. She turned as Esther passed her and caught the eye of the girl, who was glaring back from over the roof her car. She raised a finger at Margot then climbed into the car and drove away.

Guilt churned her stomach, conjuring a sour taste.

"I won't keep you long," Esther said as Margot followed her into the shop.

"It's fine," she said, even though it wasn't. Here she was allowing the mayor some food she'd denied the girl who'd looked like she could do with some sustenance. It wouldn't have hurt to have given her one of the leftover wraps and perhaps even told her about Tea on Sunday. Margot shook her head at her own lack of charity. Something about the girl had got up her nose and Margot's hackles had risen.

Esther cast a quick glance around the shop. "Things are going well here?" Despite her make-up and hair looking a bit untidy, she still looked amazing in a smart tailored two-piece suit that hugged her trim waist and a pair of very high-heeled shoes that Margot envied even though she knew she'd never manage them herself.

"Yes, we're kept reasonably busy."

"Tourists and locals alike, I suppose." Esther turned and this time her gaze swept Margot. "You're quite a worker in the community, aren't you?"

Margot shifted from one foot to the other under her scrutiny. "We all do our bit, don't we?" She thought again of the girl she'd turned away.

"But you do more than most. Supporting community events, local charities and the like. Rallying people over the nature playground showed a lot of foresight and common sense. And you were on council."

"That was years ago and only one term. Before Kath and I started the Prov."

"You're a popular person in the community."

Margot wasn't sure what to say. The praise was both unexpected and baffling.

"Have you thought of running for council again?"

"I…me…no." Margot wished she was sitting down.

"You've lived here a long time – you know lots of people." Esther cast out a hand to take in the shop. "You've obviously got a good brain for business."

"It's kind of you to say but—"

"I'm not saying it to be kind. We need people like you on council." Esther lowered her voice. "One of my councillors is… might have to retire. That would mean a by-election."

Margot shook her head. "I don't think…"

Esther lifted her arm, peered at her watch a moment then tugged her sleeves straight. "I've got another stop before I get to the next event. You should think about it." With a sharp nod she turned on her high heels and strode out.

It wasn't until Margot was locking the door behind her that she realised Esther hadn't taken anything to eat.

On a good day Roslyn walked into town to get her mail and any necessary supplies. It was only a kilometre away and downhill. Trouble was the return journey was uphill and on a bad day it felt like she was climbing Mount Everest. Today was a bad day, only she hadn't realised that until she was halfway home. Sometimes the pain surprised her but it was certainly happening more often. Now the string bag with the bottle of fertiliser and the two basil plants dragged at the end of her arm. She fought to draw air into her lungs and pain coursed down her left leg with every step. She felt every one of her sixty-seven years plus some.

She paused and leaned one arm on the stone wall surrounding the Lutheran church, admiring the architecture from afar while slowly recovering her breath. She hadn't been inside since Gunter's funeral. She swallowed the quick stab of sorrow that surprised her from time to time. She still missed Gunter so much and felt the weight of the responsibility he'd given her, which she'd kept to herself as much as was possible.

She fixed her gaze on the old church in front of her. Facing the road were two impressive arched windows, set in the white stucco walls. The whole building was topped with a new roof of deep-red corrugated steel that had taken some years to save for. Roslyn had quietly donated money even though she was no longer a parishioner. Her parents would have had they been alive, and Roslyn thought they'd be happy she carried on the custom. Her Jesser ancestors had been the original German settlers the town had been named for. She'd kept her surname when she'd married, wanting to continue the Jesser tradition.

A car swung in beside her. She cursed under her breath as she recognised the vibrant green duco. The window buzzed down. She wasn't in the mood to be fussed over by her little sister.

"Need a ride?" Margot said. "I'm on my way home from the shop. I can drop you on the way past. I'm not organised for dinner. It totally threw me to have to cover for Kath at the Providore today. And you'll never guess who called in as I was closing…the mayor."

Roslyn climbed in, pleased that Margot's focus was on other things and not on Roslyn's struggle to get up the hill. She tried not to wince as she lifted her left leg into the car. "I suppose even the mayor has to eat."

"But that's the strange thing. She said she did but she talked to me about council and—" Margot pursed her lips. "Well, it was all a bit odd, that's all. Held me up and dinner's not prepared."

Roslyn clutched the armrest as Margot's tyres spun in the loose gravel and they rocketed out onto the road. Her sister clearly had things on her mind.

"I thought Dennis was cooking a barbecue."

"He is but there're still things to finish off and the salad to make. I've brought a selection of leftover mini cheesecakes and a slice from the shop for dessert." She jabbed her thumb towards some containers on the seat behind her. "I was going to make a raspberry vacherin but covering for Kath didn't leave me time to do the meringue."

"Take me to your place. I'll cut through the yard."

Margot and Roslyn shared a fence line and easily accessed each other's homes via the gate between them. What had once been one of their parents' properties had been subdivided when their mother had died. Their father had wanted rid of the parcel of land at the top of the hill overlooking Jesserton. It had been more their mother's passion. She'd had horses and ideas to plant more vines and fruit trees. He'd split the hilltop paddocks for his daughters and kept the house just down the road in town for himself.

Margot had been seventeen and Roslyn twenty-four. It had been perfect for her. She'd been able to move out of the family home into the old stone house that stood on her portion of the property. Several years later, when Margot had married Dennis they'd built a new house on their parcel of land.

"Everyone would decide to come when it's my turn," Margot grumbled. "Not that I mind. It's lovely when we're all together but, lucky you, it was such a small gathering last time at yours. So much more relaxing. Of course, your catering style is different." Margot flicked on her indicator and slowed slightly for her road, which was coming up fast.

Roslyn didn't take offence at her sister's insinuation that Roslyn's meal was no comparison to hers. That's just how Margot spoke. Words tumbled from her lips without thought and later when she sometimes realised she might have said something unkind she'd apologise profusely. Anyway, it was true. Roslyn couldn't be bothered with the fuss of cooking while Margot adored it.

"When you say *all* are you including—"

"Geraldine." Margot flicked her a glance that dared her to say more.

Roslyn pursed her lips and stared ahead. Geraldine was Dennis's brother's ex-wife. She'd kept the house in Jesserton in the divorce settlement and also her place at Margot's dinner table. She was a dithering, skittish woman who continually apologised for anything and everything, often for something she had no need to apologise for, which drove Roslyn batty.

"You've got so much patience, Margot."

"There's no harm in inviting the woman for dinner every so often. She came a couple of times while you were in Japan visiting Jerome earlier in the year. Then she's been away in New Zealand visiting her son. She's only been back a few weeks. We're all the family she has close by."

Roslyn's snort changed to a sharp intake of breath as Margot turned the wheel and shot across the road in front of a truck powering up the hill towards them. The blare of a horn followed them as the car slewed onto their rough gravel road.

Roslyn gripped the armrest tighter. "If you're trying to kill me I'd have preferred to walk."

"The truck was climbing the hill. It was going at a snail's pace." Margot batted away her complaint with a wave of her hand. "We had plenty of time."

The car bounced over a pothole.

"Bugger!" Margot's free hand went back to the wheel. "I must get on to the council again about getting this road sealed."

"It's not that long since we sent the last letter. They've probably hardly had a meeting since then." Roslyn winced as the car bounced over another rut. Margot slowed slightly to turn into her driveway then came to an abrupt stop in front of her garage. There were a few small dents in the roller door – evidence of the times she hadn't stopped quite quickly enough.

They climbed out of the car. Margot whipped her head around and leaned across the bonnet. "Greg from the plant shop told me you were there earlier. You might have called in my way."

Roslyn lifted the string bag she'd just picked up off the car floor. "You were serving as I went by and I knew I'd be seeing you tonight." Barely a day went past when they didn't see each other, even if just to wave over the wire fence that divided Roslyn's backyard from Margot's side garden.

"There's a rumour Gunter's place has sold."

Roslyn sighed. It had taken no time at all for that gossip to spread. She'd warned the agent. "Expressions of interest closed last week so I suppose a decision would have been reached."

Margot fixed her with a sharp look. "You don't know anything?"

"How could I know anything?"

"You're working for Gunter."

"Gunter's dead."

Margot huffed out a breath and walked around the car. "His estate has you as the caretaker."

"You make me sound like the groundskeeper for an English lord."

"You're always over there. I thought you might have heard something."

Roslyn studied her sister. "Why are you so interested all of a sudden?"

"It's right next door." Margot didn't meet her look and there was a pink glow to her cheeks. "Of course we're interested."

The afternoon was pleasantly warm but a chill prickled Roslyn's arms. "Did you put in an offer?"

Margot nibbled at her thumbnail like she always did when she was nervous.

Roslyn forced her mouth to close then immediately opened it again. "You and Dennis made an offer on Gunter's place! How? Why didn't you say something?"

"It was a silent auction."

"But you might have mentioned it to me—"

"Oh hell, Roslyn, you haven't put in an offer too, have you?"

"Of course I haven't but I wish I'd known you had."

"Why are you so surprised? What difference would it have made?"

This time it was Roslyn's turn to duck away from her sister's piercing look.

"Roslyn!" Margot's hand gripped her arm then fell away as Roslyn lifted her head. "You were involved in the sale decision, weren't you?"

"Your name wasn't on the list." She hadn't meant to look but the agent had stepped out of the office for a moment and she couldn't resist glancing at the list of those who'd put in their expression of interest.

"Dennis probably used a proxy."

Roslyn shifted the weight of the bag to her other hand. Between that and Margot's disclosure she felt like she was sinking.

Margot's hand shot out and grabbed her again, her face alive with hope. "You know who the successful bidder is."

Roslyn shook her head. "I don't. Gunter's sons were making that decision with the agent."

Once more Margot's hand fell away. "When?"

"Soon, I believe, but honestly, Margot, it's nothing to do with me."

"But you must have seen the list. You said our name wasn't on it."

"It wouldn't be if you used a proxy. Anyway it's a moot point. The decision either has been or is about to be made without me. I'd better get going." Roslyn shut the car door and made off.

"You're walking funny," Margot called after her.

Roslyn stopped and turned back. "No, I'm not."

"I noticed you doing it last week. Sometimes you walk with a kind of rolling gait as if you're favouring one leg. Have you hurt yourself?"

"No. I'm just getting a bit slower, I suppose," she said begrudgingly.

"I've said before you should come to aqua aerobics with me. It's so good for your body."

"No thanks." Roslyn swam rarely and then only in the privacy of her own pool. No-one else need see her in a pair of bathers.

"I wish you would. I'm sure you'd enjoy it and it might help your aches and pains."

Roslyn drew herself up. "I'm making a tomato–zucchini bake with veggies from the garden for tonight, and I'll bring some garlic bread."

"It's not necess—"

"It's no bother. I have oodles of tomatoes and zucchinis and some baguettes that will only go stale. It's a good way to use them all up. See you at six."

She continued on before Margot could object further, careful to walk straight without favouring her bothersome left leg. The person whose house the family gathering was at, usually Margot's or Roslyn's, occasionally one of Margot's children, did the full catering. Lately Roslyn had started bringing extras.

Margot had a daughter with gluten intolerance and a son-in-law who was vegetarian, or was it pescetarian? He ate fish. She also had a daughter-in-law who was vegan and a grandchild who was allergic to eggs. Roslyn's contribution was for her own sake rather than anyone else's. She'd add some bacon to her vegetable dish and top it with cheese and breadcrumbs. At least there'd be something on the dinner table that she could enjoy. At Margot's last family dinner there had been nothing Roslyn had deemed edible and she'd overdone the wine on an almost-empty stomach. She didn't want a repeat of the headache and the rebellious digestive system that had followed that dinner. Her appetite had become finicky as it was.

three

Dinner at Margot and Dennis's

Eggplant & Chickpea Balls, Halloumi & Corn Fritters

Vegan Kebabs, Keto Fish Cakes, Pork & Honey Sausages, Mixed Grain Salad

Peanut Butter Cookie Bars, Mini Cheesecakes

Margot removed the eggplant and chickpea bites from the oven. They were looking more like blobs than balls. She'd forgotten they'd needed at least thirty minutes chilling time in the fridge before being rolled in polenta and put in to cook. It had taken far too long to roast the eggplant then scoop out the flesh – she'd had no time to waste on chilling.

Dennis strolled into the kitchen looking as fresh as someone who'd just showered and changed, which he had. While Margot had been working at the Providore and then dashed home to prepare dinner, he'd been playing golf followed by some celebratory ales at the nineteenth hole after he'd won. She'd shooed him straight towards the bathroom as soon as he'd come home.

He took a beer from the fridge, popped the top and took a sip before surveying the chaos she still had to tidy in the kitchen. "What do you want me to do?"

She pointed to the trays of food she'd just taken from the fridge. "Cook the barbecue."

"Now?" He glanced at the clock on the wall. "No-one's here yet."

"Just the sausages. The children are always hungry and I'm not sure how many of the balls and fritters they'll eat before mains."

Dennis peered at her carefully arranged platter. "Are there chickpeas in those?" He wrinkled his nose.

"Yes, and eggplant. It's vegan, no flour, no meat and no egg so it ticks all the boxes for everyone's dietary requirements." Margot beamed at him, quite pleased she'd found such a useful recipe.

"What about my dietary requirements?"

"Try one. They're delicious."

"No thanks."

"You like the halloumi and corn fritters." She pulled another loaded tray from the oven. "I've made them before."

"Mmm," he murmured with a non-committal shrug and took another sip of his beer.

"Did you hear anything about Gunter's place?"

"On the golf course?"

"Word is out that it's sold. I thought you may have been notified."

"You know I'd have told you if I had."

Margot's sudden rush of excitement oozed away. "It has to be us, doesn't it?"

"I told you not to get your hopes up—"

"But we put in a very good offer."

"As much as we could afford…" Dennis took another swig from his beer.

"But you said it was a considerable offer, higher than market value."

"We wouldn't be the only ones with our eye on that land."

"I know that but—"

"There's no point going on about it."

Margot opened her mouth to protest then blew out a breath instead. He was right. It was silly to argue about what was done. The possibility of buying the property was something she and Dennis had fantasised about for several years, ever since the first time Gunter had planned to sell then changed his mind. Back then they'd been interested in taking over his vines. It would have been another form of income, a diversification.

More recently, Emily and Cameron had been looking to move out of their small place behind their shop. Gunter's house was run-down but it had good bones. The four of them had discussed it after Gunter had died, but the cost was beyond the young family and so this time Dennis and Margot had decided to put in an offer on their own. The vines would be theirs as planned and there was the bonus of the cottage for Em and Cam. If…when they were successful they could sort out the future finances between them. Dennis knew how important it was, as much as she did. After all the waiting, it was hard to believe they'd know the result soon. They'd been friends with Gunter for almost forty years – helping and supporting each other as good neighbours did – and she hoped that might count for something.

"Margot?" Dennis waved a hand in front of her face.

"I so badly want it to be ours," she whispered.

"We've done all we can." He drew her shoulders close and gave them a squeeze. "We just have to wait on the answer."

"I know."

"Why don't I get you a drink?"

"Not yet. I'm not quite finished here." Margot recalled Esther's visit. "You'll never guess who called in last thing at the Prov... the mayor."

"She knows how good the Providore is."

"She came to sound me out, I think."

"What about? I hope you're not taking on another project. You're already involved in lots of things." Dennis took another sip of beer and poked at the sausages.

Her intrigue at Esther's suggestion dipped a little. Dennis was right. How would she fit the extra responsibilities of councillor duties into her busy life? "Community things," she said, sensing his lack of interest.

"So you want me to cook the sausages now?"

Margot pushed Esther's chat from her mind and focused back on the meal. "Yes, please."

"What're these other things?" He waved a hand over the trays of food beside the sausages. "Where's the steak?"

"I didn't get any."

"Why not?"

"There's plenty of food here. The kebabs are vegan. They'll need to be done on the grill completely separate, and you'll have to clean the plate after the sausages before you cook the fish cakes."

Dennis shook his head. "How did a simple family barbecue turn into this?"

"Please, Dennis, just cook the sausages." She turned away, too busy to spend any more time placating him or to think about council or worry over their offer on Gunter's place.

Dennis dismissed the various food requirements as trivial but each was significant. Emily's gluten intolerance and her daughter's bad reaction to eggs could make their lives miserable. Family was Margot's anchor – without it she'd be adrift and she knew how lucky she was to have the family she did. She'd been raised by loving parents, with a devoted big sister in Roslyn. Then when she'd met Dennis Margot had known she'd found her life partner and they'd raised a son and a daughter who'd found themselves well-suited partners. And now of course there were grandchildren. Every member of her family was special.

It was important to Margot that they felt welcome in her home and around her dinner table, and if that meant hours researching and preparing food it was worth it. Besides, Margot's test recipes were also useful at The General Providore, which she ran with her friend Kath. Margot hadn't wanted a business that took over her life completely so it had started out as a small shop, but they'd extended their offerings to cater for a variety of dietary needs and last year they'd expanded into the vacant shop next door.

The halloumi and corn fritters she'd made for tonight had been introduced at the Providore last summer and had become very popular. In keeping with their focus on Adelaide Hills produce, the halloumi was locally made as well. And she knew Roslyn would eat that at least.

Margot could picture her sister screwing up her nose at tonight's menu like Dennis had. She knew that was the reason Roslyn would bring her zucchini and tomato bake and the garlic bread. And if she knew Roslyn, the "simple" vegetable bake would have lots of added ingredients. No doubt Dennis would indulge in both.

Car doors slammed in the distance. The chatter of voices grew louder, accompanied by the delighted squeals of a child.

"They're here," Dennis called from the back patio.

Margot flung the fritters onto a platter, put packets and containers away in the pantry, wiped down the benches and gave the kitchen one last gaze as quick footsteps clattered across the tiled floor.

"Nanny!"

She opened her arms and bent down to receive Isabella's warm limbs wrapping around her neck and damp kisses on her cheek.

"Hello, darling," Margot crooned. "How's Nanny's favourite grand— little girl."

"Just as well you clarified that, Mum." Emily had followed her daughter in, her baby son in her arms. "She's your only 'little' girl." She brushed a kiss across her mother's cheek and handed over the squirming one-year-old.

"I'm not a little girl." Isabella pouted.

"My goodness no," Margot said as she kissed Henry's plump cheeks. "You'll be at kindy soon. That's for big girls."

"Nick and Kayla and the boys have gone round through the side gate," Emily said. "I thought you'd still be in here. Can I do something?"

"You could take out those two platters for me."

Isabella's cousins called her from the patio and she ran out to meet them.

Margot waved a hand towards the savoury nibbles she'd prepared. "There's no egg in the balls or the fritters so they're fine for Isabella and no gluten or meat either so you and Cameron can have both. Kayla should enjoy the eggplant and chickpea balls but she won't want the halloumi and corn fritters."

"You're amazing, Mum." Emily picked up the platters. "I love dinners at your house."

A burst of pride swelled in Margot's chest. She hugged Henry a little closer and kissed his soft curls. It had been a rush and she always felt a little stressed getting the final steps done but when it came to serving and cleaning up, everyone helped. For now she could relax and enjoy her guests. She hefted her grandson higher on her hip and followed Emily out. At the door she paused to look around.

She and Dennis had created a beautiful home on their piece of her parents' land and this area was perfect for entertaining without worrying about the vagaries of Adelaide Hills weather. There'd been many a gathering or event in this room over the years. She waved to her son and daughter-in-law who were chatting by the barbecue, set Henry down beside a pile of toys and kissed her two older grandsons. Dennis had put on some easy listening music and the warm spring day had evolved into a balmy evening, pleasant enough to leave the windows open. It was a perfect night.

Roslyn let herself into Margot's outside entertaining area. Adults bantering and the sounds of the children playing some kind of game mingled with music from the discreet speakers. This room was almost half the size of Roslyn's more modest home. She never understood how Margot managed all the work that went with a house this large.

Emily and Nick and their spouses welcomed her warmly as usual. The older children stopped their game long enough to wave and say hello while Henry smiled at Roslyn's approach. She bent and brushed a hand lightly over his golden curls and turned back to unpack her basket.

"Garlic bread!" Nick plucked the alfoil package from her hands. "Thanks, Roslyn." He waved it teasingly under his sister's nose and took it to the outdoor kitchen.

Next to him at the barbecue, Dennis gave her a thumbs-up. Roslyn nodded. She'd known there'd be a few who'd appreciate the buttery treat. She accepted a glass of wine from Emily's husband Cameron.

"I'm not turning down a slice or two of garlic bread either," he murmured as he moved on to fill more glasses.

Roslyn smiled. She was a widow and her only child, her son Jerome, lived in Japan with his wife and their six-year-old son. She'd had a video call with them only an hour ago. The house had felt empty when she'd ended the call and she'd been glad to have the dinner at Margot's to go to. It was sometimes comforting living on the edge of her sister's bigger family, an extension of her own small one.

"Hello, everyone," a sing-song voice called from outside.

Roslyn worked at keeping the smile on her face. The only downside was Dennis's ex-sister-in-law, Geraldine. She was a veritable pain in the derrière who continued to turn up to most family events including Christmas, unless her ex and his new wife were there but that was rare seeing they lived interstate.

Geraldine beamed at them all from the door wearing some kind of floral tent that draped like a shroud over her body.

"Hello, Geraldine." Dennis dutifully kissed his sister-in-law's cheek and more greetings were made all round.

"Oh and you're here, Roslyn, of course." Geraldine squeezed Roslyn close. "No show without Punch, is there?"

"Geraldine." Roslyn nodded and extricated herself from Geraldine's grasp.

"I'm always telling Margot how lucky she is to have a sister she gets on with so well. My sister and I rarely see each other. You two are like peas in a pod, aren't you?"

"We are lucky to be so close." Margot gave Roslyn's shoulder a squeeze. "Would you like a drink, Geraldine?"

"I'm not much of a wine drinker. I'm sorry I didn't bring anything." Geraldine flapped her hands at Margot. "But I can never compete with your catering. Oh, are they arancini balls?" She plucked a ball of food from the plate Emily was offering around, held it to her mouth then stopped. "That's not breadcrumbs, is it? I'm like you, Emily dear, I don't tolerate gluten."

"Unless it suits you," Roslyn muttered.

Margot gave her a sharp prod in the back. "They're eggplant and chickpea balls, Geraldine, and they're rolled in polenta so you'll be fine."

Geraldine popped the ball in her mouth and reached for another.

Cameron appeared with a glass of wine.

"Thank you, Cameron. Perhaps just the one glass."

Roslyn's lips twitched. Geraldine never brought anything and never hosted family dinners but she always ate well and despite her saying she didn't drink wine she usually ended up having a glass or two of whatever was going. Last time she'd come to Margot's for dinner, Roslyn had brought a particularly good bottle of wine from her cellar and Geraldine had drunk half of it.

"I'm glad you're here, Roslyn." Geraldine glanced around as Margot and Cameron moved on. She leaned closer and lowered her voice. "I want to ask you what you think. I've been getting this nagging pain here lately." She waved her hand at what Roslyn could only guess was her stomach area but with that dress it was hard to tell.

"You should see your GP if you're concerned."

"I suppose I will if it's still there on Monday. I just thought you might have an idea."

"I don't like to give medical advice."

"Oh, I'd never ask you for a diagnosis. I just wondered what you thought it might be."

"I've been retired for a few years now."

"And you know she wasn't a proper doctor, Geraldine." Dennis appeared carrying a tray of food. "She was only an anaesthetist. All they do is drug people so the real doctors can do their work." He winked at Roslyn then turned to Geraldine. "How's that car of yours going?"

"Not so well."

"I might have something perfect for you coming in next month. I'll tell you about it while I cook these." He indicated the tray loaded with kebabs and Geraldine followed him to the barbecue.

Roslyn swallowed her offence at Dennis's teasing. She was simply thankful to him for distracting Geraldine, who often bailed her up at these get-togethers with a medical question: a sore throat, an aching leg, a stubbed toe. Once it was for a toothache, for goodness sake. Roslyn wanted none of it. That was all behind her.

"Do sit down, everyone." Margot waved a hand towards the table. "It's just a barbecue so sit where you like." She didn't sit, of course, but proceeded to organise Dennis cooking the next course while the children ate what looked like rather nice sausages. Roslyn eyed them and was relieved to see there were enough for the adults as well. She took a seat beside Kayla.

"Please, everyone, help yourself to the food," Margot said as she placed plates of barbecued food on the table.

Roslyn put her casserole beside Margot's mixed grain salad and removed the foil. "There's bacon, cheese and breadcrumbs in this one," she said and earned a glare from Margot.

Roslyn ignored her sister. The garlic bread was all gone, devoured by whoever stopped to talk to Dennis as he'd cooked, and she was sure her vegetable bake would also be popular. She was glad of the distraction the food brought. It was strange but she felt anxious tonight. The list of bidders for Gunter's property that she'd seen had all been company names so finding out

Margot and Dennis had put in an offer had been a surprise. More than that, Roslyn couldn't believe Margot had kept quiet about it. And now, if the town rumour mill was right, the decision had been made, which added to the tension fluttering just below the surface.

Roslyn tried Margot's concoctions, which were surprisingly delicious. At least the fish cakes and the salad were, the latter being a mix of all sorts including pearl barley, lentils, nuts and pomegranate seeds served with a fresh herb vinaigrette. Roslyn found herself enjoying it and even dessert. Not so much the peanut butter cookie bar, which was too sweet for her liking, but the cheesecake was creamy and topped with fresh berries. She noticed the biscuit-crumb base hadn't stopped Geraldine from downing one piece and going back for seconds.

Emily and Kayla cleared the last plates and clutter from the table and went inside to make coffee. The three men stopped talking long enough to promise they'd do the dishes later then went back to their conversation about cars. Nick and Cameron were both having trouble with their work vans. The children drifted off to watch something on the television while the remaining adults sipped their choice of a port or a sticky dessert wine. Everyone relaxed, even Geraldine, who was on her second glass of the sweet wine and commending Margot on her vegan kebabs.

"You'd never guess they were vegetarian," she said incredulously.

Margot's eyes met Roslyn's for a minute and a small smile played on her lips. She tolerated fools, a quality Roslyn did not have.

The discussion moved on to next fortnight's dinner and Roslyn took the opportunity to go to the bathroom. It certainly wasn't her turn to host again. She peered at herself in the bathroom mirror. She'd never bothered with make-up, but lipstick had been her one concession. Silly when she'd spent half her working life wearing a theatre mask but it kept her lips from drying out. She searched in her bag for a lipstick and noticed her phone screen light up. There was a missed call and two messages.

Her heart skipped as she noted the missed call was from the agent in charge of selling Gunter's property. There was a voice message from her and a text from one of Gunter's sons and another from Elvin. She read the thankful and congratulatory words from the son, not exactly sure what he meant. Elvin's brief text said that he'd be in touch soon and then she listened to the voice message, which explained why the son had sent the exuberant text. It took her a while to regain her composure afterwards, and she noticed a slight tremble in her hand when she finally applied the lipstick. It was a vibrant red. In the male-dominated world she'd worked in, it had been her signature. Like it had then, the sight of it now strengthened her resolve.

Emily and Kayla were headed out as she left the bathroom, carrying trays loaded with cups, small bowls of sweet treats and a cheese platter. Roslyn took the cheese platter from Emily's overloaded arms and followed them back to the table.

She could try to leave now but Margot would wonder why and lying to say she had a headache would only raise more concern. It would be easier to drink some tea and slip off soon after.

She almost choked on the slice of cheese she'd taken when Nick spoke.

"I forgot to ask if anyone had heard about Gunter's place selling?"

Across the table Geraldine huffed herself up importantly. "Evidently it has, from what Thelma said today at the garden shop."

"I heard that from Thelma too," Nick said. "I had to go to her place first thing this morning. She had a short circuit."

"Not unusual for Thelma," Dennis quipped.

"She's got some really dodgy wiring in her place. It's dangerous." Nick shook his head. "It should be replaced."

"How would Thelma know if we—"

"You know what Jesserton's like, Margot." Dennis leaned in and gave his wife a sharp look. "Most of the rumours start with Thelma. Wasn't it her that was telling everyone that the mayor was having an affair? A load of rubbish. You have to be wary of what she says."

Roslyn put her cup of tea firmly back on the table. The anxiety she'd kept at bay over dinner had come back after the phone message and ratcheted up a notch.

"Anyway," Dennis said. "The thing with silent auctions like the one for Gunter's place is we may not know who the successful bidder was until they make themselves known."

"Looks like they have." Cameron glanced up from his phone. "I've just had a message from a mate. It's been bought by a company."

Roslyn glanced towards the door. It would be too obvious to leave now.

"Which company?" Margot snapped, her usual charm stripped away.

All eyes were locked on Cameron, who shook his head. "He didn't say."

A chorus of voices surrounded Roslyn, everyone speaking at once. Margot's gaze shifted to Roslyn.

"Do you know who the buyer is?" Her voice was the loudest and drew everyone's attention.

"Probably Hillvale," Nick said. "They've been buying grapes from Gunter for years."

"Roslyn?" Margot's gaze was still locked firmly on her.

"Why would Roslyn know?"

"I do, actually." She cleared her throat, her surge of ire at Dennis's derisive response dismissing her reserve. The agent had said it was no longer confidential. "The company who purchased Gunter's property is Meyer and Brightman."

Silence followed her words, a moment when she noted the varying looks of incredulity from those around her, and then all hell broke loose.

four

"Bloody hell. All of you shut up," Dennis bellowed.

The cacophony around the table ceased and in the silence that followed Isabella whispered, "Papa squared."

Nausea churned in Margot's stomach and there was a tightness across her forehead. A sure sign of a headache coming on.

Dennis leaned in across the table. "Are you serious, Roslyn? This isn't some joke you're playing, is it?"

"Why would I be joking?"

"I've heard of Meyer and Brightman somewhere." Emily screwed up her nose.

"They're the company who've built hotels in other wine regions," Cameron said. "Word is they've been looking for somewhere to build one in the Hills."

Margot's hand went to her mouth.

"Just because they've bought Gunter's property doesn't mean they can build a hotel." Nick looked from Dennis to Margot. "They'd have to get some kind of authorisation, wouldn't they?"

"There'd be a million hurdles to jump." Dennis snorted. "When I think of what I had to go through to expand the car yard and that was nothing like this. They won't get approval."

The tight grip around Margot's head eased a little and her hand dropped to her side. "That's right. The council has strict rules about what can and can't be built."

"They approved that luxury accommodation for one of the vineyards, didn't they?" Emily said.

"That's quite different to a hotel block. The idea has been mooted in our region before and knocked back." Dennis scoffed. "It's damned bad luck they didn't sell to locals." He glanced at Margot. "One of the wineries would have at least kept the grapes and looked after the land. Nothing will come of this."

"Well, it might."

All eyes turned to Cameron, who sunk a little lower in his chair.

"What do you mean, Cam?" Emily asked.

"Meyer and Brightman don't actually need council approval to go ahead. These days development applications over a certain value can go to the state planning authority."

"That can't be right." Nick's snort broke the silence.

"Cameron's very interested in local government," Emily said proudly. "He's been studying up on it."

"How can someone in Adelaide make a decision that will affect what happens in Jesserton?" Margot said.

"Perhaps they've got a plan that's a good one for our community and the Hills in general," Geraldine offered placatingly.

"You and Mum were interested in that land the first time Gunter proposed to sell it," Nick said. "You should have put in an offer."

Margot glanced at Dennis. He met her look with pursed lips.

"We did," she whispered.

Once more voices spoke over each other.

Dennis held up his hands, commanding quiet. "We tried. We hadn't reckoned with someone like Meyer and Brightman throwing their money around."

"Oh, Mum." Emily was the one to come and comfort her.

"We wanted it for you." Margot blinked back tears. "You and Cam and the kids. We talked about it the first time Gunter thought he might sell."

"Yes, but that all fell through." Emily glanced at her husband who was studying his phone. "I don't think we'd have the mon—"

"Dad and I thought we could renovate the cottage and you'd have that lovely space…"

"It was kind of you." Emily's hand rotated gently on Margot's back. "What a shame it didn't happen—"

"How come you were buying land for Emily?" Nick scowled at his father then at Margot.

"We weren't," Margot said. "At least, it would have been ours to begin with then we would have talked to Em and Cam about maybe living there. We thought the grapes would be a good investment for the future."

Cameron's head shot up from the phone screen he'd been scrolling through. He shrugged. "You'd never have been able to match a large company offer."

"That's as may be," Dennis huffed, "but—"

"You knew about this, Roslyn."

Roslyn met Margot's look with a stony glare.

"Why would Roslyn know?" Emily's soothing hand dropped away.

"She's been working for the estate." Margot jabbed a finger in her sister's direction. "You knew what was going on, didn't you?"

"It depends what you mean. The estate employed me to keep an eye on the place, oversee the chaps that Gunter had working in the garden for him and liaise with the winery. I suppose besides waiting for probate to be granted it was another of the reasons the expressions of interest date was so far away. The grapes are already contracted. A prospective buyer can't do anything with the land until after harvest."

"Hang on a minute, Roslyn." Dennis leaned in. "You said 'employed'. I thought you were just helping Gunter's sons out until there was a buyer. Are they paying you?"

Roslyn lifted her chin, her stony glare shifting to Dennis. "I would have kept an eye on Gunter's place anyway."

"Roslyn wouldn't have any influence on the EOI result," Cameron said. "That would be confidential and in the hands of the agent, surely."

Dennis snorted. "Depends on how much money's involved."

"Dennis!" Margot was as taken aback by her husband's barb as she'd been by the loss of the property.

"I can understand this is a shock when you'd hoped to get the property yourselves." Roslyn's voice was the only sound in the room and she fixed Dennis with one of those glares she'd perfected over the years, one that made interns and senior specialists alike think twice about messing with her. "All I can say is that the list of offers was short."

Dennis was suddenly very interested in the glass of wine he held in his hand. Margot didn't blame him. It terrified her when she saw that look in her sister's eyes.

"And I can assure you the outcome had nothing to do with me."

"We didn't think..." Margot's voice trailed off as her sister stood.

"Thank you, Margot, for a delicious meal."

"You don't have—"

Roslyn put up a hand. "I'll leave you to digest the news."

Dennis snorted and the others remained silent, fidgeting with a cup or looking at their hands. Margot's body was a lead weight stuck to her chair. In truth she was relieved her sister was leaving. Roslyn was right, they did need time to let the news settle.

The children, who'd been quiet during the excitement, suddenly came to life as the door closed on Roslyn. The two older boys began fighting over a toy. One bumped Henry and he began to cry. Isabella yelled at her cousins to stop.

"Time to go home, I think." Cameron plucked Henry from the mat and raised his eyebrows at Emily.

Kayla put restraining hands on her sons and caught Nick's eye.

"We'd better get home too," he said.

"But you didn't drink your coffee. And there's still the sweet nibbles." Margot had made bliss balls and carrot cake bites, and brought some very expensive dark chocolate from the Providore, each item ticking the vegan-friendly and gluten- and egg-free boxes.

"Couldn't eat another thing after that news." Emily brushed a kiss across her cheek.

"I can't believe it," Nick said. "Imagine having a hotel right next door."

Once more there was a pause, each adult looking down as if they'd all stopped for a silent prayer and then suddenly they were gathering their things. There was a flurry of thank yous and goodbyes, hugs and kisses.

"We didn't work out who was hosting next fortnight," Margot croaked.

Nick looked at Kayla, who busied herself tidying toys.

"Sorry, Mum, our kitchen's still not finished," he said and ushered his family off.

Cameron hovered in the doorway nursing Henry. Emily glanced his way.

"I suppose we can take a turn."

He nodded.

Emily scooped Isabella onto her hip. "Goodness knows how I'll manage with the children and work but…"

"I'll help with the food," Margot said and with final air kisses goodbye they were gone.

"Hell, what a bloody muck-up that was." Dennis poured the remains of a bottle of red into a glass and took a gulp.

Margot sighed. The headache was intensifying behind her eyes. She still couldn't believe they'd missed out on Gunter's property.

"I'd better be off too."

Margot startled. She'd forgotten Geraldine was even there.

"It was a lovely dinner, thank you both."

"You're welcome, Geraldine." Margot flapped her hands as if that would somehow set everything back to rights. "There's still so much food. Would you like anything to take home?"

"You and Dennis will eat it, won't you?" Geraldine shuffled from foot to foot, eyeing the table.

"Take these." Margot put an assortment of the sweet treats into a bowl. "They'll keep for days in the fridge. Something to have for morning tea or supper."

"Thank you."

"I'll walk you out." Margot ushered Geraldine to the door then returned to Dennis, who was staring into his empty wine glass.

He glanced up as she sat beside him. "What a shemozzle of an evening."

Margot sighed at the leftovers and dishes scattered across the table. She'd put a lot of effort into the food. "I think everyone enjoyed the meal."

"Of course they did. You always come up trumps even if some of your dishes are a bit left field."

Margot didn't bother to mention she'd seen him eat some of everything she'd made and go for more. "I really believed we'd win the bid and Gunter's place would be ours. Or ours and Emily's, at least."

"We couldn't outbid a company like Meyer and Brightman." He pushed to his feet, plucked another open bottle of red from the bench and poured a large glass. Dennis didn't like to lose. Even when he played games with the children he cut them no slack.

"Do you really think they intend to build a hotel?" she said.

"Who would know?"

"It would have been lovely having Em and Cam and the kids just up the road."

"It's out of our hands now."

Margot looked longingly at the wine bottle. It was a rather good pinot noir they'd bought a case of during the last Winter Reds festival but the vice around her head tightened and she drank a glass of water instead.

five

"You done yet?"

Amber didn't turn but shoved the last bag into the back of her car and slammed the door. Somehow she'd have to rearrange it all so she would have enough room to sleep in it tonight but for now she had to get going before the old cow behind her gave her another ear full.

Yesterday had been shit. It had started with a flat tyre that had cost a fortune to fix and had taken up most of her day. There'd been no chance to eat, and when she'd stopped at a shop to get something, the snobby hag running the place had looked her up and down as if she were a piece of rubbish, point-blank refused her then let her fancy friend into the shop. Amber had made do with a half-eaten box of savoury biscuits she'd found under the seat of her car then had returned to the caravan park to be told by the old bitch running the place that she had to leave.

"You're supposed to be gone by ten and it's almost half past," the woman's nagging voice continued. "New tenants will be here soon. I should charge you extra."

Today wasn't looking any better. Amber wiped perspiration from the back of her neck. All the trips back and forth to load her car had made her hot and sweaty. That along with the anger that seethed inside her.

When she'd turned up at the run-down caravan park a few weeks back, the woman had agreed to give her cheaper rent in an old onsite van because Amber had said she'd do her own cleaning and help out with extra cleaning of the ablution block. The woman had also said she'd write Amber a reference, but then last night she'd been waiting for Amber when she'd returned to the park and had told her she had a new full-paying booking and Amber needed to be out by the morning.

"It'll take me extra time to clean after you being there so long," the woman snarked. "Goodness knows what the place will be like."

Amber spun, unable to control her anger any longer. "It's a shitload better than when I moved in," she yelled. "I cleaned years of grime from inside. You should've been paying me to stay in that dump."

"You little bitch. I took pity on you and look what it got me."

"An unpaid worker." Amber seethed. "I also cleaned the bathroom block several times for you." She jabbed a finger at the woman. "You promised me a reference."

"That was until I realised you were doing business from my premises. I saw that bloke you had there the other night. Running your sordid business on the side. I told you no men." She glared at Amber as if she were something dirty beneath her shoe.

Amber's face screwed up into a scowl. "Tom? He's a workmate who called in for one drink."

"Yeah, right. And I'm the king's cousin. Anyway, you shouldn't be drinking in your state."

"I had one beer." Amber seethed. "What's it to you!"

"You single mothers are all the same. Get yourself up the duff then think the world owes you—"

"Yeah, yeah, yeah! Whatever!"

"You've done your dash with me. No more charity. Go find another soft touch."

Fire burned in Amber's belly, her hand clenched into a fist and she took a step forward, pleased to see the flicker of fear cross the old cow's face. Then shame washed over her. She was becoming just like her mother and without the excuse of the drugs. Her clenched hand opened and she pressed it to her belly instead. Her baby deserved better than that. She was wasting energy arguing.

She spun away and went back inside for one last look around the dingy space. It wasn't much but it had a rattly old aircon that had kept her warm at night or cool during the day, and a small fridge that had kept her food cold. The van was in a park close enough to her job at the pub in nearby Jesserton and she'd been grateful for the roof and cheap rent. The promise of the reference had been an extra carrot. The injustice of missing out on that stirred the fire in her belly again. Her head felt light, as if it wanted to float away from her body, and spots danced before her eyes. She gripped the bench and gulped in a breath as perspiration trickled down her back. She took the glass she'd left in the drainer and poured herself a drink. The water and her slow breaths seemed to help.

"What are you doing in there?"

Amber straightened, drew in another long slow breath, and spied her phone charger still in the wall plug. Her phone had little battery these days. She couldn't do without the charger. Clutching it tightly in her hand, she strode back outside and without another word started her car. She got some small satisfaction from flipping the old cow the bird as she drove away. The adrenaline rush ebbed quickly as she followed the winding road out of town and cranked the aircon up. She had a late shift at the pub tonight and nowhere to go in the meantime. The food in her esky would stay chilled for a while but she couldn't keep the car running just to keep that and herself cool.

There was no shortage of shady trees in the Hills and she'd discovered a few spots between here and the pub that were tucked away off the road. They might be okay for temporary overnight stays. The last few nights the temperature hadn't been quite so low. After her time in the van she wasn't looking forward to sleeping in the car again. She'd have to try to find something better. It was worth staying in the area. Unless she stuffed it up, her job would last until she had the baby, and she'd made a doctor's appointment she'd promised her baby she'd keep. She hadn't had a check-up since her pregnancy had been confirmed by the doctor she'd seen back in Penola.

With no prospects for work or accommodation there any more she'd made her way back towards Adelaide hoping it would be easier to find work and somewhere to stay. Work was easy enough – she could turn her hand to anything – but no-one looked twice at a pregnant woman with no references when it came to renting. She'd stopped off in the Hills where she'd been lucky enough to get the job at the pub. It paid good money and she'd been able to save a bit staying in the onsite van. The bloody tyre had put a dent in that. It had cost a fortune.

Once more the fire burned inside her as she thought of the reference she didn't get. "Bloody old cow," she yelled as she pulled up at a stop sign. She looked left and right with no real plan. A car horn tooted behind her. She chose the road towards Mount

Barker. It was a huge place and at least there she could park her car in the shade and hang out in the shopping centre before she headed to her job at the Jesserton pub.

Amber was early for her shift but Fred, the boss, was a good bloke who offered a small meal as part of her employment and she was happy to take him up on it. She found a park for her car, tucked away out of sight just down the road from the pub. She might end up staying there after work if it was quiet when she finished.

She'd spent a lot of the day in the shopping centre then driven back to the side lane behind the caravan park and used the showers there before putting on her work clothes. The old cow always watched afternoon television and never set the code on the shower block so it had been easy to nip in and out.

"Hey, Amber, after a feed?" The big ginger-haired chef welcomed her, perspiration damp all over his red face.

"Just a bit of salad will do me, thanks."

"Nah, you'll never make it through your shift on that. Busy night ahead and I've got a pizza special for tonight's menu I want you and Tommo to try. Besides, can't have Fred's two finest workers fading away." He winked and went back to his bench.

Amber glanced around but there was no sign of Ivan, the sour-faced second chef. Probably off having a smoke somewhere. He only did the basics and often nipped out for a fag or a drink.

"Help me out here, Amber. Chef's made us one each." Tom the kitchen hand had started at the pub the day after her and they'd been mates straight away. He greeted her with his big smile then turned to draw a pizza out of the wood-fired oven. Perspiration dribbled down his face and neck as well. It was extra hot in the kitchen. Amber was glad she'd be working in the bar.

The chef was loud and gruff when the kitchen was in full swing but in the weeks since Amber had started she'd noticed the extra kindnesses he'd offered to her and Tom. Maybe he guessed she had little and they both knew Tom was an English backpacker who lived from day to day.

By the look of the bowls of prepped food, Tom had already done several hours' work. He slid the pizza onto a board. "Cut that one for me while I get the next."

Amber's mouth watered as the delicious savoury aroma wafted around her. This morning she'd used the last of her milk before it went off on a small bowl of cereal and she'd had a chocolate milk drink and some savoury biscuits for lunch.

"What's on this one?" she asked as the chef reached for something over her head.

He was creative when it came to pizza. He'd had something different for the specials board every night she'd been there.

"My usual base with chicken, avocado, spinach, caramelised onion and fresh tomato."

Amber was almost drooling now.

"Chicken delight pizza is the chef's special tonight." He grinned. "Had chicken we needed to use up."

Tom and Amber took their pizzas to the small nook outside the kitchen door. Amber was already working out how many meals she'd get out of the pizza, as long as she could keep it cool. She'd slipped a couple of her ice blocks into the kitchen freezer on her way in. She picked up a slice, took a cautious nibble and closed her eyes. The flavour was divine. She knew how lucky she was to have this job, had thought the same about her accommodation until this morning. She'd learned not to rely on anyone or anything lasting. Her whole life was testament to that.

six

Margot had been baking since early morning – something for dinner and lunches, some quiches to freeze and drop off later in the week for the Tea on Sunday group and extras to give to Emily. The General Providore was closed Mondays and Tuesdays. First thing on Mondays she went to aqua aerobics in Mount Barker before doing the myriad of jobs – cleaning, baking, grocery shopping, her monthly hair appointment, volunteering at the op shop once a month and so on – that she packed into the day.

Tuesdays were meant to be her pamper day, when she'd get a massage or her nails done. Sometimes she'd go to a movie with friends or they'd drive down to the city and browse the shops and go out for a boozy lunch. Once a month it was book club and that seemed to be the only thing she reliably attended these days. Since Emily and Cameron had taken on their homeware and furniture business in Hahndorf and had children, Margot's Tuesdays were often spent babysitting or cooking, even cleaning, for them.

This afternoon she'd have Henry while Emily took Isabella to an introductory kindy session. If only they lived next door, as she'd hoped might happen if they bought Gunter's place, life would be easier for all of them. It seemed Sunday's rumour was reality. There'd been a brief report in the business section of the paper. The successful bidder had been Meyer and Brightman. She'd sobbed at the harsh reality of it. Dennis had spouted on about how she shouldn't have got her hopes up and there'd been no guarantees, but she'd set her heart on it.

She swallowed her mix of emotions and rubbed harder at the benchtop she'd been wiping down. There was chagrin that a big company, who'd care little about Gunter's beautiful gardens and his beloved vines, should take over the property mixed with worry about what they planned to do with it. And then the heartbreak that Emily and Cameron wouldn't get the opportunity to live next door. Margot had been imagining it over the last few months as if it was a certainty.

"Damn it."

She tossed the cloth into the sink and glanced at her watch. It was time for a coffee. She wondered if Roslyn was home. She'd been wanting to quiz her sister to find out if she knew anything more about what Meyer and Brightman intended. Margot put together a container with an assortment of her home-baked biscuits and slices. Roslyn rarely baked. It was always bought biscuits for morning tea, if she had anything at all.

Just as she crossed her backyard, Margot stopped and diverted to her garage instead. She'd take her car and drive via Gunter's place. Just one last look for old times' sake.

The trees lining their curved driveway were flush with the leafy green cover of late spring. The thick canopy provided shade and privacy and also helped to keep down the dust in summer. Margot loved that their house was not visible from the road. At the gate she turned left and drove the few hundred metres to Gunter's equally long and secluded driveway. The large sign declaring *For*

Sale seemed to mock her as she drove past. She pulled up in front of the old house then paused. She hadn't been here since Gunter had died and a wave of nostalgia swept over her.

His house was situated just below the crest of a steep hill. From the front she looked across his vines and fruit trees, out over a wide valley and to the hills beyond. There'd been some good rain a few weeks back, freshening the green in the vines and trees as far as the eye could see. It was a pretty sight. What if the vines were ripped out? She pressed a hand to her stomach against the small punch of loss at the thought of a developer spoiling it all. Then tried madly to think of an explanation for her presence as a ute came slowly up the hill from the direction of the vines.

It stopped beside Margot's car. She was relieved both to see the Hillvale Winery sign on the door and that she vaguely knew the driver.

"Hello, Mrs Pedrick."

"Checking the grapes?" Margot asked the viticulturalist, who was younger than her own children but had grown up in the area.

"Yes. All looking good."

"I just popped in for a look around, make sure all's okay."

He nodded. "No worries. I'll leave you to it." With a wave he moved off.

Margot waited until his vehicle had disappeared from her rearview mirror and got out of her car. She gazed at the old ramshackle house then took the three steps to the verandah. She was surprised to see a couple of old wicker chairs and a table still perched at one end, exactly where they'd always been when Gunter was alive. It had been his favourite place to sit. She'd heard his sons had emptied a lot of his belongings into a skip before they'd even held his funeral, and taken the rest to the op shop. Perhaps the chairs had been forgotten or deemed too old.

She flicked leaves and dirt from one of the cushions then picked it up and shook it before replacing it and sitting. She'd had many a cup of coffee here with Gunter when she'd brought him something she'd baked. Beside her, the sash window to his bedroom was still wedged open a sliver by a thin block of wood, and beneath her feet the cement was cracked and broken. The house might be in disrepair but the view…She looked out across the valley again.

She remembered the conversation she'd had with him several years earlier when he'd been thinking he'd put his place on the market. She'd sat on this very chair and set the food she'd brought on the table. Gunter had made them coffee.

"Here we are." He'd carried a tray loaded with his stove-top coffee pot and everything else they'd need to make the coffee. He'd put it on the table next to the plate with her date-and-banana cake and proceeded to pour.

Margot preferred coffee from her shop but next best was Gunter's and with cups in hand they'd settled back and turned to the view. One of the men Gunter had taken under his wing was moving slowly between the vines. Margot followed his stilted progress, unsure how she was going to start the conversation she'd been planning without sounding mercenary. She took a sip of the coffee. The intensity hit the back of her tongue then mellowed. Beside her Gunter cleared his throat.

"You've probably heard I'm thinking of selling…" His words trailed off and he looked down into the cup he gripped in his hands.

"We did hear that, yes." He looked so vulnerable Margot's heart broke for him and for a moment she wanted to leave things be but it was too good an opportunity to miss. "That's what I've come to see you about actually. Dennis and I would like to make you an offer."

Gunter's eyes went to the cake.

"That's not why I brought the food," she added quickly.

He smiled and picked up a slice. "I have been the lucky recipient of many fine dishes from your kitchen. I'm most grateful. I miss my dear wife's cooking."

"Dennis...well, Dennis and I are worried for you, Gunter."

"Why?" He looked genuinely surprised. "I'm not unwell. Just a little weary of managing on my own. My sons suggested I downsize." He looked out across the valley. "I've had a good life here. I hope my good fortune might be of more use to others."

Margot frowned.

"I could use the money from the sale to help with local people down on their luck."

"You're a kind man, Gunter."

He volunteered at the Hills Community Hub in Mount Barker and often had some of the clients work with him. He believed new skills and some supportive words were sometimes all someone needed to build self-esteem. Gunter was one to action his principles, a quality Margot found admirable. He'd helped many men get back on their feet over the years.

Gunter cleared his throat. "The money left over after I get myself a small place in town would be useful at the Hub."

"You haven't actually signed with an agent yet, have you?"

"Not yet."

"Oh, that's good, we—"

"But I've been talking with one who's been very helpful. Unless there's something wrong, I'll stick with her. I will not go back on my word."

"But Dennis and I could make you a private offer." Margot lurched forward. "It would be market value plus some extra, of course, and it would be straightforward."

"Straightforward?"

"Cut out the middleman. It's more money for you, for your charity."

"Oh, yes. I understand, but my sons have been advising me and they think it best it go on the open market."

Margot swallowed her annoyance at his sons, who rarely visited and no doubt were thinking of the future when they might get a bit of Gunter's money too.

"I don't want anything to be awkward between us, that's why I'm thinking of going with the agent." Gunter smiled kindly. "That doesn't mean you might not buy the property, just that the agent would deal with it all. It's kind of you to think you might save me some money by not having an agent but we don't want money discussions to come between friends."

The image of his kindly smile dissipated as Margot was startled out of her reminiscing by hammering. She looked towards the sound coming from further along Gunter's driveway, but the curve in the tree line blocked her view of whatever it was. She stepped down from the verandah and moved cautiously along the drive. There was a dual cab parked up at the entrance and a man was putting up a sign. Another lay at his feet. She went back to her car, wondering what she'd do if it was someone from Meyer and Brightman and they'd come to view the property. She sat hunkered down in her seat like a sneak for several minutes and finally decided to simply drive right out. She was a neighbour checking on the place, that was all.

When she approached Gunter's gate the dual cab was gone but a sign had been hammered in beside the gate, replacing the *For Sale* sign. She pulled up beside it, reading with astonishment. The site was the proposed location for the Adelaide Hills' newest accommodation, a boutique hotel. All enquiries were to be directed to Meyer and Brightman. There was a name and contact details.

Margot selected Dennis's number with trembling fingers but her call went to voicemail. With shaky hands she took a picture of the sign and sent it to him as warm tears began to course down her cheeks. Not only had they missed out on buying it, but there really was to be some kind of huge hotel development right next door.

Roslyn looked up at the sound of wheels crunching on her gravel drive followed by a sharp skid as brakes were applied. She wasn't expecting visitors. A car door slammed. She struggled to her feet just as someone knocked on her front door.

"Roslyn?" The voice was Margot's.

She paused to steady herself and there was another knock and call. Roslyn crossed the lounge, ignoring the pain in her hip and knees. She flung open the door before Margot could knock again. "You don't usually drive—" She was silenced by Margot's wail and her arms being flung around Roslyn's neck.

"What on earth's happened?"

"It's all too terrible."

A small stab of concern caught Roslyn in the chest. "Is Dennis—"

Margot wailed louder. Roslyn drew her to the couch, sat her down and took a wad of tissues from her pocket. She handed them to Margot without bothering to see if they were clean.

"Catch your breath and tell me. What's happened? Where's Dennis?"

Margot stopped her sniffling, blew her nose and fixed Roslyn with a surprised look. "At work."

Roslyn huffed out the breath she didn't realise she'd been holding. "So he's okay?"

"He was fine when he left this morning."

"The children?"

"They're fine too. I've been to Gunter's place."

"Is something wrong there?"

"Yes! No! Well, yes and no."

Roslyn sat back, perplexed. Sometimes talking with Margot was as if she'd entered a theatre late and missed the first scene of a play.

"I know we didn't get the place but I wanted to look at it again, one last time." She blew her nose. "I rang Dennis but he didn't answer so I sent him a photo."

Roslyn pursed her lips. "You sent Dennis a photo of Gunter's place—"

"No, not the house or anything. There was a sign."

"What sign?" Roslyn snapped, her patience wearing thin.

"While I was there someone put up a sign." Margot flapped her hands in the air. "It was what I feared but Dennis said we should wait and see."

"Wait and see what?"

"Meyer and Brightman have put up a sign at Gunter's gate. Well, at least, one of their minions did it, I suppose." Margot's tears were all gone now but her eyeliner had smudged below her eyes.

"A sign that said what?"

"Oh, for goodness sake, Roslyn, pay attention. They're actually going to do it."

Roslyn pursed her lips. Margot would surely make sense eventually.

"They're going to build a hotel on Gunter's land, right next door to our place."

"That's what was on the sign?" Roslyn knew about the hotel but it was still in planning as far as she understood.

"Proposed hotel, it said." Margot's nose was red from blowing and her bright pink lipstick was smudged as well as her eyeliner, giving her the appearance of a surprised clown.

"These things take time," Roslyn said. "Big companies do this kind of thing. It could take years or never come to anything." She used an authoritative tone but from what she understood Meyer and Brightman had been doing their homework. She stood. "I've not long had a coffee but I might have another. Would you like one?"

"Proper coffee?"

"Of course. My machine's been fixed."

Margot nodded and followed her to the kitchen, taking a seat on the couch where Roslyn had been working before her arrival.

The buzzing and hissing of the machine prevented further conversation for a while and allowed time for the pain in Roslyn's leg to ease. She was walking steadily by the time she'd filled the mugs. She took them across to the sunny sitting area.

Margot looked around as Roslyn set the mugs on the little table between them then leaped up. "I forgot I brought you biscuits and slice. They're still in the car."

"Please don't get them on my account. I'm trying to cut back on sweets."

Margot raised her eyebrows but instead of saying more on the subject she waved at the papers Roslyn had left spread across the coffee table. "What's this?"

"Kei's teaching me Japanese."

"Oh, how sweet."

"We've only been doing it a while. We end each video call with a lesson and I'm supposed to practise in between. It helps that I've visited them and spent some time in Japan but I'm not much good at it." It was wonderful to have something to work on together with Kei though, that's why she did it. Her only grandchild lived so far away; Roslyn badly wanted to continue to make connections with him.

"I'm sure you'll get the hang of it." Margot smiled. "Nick's boys used to enjoy baking with me but we haven't had any cooking sessions for ages, not since they started school, I guess. They get busy. Isabella and I have a date to make gingerbread biscuits before Christmas."

They sipped their coffees.

"I really am worried about the possibility of a hotel being built right on my doorstep."

"I'd agree if it was on your doorstep but it's—"

"I knew you'd be on my side, our side."

"It's not a matter of taking sides. The hotel won't be right on your doorstep – there's a lot of land between you."

"But surely you don't want a hotel so close."

"I don't know enough about it yet."

"It's such a shame," Margot moaned. The look on her face made it clear she wasn't listening.

"What is?"

"To not have Em and the kids move to Gunter's."

"I think you have to accept that that horse has bolted, Margot. Something else will come up."

"Not close like Gunter's." Margot fixed her with a glare. "Unless you're selling?"

"No. I'm not. They can cart me out in a box when my time comes. I've made that clear in my paperwork." Although the way her body was letting her down, that might be sooner rather than later.

"That's how I feel too. And how good would it be to have my daughter, your niece, nearby as we get older."

"I wouldn't expect Emily to run around after me as well."

"You're on your own now, Roslyn. Jerome's too far away to be any help."

"I don't need any help."

"Yet."

Once more Roslyn eyeballed her sister.

Margot sighed. "Having Emily at Gunter's would have been perfect."

"You can't dwell on it, Margot."

"Goodness, you sounded just like Dad then." Margot sat up straight, pulled a serious face and cleared her throat before putting on a deep voice. "You mustn't dwell on it, Margot. You'll only get grey hair and wrinkles for no reason."

They both smiled at the memory of their dear dad who'd died only a few years prior. Roslyn settled back against her chair and Margot did too.

"What I mean is it may never have happened anyway." Roslyn spoke softly this time. "What if Gunter had lived on merrily for many more years?"

"His place is a lot more work."

"I know but he could have got help in. Lived there for another ten or twenty years. He was only in his seventies. If Em and Cam truly want to move they should be talking to agents about where and what they want. Another great opportunity might be just around the corner."

"You're being very positive."

"Aren't I always?"

"I'd describe you more as...direct but..." Margot looked her up and down. "You know, I think you've softened around the edges since you retired."

"Got rounder, you mean." Roslyn sat a little taller. She'd put on a few kilos in the last two years.

"Maybe a little but that's not what I meant. You are perhaps...well...not so forthright as you were," she finished lamely.

Roslyn sniffed. "I've never been one to beat around the bush when there was a direct path."

"Sometimes I wish I could be like that."

"Do you?" That surprised Roslyn. Margot was as soft as butter when it came to differing opinions. She was no good at dealing with conflict. Which could be a good thing in regard to the hotel being mooted for next door. Margot might get a little hot under the collar for a while. Fire a few bullets supplied by Dennis, and then as soon as someone took the opposite side she'd back down. This current animosity would blow over. "It's important to stand up for what you believe in but sometimes it's a difficult path. That's when you have to weigh up the pros and cons. Make sure you take the emotion out of it."

"You're right, I suppose." Suddenly Margot's eyes sharpened. She glanced at her watch. "Thanks for the chat and the coffee. I'd better get home. I'm having Henry for the afternoon and I've got lots to do." She made for the back door.

"Aren't you forgetting something?" Roslyn nodded towards the front of her house.

"Oh." Margot put a hand to her forehead. "I came in the car. Silly me. Forget my head and all that." She chuckled as she went the other way. It was an odd, forced clucking sound. "See you."

Roslyn was thankful she'd gone. The blasted pain had returned, this time in her lower back, and she'd become uncomfortable in the chair. She didn't diagnose other people's ailments but she'd done her own and she knew it wasn't good. She couldn't avoid it any longer. The time had come to make an appointment with her GP. If only some of her earlier positivity towards Margot translated to herself.

seven

"Here's your mumma and your sister back from kindy," Margot crooned in Henry's ear. She'd been watching out the window for Emily's car for the last thirty minutes.

He cried and reached for his mother as soon as she came inside. She took him and Margot's arms fell to her sides, aching from the weight of him.

"What's up?" Emily cuddled him against her shoulder.

"He was fine till he woke up from his nap. He's a bit flushed. I wonder if he's teething."

"Ugh, surely not again."

"Nanny, look what I made at kindy." Isabella tugged on her arm and held up a page with her name on it, colourful pompoms glued to each letter.

"Won't that look nice in your room," Margot said.

"What's all this?" Henry had stopped crying and Emily was gazing at the papers spread across the table. Margot had been trying to read and sort them while she'd jiggled the baby.

"That blasted Meyer and Brightman are definitely planning to build a hotel next door. They've put up a sign declaring it."

"Oh, Mum, it'll be awful. Your lovely quiet road…" Her voice trailed away and they both stared at the assorted papers.

Margot started scooping them up. "I've been scanning the internet trying to find out what I could do about it."

"What do you mean?"

"There has to be some way to stop it."

"Do you think there is?"

"I'm going to do my best to find out. I won't let them spoil our beautiful town without a fight."

"Go, Mum."

Henry started to grizzle again and Margot ran a hand over the soft curls on his head. "He's not himself. You'd better get him home."

At the door Emily turned back. "Will you have time to help with food for the family dinner?"

"Of course I will. It'll be my weekend off so I can help with the children and I'll make something. I'll think on it and let you know."

Margot waved them off then hurried back inside. She'd only been able to skim some of the information she'd printed before Emily had dropped Henry off. She collected the papers and moved into the office.

Margot heard Dennis coming in from the garage and glanced up at the clock. Damn, it was after six and she hadn't thought about dinner. After her cooking spree first thing that morning she'd cleaned up and not gone back into the kitchen except to make herself a sandwich for lunch.

"Margot?"

"In the office," she called. "You're late."

"Few problems at work." He waved a hand dismissively, looked at the stacks of paper all over the desk then back to Margot. "What are you doing?"

"Working on the plan."

"What plan?"

"The 'stop Meyer and Brightman building a hotel on our doorstep' plan."

Dennis scratched his head. "I heard a rumour today about the price they paid. Even if it's half true, it was way out of our league. They wouldn't be paying that much money if they were going to change their minds."

Margot sagged into her chair. "Oh." She'd been so carried away with her research she'd imagined it would be easy to stop them.

"What's this?" He crossed the room and picked up one of the stapled piles of paper.

"Part of my plan." She sighed.

Dennis lifted the paper closer. "*We, the undersigned, petition the Council to stop the building of a multistorey hotel in Jesserton.*" He frowned and peered at her over the page. "You've drawn up a petition?"

"It was the logical next step but..." She shrugged. Perhaps she'd been wasting her time.

"I thought Cameron said it's out of the council's hands."

"They can fight it though." Margot sat up. "On things like noise and waste water and probably more – I just haven't found it yet."

Dennis scratched his ear. "You could be right. It might not be as easy as Meyer and Brightman seem to think. We can have a say in what happens on that land." He waved the petition at her. "I'll put some of these at work."

Margot brightened. "And I can put some in the Prov. Greg will put one in the plant shop. I'm sure all the local businesses will take them."

"Of course they will. None of them will want a lumbering great hotel towering over the town, ruining our peaceful lifestyle."

Margot picked up a pen to make a list. "Emily and Cameron will put petitions in their shop. Nick can take them with him and when he's on a job there might be places he can leave them. Roslyn's got a few connections she can follow up and Geraldine will take some around, I'm sure. Between us all we can spread the petition far and wide." Perhaps her work hadn't been wasted. Dennis's initial reaction had taken the wind from her sails but with him on board she was excited again.

"Well done, Margot." He patted her shoulder and smiled.

"I haven't had time to think about dinner."

"How about we go to the pub? Take one of your petitions for Fred. I'm sure he'll be keen to have one. He won't want a hotel springing up so close to his doorstep."

They were ready and out the door in no time at all. Margot was looking forward to a drink and not having to think about what to cook for dinner was an added bonus.

She paused to take in the sleek black car in their driveway.

"What's this?" she said as he shepherded her towards the driver's side door.

"Part of the reason I was late. A new EV." He opened the door and the smell of new leather wafted out.

They owned a Renault dealership and one of the perks was Dennis changed vehicles regularly – almost as often as his underwear.

He patted the roof lovingly. "It's top of the range. I thought you might like to drive."

"You know it makes me nervous."

Several years ago she'd scraped the side of his latest car, a fact he rarely let her forget, and she'd hated driving one of his ever since.

"You'll love this, Margot."

"Are you sure?" She hesitated but Dennis opened the door and guided her in then hurried around to the passenger side.

By the time she pulled up down the road from the pub – they never parked Dennis's car in a car park in case of bumps from other cars – she was in love.

"What do you think?" He grinned at her.

"It's a beautiful car and it drives like a dream."

She ran her hands over the leather seat as she got out. Silly really – there was no point in becoming attached to his demo models. At least she got to keep her own car for a year or two before he upgraded her to a newer model.

"You know we have to be a mobile advertisement for the dealership," he'd say whenever he brought her next car home.

"Oh, damn." Margot put a hand to her head. "In the rush to get out the door I left the petition behind."

"Never mind. We can talk to Fred about it and you can drop it in during the week."

As it turned out Fred had time to join them for the meal.

"I don't get a chance to sit and enjoy food from my own kitchen very often," he said.

"You've got a few new staff members." Margot glanced around. There was a young woman behind the bar and a new chap she'd noticed through the kitchen door.

"Thankfully or my permanent staff would be burned out by now. It's been tough finding the right people. These two are proving useful, although I'm not sure how long either will stay. Amber's pregnant and on her own and Tom's a backpacker."

"But at least he can't get pregnant," Dennis quipped.

Margot ignored the two men's grins and tried to get a better look at the new barmaid.

"Amber's no slouch," Fred said. "If it wasn't for her small bump you'd never know she was pregnant. She's a good worker."

Amber turned to a customer and the bright light at the end of the bar illuminated her purple hair. Margot clicked her tongue. "Well, I hope she's polite to your patrons."

"She gets on well with most."

"She was rude to me in the shop the other day."

"Really? She's been great here," Fred said. "Doesn't take any nonsense though."

"How long till she has the baby?" Margot was relieved the girl had a job. She swallowed her guilt for turning her away the previous Sunday.

"Don't know. She seems to think she'll make it to the end of summer and that suits me."

Amber laughed at something her customer said and Margot saw a very different face to the surly girl who'd flipped her the bird.

"Have you heard about the development on Gunter's land?" Dennis asked.

Margot turned her attention back to the two men.

"So it's true?" Fred's loaded fork hovered in the air.

Margot nodded. "They've put up a sign saying it's the site for a new hotel."

"The ink would be barely dry on whatever deal they did," Dennis said.

Fred's fork hit his plate as he swore. "We've just started making some headway with this place."

"No-one wants another hotel. Especially the size Meyer and Brightman have proposed," Dennis said.

Fred pushed back in his chair and swore some more. "Four generations this pub's been in my family. We nearly lost it during Covid, now this."

"I've made a petition for the council to stop it," Margot said. "I was hoping you'd put a copy somewhere here."

"And I reckon we need to rally a few key local figures for a meeting." Dennis clapped a hand on Fred's shoulder. "We've all got to pull together to stop this hotel before it gets any traction."

"I'll put the petition on the front bar." Fred's eyes blazed. "And if you need a space for meetings you're welcome to use the front dining room here."

"Thanks, Fred." Perhaps it was the second glass of wine but Margot felt the tension of the last few days ease. Fred was a larger-than-life figure in the town and ran a business most locals frequented. It was a relief to know he was on board.

eight

Roslyn kept her eyes on her tablet. She had her current book open on the screen but she'd barely read two sentences since she'd checked in at the medical centre. The tablet was more a shield. Tucked away in the corner of the waiting room, she didn't want to look up in case she knew someone and that might require conversation and from her experience conversation in a doctor's waiting room was always awkward.

There'd been so many times she and Richard had sat together, here first and then at various specialists' rooms. The news the doctors imparted had rarely been good. Roslyn had hoped she'd never have to visit one again, but at sixty-seven avoiding a visit to the doctor was as likely as avoiding death and taxes.

Someone sat in the next closest chair. The seats were spread out at least and Roslyn didn't look up. She stared hard at the words on the screen.

"Oh hello, Roslyn. Fancy seeing you here."

She pursed her lips and forced herself to glance up. "Geraldine."

"How are you?"

Roslyn's hands gripped the tablet tighter. That had to be the stupidest question someone could ask in the waiting room of a doctor's surgery. Thankfully Geraldine didn't wait for an answer.

"I took your advice and made an appointment."

Roslyn frowned and Geraldine leaned closer.

"You suggested I see the GP about my pain." She waved in the general direction of her torso, which today was covered in a floral blouse and loose pants.

Roslyn nodded. "Yes, good idea."

"Geraldine?"

They both looked up at the doctor's call.

"Hello, Roslyn," he said.

"Gareth." Roslyn nodded and then watched sour-faced as Geraldine followed him back to his consulting room.

Gareth had been Richard's GP and then hers. He knew all about her. It was such a nuisance to have to explain everything to someone new. A week had gone by since she'd picked up the phone to make an appointment and she'd not been able to get one with Gareth but neurotic Geraldine had. She glanced back at the tablet but she was too annoyed to focus. When she'd rung to make her appointment no amount of bluster had got her past the iron fist of the receptionist. Gareth had no appointments left this week and then he was away for two weeks. They'd offered her an appointment with a Dr Wu and she'd almost said no but she'd already been putting off this visit for a while.

"Dr Jesser?"

A young man glanced around the waiting room. His glasses had slid down his nose and his stethoscope hung precariously around his neck looking equally in danger of slipping. The only other person left in the waiting area was a young woman, pregnant, if the small bulge under her tight t-shirt was any indication. She gave a sullen glance then went back to her phone.

The doctor's gaze came to rest on Roslyn and he smiled. She rose to her feet, looked him up and down then followed him along the corridor, past Gareth's door, which was firmly shut, and into the consulting room. Dr Wu closed the door behind her.

"Dr Jesser." He waved her to a seat.

"Retired doctor. My name is Roslyn."

"Of course." He smiled. "I'm Dr Joseph Wu. Please call me Joe."

Her first impression had been how young he looked, but up close he looked younger than young. She did the maths. He was a GP registrar – he had to be in his mid-twenties at least.

"Thank you for seeing me, Joe. I usually see Gareth, Dr Jones, but he had no appointments. All my information will be in my notes." She waggled a finger towards his computer.

His gaze remained fixed on her. "How can I help you today?"

"I…I need a hip replacement," she blurted.

"Oh." He turned to the computer and pushed his glasses up his nose. "I didn't see that in your recent notes."

So he'd read her file at least. "No. It won't be there. This has been a gradual decline in the last year and I think…I believe my hip is wearing out."

Joe stopped peering at the screen and turned to her, leaning back in his chair, his expression holding the merest hint of surprise. "You've not had this investigated before?"

"No. At my last annual check-up about a year ago—"

"Eighteen months."

Roslyn frowned. "Surely it hasn't been that long?"

He glanced at the screen. "Your last visit here was for a general check-up and no follow-up was required. That was…" He leaned in closer to the screen then glanced back to her. "Exactly nineteen months ago. You've not attended this surgery since. Perhaps you went somewhere else, saw a different doctor?"

"No." Roslyn sat straighter in her chair. Did he think she was losing her marbles? "Anyway, when I saw Gareth last, the pain was a mild niggle. I thought I'd jagged my leg, slept wrong, done something. I didn't bother to mention it then." She adjusted her position on the chair. If she was being honest the pain had been more than that. She didn't mention the pains in her fingers and feet and the regular ibuprofen and paracetamol she took.

"And now the pain is a problem."

"Sometimes."

He raised his eyebrows.

"More often," she conceded. "My hip is the worst. Some days I can barely get off the bed and then once I get going I'm usually okay but…anyway. Hip replacement seems inevitable."

He held her gaze, his expression that of a person in deep thought. Then he smiled benignly as if she was a child that needed placating. "I think we need a lot more investigation before we order a new hip."

Roslyn thrust out her chin. "I am a medical doctor. I think I'd know—"

"Retired, you said."

"I still have a functioning brain and a good memory."

"Excellent. So as you know there could be many reasons for a bothersome pain. Let's explore all the possibilities before we leap to surgery." He continued to stare at her. His smile might be sweet but his look was steadfast.

She shrugged. "Very well, Dr…Joe, investigate away."

By the time Roslyn left the doctors' surgery her years of denial about her condition had been exposed to Joe's scrutiny. She was fed up and her hip and back ached from all the poking and prodding.

She had scripts to fill and a hand full of requests for tests from blood to CT scans and a referral to a specialist. And to top it all off, her normally excellent blood pressure had been high.

"Any wonder," she muttered as she made her way to her car, which, thankfully, was in the shade of the only tree in the car park. It was a hot day with a wind from the north that added to her irritation.

She swore under her breath as she approached. She'd backed into the space and the only other car in the park, a station wagon, was close in beside her door. She'd put on a few kilos but even before that she'd never have managed to get between the two cars, let alone open her door. As Roslyn strode towards the passenger side of the other car she realised the motor was running and all the windows were up. She drew level with the front door and bent to peer in. Every space in the car was filled with bags and boxes and bedding with only the driver's seat spare for the young woman who sat there, head back, eyes closed, a lank strand of purple hair flopped across her pale face.

Adrenaline shot through Roslyn's veins. She pummelled on the window.

Amber shot forward and bumped her rounded stomach on the steering wheel. She'd only dozed for a minute, before being startled awake by a thudding noise. Dazed, she looked around then jumped as someone knocked loudly on her passenger window.

"Are you all right?" The question was sharp.

A woman was staring at her through the glass, her face almost pressed flat.

Heart still thumping in her chest, Amber lowered the window a crack. "I was fine till you scared me half to death," she snapped.

The woman exhaled sharply. "I can't get into my car."

Amber glanced sideways. She'd only planned to wait in the shade till the owner of the car appeared. She hadn't meant to doze off.

"You would if you'd parked properly. Taking up all of the shade for yourself." Amber couldn't help being snitchy. This was the woman who'd given her an appraising look in the doctor's waiting room and dismissed her as if she was nothing. Amber had seen a lot of those looks recently and she was in no mood to ignore it.

"I'm sorry." The woman fanned her face with her hand. "If you'd just shift out I'll be on my way and you can have the whole space to yourself."

Amber hit the window button and shoved the gear stick into reverse. The woman took a quick step away as Amber's car shot backwards. The car park was empty but for the two of them. The surgery closed over lunch or she'd have waited inside. The blasted doctor had wanted Amber to come back later for her test results. She'd have gone otherwise, found a better spot, but she hadn't slept well in the car overnight and the cool of the aircon and the hum of the motor had lulled her into a doze.

The older woman drove forward and passed Amber, glaring as she went. Amber was tempted to flip her the bird but resisted the urge. Instead she kept her gaze focused on the space the woman had vacated. The lone tree offered thick shade. It wasn't ideal but her fuel was getting low. She could turn off the motor, put down the windows and wait till her appointment. Before she could put her plan into action her engine spluttered and stopped. Her heart skipped as she tried to restart it. She stared at the useless fuel gauge. It never dropped below quarter full so she was always guessing, making sure she kept it topped up, but she hadn't driven much the last few days. She tried again to start the car but there was nothing.

Amber thumped the steering wheel and yelled. Why did bad shit always happen to her? Her shitty, shitty life just got shittier and shittier. She took a deep breath and pressed her hands to her stomach.

"I'm sorry, Beetle," she whispered. "It's not you." She took some deep calming breaths. The doctor had said her blood pressure was low and she was dehydrated. That's why he'd done the tests. She cradled her belly and rocked back and forth as if the baby was in her arms. Tears rolled down her cheeks. It didn't matter what happened to her but she couldn't let anything happen to her baby. It was the only reason she'd decided to stay and wait for the tests.

There was a tap on her window, gentler this time. "Are you all right?"

Amber glanced sideways. It was that bloody woman again. How was she going to get rid of her? She blinked the tears from her eyes but black dots danced before her vision and her head felt as if it was about to explode.

The door flung open. The hot air from outside rushed in but its freshness made her suddenly aware of how quickly the heat had built up inside the stationary car.

"Are you trying to cook yourself?" The woman leaned in. Her face shimmered and Amber couldn't quite focus on her.

"Get out of the car," the woman commanded.

"Piss off." Amber felt a tug on her arm. The black dots danced faster. She was powerless to resist or assist. An arm slid behind her and dragged her towards the door. Amber managed to get her rubbery legs to swing out and the woman supported her to stand. They struggled to the base of the tree where Amber sagged to the ground.

"Do you have some water?"

Amber opened her mouth but no words came out. Feet in a pair of expensive orthotic sandals retreated. Amber tipped to one side and bile rose in her throat. Something cool and wet wrapped around her neck and a hand eased her up straight.

"Take some sips." The woman's voice came from a long way away.

The rim of a bottle pressed to Amber's lips. She opened her mouth and water trickled in and ran down her chin. It was warm but she swallowed and then took some more.

The damp cloth lifted from her neck and pressed against her cheeks and her forehead then went back to her neck.

Amber's eyes fluttered open. The dots had receded and the concerned face of the woman leaned close.

"Lie back," she said, her voice gentler this time.

A hand guided Amber back and she didn't resist. She had no strength for argument. Something soft cushioned her head.

"I'm putting your feet up against the base of the tree for elevation." Her rubbery legs were raised as if they weren't hers. A firm hand pressed her shoulder, patted then dropped away again. "Stay put a moment. I'll be back with help."

"I'm fine." Amber was sure she'd spoken but the woman retreated regardless and disappeared beyond the back of Amber's car.

She shut her eyes, willing herself to feel stronger so she could get up and get away but the thought of moving was all too hard. She lay still, her mind drifting. Why was she even here? She lifted a hand to her belly, reassured by the small bulge beneath her palm.

"She's here."

Amber turned her head as two pairs of legs came towards her. The woman was back with a man.

"Joe is a doctor. He can have a quick look at you."

He shook his head when he saw Amber. "I'll check her over but I think she'll need an ambulance."

"No." Somehow Amber managed to make the sound.

"We're a doctors' surgery, not a hospital. You need some care – probably fluids through a drip. An ambulance and hospital is the best option." He pulled something from his bag – one of those fancy thermometers.

Amber had enough strength to shake her head but that made the dots dance again. She kept still as he put the thermometer in her ear.

"Is an ambulance really necessary, Joe?" the woman asked. "One of the doctors in your practice has just seen her. She's been sitting in a hot car. She's probably just overheated and a bit dehydrated."

"That's your professional diagnosis is it, doctor?"

"No need for that," the woman snapped.

The thermometer beeped. Amber put a hand to her throbbing head. "Go away," she snarled, but in reality the words came out as barely a whisper.

Joe took a step closer and bobbed down beside her. "Which doctor did you see?"

"An old guy. Don't remember his name." Amber's voice croaked and the woman lifted her head and pressed a cup of water to her lips. It was cool. She sipped.

"Let me check your blood pressure." He pulled more gear from his bag.

Amber didn't have the strength to argue and there was no way she was going to mention the other doctor had said she had low blood pressure. This one'd call an ambulance for sure.

"Do you think we could help her inside to cool down? Find out who she saw." The woman spoke with an edge of irritation. She adjusted the cloth on the back of Amber's neck. It was cool for a moment.

"Pressure's low. She needs observation and nursing," he said firmly.

"I'm fine." This time Amber managed to make the words sound normal. She lowered her feet and slowly sat up. By placing a hand against the tree she got herself to a standing position.

"You don't look fine." The woman reached out a hand to steady her.

Amber took a deep breath, filling her lungs with air, and stepped forward. She remained upright and continued hobbling to the door of her car. She bent to look inside. The ice blocks would be melting swiftly in this heat and her few fridge items would be ruined. Her phone made the chimes to announce it was going flat.

"Where's the nearest petrol station?" She turned back. The two doctors were both staring at her as if she'd grown another head. "I need fuel, that's all. If I hadn't run out I'd be long gone."

"I don't think you should drive," Joe said, his tone softening. "Look, I can't force you, but I recommend we call you an ambulance right now. Or at least that you come back inside and let us look after you there."

"No way." Amber shook her throbbing head carefully. "I'll come back later, like I told the other doctor."

Joe pursed his lips then bobbed down to pack away his things. "She really needs someone to keep an eye on her in the meantime." He was talking to the other doctor who studied Amber as if she were summing her up.

Amber leaned against her car. She was used to that kind of look from women like this one, entitled snobs who saw young and pregnant and equated it to stupid and useless. She set her jaw and reached into her car for her purse and keys.

"I can drive you to get the fuel at least," the woman said.

Joe's gaze rested on Amber a moment then he nodded and headed back towards the surgery.

"It's quite a walk from here," the woman continued. "And far too hot a day."

"Aren't you busy…doctoring."

The woman frowned. "I was here as a patient. I'm retired."

"Oh." Amber faltered. She still felt as if her head might float right off her shoulders and her legs were like those of a puppet on strings that she wasn't in control of. "Okay, thanks."

"I'm Roslyn."

A hand thrust towards her. Amber glanced at it then back at the woman. "Amber," she said and slammed her door shut, making sure it was locked.

nine

"Bit quiet today," Kath said as she took the tally from the till.

"The hot wind always keeps people at home." Margot wiped the counter around her friend.

"Sunday was perfect. A lovely day." Kath took the money from the trays. "Lani said you were busy but you sent her and the casual girl home early…again."

The word hung in the air. Margot kept her back to Kath and rubbed at a stubborn mark on the glass of the cake display. "Not until the rush died down."

"You shut before Greg. He saw a few people peering in our window."

"The street was dead at two o'clock," Margot huffed.

"Greg had a busy afternoon."

"He's a plant shop. It's a different trade."

"We advertise being open till three on Sundays, Margot. You did it the previous Sunday too, when you covered for me."

"Are you keeping tabs on me?" Margot kept her voice light but her insides fluttered with unease. She and Kath had been friends since meeting at a mums-and-bubs group when their children were babies, had both worked and lived locally, and had finally achieved their dream of opening The General Providore together several years prior. It wasn't that they'd never had a cross word but for some reason Kath was pushing to keep building the business while Margot liked it the way it was, busy enough but not too demanding. She thought they'd decided that together from the beginning. And Kath was a stickler for keeping to the hours even if there were no customers. Margot didn't argue. She often conceded easily to any differences to keep the peace then quietly did things her way. It seemed to work.

"Of course I'm not, but you know this town. Everyone else keeps an eye on whatever you do."

"The street was dead," Margot repeated. "It doesn't hurt for Lani to get an early minute sometimes, she's such a hard worker, and it's not worth paying the casual girl wages when the shop's empty."

"Fair enough. I've done that myself but I stay on, just in case. People know we're open till three. It says it on our door and on our socials. If someone comes specially and we're shut, it's not a good look. We don't want any bad reviews."

Margot rinsed out the cloth. Kath was obsessed with their social media presence. Margot hardly bothered to look at it. "We've been busy today, at least."

"Yes, and now that we're closed I wanted to talk to you about the outdoor area."

"It was a bit hot out under the verandah today. People prefer indoors on a day like we've had."

"I've had an idea about how to make the verandah more weatherproof. I've been looking at those roll-down shades. They could fit between the verandah posts."

"They're rather expensive."

"They'd soon pay for themselves. People would be more inclined to sit outside if the sun's not beaming down on them in summer and it would protect them from the wind a bit on a day like today and the rain in winter."

"We've managed all this time without them, Kath." Margot kept her tone neutral, not wanting to upset her friend but not wanting to encourage her either. "People come for our good food and the quaintness of our shop. They won't be able to see past the path if we have blinds."

"I think of them as an enhancement. We've got competition in Sheffield now."

"Sheffield's a ten-minute drive away."

"That's nothing to people these days. Especially as quite a few locals go from here to the supermarket there. It stocks a bigger selection than ours and it's open every day. Instead of getting their coffee here they might get it in Sheffield."

"I've called in at the new cafe. It's more like a bakery with pastries and buns. It doesn't have the same vibe or variety of food as The General Providore."

"But they're bigger, with lots of undercover seating."

"We've already opened up into the space next door. It will change who we are if we become too big. We don't want to lose the charm of the place." And increase their workload, but Margot didn't want to mention that. Margot's Mondays and Tuesdays were precious to her. She and Kath were already overcommitted without adding more but lately Kath had been pushing for just that. Margot didn't understand it. Kath ran a cleaning business on her days off from the Prov but, now divorced and with her youngest almost finished uni, she had fewer financial commitments and was practically flying solo these days. Margot almost envied her.

"We need to make a few improvements. Make it more comfortable for people."

"I suppose it could be a positive improvement. Perhaps we could get a quote. See what it'd cost." Margot didn't like arguments and she could see her partner was working up to one.

Kath smiled. "I've checked out two places that sound possible. I'll see what they say."

"I haven't had a chance to catch up with you about the hotel."

"Fred's?"

"No. Gunter's property has been bought by a developer."

"Oh? I assumed you and Dennis would buy it. You were keen once before."

"We couldn't match whatever the developer paid."

"I'm sorry."

"We'll all be sorry if they build a hotel on the site of Gunter's cottage."

"Is that their plan?"

"That's what the sign at the gate says. And I assume there'll be eating places as part of it and they'll be open to the public. Won't do our trade any good."

"Surely council haven't approved it. I haven't heard anything."

"I've made a petition." Margot put down the cloth and picked up the envelope she'd brought with her. "I thought we could put one on the counter here and I'm going to call in at all the other businesses. Fred's put some in the pub." Margot took one out and placed it on the counter with a pen.

"Hang on a minute." Kath swiped up the petition. "What does it say?"

Margot's mouth fell open and a little jab of hurt stung in her chest. "Good heavens, Kath."

"What?" Kath glanced up from the paper. "We don't put anything like this in the shop without discussing it."

"Of course, but you'll agree to this, surely. You won't want a multistorey hotel looming over our dear little town. It would be totally out of sync with our community."

Kath shrugged. She read the petition and placed it back on the counter. "That sounds fine to me."

"I'm glad you approve." Margot tried not to let her hurt sound in her voice.

"Don't be upset. We've always made decisions together about what's best for our business."

"Of course we have." Margot's words gushed with relief and at the same time she smothered the thought that lately it seemed Kath was pushing for change without regard to Margot's input.

"I'll sign it, of course." Kath picked up the pen. "We've worked hard to build this business. Don't want some outsider with fancy ideas taking it away from us."

Margot nodded. They felt the same about that at least.

Roslyn waved a hand in front of her face to dispel the petrol fumes. After driving Amber to the service station she'd insisted on carrying the heavy fuel container for her. Now she watched as the young woman defiantly poured it in unassisted. Once the can was empty Amber lowered it to the ground and glanced at Roslyn.

"I told you not to stay," she said and screwed the fuel cap back on. "I've done this before. Dodgy fuel indicator."

Roslyn stood her ground. She was hot and in need of a drink – she'd given her water bottle to Amber earlier – but she wasn't about to leave this young woman despite her assurances she'd be fine.

Amber opened the back and slid in the empty container. Roslyn caught a glimpse of a bedding roll before the tailgate slammed shut.

"You can go." Amber flapped her hands at Roslyn and got into her car, leaving the door open. She tried starting it but the engine didn't catch. She tried several more times before cursing and thumping the steering wheel.

"I could call for help. It might need priming or something." Roslyn had no idea about what went on under bonnets of cars but it sounded plausible.

"Like I said, it's happened before," Amber snapped. "It'll start eventually." She had several more tries with no luck and the motor was starting to sound sluggish.

"You'll flatten the battery." Roslyn knew that much. "I could call roadside assist."

"I don't have that."

"I know someone else who could help."

"Damn." Amber was peering at her phone. "It's time for me to see the doctor again."

"I'll call while you're inside."

Amber glanced from her phone to Roslyn. "Okay." She got out of her car and gave Roslyn the keys. "Thanks," she muttered and stalked away.

Roslyn called Dennis. His car yard wasn't far away. She asked if he could spare one of his mechanics. He'd been reluctant but when Roslyn had explained the situation, he'd given in.

While she waited she stood in the shade and inspected Amber's car. It was a leafy grey and shiny clean. Its Holden badge reflected the sun, making her wince. Inside it was a different story. It was a quagmire of boxes and bags that spilled in every direction. Roslyn suspected from the gear in the back that Amber had been sleeping in the car. That was no life for anyone let alone a young pregnant woman.

The mechanic arrived and started the car again in no time, as Roslyn had thought he would. He was just driving away when Gareth spoke from behind her.

"Hello, Roslyn. I didn't realise it was you waiting for Amber."

"I wasn't."

Amber glared at her from beside him.

"At least..." Roslyn twisted her lips sideways. "We've only recently met. I was just helping her out."

"That's kind of you and I'm glad it's you because she needs a bit of TLC and a place to stay for a few days."

"Oh."

"I told you, I'm fine," Amber snarled.

"Well, not exactly. Your test results are borderline okay and your blood pressure's still on the low side." Gareth smiled. "But I'm sure you'll improve if you get more fluids into you—"

"I can't give up my job." Amber's hands went to her hips.

"I understand but you need a decent place to sleep and some proper meals." He looked at Roslyn.

She stared back. "You want me to take her in?"

"I don't need you to," Amber snapped. "I've got another place lined up. Only slept in my car for a few nights 'cause...I had to leave my last place early." She snatched her keys from Roslyn's hand and got in her car.

"She needs a little help," Gareth murmured.

"Have you gone mad?" Roslyn hissed.

"Just for a few days."

Roslyn shook her head. This from the man who was too busy to see his long-term patient but somehow managed to fit in appointments with a young blow-in.

"My house isn't suitable for visitors."

"What about your cottage?"

"But—"

"Can you two move?" Amber was leaning out of the window glaring at them.

"You have to think of your baby's health as well as your own," Gareth said sternly and once more turned his questioning gaze on Roslyn. "She needs a few days so we can be sure she gets rehydrated and she needs to come back for a check-up in a couple of weeks."

Amber's car revved to life.

"Good luck." Gareth gave an apologetic grimace and returned to the surgery.

Roslyn watched him retreat then startled as Amber's car edged back. Damn young fool was no concern of Roslyn's. She stepped out of the way and Amber swung her wheel to turn. A loud crunch came from behind.

Another string of foul-mouthed expletives came from the young woman's mouth as she lurched the car forward again. Roslyn glanced from the brick garden bed, which seemed none the worse for the collision, to the back of Amber's car where there was a small dent in the bumper.

Amber got out and came around to inspect the damage.

"Shit, shit, shit." She rubbed the bumper with her hand.

"It's not much of a dent," Roslyn said. "And no damage to the garden bed so you won't have to fix that."

"As if I'd—" Amber sunk down, squatting at the back of her car. "What's the point," she hissed and her head slumped forward and rested against the metal.

She looked so forlorn and she couldn't be that old, barely out of her teens. Roslyn sighed. "Do you really have somewhere to stay tonight?"

There was a moment's pause then Amber's head shook and she pushed herself upright. "But I'll be fine. There's a place near the pub where I work that's quite good. Out of the way and not far from public toilets."

"Which pub?"

"Friedrich's Gasthaus."

"That's just down the road from my place." Roslyn paused. How could she turn the girl away now? "I've got an empty cottage. You could stay for a few days."

"I told you I don't need—"

"We both know you're lying. Anyway, Gareth's right. You need to take good care of yourself or it'll be the baby that suffers."

Amber's hand went to her stomach and Roslyn knew she'd found a way to get through to the stubborn young woman. "You'd have your own space, a comfortable bed…"

Amber looked wistful at that.

"A few days till you can find another place." Roslyn patted the car key in her pocket. "I'm on my way home now. Why don't you follow me? Have a look. If you don't like it, I certainly won't stop you from finding another place."

Amber wiped away a dribble of perspiration at her neck. "Is it cool?"

"There's only a small aircon in the main bedroom but the walls are thick stone and the loft helps keep it cool and there's a fan and…" Roslyn's words dried up. She was babbling and she never babbled. Something about Amber put her on edge. And, really, did she care if the girl accepted her offer or not?

"I'll come and check it out."

Roslyn glared at her. A little humility would go a long way.

"Thanks." Amber's lips turned up in an almost-smile.

"Follow me." Roslyn moved as fast as she could back to her car before she could rescind her offer.

"This is it." After fumbling with the key Roslyn used some extra force to push open the old wooden door of the cottage. "The door catches at the bottom on the slate – you just need to give it a shove."

Amber stood behind her, craning around her shoulder to see in.

"Have a look. It should have everything you need." Roslyn stepped into the small entrance. She was met by warm stuffy air. "I haven't been in here for a while." She waved at the door on her right. "The bathroom's in there and there's a small washing machine. It's all on rainwater so no long showers and don't fill the bath." She continued on to the lounge and opened a window.

Amber followed her inside. Her face lost its sullen look, replaced by surprise as her gaze swept over the plush couch, the loaded bookshelves and up to the overhead loft. Roslyn's head filled with doubt. After all, she knew little about this young woman, other than that her blood pressure was low and that she was doing it tough, but not why.

Now that she was here Roslyn worried she might not be able to get rid of her. What if she took ill, lost her job, invited friends? Possession was nine-tenths of the law, as Roslyn was well aware. It was silly to have made such a spur-of-the-moment decision.

Amber peered into the kitchen and then moved through and into the main bedroom. Roslyn took pride in knowing it was all neat, comfortably furnished and well equipped. The cottage had been done up years ago, first as Richard's den and then later for their son, Jerome, when he started uni. The main house had three bedrooms but only one bathroom and Jerome had appreciated his own space out here. And it made a great guesthouse when he and his family came back from Japan for visits.

Amber returned to the living room, peeped into the second bedroom then turned back. For a brief moment vulnerability crossed her face before her eyes narrowed and her jaw hardened.

"I can pay rent but not at the rate you'd want for this place."

"You don't have to pay me—"

"I suppose you want a free housekeeper then?" Amber snapped. "I told you I work at the pub but I could do some cleaning."

Roslyn put up her hand. "As I said, you're welcome here a few days while you look around for somewhere else to stay. There's no need to pay me. The place is empty…at the moment," she added, to give the impression it wouldn't always be.

ten

Instead of stacking the outside chairs Margot sat on one. They'd had a steady stream of customers all day and one of the casual girls had gone home sick. She was glad it was Friday afternoon and not her weekend on.

"Gad, it's been a busy day." Kath put two coffees on the table. "Neither of us got our morning coffee so I thought we should have one now. Lani's finishing up inside."

"Thanks, Kath. The weekend weather is supposed to be mid-twenties like today. Should be a gorgeous final spring weekend. I hope you won't be too busy. I've got errands to run tomorrow morning and then I'm looking after Isabella and Henry in the afternoon but I could help over lunch if you get stuck."

"Thanks, but my youngest will be around all weekend. She can help if I need."

Kath's daughter had worked in the shop during her school years and still helped out the odd times they'd needed an extra between her uni studies.

"That's good."

"I've got some quotes for the blinds." Kath put some papers on the table.

"Already."

"The sooner they're in the better."

"You were just getting quotes, you said."

"Yes, and I have." She spread the papers out in front of her. "There's not much difference in the actual blinds and the price between the two but one place says they can install them in a couple of weeks. The other was going to be after Christmas."

Margot picked up the pages. "Goodness, that'll knock a hole in the profits."

"Like I said, I think it'll encourage more people to stay if they've got protection from the weather. And they're see-through, so it doesn't block the view of the street."

"But you won't see our sandwich boards."

"I've been thinking we need some different signage anyway. It's a pain to lug those heavy boards out and in each day. Some nice flags that hook to the verandah posts would be easier."

"Another cost."

"Our planters will still hang from the verandah outside and with some creative signage it'll give us an easy facelift."

Margot was tired but Kath's enthusiasm was catching. "I guess so," she said.

"Great." Kath snatched up the papers. "So we'll go with the slightly cheaper and quicker option. I'll ring them now. They might be able to fit us in even sooner. Summer begins next week."

Margot sipped her coffee and stared along the street while her friend spoke to the installer. The General Providore had only been meant to be a small business, just the two of them and a casual. Now it was the two of them, Lani, who was permanent, and four casual staff. Both Margot and Kath were already stretched for time. Kath had her cleaning business and Margot kept her days off for her volunteer work and her family. It was different now that she had grandchildren. She wanted to be able to spend time with them, help care for them sometimes when their parents needed an extra pair of hands. The bigger and more complicated things got with the Prov the harder they were to manage. There were extra pressures when staff called in sick. Kath was creating an empire while Margot simply couldn't devote any more time or energy to it.

Her gaze drifted to a group of people near the post office down the road from the plant shop. Thelma was one of them and a couple of women from Margot's book club. As she watched, someone else came out of the post office. They were all gathered around the community noticeboard.

"They can do the blinds." Kath sat and picked up her coffee cup, her smile wide.

"That's good." Margot tried to summon some enthusiasm.

"They'll be here Monday to measure. I'll come in and meet them."

"Okay."

"What's going on down there?"

Margot followed Kath's gaze back down the footpath. There were about eight people by the noticeboard now – a very unusual sight for Jesserton at four o'clock on a Friday afternoon.

"I'll wander down and find out."

"I'll come with you."

They'd nearly reached the group when Thelma saw them coming.

"There's to be a meeting," she blurted. Her eagerness to share lit up her face. "About the fancy new hotel."

A rumble of comments rose from those around her.

"What's going on?" Greg had followed them down the footpath.

The people closest to the noticeboard stepped aside to reveal a bright new poster behind the glass. It stood out, shiny and fresh, pinned between the ad for the upcoming New Year's Eve celebration and an old missing cat flyer.

The headline jumped out at Margot – *Community Meeting* – then underneath in slightly smaller font *Come and find out all about the new boutique hotel concept for Jesserton*. Below that was one of those artist's impression-style photos of a fancy-looking hotel. Margot counted the levels that staggered up the side of the hill, which she presumed was the one on Gunter's property. There were five storeys.

"These Meyer and Brightman fellows are all about big projects in small communities that don't want them, aren't they?" Thelma said.

"Did you know about this, Margot?" Kevin from the butcher shop's tone was accusatory.

They were all staring at her.

"I only live next door," she blustered, hating to be the centre of their attention.

"I didn't realise that jolly company had plans already," someone called from behind. "I thought it was just an idea." There were several murmurs of dissent.

Kath stepped in closer to Margot. "I guess it is just an idea but we have to nip it in the bud."

Margot nodded. "That's why I started the petition."

"What petition?" Kev asked.

"I left one with your sales assistant on Tuesday."

Kev scratched his head. "He must have put it somewhere safe."

"It's on the shelf by your rubs and seasonings," Thelma said. "I signed it this morning."

"We've got a few signatures on the one in our shop already," Kath said.

"Me too," Greg said.

"I've signed both of them and the one in the post office." Thelma gave a determined nod of her head.

They all looked at her.

"Oh," Margot said. "I don't think you're supposed to—"

"They can't build something like that here," Kev barked.

"That drawing looks as if they plan to." Sandy from the hairdressers stabbed a finger towards the poster.

"Sure looks like they think they can," a grumpy voice called from the back and then everyone started speaking at once.

"We've got…" Margot's words came out in a croak. She cleared her throat and spoke up. "We've got to stop them."

The cacophony of voices silenced and once more all eyes were on her.

"Margot's right," Thelma said. "We should boycott this meeting."

"Good idea," Kevin said.

"Well, actually." Margot cleared her throat again. "I think we should all go."

"Seriously?" It was the querulous voice from the back again. Margot realised it was Martin Threadgold.

"At the moment they've got an idea and an artist's sketch of their plan. But the ink's barely dry on the sale. They can't have got too far with it all. We can hear what they have to say, ask questions and be better informed to put a stop to it."

"Margot's right," Kath said. "This will affect everyone. The whole town should be there."

Margot gave her friend a grateful smile as the voices around resounded in agreement.

"We should ask lots of questions," Kevin suggested.

"How will we know what questions to ask?" Sandy frowned.

Kevin scratched his head. "We could make a list and hand it out so everyone takes a turn."

"Perhaps someone from the council will be there." Thelma pointed a finger in the air then tapped it to her chin. "Although I think there's a bit of turmoil there with Councillor Higgins taking sick and the mayor playing up."

"Ooh, yes, I heard about that," Sandy said.

"Let's stick to the facts about the meeting." Martin's sharp retort nipped the gossip in the bud. Margot was thankful – it was so easy for people to get sidetracked.

"You've been in touch with the council, haven't you, Margot?" Kath asked. "To get the petition organised?"

"I only spoke to customer service about preparing a petition. They were very helpful. None of the councillors were available at the—"

"I told you they're in troub—"

"I'll ring a couple that I know if you like." Greg's quick reply cut Thelma off. "Make sure there'll be someone there."

"Thanks." Margot nodded. "In the meantime I think Kevin's right about preparing some questions. Fred said we can use the dining room at the pub for meetings. Why don't we meet there on Monday night? Fred will want input, I'm sure."

"I've got late appointments on Monday," Sandy said.

"I can't be there Monday night either." Kath gave an apologetic wince.

"That's okay. Let's say seven o'clock for those of us who can make it." Margot looked around and got several nods.

"Gunter would be turning in his grave if he knew about this," Kev said.

"He and his dear departed wife, both," Thelma nodded. Her sad look changed to one of resolve. "I'll be at the meeting."

"Great! Spread the word, everyone," Margot said. "We don't want any spare seats left in the Lutheran church hall next Wednesday night."

They began to disperse but a loud "Well, I never" from Thelma stopped them. She was pointing towards the little supermarket across the road where a sign had just been stuck up inside the window, SOLD.

"Who'd have guessed that would happen?" Greg scratched his head and there were other murmurs of surprise.

"Teakles' has been on the market for years," Kath murmured. "I honestly thought they'd walk out or drop dead before it sold."

Margot nodded. She only shopped there if she was desperate and often they didn't have what she was looking for anyway. The Teakles were a lovely couple but they'd long ago lost interest in running a business.

"I'll go and find out what's going on." Thelma nodded emphatically and strode off, her sturdy walking boots pounding across the road.

Martin followed her but everyone else dispersed and Kath and Margot strolled back to the Providore.

"You've certainly taken the lead with this hotel business," Kath said as they cleared away their coffee cups.

"What do you mean?"

"You'd usually be one to agree a blue sky was pink if that's what everyone else said."

"Are you saying I'm fickle?"

"No." Kath batted a hand at her. "But you usually avoid confrontation."

Margot frowned. Roslyn had said something similar just the other day. "I see myself as a peacekeeper. That doesn't mean I'm a pushover. Especially when it comes to something important like the wellbeing of our town."

"Well, I think it's good of you to show some leadership with this. You're a strong voice for Jesserton and I'm right behind you." Kath carried a stack of chairs inside.

Margot paused, bent over the other stack of chairs. Showing leadership? Was that what she was doing? It hadn't been her plan to be a voice for the town when she and Dennis had first discussed putting a stop to the hotel. She got a stronger grip on the chairs and straightened, her earlier concerns replaced by a sense of resolve she'd rarely experienced before.

eleven

The fact that Amber had wasted her Saturday was confirmed as she drove past the last rental on her list. It was on the edge of Sheffield, a small town close to Jesserton. The house looked old and run-down with an overgrown weed-filled yard, and she almost kept driving but there were few cars parked outside and no line of people waiting like there'd been at the previous three places she'd visited. Maybe she had a slight chance. She found a park a bit further along the street, dragged her unruly hair back into a ponytail and rubbed at the sauce mark on her t-shirt. There'd been a sausage sizzle at Bunnings where she'd had to park for the last inspection. The smell of the onions had drawn her to it.

She burped and swallowed the acidic taste that singed her throat. She was paying for eating the onions now. A few gulps of water, a quick look to make sure her face was clean – too bad about her t-shirt – and she got out of her car and made her way back to the property.

It was a private rental, not via an agent, and the obvious lack of other prospective tenants allowed her a small sliver of hope. Amber reached the gate, which hung open, one hinge not attached to the rusted frame. She was halfway along the path when a couple of blokes hurried out the front door. They were so intent on their conversation they barely acknowledged her as she stepped to one side to let them pass.

She caught the words "kidding" and "disgusting" before she made her way up the three crumbling steps to the door. It could loosely be described as a screen door but it was more holes than screen. She pulled it open and stepped inside to be met by the smell of damp and decay. Amber wrinkled her nose and took two more steps. Her foot almost snagged in a hole in the threadbare carpet. She moved on carefully.

"Who's there?" A man stepped into the doorframe at the end of the short passage. He was slightly stooped, with a few wisps of silver hair swept across his head.

"I've come about the rental."

"Are you pregnant?"

Amber frowned then looked down. Part of her t-shirt was stuck in the elastic waist of her pants and accentuated the small round of her belly. She tugged it away. She could just say she'd put on weight but she knew the rest of her was too thin. "Yes." She nodded, thinking that was the end of her chances.

The man beamed at her. "A baby is wonderful. Come in, come in." He beckoned. "You have a look around, okay?"

Amber gave a quick glance into the two front rooms, both gloomy and empty of anything except stained floor coverings and ratty blinds half down over small windows. Her heart sunk further. She had no furniture.

"Come look at the kitchen. It's got a new oven. I just put it in."

Amber reluctantly followed him into the small kitchen.

The man stood beside a compact upright oven that reminded her of the cooker from her childhood neighbour's house. The woman had been a grandmotherly figure in Amber and her brother's lives during the time they'd lived next door to her. She was always cooking biscuits that she gave to them with mugs of warm chocolate milk. No warmth or deliciousness emanated from this stove. There were gaps between it and the rough benches either side, and exposed wall behind it, as if something bigger had been there before. She could see wiring in the gaps.

"I got it for a song." He opened the oven door. "But it's all clean and in good order. Do you like to cook?"

Amber nodded, not putting a voice to the lie. She crossed the worn linoleum floor and stepped into a bigger room where the larger windows let more light into the dingy house. At least there was a table and two chairs. Beyond the glass there was a yard, as overgrown as the front.

"Lots of room for a family."

Amber turned. The man was smiling at her.

"Does your husband have work nearby?"

"I'm...I'm on my own."

"But your baby." He waved a hand in the direction of her belly. "How are you going to pay the rent?"

Amber drew up her shoulders. "I've got a job and money put aside."

"On your own you won't manage. Babies take lots of work."

Amber stiffened. "You don't need to worry. I'll manage."

"You have references?"

Annoyance dissolved her sliver of hope. "My partner paid the rent at our last place."

"No, no, no." He shook his head vigorously. "I know what will happen. You move in here then you can't pay."

"You don't know that."

"I know." His look was full of disdain and he shooed her with his hands as if she were a dog. "This is no good. You go."

Amber's annoyance fizzed and erupted as anger. "This place is a dump anyway," she snarled as she barrelled past him. She caught her foot properly in the ragged carpet this time and stumbled against the wall, making a larger hole as she tugged her foot free.

"You damage my property!" the man yelled after her. "No respect, you young people."

Amber flipped him the bird. Respect was supposed to be a two-way street but in her experience it was rare she was given any. She recalled the way the woman at the first unit she'd visited that morning had looked her up and down. Amber's clothes had been clean then but the woman's gaze had lingered on her belly and her face had pinched in tighter. Amber had been careful to make sure her t-shirt hung loose after that, until now. This house was a dump but she knew she would have taken it at the right price.

By the time she arrived back at Roslyn's place her anger had subsided a little. She switched off the car and sat a moment, staring at the stone walls. The cottage was an old building, but Roslyn, or someone she'd paid no doubt, had managed to make it comfortable. Absolutely no comparison to the dump Amber had just left but she had to find a place soon and, as she'd been told a few times too many lately, beggars couldn't be choosers. Roslyn had made it clear this was a temporary thing and Amber had stayed three nights already.

She let herself into the cottage and dumped her bag on a chair where it immediately slid sideways disgorging the contents all over the floor. She marched on into the kitchen and gulped down a big glass of water. When she'd seen the doctor he'd told her she should be drinking lots but the trouble with that was she had to pee more often. She'd get a bad rep at work if she was in the toilet every five minutes.

Back in the lounge she looked at the scattered contents of her bag. The page of rental listings lay on top, teasing her with the string of addresses that had filled her with hope. She'd copied them out the previous night just in case her phone went flat. What a waste of time and petrol that had been, and she'd had to get up extra early to make the first one. She'd driven to three different suburbs across Adelaide where the queues had been long to inspect properties she had no hope of being accepted for, then ended up close to Jesserton at that dump of a place, not fit for a dog let alone Amber and a baby. She swept up the paper, scrunched it in her hands then shredded it.

"What's the point!" she raged and flung the pieces across the room where they fluttered every which way to the floor. She groaned and sagged onto the couch. There were several pillows too many on it and she tossed them to the floor as well. One of them probably cost as much as she spent on food for a week. The unfairness of it fuelled her anger. She struggled up from the couch and kicked the cushions. "Bloody fancy rubbish," she ranted.

"Hello?"

"Shit!"

Roslyn was peering in at her through the screen door. Amber hadn't seen her since the afternoon she'd moved in. She hurried forward, hoping the woman hadn't seen her flinging her cushions about. Amber pushed open the screen and stepped out, forcing Roslyn to hobble backwards.

"I heard your car." Roslyn peered over Amber's shoulder.

"I've been out looking for another place," Amber said quickly, trying to fill the doorway so Roslyn wouldn't see the mess.

"That's good."

Amber tensed. "I've been to four places today but no luck."

"I see."

"I'll try—"

"I thou—"

They both spoke at once then faltered. Amber glared at Roslyn who stared back, her eyes narrowed, her nose in the air.

"I thought you must have been at work." Roslyn raised her hands. "I brought you this."

They both glanced down at the tea-towel-wrapped bundle.

"It's a banana cake and a chicken pie. I made two and thought—"

"I *can* cook." Amber glared at Roslyn, whose brow creased to a frown.

"I wasn't suggesting..." She blew out a sharp breath. "I made extra and I thought as you seem to be working...or out, that you might appreciate not having to cook but if you don't want it I'll put it in my freezer."

Their eyes met again. Roslyn's stare was resolute. Amber glanced at the bundle in her hands. The smell of warm pie pastry wafted her way. She swallowed as saliva pooled in her mouth. She hadn't shopped in a while. She'd had the last piece of her Wednesday night pizza for breakfast this morning and she was on the late shift tonight so she'd miss the chef's free meal.

"Thanks," she said.

Roslyn handed over the food but stayed put. "How are you feeling?"

"Fine."

"No more dizzy spells or headaches?"

"I thought you were a *retired* doctor."

"I am," she snapped. "It's not a consultation, just a neighbourly enquiry."

Amber wilted a little under her glare. "I'm feeling fine." It was the truth as far as her physical health was concerned. She'd worked shifts at the pub each night since she'd moved in at the cottage but the comfortable bed and safe surroundings had meant she'd slept well and woken each morning feeling refreshed – something she hadn't experienced in a long while.

"Everything's all right in the cottage?" Once more Roslyn tried to peer past her shoulder.

"You can come in and check if you like."

"I'm not checking up, simply asking if there's anything else you might need."

Amber blew out the breath she'd been holding. "No... thank you."

"Good, well, I'll leave you to it." Roslyn turned on her heel and walked two steps before she started to limp. Amber had noticed she'd done it the first day they'd met. She'd insisted on carrying the jerry can with the fuel for Amber but she'd almost lost her balance at one point. There was obviously something wrong with her leg.

Amber opened her mouth to ask if she was okay then thought better of it. Roslyn was as prickly as an echidna; no doubt she'd not appreciate questions about her health.

Roslyn did her best to make a dignified retreat. The doctor's pulling and prodding had stirred things up and it was still difficult to find a comfortable way to walk. The hairs on the back of her neck stood up, not just because she felt Amber watching her but because the girl's behaviour had set off warning bells.

It had been impossible to see much of the cottage but the bit of floor Roslyn could see had been littered with rubbish and cushions. The cushions hadn't been expensive but she'd spent a lot of time scouring op shops looking for something to replace the originals whose demise she'd prefer to forget.

Amber herself had looked terrible, even though she'd said she was fine. Her streaky purple hair was lank and part in, part out of a tangled ponytail, her face flushed and the clothes she'd been wearing looked like they were in need of washing. The brief moment Roslyn had been close she'd caught a strong whiff of body odour. No wonder she'd made no headway finding accommodation if she'd presented like that.

Roslyn managed to get herself inside and propped in a semi-comfortable position at her kitchen bench. In front of her the dishes from her baking were still scattered over the sink. She'd tackle them later or even leave them till after dinner – what did it matter? More important was the situation with Amber. Roslyn had given the young woman some time, hadn't hassled her, but now she wondered how much effort Amber was putting in to finding herself accommodation.

She glanced at the clock then at the painkillers Joe had prescribed. She'd put aside a nice bottle of red for her steak dinner and it was close enough to five o'clock. She'd have a glass of wine instead of a pill.

She'd just poured the wine and taken her first sip when her back door rattled and Margot bustled in.

"Have you read the paper today?" She waved a folded newspaper in the air.

Roslyn glanced at her tablet lying on the side table. She never bought a paper copy these days, preferring the digital version. "Not yet."

"There's a write-up about the proposed hotel. That blasted Meyer and Brightman lot are unbelievable." She paused. "Are you on the wine already?"

"It's five o'clock." Roslyn wasn't sure why she needed to justify the time of day to her sister.

"Is it? I might join you then."

Roslyn didn't bother to get up but picked up the paper that had been tossed aside as Margot helped herself to a glass and some wine.

"Dennis not home?" Roslyn asked.

"He's at work."

"On a Saturday afternoon?"

"Someone's sick." Margot paused to look at the sink. "Have you been baking?"

"A simple chicken pie and a banana cake."

"You never bake."

"I do sometimes. Anyway, I had some soft bananas needed using up. Thought I could take cake to Emily's tomorrow."

Margot quirked one eyebrow then waved at the paper as she came and sat down. "The stuff about the hotel is all in there. Meyer and Brightman may have only just bought the place but they've been working on this hotel idea for a long time already."

"Biding their time till they found the right property, I'd suspect."

Margot's eyes narrowed above the glass she'd raised to her lips. "Did you know about it?"

"No. But a company like that would be looking and coming up with ideas all the time and well before they made a commitment."

Margot snatched the paper from her and began to turn the pages. Roslyn took a sip of her wine. The proposed hotel was not high on her list of concerns.

"Listen to this." Margot began to read from the paper. *"New bespoke hotel proposed for the Adelaide Hills. Developers Meyer and Brightman, who have built unique accommodation in other tourist regions* both in South Australia and interstate, have applied to build a hotel with eighteen rooms and two penthouse apartments. Nestled against the side of a hill outside Jesserton, each room will have private balcony views across the valley to the hills." Margot glanced up. "All those people looking over my backyard."

"I don't think—"

"There's more." Margot continued. "*The hotel is designed to accommodate those wanting a little more luxury and will encourage visitors to remain longer, stay overnight and see more of the region.*"

"Surely that would be a good thing for local businesses," Roslyn said.

"Not in Jesserton. They're hardly likely to visit the cafe or the pub if there's a restaurant in the hotel, and I can't see them popping into Sandy's for a haircut – she's hard enough to get into as it is." Margot waved the hand with her glass in the air and the red wine slopped wildly from side to side.

"Don't waste my wine," Roslyn snapped. "That's an expensive bottle."

Margot continued as if she hadn't spoken. "They won't be spending money at Greg's for a plant or…or the butcher shop for meat…"

"Perhaps on their way home?" Roslyn ventured, which earned her a glare from Margot who sniffed and turned back to the page.

"'*Our key focus is sustainability,*' said the hotel's designer. '*The objective of the development's methodology and the servicing and operation of the hotel is to deliver a well-appointed accommodation experience, which is heightened by the adoption of contemporary environmentally sustainable design.*'"

The paper flopped forward and Margot stared over it. "What does that even mean?"

Roslyn didn't need to answer. Margot snapped the paper upright and kept reading.

"'We think our bespoke hotel will provide our guests with luxury accommodation right in the heart of the Hills, nestled alongside picturesque Jesserton and nearby wineries and tourist attractions.'"

"Something that's lacking in this area," Roslyn said, but once again she was ignored.

"This is what I can't believe." Margot stabbed a finger at the paper and continued. "*'We've now reached a point where council is happy with the concept.'*" She looked up. "Council is happy with the plans!" she repeated, her hands scrunching the edges of the paper. "How can it have come this far without anyone knowing?" Her eyes narrowed. "They've only just bought the land. And now there's suddenly a plan and council knows about it already."

"They're the kind of company that would know all the rules. They've probably had ideas, even a basic outline, for ages and been on the lookout for the right land. As soon as they found it, they were ready and waiting with their well-thought-out plans."

Margot's mouth dropped open. "I can't believe you're on the side of the hotel."

"I'm not on anyone's side. I think the key words in that article are *council is happy with the concept*." Roslyn wagged her finger to underline her point.

"Don't get all high and mighty with me."

"I'm simply pointing out that it's still in planning and might not go ahead."

"Might not." Margot leaped to her feet. The newspaper slid to the floor. "It won't! The rest of the town is up in arms."

"The whole town?" Roslyn raised an eyebrow.

"Everyone. This is not a joke, Roslyn. You always do that."

"Do what?"

"Play the high-and-mighty big-sister card as if you know all the answers and I know nothing."

Roslyn clamped her lips together then changed her mind and opened them for another mouthful of wine.

Margot swished the paper through the air. "You're always so bloody smug." She spun and waltzed out the door.

Roslyn listened to the angry clack of her sister's heels retreating along the path and the bang of the garden gate, and then the quiet settled. She looked at the partly drunk glass of wine that Margot had left behind, tipped it into her own, took a sip and wondered how she was going to get Amber out of her cottage.

twelve

Dinner at Emily and Cameron's

Hummus Dip with Veggie Sticks & Corn Chips

Asparagus Stir-fry, Vegan Lasagne, Green Salad with Lemon Dressing

Fruit & Yogurt Granola Parfaits, Tahini Almond Cookies

"Thanks, Mum," Emily said as Margot put her lasagne in the oven.

"It's just to keep warm," Margot said. "And I've made a couple of simple sweets. I think everyone will like the cookies and your dad's got the parfaits in the esky."

"You're the best." Emily hugged her. "We've had such a busy week I nearly called off dinner but Cam volunteered to do his famous asparagus stir-fry." She smiled at her husband as he popped a bottle of champagne. "That's a sound I'm pleased to hear."

Dennis hefted the esky up onto the kitchen bench, accompanied by the rattle of clinking glass.

"Careful of the parfaits," Margot chided. "There's no need to put it on the bench. We can leave the esky in the laundry until dessert."

"No room," Cameron said. "I've got the drinks on ice in there."

Dennis tucked the esky against the end of the island bench and brushed a kiss across his daughter's cheek. "I hope you've got something with meat in it, Emily. I don't like the look of your mum's vegan lasagne."

Henry tugged at Dennis's trouser leg, distracting him, and Emily made a wincey face at Margot as Dennis scooped up the little boy and took him outside.

"He makes a fuss but it doesn't hurt him to not eat meat once in a while," Margot soothed. "Nick and Kayla are running late. I think he's had trouble with the work van again. Oh, and here's Geraldine."

"Can you get everyone to stay out in the courtyard, Mum?" Emily flapped her hands towards the door. "It'll be chaotic if they all come in here."

"Here, give me the champagne. I'll take it out."

"Glasses are already out there." Cameron handed over the bottle. "I'll bring the wine and some beers."

The home Em and Cam had created behind their shop in the main street of Hahndorf was little more than a flat. Two bedrooms and a living area. Not a lot of room for extras. Margot stepped out into the courtyard. It was also small but shady and pretty with one wall and the rafters covered in glory vine.

There was the usual ruckus as everyone caught up. Nick's two boys were at a birthday party, which Margot knew Emily would be happy about. Two less to find a space for. Roslyn was the last to arrive.

Margot brushed a kiss over her sister's cheek. She was still a little miffed with Roslyn for her flippant response to her concerns over the hotel but she swallowed her annoyance for the sake of peace.

"Is that your cake?" Margot reached for the foil-covered plate Roslyn had surreptitiously slipped onto the table. "I'll pop it inside for later."

"No, that's some savouries. This is the cake." Roslyn produced a smaller plate with her cake wrapped in plastic film. "And I brought wine." She handed a bottle of red to Cameron.

"What have you got under here, Roslyn?" Dennis had divested himself of his grandson and held a beer in one hand while he tugged at the corner of the alfoil with the other.

"Just a few sausage rolls." She smiled at Emily as she came outside. "I know you two are busy with the shop and family so I thought I'd help out with food."

"Since when have you ever made sausage rolls?" Margot asked.

"I didn't make them. I called in at that new cafe in Sheffield to see what it was like and they had them. They're cocktail size so I thought they'd be handy as pre-dinner nibbles."

"I had coffee there the other day," Geraldine said. "It's a lovely cafe."

Dennis finally got the alfoil off. "Better try one then." He put it in his mouth and nodded before picking up a second. "They're good."

"Sorry, they're not suitable for vegan or gluten-free or vegetarian but I thought you'd have that covered. Oh, and they said they don't use egg." Roslyn smiled at Isabella, who looked pleadingly at Emily.

"You can try one," Emily said.

The savoury scent wafted in Margot's direction making her mouth water but she resolutely held back. The men took their beers and went to have a look at Dennis's car while the women settled around the table.

Emily chewed on a carrot she'd dipped in the hummus and screwed up her nose. "Cam says I've put too much tahini in it. He might be right."

Margot avoided the sausage rolls and took a scoop of the hummus on a corn chip. She smiled to cover her reaction to the bitter dip. "It's fine."

Kayla tried some and sucked in a breath. "Did you use unhulled tahini? It can make a difference to the taste."

Emily eyeballed her sister-in-law. "It's not easy hosting family dinners, you know."

Kayla was suddenly very interested in something in her lap.

"I seem to be able to tolerate a little gluten these days." Geraldine reached for a second sausage roll and Emily transferred her testy gaze to her.

"How have you got on with the petition in the shop, Emily?" Margot asked, keen to draw the topic away from the food.

"I'm not sure." She ducked her head to gather up a toy Henry had dropped. "A few, I guess."

Margot studied her daughter but she was intent on giving Henry back his toys. She'd thought there'd be plenty of signatures on it already.

"What petition?" Roslyn asked.

Margot lifted her chin. "I've made a petition to stop the hotel being built."

Roslyn raised her eyebrows, accompanied by a barely audible snort.

"Good on you, Margot." Geraldine beamed. "I'll sign it."

"I hope you're all coming to the meeting this week."

"What meeting?" Roslyn asked.

"For goodness sake, Roslyn, sometimes I wonder if you're a part of the town or not for all the interest you take. Meyer and

Brightman are holding a meeting this Wednesday night in the Lutheran hall about the hotel."

"Oh, I see. I suppose…"

"And tomorrow night a few of us are gathering at the pub to prepare for the meeting and make a list of questions we want answers to."

"I can't do tomorrow night."

Margot frowned at her sister.

"I've got a Zoom meeting with the outreach services group."

"I thought you'd stopped volunteering."

"I don't physically provide the service but I still have support input."

Margot shrugged. She couldn't argue against Roslyn's volunteer work but she'd hoped for her sister's support with the meeting preparation. "You'll come to the meeting Wednesday though."

Roslyn's nod was stiff.

"Nick will be there," Kayla said brightly.

"And me." Geraldine smiled and helped herself to another sausage roll.

"You should pace yourself, Geraldine," Roslyn said. "I'm sure Emily has a lovely dinner for us."

"But they're not very big, are they?" Geraldine popped the small pastry into her mouth. "What have you made us for dinner, Emily dear?"

"We're having Cam's asparagus stir-fry and Mum's made a delicious vegan lasagne."

"Lovely," Geraldine said with a smile but her gaze went to the dwindling number of savouries Roslyn had brought.

It irritated Margot that Roslyn always brought not-so-healthy food and those without food intolerances devoured it. Last fortnight it had been the garlic bread and the vegetable bake with bacon and cheese added, and this time sausage rolls and cake.

The sound of male voices drifted from the side of the house.

"We'd better get the mains out." Margot stood while Emily handed Henry to Kayla.

"Can I help?" Roslyn asked. She had no idea what had got up Margot's nose but if she held it any higher in the air she was bound to trip over.

"No thanks, Roslyn. Mum and I can manage," Emily said. "There's not much to bring out. Can you ask Cam to refill the drinks?"

"This hotel business must be such a worry for you," Geraldine said as the glasses were topped up and she took a seat beside Roslyn.

"Not really," Roslyn said. "It's all still only on paper. It may not happen."

"It certainly won't if Margot and I have anything to do with it," Dennis said as his wife put a large dish of lasagne on the table. "Margot's been sensational, getting a petition going and organising people to prepare questions for Wednesday night's meeting."

"I'm not really organ—"

"The hotel hasn't got a chance if Margot's in charge." He cut off his wife's protest and winked.

Roslyn studied Dennis for signs of too much alcohol. He was rarely so effusive about Margot's talents.

"I don't suppose you're coming to the meeting?" he said.

"I've only just heard about these meetings."

"Margot's been doing lots of research. We want to get all our facts straight and questions sorted ready for Wednesday night. Your sister could do with your support."

"I can't come tomorrow night."

Dennis frowned.

"But you'll be there Wednesday, won't you, Roslyn?" Margot was standing at the head of the table, one hand holding a serving spoon and the other reaching for Roslyn's plate. "Lasagne?"

"I'll be there." Roslyn turned to Emily who was dishing from another pot. "I think I'll try Cameron's stir-fry to begin with."

Roslyn wasn't a fan of asparagus but there was no way she was eating that lasagne. It was full of things she either didn't like or didn't agree with her. She kept her head down and was glad when the conversation turned back to Dennis's new car and Isabella's kindy forays.

"How did you get on at the doctor's?" Geraldine's voice was low in her ear.

Roslyn stiffened. "Perfectly fine. Just a check-up. And you?" She immediately regretted the question as she then had to sit through Geraldine relating her medical history in great detail.

"The doctor suggested I see a counsellor, you know." Geraldine's voice had dropped so low Roslyn nearly didn't hear her. "I get so tired some days I can barely drag myself out of bed. He thought maybe it was depression."

"Perhaps you should then."

"I wasn't going to but you think I—"

"Always best to follow your doctor's advice," Roslyn said, aware how pompous she sounded even to herself.

She was relieved when the plates were empty and she rose as soon as Emily and Margot began to clear away. "Let me help with the dishes."

She followed them into the house. Emily had to take Henry for a nappy change so it was just Margot and Roslyn scraping plates and stacking the dishwasher.

"We'll only fit in one more Sunday dinner before Christmas," Margot said. "And I'd like to host Christmas." She looked expectantly at Roslyn.

"You'll get no argument from me but you know I'll bring something."

"Of course, thank you. Everyone does when it's Christmas." Margot pressed her knee against the dishwasher door and shoved it shut. "I wondered if you'd host next fortnight's dinner."

Roslyn started rinsing glasses that hadn't fitted in the dishwasher. There was the problem of Amber but surely she'd be gone within the next two weeks. "Maybe Nick and Kayla woul—"

"Nick's still renovating their kitchen," Margot said. "It's hard for them to entertain."

Nick had been working on the kitchen ever since they'd bought the house in Jesserton eighteen months ago. They'd hosted a family barbecue the month they'd moved in but hadn't taken a turn since. "What about Geraldine?"

Margot glared at her.

Roslyn shrugged. "I suppose I could."

"Perhaps the pool would be warm enough for the children by then."

"Perhaps." The pool was the bane of her life these days. Richard had been the one to look after it but since he'd died she had to pay someone to come and see to it, turn on the solar and get it ready for the summer months.

Margot looked around the small kitchen. "I should take out the dessert."

Roslyn helped her lift the parfaits from the esky. "What's in these?" she asked.

"It's an easy recipe that I'm sure everyone will love," Margot said. "And so simple. It's oats and assorted nuts and berries, maple syrup and yogurt."

"What about Kayla?"

"It's vegan yogurt." Margot beamed as if she'd won first prize at the show. "And the tahini cookies are delicious. I'll definitely be keeping them on the menu at the Providore while pomegranates are in season."

Roslyn was a fan of pomegranate at least, but goodness knows what else Margot had put in the biscuits. "And there's my banana cake." She wasn't feeling like dessert herself but she thought there'd be a few around the table who'd appreciate her contribution.

"You always do that, Roslyn."

"Do what?"

"Bring extras."

"You brought food."

"Yes, because Emily asked me to and, anyway, I brought things everyone can eat."

"Not everyone. My stomach does not tolerate red lentils." There had been that one time and it may not have been entirely the lentils' fault but she hated being forced to eat food she wasn't keen on. "And I dislike tofu."

"You had the asparagus stir-fry."

"What other choice was there? My sausage rolls disappeared in quick time."

"We don't have to have meat at every meal."

"Why not, if it's what we like?"

They glared at each other across the kitchen bench. Margot had become quite snippy of late. This hotel business was obviously stirring her up but Roslyn wasn't buying into it.

"If there's no meat for Christmas dinner I'm not coming," she snapped.

"Me either." Nick carried in the still half-full lasagne dish. At a glare from his mother he put it quickly on the bench and held up his hands. "Just kidding. Can I help bring out dessert?"

"Henry's gone to sleep." Emily arrived back in the kitchen. "Hopefully he's down for the night." She looked at each of them then at the tray of parfaits. "Oh good, you're organising dessert. Is there still champagne? I think Cam's got a bit of an announcement to make." She picked up the plate of biscuits and went out to the courtyard and Nick followed her with the tray.

Roslyn indicated her cake. "I'll take this out." She smiled at Margot. "Then there's something for everyone."

Outside Cameron was topping up the glasses again. Emily gave a small clap of her hands.

"Cameron's got some news." She beamed at her husband and they all turned expectant gazes in his direction.

Cameron cleared his throat. "I expect you've heard that a councillor has retired due to ill health."

"Poor man," Geraldine murmured.

"Yes, not the best circumstances," Cameron said. "And I've heard from a reliable source that the mayor is also resigning…she's moving interstate, I believe."

"Maybe some truth to that affair rumour," Nick said.

"Oh, yes, I heard that too." Geraldine nodded. "No smoke without fire, is there?"

"She cited personal reasons," Cameron said. "Regardless, it means there will have to be a by-election and—"

"Cameron's going to stand," Emily burst out, full of pride.

"For mayor?" Roslyn asked.

"No. That's a much bigger role that I don't have the expertise or time for." Cameron shook his head. "But I think I can make a decent go of being a councillor."

"Good on you, Cam." Dennis raised his glass. "A sensible head might help with all this proposed hotel business for Jesserton."

Margot leaped up and raised her glass. "Yes, wouldn't that be fantastic."

Cameron's smile dropped away. "We'd better not get too far ahead of ourselves. I'm not sure how much input I'd get into that and, anyway, I have to be elected first."

"To Cameron." Emily tapped her glass against her mother's.

Roslyn raised hers and joined the chorus. She was quite sure Cameron would make a very good elected member but she wasn't so sure his family understood what that might mean when it came to the development.

thirteen

Margot glanced at her watch then at the empty drive stretching away beyond the curve lined with leafy trees. Today they were ripples of variegated green, stirred by a gentle breeze that was keeping the temperature to a pleasant mid-twenties. It was a beautiful day. She glanced at her watch again. It was the first Tuesday of the month, they had book club, it was Roslyn's turn to drive and it was nearly two o'clock.

Margot pulled out her phone to ring and startled as it vibrated in her hand with the tone of an incoming message. There was a number on her screen rather than a name so no-one from her extensive contacts list. The first line caught her attention.

Hello Margot, its Esther.

Margot opened the text and read on.

I'm sure you've heard the million rumours. Truth is I've left my husband and I'm moving away with my new partner. As much as we've tried to maintain our privacy its been difficult. I've given a lot of my life to public service and now I'm taking time for me. I think you're invested in this community and would make a good mayor.

Margot gasped. The phone slipped in her fingers and she gripped it tighter as she read the last two lines.

I sincerely hope you'll give it some thought. You have my number now if you'd like to talk.

Margot stared at the screen until the text blurred. Several years ago she'd done one term as a councillor. She knew how busy she'd been then. She wasn't sure she'd have the energy to devote to being a councillor now, let alone mayor.

A car slowed on the road beyond her driveway. Margot tucked her phone away. She wouldn't mention the message to Roslyn. She'd pooh-pooh the idea straight away and she'd no doubt be right but Margot wasn't in the mood to be told by her sister.

Tyres crunched on the gravel and Roslyn's Mercedes rolled towards her. Dennis had been annoyed when Roslyn bought the car. First because she didn't buy it from him and second because she'd got an EV before he had. She recalled his excitement at bringing home his sleek black EV the previous week and sighed. It had certainly been a nice car and cars were his livelihood but Margot could never summon the care factor he did.

The sleek white car rolled to a stop beside her and Roslyn gave a brief wave over the steering wheel.

Margot waved back. She hadn't seen or spoken to her sister since Sunday evening. It was more that Margot had been too busy rather than that she was still annoyed with Roslyn over the food thing, although it was irritating that she didn't seem to take it seriously. And on Monday she'd been busy preparing for and then attending the planning meeting at the pub.

"I thought you'd forgotten me," Margot called as she put her basket on the back seat.

"It's not two yet. And book club never starts on time," Roslyn said. "Especially when it's at Helen's."

"Why does she pick such fat books?" Margot glanced across at her sister. "Have you read it?"

"Yes."

"Of course, you'd have time."

"We have the same amount of time, Margot. It's how you choose to use it that makes the difference."

Margot stiffened. Roslyn was using her imperious big-sister voice again. "You're retired though."

"I don't sit around reading all day."

"I'm so busy," Margot groaned. "The month flies by. Most weekends if I'm not working, I'm looking after grandchildren. And now this hotel business has added an extra load." Margot drew a breath. "I thought you might have at least called in for coffee yesterday. I could have done with your input before our planning meeting last night."

"I went out...for lunch."

Margot glanced at her sister. Roslyn was focused on making a right-hand turn.

"You could have come over after that."

"I thought perhaps you might still be annoyed about the food..." Roslyn shot her a quick glance. "And you didn't ask me to come for coffee."

"For goodness sake, Roslyn, I do get annoyed with your superior attitude sometimes but we're sisters. You don't need an invitation." Margot remembered the car she'd seen that morning waiting to turn out of Roslyn's driveway as she'd passed. "Did you have visitors? I saw a strange car leaving your place on my way to the shops this morning."

"Might have been the pool man. He came this morning."

"Doesn't he drive a va—"

"Which reminds me, I was going to talk to you about aqua aerobics," Roslyn said quickly. "I thought I might join the class."

"Really?"

"Don't sound so surprised. You've been at me to join."

Margot's hand shot across and patted Roslyn's arm. "I'm glad for you. I'm sure you'll be so much better for it."

"So you've said. Are there any times other than first thing Monday?"

"Several. I've got a program at home. I'll get it for you when you drop me back."

Roslyn pulled up down the road from Helen's house. Margot glanced at the cars lining the footpath either side. "Looks like they're all here. Any quick hints you can give me about this blasted book?" she huffed. "I really did try but I couldn't get into it."

"Just mention a few things like 'brilliant description', 'wonderfully written' and 'superbly drawn characters' and you'll muddle through till the wine's poured and then they'll move on to other topics."

They both reached into the back for their books and bags. It was their last book club for the year so it had a Christmas theme and they all brought gift-wrapped books to swap.

"I've got copies of the petition for Helen."

Roslyn frowned at her over the roof of the car. "She doesn't have a business in town."

"Their pizzeria's in the next town. Sheffield will be affected by the hotel too and she might hand some around to other businesses."

Roslyn opened her mouth then pursed her lips and turned to walk up the path.

Margot paused at the gate and glared at Roslyn's ramrod straight back. "What is it?"

Her sister stopped, half turned. "Nothing…except…"

"Out with it."

"Just remember not everyone will be opposed to the idea of a hotel."

"Of course they will. Even in Mount Barker, Dennis thinks a lot of people will be against it. He says a hotel like that in Jesserton will dominate the landscape and stifle small business. And now that Cameron's running for council, that'll add some common sense to council decisions."

"I'm not sure if it's as easy as that," Roslyn said.

Margot swallowed her annoyance, glad she hadn't mentioned Esther's text. Ahead of them the front door of the house opened.

"Hello, Helen." She plastered a smile to her face, strode past Roslyn and air kissed their hostess's cheeks. "I'm looking forward to today's discussion. It was a wonderfully written story, wasn't it?"

⁂

Amber stepped into the bath and slowly lowered herself into the encompassing warmth. It was one of those long, deep baths that stood on large claw-like legs in the corner of the bathroom that she'd only ever seen in pictures of fancy houses. This one wasn't shiny and it had little chips in places so Amber suspected it might be as old as the cottage itself but that didn't matter. Her belly was like a small island in the centre. She blew out the breath she'd been holding and closed her eyes, gently inhaling the soft scent of the lavender oil she'd purchased on her quick visit to the shops that morning.

She'd woken early and headed to the supermarket for a few supplies. She'd had a craving for toast but had run out of bread. The bath oil had been in the mark-down pile at the end of an aisle. It was supposed to be calming and have a relaxing effect on the body.

Roslyn had been waiting for her when she'd arrived back from the shops, this time with some tomatoes and zucchinis from her garden. Amber wasn't a fan of either but she'd done her best to seem grateful.

After she'd eaten tomato on toast and surprised herself for actually enjoying the juicy treat, she'd decided it was time she got everything out of her car and sorted it. She'd made piles all over the lounge: a small one of items she'd collected for the baby, a slightly bigger stack of her own clothes, a box of shoes and bags, a crate of pots and pans and a kettle. She had a plastic tub with a lid for food items like pasta, two-minute noodles and tins of baked beans that she bought when they were on special. The esky was already empty, its meagre contents in the fridge along with the remains of the pie and the rest of the vegetables Roslyn had given her. Also draped over a chair in the lounge was the thin mattress she rolled out in the back of the station wagon when she needed, a sleeping bag, a few extra towels and sheets, and that was almost the sum of her possessions.

Later Amber had been outside. The day was mild and she'd been drawn out to the garden that made a colourful wall between the cottage and Roslyn's backyard. Amber had basked in the early afternoon sunshine, stretching like a cat. She'd taken her mug of tea and carefully explored the garden area, not wanting Roslyn to catch her snooping. There'd been a van over to one side of the big space between the cottage and Roslyn's house. It was parked beside some kind of enclosed verandah and had *Hills Pool Care* written across the side. Roslyn had come out dressed in a smart blue jacket and pants and spoken to the man with the van, then she'd put some things in the back of her car and driven away. Not long after, the pool man had also left and Amber had taken a chance for a quick snoop.

Under a see-through corrugated roof with three walls enclosed by pull-down blinds there was an in-ground swimming pool. The water sparkled clear and clean over vibrant blue tiles and looked good enough to swim in. She squatted down and dipped her hand in, expecting the water to be icy cold, but while it wasn't warm it didn't have the chill she'd anticipated. There had to be some form of heating.

She'd stared at the large body of water again and then went straight back to her cottage and ran the bath. She'd had several shifts at the pub over the weekend and this was her first full day and night off since she'd started working there. She told herself she deserved it.

Soaking in the bath, she pondered her few possessions. The car was the most important. Without it she really would be stuck and homeless. She hadn't had much when she'd moved to Penola but living with Tyson she'd begun to take pride in their flat and had bought a few things, which thankfully she'd managed to retrieve after he'd thrown her out. He'd wanted her gone, threatened her and the baby. Just thinking his name made her shudder.

She sank deeper into the water and stared up at the ceiling, dragging her thoughts from the man who'd dumped her like a rotten potato as soon as he'd found out she was pregnant. She drew in a long, slow breath and focused on the small water stain above her. The paint was peeling in a couple of patches too but she'd seen far worse and it was a million times better than sleeping in her car. While she'd eaten her toast that morning she'd checked the real estate rental pages but there'd been no messages for her on any of the sites she'd listed her details. Without rental history or referees it was useless but stubbornly she checked anyway.

Movement inside her drew her hand to her belly. The doctor had asked if she'd felt the baby move yet. Was this it or simply the curry she'd had at the pub the night before? Under her hand she felt the strange fluttery sensation again. Amber smiled.

"Hello, Beetle," she whispered.

She lay there cradling her baby long after the movement had stopped. She was going to be a mother. She had no idea what that meant except she was going to be better at it than her own mother.

Her phone rang from the other room. She didn't rush to get it. She didn't have the energy, and the most likely caller was Fred asking her to do another shift. Amber sighed. She needed the work but she'd also been desperate for a day off. He'd already booked her for the lunch and dinner shifts tomorrow. The phone pinged with a message. The water had lost its warmth and the wondering got the better of her.

Amber hauled herself up and stepped carefully out of the bath, wrapping herself in her old towel that barely dried her these days. She thought of Roslyn's thick white towels in the cupboard. Amber had put them away, preferring to use her own stuff, but she flung open the door and tugged one out. Dropping her towel on the floor she dried herself, slipped on the robe that hung behind the door and wrapped the fluffy towel around her wet hair.

In the lounge she picked up her phone and smiled at the name on the screen. It was Immi, the only person she'd kept in touch with since she'd left Penola. She listened to the message and quickly lost her smile. Tyson had been asking after her, wanted to know if Immi knew where she was. Immi had assured him she didn't. Which was true. Immi knew she'd headed home to Adelaide but not that she'd stopped along the way and ended up in this cottage tucked away in the Adelaide Hills. Tyson knew her mum's address, of course, but Amber hadn't been in touch with her mum since she'd left home eighteen months ago.

Tyson had made it clear he wanted nothing to do with the baby, or her. He'd kicked her out and quickly taken up with someone else, and Amber had lost her job. Tyson was a barman at the pub where she'd also worked but she'd been casual and when he'd given her the flick so had the boss. Amber had thought she'd escaped him and got away with it. There'd only be one reason he'd be looking for her and it would have nothing to do with her or her baby.

She made herself some more toast, cut a slice of the marked-down cheese she'd treated herself to, added another slice of Roslyn's tomato and munched while she flicked through Facebook on her phone. Tyson had made one post since she'd looked last. It was a blurry photo of him and a few of his mates, arm in arm. He'd called it "boys night". She scrolled through pages for anyone she knew but there was little to see.

Her body felt heavy and her eyes drooped. She eased back onto the couch and curled into a ball, letting the soothing escape of sleep take her.

Roslyn dropped Margot at her door and headed back along the driveway, recalling the events of the afternoon. If she had to describe it in one word, she'd say interesting. Helen had provided plenty of afternoon tea but the book discussion had been scant. Roslyn had enjoyed this month's book and had been looking forward to sharing her thoughts and hearing other people's, but after a cursory discussion the conversation had moved on to different topics. Roslyn suspected that, like Margot, half of the women there hadn't even read the book.

When she'd still been working she'd belonged to a book club in the city. They'd all been professionals like her and met in the back room of a wine bar, where they'd discuss the book they'd read over a meal. It had always been a detailed discussion, not that they'd all agreed — sometimes the debate had been quite heated — but Roslyn had found it stimulating. Once the topic of the book had been exhausted, they talked other books, politics, travel, theatre.

In Margot's group there might be a bit of an exchange about theatre or a movie but otherwise it was the failings of husbands, the amazing feats of grandchildren, gardens, recipes and so on. Roslyn contributed to a degree but since she'd retired she missed the stimulation of her previous book club, which sadly had disbanded. Margot had encouraged her to join her group more than a year ago but Roslyn still felt like an outsider.

Then there'd been the awkward moment when Helen had refused to take Margot's petition. She'd said she and her husband wanted to find out more before they got all political. A bit of a heated discussion had taken place, with some of the women agreeing with Helen and others taking the petition to share around. Margot had ranted about it all the way home, upset that some of her friends hadn't sided with her. Roslyn had swallowed her "I told you so" and remained silent.

She pulled in under the carport. Ahead of her down the extended drive she could just see the back of Amber's station wagon parked at an angle close to the cottage. Roslyn had noticed the tailgate had been up when she'd left and it was still like that. She wondered why.

She made her way slowly along the drive. The car was totally empty. Roslyn took a step closer to the door of the cottage. The wooden door beyond the screen was open but there was no sound of movement. She glanced back at the car. Surely the battery would go flat if the tailgate stayed open too long.

She tapped on the screen door. "Amber?"

There was no answer and the door swung out as she rattled it. Roslyn took a tentative step inside. Perhaps the girl was resting. The bathroom door was wide open and from where she stood Roslyn could see the bath had been used, was still full of water. She huffed. Amber obviously hadn't understood about conserving water. Roslyn couldn't help glancing around the bathroom. There were clothes overflowing from a bag beside the washing machine, towels in a heap on the floor and toiletries spread across the bench.

Roslyn startled at the sound of her phone ringing in her pocket. She grabbed at it at the same time Amber called, "Who's that?"

Roslyn jabbed end on the call from the unknown number – blasted nuisance calls. Amber stumbled to the door, clutching a robe tightly around her chest with one hand and holding a saucepan in the air with the other.

"Roslyn!" Her mouth fell open. She lowered the pan. "What the f—"

"I'm sorry. I didn't mean to intrude but it seems as if your tailgate's been open all afternoon. I called out and you didn't answer and the door was open…"

"Bloody hell, I forgot I'd left the car open." Amber snatched her keys from among the empty chip packets, pens and papers scattered on the hall table, and pushed past Roslyn and out the door.

Roslyn hovered just inside the living room. Once more she'd been babbling. It was not something she ever did but there was something about Amber's ferocious stare that set her off. The tailgate thudded shut then there was the sound of the car turning over.

Roslyn took in the boxes and bags overflowing with household items, the empty noodle packets, a pair of discarded shoes and the still-scattered cushions. From where she stood she could see the kitchen was hardly in a better state. Perhaps Amber had lived in her car so long she wasn't capable of managing a house.

The screen door banged and then the bathroom door clunked shut, no doubt to hide the evidence of the bath.

"The battery hadn't gone flat." Amber rubbed her hair with the towel that had been wrapped around her head. "I borrowed some towels," she stammered. "Mine were all…I need to do some washing."

Roslyn was stuck to the spot. She wanted this girl gone and yet she didn't want to appear uncharitable and renege on her offer of somewhere to stay.

"I had a day off so I cleaned out my car." Amber waved a hand at her scattered belongings then it dropped to her side. "Ready to repack."

"Have you found accommodation?" Roslyn could hear the eagerness in her own voice.

"No…not yet, but I've got my name on lots of lists. Something will turn up." Amber pulled the thin cotton robe Roslyn left for visitors tighter around her. Except for the bulge of her baby she was very thin.

In spite of Roslyn's apprehension, she couldn't just toss the girl out. "When's your follow-up appointment with the doctor?"

"Next Wednesday."

"Good." Roslyn nodded. "Well…I'll leave you to it."

"Thanks."

Amber followed her to the door and it shut with a thud behind her.

fourteen

"Why does everyone have to be late tonight?" Margot snapped at Dennis as they pulled up in front of Roslyn's place and there was no sign that her sister was ready. "Tonight's community meeting with the developers has been on everyone's calendar, surely?"

"We'll be there in plenty of time," Dennis said.

"But I had planned to be early." Margot wanted to select the perfect seats, close to the front of the hall but not in the front row.

"Take a chill pill."

Margot glared at Roslyn's front door and flicked her seatbelt undone. "She's not coming. I'd better go and—"

The front light came on and Roslyn's door opened.

"There you go," Dennis said. "Perfect timing."

"If you hadn't been so late home we wouldn't be rushing now."

"Let it go, Margot."

"Work is taking all your time lately and—"

"For goodness sake, Margot, I have to work. You always harp on."

Margot gasped and put a hand to her cheek as if he'd slapped her. Dennis rarely used that tone. Roslyn opened the back door, flooding the car's interior with light. Margot ducked her head, blinking back hot tears.

"Thanks for the ride, Dennis," Roslyn said, oblivious to the tension. "I haven't had a good look at the new car."

"What do you think?"

"Very nice. But how did you end up with an Audi?"

Margot's head shot up. She hadn't even noticed it wasn't a Renault.

Roslyn closed her door and the light faded.

"Just testing it," he said. He manoeuvred the car out onto the road.

Margot stared at him but his focus was on driving.

"I thought perhaps Pedrick Motors was branching out." Roslyn chuckled.

"Would you like to drive on the way home? Margot's impressed with it. I think you might like it better than your Mercedes."

"Really?" Roslyn's response held a hint of disbelief.

"And here we are already," Dennis said. "Look at all the cars."

Margot swallowed her annoyance as they cruised past the Lutheran church and hall, where not a space remained within cooee, and turned down a side street.

Dennis pulled in. "This might be the closest we'll get."

Still smarting from his earlier harsh words, she remained silent as she gathered her bag and notebook and got out of the car. She was anxious about the meeting and Dennis had only unsettled her more.

"Do you know much about what's happening tonight?" Roslyn asked.

"Several of us have planned questions to ask," Margot said brusquely and jabbed one of the slips towards Roslyn. "This one's for you."

Roslyn frowned at it. "I've come more to listen."

"Surely you can ask a question about traffic. It will affect you, being right on the corner."

Roslyn gave a vague nod and pushed the paper into the pocket of her wallet. They walked together up the hill towards the hall. Roslyn was being very slow.

"Is that leg still bothering you?" Margot asked.

"A bit. You two go on ahead. I'll be fine."

"Don't be silly – the meeting's not due to start for ten minutes," Dennis said. "We don't need to rush."

Margot swallowed her agitation and tried not to allow her footsteps to quicken. In her hand she clutched the list of carefully prepared questions they'd set out Monday night at the pub. It had been a small gathering – Fred, Dennis and Margot, of course, then only Kevin and Martin had turned up. They'd worked on the questions and taken some to hand to others. "Looks better if a cross-section of people ask," Fred had said. "Rather than the same few."

Inside, the hall was almost full, buzzing with voices and expectant energy and, as Margot had worried, the only vacant chairs were in the front row. Geraldine smiled and waved from her seat near the back. At the front of the hall a small podium had been set up with chairs and a microphone, and a large banner with the artist's impression of the proposed hotel stood as a backdrop.

They continued on down the central aisle, speaking to people as they went. Margot had a sudden recollection of Emily's wedding and being mother of the bride, but instead of walking alone this time she had Roslyn and Dennis with her. Or at least she had. By the time they got to the front row, Dennis had disappeared. She glanced around and finally spied him to one side talking to another man who owned a business near their dealership in Mount Barker. Seated in front of him were the Teakles.

The sale of their supermarket was still the talk of the town. No-one had thought it would happen. Evidently they'd got a good price from a company that wanted to keep the footprint but renovate and make it a seven-day-a-week business. Everyone agreed that had to be good for Jesserton. She'd also seen Kath in the crowd and Helen from book club – that had heightened her anxiety – and a few others she recognised who didn't live in Jesserton. There were certainly people from all over and she was glad to see one of their local councillors as well. That helped settle her nerves as she and Roslyn took their seats.

The presentation was slick. A man and a woman from Meyer and Brightman introduced themselves as Max and Carlene and took turns to present the outline of the proposal. It was similar to what had already been reported in the paper but with more explanation about the uniqueness of the rooms and that the venue would be suited to small weddings, corporate events, romantic getaways and general visitors to the region. There were also plans for some kind of food prep space for caterers and breakfast provisions would be provided on request, but they didn't intend to have a fully functioning restaurant.

That brought a murmur from the crowd.

Max held up his hands. "Research conducted by the South Australian Tourism Commission has confirmed a real need in this region for the kind of accommodation we're offering."

He went on to say he believed the hotel would enhance the local community and finished with a spiel about employment opportunities then asked for questions from the floor.

"Where do you expect all these visitors to eat if you're not having a restaurant?" Fred called from somewhere behind.

It wasn't quite the wording from the list of questions they'd planned but it would do.

"A good question, sir." Max opened his hands in a welcome gesture. "May I ask anyone with a question to state your name first, please? It would be helpful for us all."

"Everyone here knows me. I'm Fred and I own Friedrich's Gasthaus just down the road. Been in my family for four generations."

"That's good to know." Max smiled magnanimously while Carlene scribbled in a notebook. "We'd like to work closely with you." Once more Max opened his arms wide. "And any food and catering business who'd be interested."

Kev leaped to his feet. "My name's Kevin and I own the butcher shop. I can't see how a hotel without a kitchen will help my business."

Margot frowned. Kev lived not far from the other side of the proposed development. He was supposed to ask about noise from people and music and traffic and so on.

"The rooms will have basic cooking facilities," Carlene said. "We've some ideas for self-catering we'd like to talk to you about." Her smile radiated charm. "But we're probably getting a bit ahead of ourselves." She glanced towards the side of the hall. Margot had noticed her do that a few times. She turned to follow her gaze and noted a man in a smart jacket, arms folded, leaning against the wall. Margot didn't recognise him as a local.

"The hotel is still in the planning stage," Carlene continued. "We were hoping to answer any questions more directly related to its design and function. We want to know what you think."

"It'll be an eyesore towering over the town."

"Hello, ma'am." Carlene's smile remained stuck across her face. "May I have your name, please?"

"Thelma Schmidt. I've lived in Jesserton all my life. It's a beautiful town and a huge hotel will spoil it."

More murmurs and grumbles followed. Thelma hadn't been at Monday night's meeting but her comment was similar to one of the questions Margot had said she'd ask. She took a breath and rose on trembling legs. The voices went quiet.

"My name's Margot Pedrick. Like Thelma, I've lived here most of my life. I run The General Providore in town with my friend Kath." She glanced back and Kath smiled and nodded. Margot lifted her chin and stared directly at Carlene. "My husband and I actually live right next door to your proposed development and we want to know how you plan to maintain our privacy and that of the other people's properties that your hotel rooms will look over."

Behind her there were mumbles of support as she sat back in her chair with a small whoomph.

"Thank you, Margot." Carlene nodded, the smile still in place. "Each room and balcony will be partitioned to prevent overlooking each other and everything else but the gardens and valley in front."

"What about those top rooms?" Thelma called.

"The final height of the hotel is still to be determined," Max said then waved a hand towards the back. "You have a question, sir?"

"My name's Martin Threadgold. My wife and I have several holiday rentals which we've run here for many years. I'm sure you're aware of the difficulties we have with water supply in this area and then waste water disposal. How will a big structure like yours, catering for a large number of people, manage that?"

At least Martin was sticking to the question list.

"A great question, thank you, Martin," Max said and moved closer to the large poster. "There is an existing and well-maintained turkey nest dam, and also part of the hotel build would incorporate water catchment and storage." He pointed to the sketch. "You can't see it here but storage tanks will be built into the hill underneath the hotel, a tank for each level of rooms but with interconnectivity. In the same way we're also dealing with grey water, which will be used in the extensive gardens surrounding the hotel. Which, by the way, we hope to have open to the local community most of the time. A place for a picnic or to walk your dog." Once again his smile stretched wide with his open hands.

Dennis asked the prepared question about the traffic that would go past their place on the unsealed road that had been discussed at length at their planning meeting, and Fred asked about a liquor licence, another question not on their list. People Margot didn't know asked more questions and each time Max or Carlene had a smooth answer.

"You have a question, sir?" Max nodded to a man across the hall from Margot.

"Good evening. I live in Jesserton and work in the city. Like everyone else here I enjoy the lifestyle." He glanced around and Margot recognised him as one of the Prov's regular weekend customers. "What would be the benefits for our community to have your hotel here?"

"Thank you – an excellent question. There will be employment opportunities, of course, both during the build and once the hotel is complete. We're also committed to work with local businesses who we hope will benefit greatly from the experience and—"

"*Hope* is all well and good." Fred's voice boomed around the hall. "But council have been very quiet about something that will have such a huge impact on our community. Why is that, Councillor Moss?"

Voices of support for Fred's question echoed around the hall and Max put his hands up for silence. Margot turned as the councillor rose to his feet. He glanced from side to side, waiting for the final rumbles and mumbles to cease. He was about the same age as her kids and while he didn't seem fazed by the hostility in the air, Margot did feel a little sorry for him.

"Good evening. I'm Brett Moss. I don't live in Jesserton but I do live in Brunville across the freeway and—"

"Speak up, man," called a voice from the back.

The councillor stood taller, turned as if he was looking for the interjector then continued in a louder voice. "While I am a councillor I have no influence on this decision."

"What's the good of you then?" someone interjected and there were a few chuckles.

"From what I understand, this project is in the consultation phase," Brett said.

"From what you understand!" The interjector's voice rose a notch.

"A proposal of this scale goes to—"

"Speak up," the voice called again.

Brett cleared his throat. "There's plenty of time for discussion once we have more facts but approval is not—"

"What about our approval?" a voice shouted.

"We want more than smooth placations," called another.

"When's the next council meeting?" Kevin shouted over the growing rumble of voices. "We should all be there."

It took a while for Max to restore order, and when he did he asked people to take a brochure and direct further questions via the company website. He closed the meeting and he and Carlene began to pack up their things as once more pockets of loud conversation broke out around the hall.

Roslyn rose to her feet. "I think it's time to go."

Margot looked around for Dennis but she couldn't see him. The councillor who'd been howled down was pushing his way ahead to the door.

"We'll find Dennis outside," Roslyn said.

Margot followed a pace behind her but Kevin stepped in her path. "Good job organising us to have the questions ready, Margot."

"Oh, it wasn't just—"

Thelma grabbed her arm. "Well done for organising this, Margot."

"I didn't organise this—"

"You've done a great job." Fred beamed at her.

"Well, thank you." Their praise spread over her like a warm blanket. "But we all did our bit."

"When's the next meeting?" Fred asked.

Margot frowned. She hadn't thought past tonight. Somehow she'd imagined everything would go back to normal after the meeting. The proposed hotel would be stopped and simply go away. Instead it felt as if nothing had been resolved.

"We should get together to be ready for when council discusses this next." Kev's fervent gaze fixed on her.

"Okay...yes...I'll find out and be in touch."

Thelma clapped her hands excitedly. "We could have one of those Facebook group thingos to share ideas and keep everyone up to date. Like we do for our craft group."

"An online group's a good idea," Fred said. "Shall I organise that?"

Those gathered agreed and Margot's flagging spirits lifted.

"Come on, Margot." There was a hint of irritation in Roslyn's voice. Margot wasn't sure why she should be annoyed other than she didn't use social media. Roslyn hadn't even asked the question

Margot had given her about the extra traffic that would be turning off the main road, which was a designated eighty kilometres zone, onto their narrower gravel road.

They made their way outside with Margot receiving more praise for her proactive stance. Groups of people stood around talking. To one side Dennis was deep in conversation with the man who'd been standing at the side of the crowd in the hall. As they approached, the two shook hands and the man moved away.

"Who was he?" Margot asked.

"Xavier Zamon – he's the project manager for the hotel."

Margot studied the suave-looking man, who was now chatting to Fred. "Why wasn't he up the front speaking and taking questions?"

"That's what Max and Carlene were for. He said he likes to get a feel for the community—"

"Humph! Why didn't he do that earlier?"

"He's been in the region several times before this."

"What was he talking to you about?"

Dennis broke into a grin. "Cars, of all things. He's in the market for a new EV like mine."

"Yours?" Margot frowned. "I thought it was a demo."

"It is." Dennis put up a hand. "You two wait here. I'll go and get the car and come back for you. That leg seems to be really troubling you tonight, Roslyn." He shot Margot a smile and then he was gone. Margot stared after him a moment. She was glad he'd lost his earlier churlishness but she still couldn't forget his harsh words as they'd been waiting for Roslyn.

She turned her focus back to her sister.

"That leg does seem to be bothering you. Perhaps we'd better have the next Sunday dinner our way after all. If it's a nice day we could always take the children over for a swim at yours afterwards."

"That's still several days away and I'm perfectly well enough to host dinner."

They lapsed into silence and Roslyn shifted her weight from one foot to the other.

"Have you seen anyone about it?" Margot asked.

"About what?"

"Your leg."

"I've seen a doctor."

"And what did the doctor say." Margot shook her head. "Honestly, Roslyn, it's like pulling hen's teeth."

"There's no need for a fuss. I'll probably need a hip replacement, that's all."

"That's all." Margot gaped at her sister. "When did you find out about that?"

"I haven't yet for sure. I had some tests yesterday and I'm seeing a specialist next week."

"Goodness, that's quick. We'll have to make a plan for when it happens. You'll need home care, or perhaps you can stay with us for a while until…oh." Margot tapped a finger to her lips. "But that would depend on when. If I'm at work I won't be much help to you. We might need to employ someone."

"Take a breath, Margot. I haven't even seen the specialist yet. Let's not get ahead of ourselves." Roslyn edged towards the kerb. "Here comes Dennis."

fifteen

Margot was in the shop kitchen humming to herself as she stirred the baked beans she was cooking for the weekend breakfasts. They'd been extra busy for a Friday, which was to be expected with only two-and-a-half weeks to Christmas. People were holding festive end-of-year events and it was good weather for tourists. Unfortunately they'd had to send their casual girl home again. Poor thing suffered terribly from migraines. Between Margot, Kath and Lani they'd managed and with the rush now over Margot had set to work on the baked beans.

There'd been no time to do anything about stopping the hotel but it was never far from her thoughts. She wouldn't get a chance until her day off on Monday, when she planned to do a lot more research and rally the locals to continue their campaign to halt its progress.

She turned off the gas and transferred the pot to a trivet to cool. In the brief silence Thelma's voice carried from the shop. She was banging on about the scandal with the mayor again.

"And I hear Cameron is going to stand for mayor in the by-election," Thelma announced.

Margot hurried out and glanced around the shop. Thankfully all the other current customers had been served and were seated. Lani was clearing plates outside. The only person standing on the other side of the counter was Thelma. Margot moved up beside Kath and leaned over slightly, keeping her voice low.

"Actually, Thelma," she said, "Cameron's not standing for mayor."

"Oh, that's not what I heard," Thelma huffed. "And I believe he's in favour of the proposed hotel."

"That's nonsense. As Cameron's my son-in-law I do happen to know the facts about this." Margot straightened. "He's definitely opposed to the hotel and he's going to try for the vacant councillor position."

Thelma's mouth flapped then drew in as if she'd just sucked on a lemon. "And do you also know the facts about your son's business? I've just received his bill for coming to fix my electrical fault the other Sunday. It's outrageous. Otto never charged me anywhere near that."

"Otto was too soft for his own good," Kath said. "Now that Nick's taken over he's got to run the business his way. He's got a family to support and good service doesn't come cheap these days. You were lucky to get an electrician on a Sunday."

Margot threw her friend a grateful glance as Thelma gave a small humph.

"Now, we've got some of your favourite lemon cake left," Kath said. "Would you like a slice with your tea, Thelma?"

Thelma smiled, her ruffled feathers smoothed at the thought of the cake. "Thank you, dear, that would be lovely."

"You take a seat and Lani will bring it over."

Several people came in then and it was all-hands-on-deck again. A couple Margot didn't know were looking at the petition.

"A hotel here would be perfect," the woman said. "There's nothing like it in the region."

The man nodded and looked from Kath to Margot behind the counter. "Who owns this place? Surely they'd want a smart hotel nearby."

"We own the Providore," Kath said and glanced at Margot.

"It wouldn't be good for our business," Margot said.

"I don't see why not," the man continued. "When we stay at hotels we like nothing better than to wander the local community and support the businesses where we can. We'd definitely stay more often if there was a hotel here in the Hills."

The woman beside him nodded and then they placed their orders with Kath. Margot went back to the kitchen to start on the tomato burrata salad and mushroom gnocchi they'd requested. It was all right for people who didn't live here to like the idea of a hotel and she didn't agree with the man's suggestion that it would support local businesses. It might bring a bit of extra traffic the Prov's way but they were already busy and there weren't many other businesses for tourists in Jesserton. Besides, Margot didn't trust the developers not to put in dining facilities. People would dine in the hotel more often than out if that happened. And locals would go there. It would be competition, not complementary, for those in business.

It was hectic again with a few new customers wanting coffee and food then finally it was quiet enough to have just one in the shop serving. Kath left Lani to it and came out to help Margot in the kitchen.

"I have been wondering about the new hotel," Kath said.

"Haven't we all?" Margot transferred the cooled pan of baked beans to a container.

"I've been thinking on what the chap from the hotel said."

Margot frowned. "What chap from the hotel?"

"Xavier someone." Kath patted her back pocket. "He gave me his card. I was—"

"Was he the project manager who was hanging around at the meeting on Wednesday night?"

"Yes." Kath pulled out the card. "Xavier Zamon was his name."

"Why were you talking to him?"

"I didn't intend to but he approached me."

"Why?"

"Said he wanted to find out more about what each local business had to offer. And how we could support each other."

Margot's face tingled as if it had been slapped. "And you discussed this without including me?"

"He caught me as I was leaving the hall. I had no idea where you were. It's not as if I was doing something shonky, Margot."

"But you haven't mentioned it."

"To be honest, I hadn't given it another thought until that couple brought up the hotel earlier, but it has made me think about it."

"Think about what?"

"This Xavier chap said they'd only be having a basic coffee and wine bar in the hotel."

"If you can believe them."

"He said the idea is to encourage their guests to dine out in the local area."

"What?" Margot scoffed. "They'll all come down here for breakfast and lunch and go to Fred's pub for dinner?"

"There's more than our businesses in the region but he did say something about wanting to involve local businesses in some of their in-house catering options."

The spoon Margot had been holding clattered into the sink. "We're busy as it is. You want us to be delivering food to his hotel as well?"

"It's all in the planning at the moment. He was only putting out feelers. I don't remember seeing him but evidently he's called in here a few times and liked what he's tried. He thinks we'd be a good fit with the self-catering ideas they have for the hotel. He had lots of suggestions and possibilities."

"And you hadn't remembered that until now?"

Kath screwed up her face. "I wanted to talk to you about it but you get so…irate about the hotel whenever it's mentioned."

"Of course I do. It'll be terrible for our community. I'm not sure what spell he's put you under—"

"What do you mean by that?"

"He was good looking. Probably had an accent and laid on the charm."

Kath's cheeks turned pink.

"You know how easily you're attracted to those kinds of men." Margot had picked up the pieces for her friend on several occasions after her online dating choices had gone wrong.

"You think because he was good looking and had done his research that I couldn't see past that and listen to the truth in what he was saying?"

Margot's stomach lurched. Kath was upset now and she'd been the cause of it but the truth was her friend had been single a long time and she was easily swayed by a charming man. "That's not what I meant."

"Really?" Kath's finger jabbed in the air. "Well, I'm telling you what I mean. We need to rethink the pros and cons of having some unique hotel accommodation in Jesserton and until we do, that petition of yours can stay off the counter."

"Hey, Kath." Lani spoke from behind them and they both turned. "Keep it down. I can hear you out here."

A wave of mortification swept Margot as if she'd stood naked in the main street.

"Mind your business, Lani," Kath snapped.

The young woman ducked her head and spun back to the shop. Kath glared at Margot. "The rush has died down. Why don't you go home? I can stay on with Lani. We both know I don't have a life," she snarled and began unpacking the dishwasher.

Margot gasped and gripped the counter. It was all too awful. They'd disagreed before but never had words, at least not hurtful words. There was this weight in the air between them like a lead roof about to fall. Tears brimmed in Margot's eyes. She snapped the lid on the baked beans container and shoved it in the fridge then glanced at her friend. Kath was stacking plates, her body stiff and no sign of her relenting. Margot took her bag from the hook and almost ran out the back door.

sixteen

Amber sat in her car watching the groups of people waiting outside the rental property. She'd counted fifteen before she'd given up. It was the third inspection she'd attended that afternoon in Mount Barker and the property was at the highest end of her budget. Looking at the line-up, she knew she'd be wasting her time even getting out of her car. At the previous place the woman in the suit at the front door had looked her up and down and told her not to bother. Here she made the decision for herself and drove off.

She was halfway back to Jesserton before the tears of frustration clouded her vision, forcing her to pull over. She parked on the edge of the road and raged at the unfairness of it all. She'd be a good tenant but she'd never get the chance to prove it. She wiped angrily at the tears. There were several fluttering movements in her belly, which she now recognised as the baby moving. She sniffed, blew out a long, steadying breath and pressed one hand to the bulge.

"Sorry, Beetle," she whispered.

She couldn't keep doing this – using precious fuel for no gain, getting her hopes up only to have them smashed – and each time it got harder to try again. She hadn't felt this low since Tyson had kicked her out.

She put two hands on the steering wheel and rested her head against it, taking slow steady breaths. It wasn't all bad. She had a job for as long as she could keep working and she was managing to put some money aside, thanks to Roslyn's generosity. Still, she couldn't stop the fear that wormed inside her whenever she tried to plan more than a few days ahead. At the moment she only had one option as far as she could make out and the thought of it only added to her anxiety.

A car coming towards her slowed. Her heart skipped a beat. It was a police car. She flicked on her indicator to show she was about to move on. The lone policeman stared as he passed but continued on. She sucked in a deep breath, blew it out and pulled back onto the road. The last thing she needed was police attention.

Her stomach growled. It was well past lunchtime. At least she'd got some fresh bread and sandwich fillings while she'd been in town. She'd go home and eat while she came up with her plan.

"The things I do for you, little Beetle," she said.

Roslyn's car was under the carport as Amber drove slowly along the drive but she wasn't sure if that meant the older woman was home. When Amber had left that morning Roslyn had been getting into a fancy black car pulled up at her front door. Amber had only caught a glimpse of her but Roslyn's red lipstick had stood out and she'd been smartly dressed in black trousers and jacket with a white shirt. Maybe she'd been going on a hot date. Amber had smirked at the thought.

Just as she drew level with the front of Roslyn's house Amber noticed a woman peering in the front window. It wasn't Roslyn. Amber stopped her car and the woman turned and came towards her then halted as recognition dawned for both of them.

"What are you doing here?" the old bag from the town cafe asked.

"Same to you," Amber batted back.

"I live here."

"You do not. This is Roslyn's house."

"I'm Roslyn's sister. I live right next door. I came to see her."

"She's gone out."

"How do you know and why are *you* here?"

"I live here."

"With my sister?" The woman's tone was incredulous.

"Not exactly with her. In the cottage down the back."

"I don't believe you."

Their stoush was interrupted by the sound of tyres on the gravel drive behind Amber. She glanced in her rear-view mirror. It was the black car she'd seen Roslyn get into earlier.

"You can ask her yourself," she said and drove on towards the cottage.

She couldn't believe the cow of a woman who'd refused her service at the cafe the other day was Roslyn's sister. They looked nothing alike. Roslyn was tall and angular with cropped grey hair and she never wore make-up except for lipstick. Her sister was shorter, had hair that looked like she'd just stepped out of a hairdresser and wore layers of make-up. And she lived next door. Roslyn hadn't so much as mentioned a sister, let alone one who lived so close. She glanced in her mirror again, in time to see the cafe woman gesturing at Roslyn as the black car drove away and then Amber pulled up by the cottage and they were lost from her sight.

Roslyn waved off the car. She took a breath and turned to face her sister's wrath.

"You've taken in a tenant and you didn't tell me." Margot's eyes narrowed with disbelief.

"I haven't exactly taken in a tenant." Roslyn blew out the breath. "It's complicated."

"I can't believe you'd have someone in there after what happened last time. And that offensive girl is the last person I'd expect you to open your home to."

"Offensive?" Roslyn frowned. "Amber can be a bit forthright…"

"Rude is what I'd call her."

"Hmm. I need a cup of tea. Why don't you come in?" Perhaps it was the several wines she'd had over lunch, or the news Elvin and Gunter's sons had imparted or both but Roslyn felt inclined to be affable with her sister. The Amber problem was perhaps the easier to explain of the two secrets she'd been keeping and a good distraction to deflect Margot from digging deeper into the lunch Roslyn had just returned from.

"You know I don't drink tea."

"Coffee then. Come in. It won't take long for the machine to warm up." Her heel wobbled in the uneven gravel and she gasped as pain shot down her leg and across her back. "Blast."

"Roslyn?" Margot's arm went around her waist.

"I'm all right. I shouldn't have worn heels."

"They're hardly what you'd call heels." Margot leaned in and sniffed. "Have you been drinking?"

"Of course I have. I've just enjoyed a lovely long lunch at a winery with…some friends. So yes, we did consume some rather good bottles of wine."

"Was that a hire car that dropped you home? It looked like that Elvin man in the front."

"A courtesy car." It wasn't exactly a lie. Elvin had ordered a chauffeured car so none of them had to worry about driving.

"Fancy car for a courtesy—"

"Let's go inside so I can get my shoes off and you can quiz me about Amber." Roslyn went on ahead. "What are you doing here at this hour on a Friday anyway?" she asked as she flicked on her coffee machine.

"It was quiet so Kath said she'd do the last hour and finish up." Margot didn't sit but came to the bench and watched Roslyn while she made the coffee. "I haven't seen you since the meeting."

"That was only two nights ago."

"I know but I was worried about you."

"Why?" Roslyn passed her a coffee and picked up her own. "Let's sit."

They moved to the comfy chairs in the corner and Roslyn prised off her shoes. Margot was right – they were hardly heels. They were only a few centimetres higher than flat but she shouldn't have worn them all the same. Her body cursed her for it.

"Your leg." Margot's brow creased. "I don't like to think you're in pain."

Roslyn's attitude softened as she took in Margot's fretful look. "I'm off to the specialist next week and I'm sure he'll have some answers. In the meantime don't worry about me." Roslyn didn't want to add her sister's angst to her own. She was fairly sure she knew what the outcome would be.

Margot sighed and took a sip of her coffee. "And what about this girl you've taken in? I still can't believe you'd be so...so irresponsible."

"That's an odd choice of word."

"Have you forgotten what happened the last time you had someone in there?"

"Of course not." It had been a terrible experience made all the worse because it had been when Richard was so unwell. "This was a favour...for Gareth."

"Your GP?"

"Yes. Amber wasn't well and needed a place to stay for a few days."

Margot frowned. "What's wrong with her?"

"She was dehydrated. Low blood pressure, poor nutrition I suspect, but she's doing much better."

"How long's she been here?"

"Oh…" Roslyn had to think on that. Time seemed to have slipped by quickly since her visit to the doctor the previous week. "A few days…maybe a week."

"A week! And you haven't mentioned it! How much longer is she staying? Is she paying board? Did you know she works for Fred at the pub?"

"For goodness sake, Margot, slow down." The glow of the long lunch was beginning to wear off as was the earlier warmth she'd felt from Margot's concerns for her health. "I didn't mention it because I knew you'd get in a tizz."

"I'm not in a tizz. I worry about you."

"Well, don't." Roslyn set her half-drunk coffee firmly back on the table. It was her fourth cup for the day and the caffeine was buzzing in her veins. She really should have had tea. "I am perfectly capable of managing my own affairs, you know."

They glared at each other, the problems with the previous tenants hanging unspoken in the air between them. Roslyn had needed help that time.

Margot sniffed. "Well, I suppose she's got a decent job so at least she can pay her way."

Roslyn looked down at her trousers and rubbed at a mark to avoid her sister's gaze. So had the previous tenant.

"Let's just hope she doesn't do any damage."

"I don't think that's likely." Roslyn looked up.

Margot arched her eyebrows, then with a huff took her cup to the sink. "I'd best be off then."

Roslyn followed her out and was surprised when Margot turned back suddenly and kissed her cheek. Her concerned gaze lingered on Roslyn. "I hope it doesn't come back to bite you like the last time."

"It won't," Roslyn said with as much affirmation as she could muster then watched her sister follow the path across the yard and past the veggie patch, until she disappeared around the fruit trees. Margot finding out about Amber had definitely been the lesser of two evils. Roslyn didn't want Margot catching wind of the lunch meeting she'd just had. Not until she got it all straight in her own head. She chuckled. "All hell would break loose."

"Roslyn?"

The older woman spun, grabbed at her thigh and muttered under her breath.

Amber approached cautiously, looking around for whoever Roslyn had been talking to. She thought she'd seen the sister leave. "Are you okay?"

"Yes." Roslyn sucked in a breath. "My blasted leg plays up sometimes, that's all."

"Do you need help...to sit down or something?" Amber glanced around. "Do you have one of those walkers?"

"No, I don't," Roslyn snapped.

"Okay, okay, just trying to be helpful."

Under Roslyn's intense look the words Amber had prepared suddenly deserted her and she took a different tack. "Did you get into trouble?"

"Trouble?"

"With your sister? She didn't look too happy that I was here."

"She's not. She says you were rude to her."

"She started it." Amber lowered her gaze to her feet and poked at a weed in the path with her shoe, wishing she hadn't come.

A deep sigh came from Roslyn. "I don't doubt she did. What was it you wanted?"

Amber looked up. Roslyn studied her with no sign of her sister's condescension. "If it's a bad time I can come tomorrow or—"

"Why don't you come inside and tell me what it is you want? I've got something for you." Roslyn looked her up and down. "Or are you on your way to work?"

"I'm ready to go but it's not time yet."

Without another word Roslyn walked towards her back door. Amber was obviously expected to follow.

Inside the light and airy kitchen-come-family room, Amber paused and looked around. The room was not over-the-top grand like she had imagined it might be. The floor was wood, perhaps the original – the outside of Roslyn's house didn't look much newer than the cottage. At one end of the room, beside the door they'd just come through, was a cosy couch and an armchair, and at the other a kitchen with an island bench. The kitchen cupboards were the colour of golden honey. There were a few books and papers on the coffee table and a tablet but otherwise there were no ornaments or photos. A single tall plant sat in a corner and the walls were bare except for two paintings and a weird set of flying ducks.

Roslyn had her head in the fridge at the far end of the kitchen. "Sit down," she called.

Amber perched on the edge of the pale blue couch.

"I was going to bring you some of this savoury tart I made." Roslyn carried a container over and placed it in a space on the low table in front of Amber then took a seat opposite.

"You don't have to keep feeding me."

"I know but as you probably understand, cooking for one isn't that wonderful. I either can't be bothered or I end up with way too much."

Amber glanced at the container. "Thanks."

"You might not thank me. I think I overdid the onion. My sister's the one who can cook. That gene skipped me." Roslyn smiled and a whole new woman was revealed.

"She sure doesn't like me."

"Take no notice of Margot, she can be a bit—"

"Rude."

Roslyn quirked an eyebrow. "Protective. Don't be too bothered by her. She's as soft as butter underneath."

Amber's resolve returned. "I've been looking for rentals again."

"No luck, I assume."

"No, so…I was wondering if I could stay on for…for a while. I'll keep trying to find a place but it's not easy."

"So I understand."

"I'll pay though, if I could stay a bit longer."

Roslyn frowned. "When you say 'a bit longer' you mean…?"

Amber winced. "I don't know."

Silence fell between them and once more frustration flared and gnawed inside Amber, an incessant ache she never seemed to be able to fully extinguish. Here she was begging again and what for? To keep a roof over her head instead of sleeping in her car. Roslyn had said she could only stay a while and she'd been here well over a week already. It had been silly to think it might go on. She leaped to her feet and made for the door.

"Amber, I—"

"Forget it!" Amber stalked out the door and shut it loudly behind her. Hot tears of rage dribbled down her cheeks. She batted them away and swore all the way back to the cottage.

Roslyn sat for a moment in the silence that followed Amber's departure. It had been such a mixed bag of a day, unexpected in so many ways. The sale of Gunter's property had been finalised and her portion of the final amount was significant, but it was the rest of Gunter's wishes that had surprised her the most.

He'd wanted his dear friend Roslyn, as he'd called her in his bequest, to work out the best way to spend or invest the rest of the money from the sale of his property to benefit those in need in the local community. Roslyn had at first been speechless and then protested, of course. What did she know about charity work except that she donated money to it? Elvin and Gunter's sons had reassured her that she was the right person for the job and that Elvin would be her support and the one to oversee any plan into action. They'd also urged her to keep her research and plans secret, lest she be inundated by any group or organisation that got wind of the money. And now there was Amber's request, which just added to the oddness of the day.

Roslyn straightened the two magazines on the table and glanced around her comfortable home. Life hadn't been easy for her but her hard work had brought many pleasures. She'd never had to worry about keeping a roof over her head, never been without the support of family, never been pregnant and alone. In light of all that had been revealed by Gunter's sons and Elvin at lunch today, more good fortune was coming her way. All due to Gunter, of course. Her gaze focused on the ducks and a smile twitched at her lips. Only because they were his would she allow them to sprawl across a space in her otherwise sparsely adorned home. She contemplated her dear friend and wondered what he'd make of Amber and her situation. She was fairly sure she knew the answer.

She pushed backwards, arching against the pain in her back, then rose carefully to her feet, picked up the tart container and let herself out. At the cottage door she hesitated. The old wooden door beyond the screen was shut but Amber's car was still there so Roslyn assumed she was inside.

She pulled back the screen and knocked.

There was no sound beyond the door. No indication that Amber had heard her. She lifted her hand to knock again as the door lurched open, the bottom scraping loudly on the slate floor in protest. Amber stood beyond it glaring back at her.

Roslyn held up the container. "You forgot the tart."

The girl made no move to accept or to retreat.

Roslyn drew the container back to her body and straightened. "And you didn't let me finish what I was going to say."

One of Amber's arched eyebrows tweaked.

"May I come in?"

Amber stepped back. "It's your place." She spun and walked back into the cottage.

Roslyn followed then paused at the lounge door. The room was neat and tidy. So different to the last time she'd visited. Except for Amber's bag on the couch, some plastic crates stacked against a wall and several of the books from the bookcase sitting on the end of the dining table, it was as if no-one had been there. She crossed to the table, put down the container and picked up the top book. It was a well-thumbed copy of Dion Leonard's *Finding Gobi*. Roslyn smiled. She put it back and turned to Amber, who was standing with her arms folded defiantly over her chest, the scowl on her face even deeper.

"There's no TV so I thought I'd read."

"You're most welcome to the books." Roslyn waved a hand at the overflowing bookcase that filled one wall. "They were my husband's. Richard read widely and often. I'm sure he'd have been happy for you to enjoy them."

"I've never been much of a reader."

"I'm sorry about the TV."

Amber's scowl softened to a slight frown. "Why?"

"There is one that belongs in the cottage but it's in the spare room at my place. I'd forgotten."

Amber shrugged. "Doesn't matter. I'll be leaving soon anyway."

This time it was Roslyn's turn to frown. "But you asked to stay here."

Once more Amber shrugged.

Roslyn shifted her weight to her other foot to alleviate the ache in her leg. "Can we sit and talk about this?"

Amber remained tight-lipped but moved to the other side of the dining table. They both pulled out chairs and sat.

"I prefer plain speaking." Roslyn adjusted the position of the container she'd put on the table. "The reason I've been reluctant to have anyone here is twofold. I like to have the place available for my son and his family and some of my friends whenever they visit and…" She clasped her hands firmly together. "I had a very bad experience the last time I had people here on a longer-term basis."

Her confession was met with stoney silence from across the table. The girl was not going to give an inch.

"Anyway," Roslyn continued. "It's unlikely my son will be back in Australia until sometime next year. And I have two spare bedrooms in the house to accommodate friends so I can manage without the cottage for a while longer."

Amber leaned a little closer, her look wary. "Are you saying I can stay?"

"With certain conditions."

"Here we go." Amber flung herself back in her seat and folded her arms.

Her attitude was beginning to annoy Roslyn. Maybe Margot had had a point. "Don't get on your high horse. I'd expect you to pay some rent, keep the place tidy and be mindful of water use."

A small look of contrition flitted across Amber's face before the scowl returned.

"And," Roslyn continued, "I don't mind you having a friend or two over but no parties."

Amber snorted. "And here I am such a party girl with a zillion friends."

This time Roslyn remained silent. Behind her a phone beeped, the sound one made when its battery was low.

"How much is the rent?" Amber asked.

"We can work something out, just to cover the electricity et cetera."

"You don't want me to do anything else?"

"Like what?"

"Clean for you, mow the grass."

"I'm quite capable of cleaning my own place and I already pay someone to mow the grass. All you have to do is pay a bit of rent and look after the cottage. Let's see how that goes."

"Okay."

"I'll work out a figure and get back to you."

"Okay."

"Good." Roslyn stood and Amber did too. She followed Roslyn to the door.

"Thanks," she said as Roslyn let herself out.

"You're welcome."

"And for the food," Amber called after her as she walked away.

Roslyn waved over her shoulder. At least the girl's scowl was gone. Roslyn had hoped she was doing the right thing when she'd made her way to the cottage. It might come back to bite her like last time but the look on Amber's face at the offer of a roof over her head for a while longer was worth it – Roslyn glanced towards her side fence – and she could be truthful now if Margot quizzed her on the rent.

seventeen

Margot wandered aimlessly around her garden. She'd marched inside after her words with Roslyn but the house had felt hollow and empty and she'd come straight back out. It was a beautiful afternoon and the garden bloomed with roses, lavender and rhododendrons. The bees were loving the lavender and butterflies flitted over the flowers and in and out of the shadows cast by the magnolia and Japanese maple trees. The warm scent of summer filled the air but still Margot felt cold.

She huddled into herself as she rambled along the path towards the back of the yard. Her dad had helped her plan this garden when the house had been built. It was extensive and had been added to over the years to include the lawned area with children's swing and slide that the path skirted around and went on to reveal a hidden gazebo and an arbour of bigger trees. She stopped before she reached them. The path continued on, leading to the vegetable and fruit garden at the back. It was a lot of work. She and Dennis had done much of it themselves under her dad's direction. The garden had grown as her children had grown and now her grandchildren got to enjoy it too. These days they employed someone to do most of the heavy work but Margot still oversaw it and did some of the easier jobs herself. Trouble was, today the sight of it didn't bring her any joy.

After her argument with Kath, the real reason she'd left work early, she'd gone to Roslyn's for a sisterly shoulder to cry on. Instead of finding her sister there'd been the shock of that awful girl being there and Margot had been horrified to learn she was living in the cottage. Then when Roslyn had turned up they'd had a row and now here she was, alone and miserable. Dennis wouldn't be home for hours and there were things she could do inside but she didn't feel like sorting through the clothes she'd been planning to donate to Dress for Success or stripping the spare beds Nick's boys had slept in when they'd last stayed over or cleaning the oven, which had been on her list a while now, nor did she feel like preparing dinner.

She imagined sitting with Roslyn by her pool, sharing a bottle of wine. It had been their ritual for years. Dennis usually put on drinks for his staff on a Friday and Richard had often done something with his university colleagues. Friday was usually Roslyn's early finish – she'd always worked such long hours and so hard. The two of them would spend a couple of hours mulling over the week that had been. Roslyn brought a sense of calm to Margot's frazzled life and Margot liked to think she brought some light and humour to Roslyn's more serious, studious world. Of course it had been interrupted when poor Richard took sick and then died but they'd resumed their weekly catch-ups, although sometimes it would be Saturday or even Sunday if Roslyn's roster changed or other events took precedence.

Since Roslyn had retired two years prior and The General Providore had become busier, their weekly chat had become more haphazard. They still saw a lot of each other – the family dinners, dropping in with veggies, calling in for a coffee or to borrow something – but they weren't the same as their regular chewing-the-fat sessions.

Margot could swallow her pride and go back to Roslyn's but the worm of annoyance and hurt still squirmed inside. She was often the peacemaker, turning the other cheek to Roslyn's sharp tongue. Margot understood her sister never meant harm, it was just the way she was, but today her barbs had hurt more than usual and Margot wasn't quite ready to forgive her. Her dad would have said she was cutting off her nose to spite her face.

Margot smiled. "Dear Dad," she murmured. He'd been gone several years but how she missed him. His good common sense, that was often dished out abruptly but without the barbs Roslyn was capable of, and his warm welcomes, as if Margot was the most important person in his life. Towards the end she assumed she truly was. It was Margot who'd cooked for him, taken him to appointments, did the jobs around the house that the support people didn't.

Her phone pinged. A message from Em. She beamed at a photo of Henry playing in the sandpit, one hand on a digger and the other hovering mid-air, and a look of determined concentration on his cherubic face. *Had a good day at childcare* was the caption. Margot had forgotten it was his first day. She sent a love heart emoji back and opened her Facebook page, scrolling through the ads for clothes, some posts from chefs she followed, travel photos from interstate friends, and then remembered the group Fred had set up, Jesserton Jabber, he'd called it. She'd sent a join request a few days earlier and she'd been accepted. Fred had put up the usual admin rules and several people had thanked him for creating it, including Thelma, whose responses were invariably in capitals.

Margot started a post saying she had an appointment with the council planning officer for next Monday and that she'd organise a date for a meeting after that to share the information. She'd barely pressed post when someone began typing. She watched the small dots dance on the screen.

Thelma: THANK YOU MARGOT.

Thelma had been in for her daily coffee as usual and seemed to have forgiven Margot for Nick's bill. More dots danced.

Sozz PO: *Good that youre on it already*

"Sozz" was Sarah from the post office. After Thelma, she knew most about what was happening around town.

Greg: *Good luck*

The dots danced again, back and forth, taking an age, until finally a message appeared.

Thelma: *TELL KATH THE NEW SLICE I TRIED THIS MORNING WAS DELICIOUS.*

Margot resisted the urge to respond that Kath was also a member of the group. Then another message appeared.

Golds: *Give them what for from us*

It was one or other of the Threadgolds – she assumed Martin; it didn't sound like a comment the more gently spoken Anne would make. Tyres crunched on the driveway and Margot put her phone away. She wasn't expecting anyone at five o'clock on a Friday but she welcomed the interruption, even if it was only a parcel delivery.

She went through the side gate and was surprised to see Dennis's black Audi, as she now knew it to be, in the garage and the roller door slowly descending. She retraced her steps to the back of the house as she heard him calling her. They both arrived in the outdoor room at the same time, Dennis almost hidden by a huge box wrapped in cellophane and tied with a black, white and red ribbon.

"What's going on?" she asked as he lowered the box to the table and swept her up in a hug.

"We've done it, Margot."

"Done what?" She glanced over the box of expensive food and spied a bottle of Dom Pérignon tucked into one corner.

Dennis gripped her hands and looked directly into her eyes. The excitement in his gaze lifted her spirits.

"Has something happened? A change with Gunter's land…"

He frowned and dropped her hands. "Not that I know of. This is about the car dealership. We've been given the go-ahead to expand and Audi like our application so far. This box is from them." He swept his hand in the direction of the expensive gift but Margot was busy swallowing the bitter taste of disappointment all over again.

"Sit down." He pulled out a chair. "The Dom's not cold but I brought home a bottle of the Pol Roger that you like so we could celebrate."

He went inside and Margot had barely lowered herself to the chair before he was back, a bottle in one hand and a platter in the other.

"I stopped by the gourmet shop and picked up one of their cheese boards."

"What's this about, Dennis?" she asked as he poured her a champagne and one for himself.

"The expansion of our dealership."

"We canned that idea last year."

"Not canned, just delayed. Things have changed and people are clamouring for EVs."

"You didn't discuss it with me."

"I've mentioned it several times, Margot."

She frowned. She supposed he had. "I thought you were just keeping the idea alive."

"I was." He leaned forward, his look earnest. "Margot, there's no secret here. I knew you weren't really paying attention when I brought it up. You seemed happy for me to deal with it."

"I was…am. It's just that it seems to be done and dusted and—"

"Not quite. You knew we were working on expanding."

"Yes, but I thought that was with Renault."

"It is, but there's plenty of room for a second dealership since we did the extensions. Audi and Renault have agreed in principle, and there's scope for both in the region. My last big meeting with Audi was around the time Gunter died."

Margot frowned. "I do remember you throwing around some ideas."

"It was more than throwing around ideas, Margot." He shook his head. "You had a lot on your plate and you were very focused on getting the land."

"So were you."

There was a heartbeat of a pause before Dennis spoke, a moment when she saw ambiguity in his usually steadfast look.

"We missed out on the land," he said. "It's probably just as well. It would have been some time before we'd see a return on our investment or for Emily and Cameron to pay us back. The Audi dealership will see income for outlay."

Margot was puzzled by the whole discussion. "Surely there was paperwork, things to sign?"

"We did the initial stuff last year but, yes, we'll need to sign the rest of the documents soon. It's not quite finalised. Renault and Audi both had a few more stipulations about the showroom layout but this gift from Audi is a good sign." He gripped her shoulders and hugged her close.

Margot shook her head. She did remember their first talks with Audi. There'd been rules about showroom and workshop space, particular colour schemes and uniforms, specifically trained mechanics.

"We're meeting our Renault target well and truly so they're happy." He grinned. "You're going to love your new car."

"I love the one I've got."

Margot's head was spinning. Dennis's phone buzzed. She took a sip of champagne while he answered.

"Hello, Nick." Dennis glanced at Margot. "Yes, we're both home."

He listened then lowered the phone to his side. "Kayla's at her mum's with the boys for some family thing. Nick wants to come over. Something he wants to talk to us about. Have we got enough to include him for dinner?"

"I haven't started dinner but there's a lasagne in the freezer I could defrost."

Dennis's eyebrows raised.

"With real meat and dairy," she said.

"Sure, Nick, Mum's got one of her proper lasagnes on the go."

Margot rose to her feet and went to take the lasagne from the freezer. Thank goodness her new microwave had the best defrost function. While she was throwing together a tossed salad Dennis came in to top up her glass.

"Not sure why Nick is coming over. He was cagey on the phone." Dennis picked out a slice of cucumber and munched it slowly. "You don't think they want to move back in with us?"

"Why would they want to do that?" Nick and Kayla and the boys had stayed with them for almost two years before they'd bought the house they now lived in. "They've got their own place now."

"It needs so much work."

"It's got good bones. You said so yourself."

"But Nick's done hardly anything to it."

"He's been working such long hours since he took over the business from Otto."

"But that kitchen isn't workable since he stripped it out. He shouldn't have done it if he wasn't ready to fix it."

"I think he was hoping you might work on it with him. You did kind of imply you would."

"When I had spare time. The kids have all moved out but it seems like we're busier than ever. Nick could at least have made a start. All these dealership changes are going to keep me extra busy for a while." Dennis drained his glass and poured some of the remaining champagne into hers. "I'll get a bottle of red to go with the lasagne." He headed off to the wine cupboard in the other room.

Margot was happy for the subject to be changed. She picked up her knife and sliced some extra cucumber. It wasn't like Dennis to criticise Nick. The two of them used to be as thick as thieves, although their relationship had started to strain by the time the young family had finally moved out. Dennis was less patient with the children towards the end of their stay, which had sometimes meant Nick would have a go at his dad, and Margot had bitten her tongue to the point of almost chewing it off at Kayla's lack of assistance with meals. She prepared her own but both the boys and Nick had mostly preferred Margot's cooking to Kayla's vegan dishes and sharing the kitchen had become a source of aggravation.

The microwave binged and Margot transferred the lasagne to the oven. She didn't mind eating vegan meals sometimes, but it could be a challenge when Dennis arced up. She had to admit she preferred real meat to the meat alternative too, but she'd done her best to accommodate her daughter-in-law.

Nick walked in with flyers in his hand. "Cam hasn't wasted any time. I saw Em earlier and she asked me if we could distribute some of these." He put the bundle on the bench. "You should have yours ready, Mum."

"My what?"

"Application. You're already on the bandwagon with the hotel. You should stand for mayor."

Margot studied her son for signs of guile but his smile seemed genuine. The forgotten text message from Esther popped into her head. She'd never responded to it and Esther had already left town. The mayor's position was indeed vacant.

"That'd be funny," Dennis said, handing Nick a beer.

"Why?" Nick and Margot said in unison.

She was annoyed at Dennis's dismissive tone but buoyed by her son's support.

"I'd hate to see you any more stressed, Margot." Dennis's tone turned serious. "There can be a lot of conflict in public office, people hounding you about all sorts, and you hate public speaking. You were glad when your stint as councillor ended."

Margot shrugged at Nick. "It's true. I don't like the limelight."

Dennis nodded in an I-told-you-so way and asked Nick if he'd seen any of the cricket. Margot picked up the flyers. It was a nice photo of Cameron, and his list of achievements and interests and what he thought he could bring to the role of councillor was very impressive. She ran her gaze over it again. There was no mention of opposition to the hotel. Still, he lived in Hahndorf so it wasn't such an issue there, she supposed.

She stacked the pile to one side and got out the plates for dinner. Dennis was right. She wasn't courageous enough for public office again even if she was devoted to her community as Esther had suggested. Margot had been a bundle of nerves during last Wednesday's meeting and it had taken all her courage to ask her question. How on earth would she go if she was mayor?

They'd finished the lasagne and the two men had almost emptied the bottle of red – Margot had stuck with the champagne – before Nick broached the topic he'd obviously come to discuss. Nick was very like Dennis in looks and mannerisms but he had a vulnerable side that he kept hidden from others. Margot had noticed the unease in him all evening – the extra laugh at his dad's jokes, the over-enthusiasm for a simple lasagne and salad.

He was fiddling with the stem of his empty wine glass and as he looked up Margot glimpsed the hardening of his face, so like Dennis. She steeled herself. He and Kayla couldn't be breaking up, could they? There was so much of that these days.

"Your new van should be here before Christmas." Dennis spoke before Nick did.

"Oh, right."

"What new van?" Margot asked.

"That van Nick inherited with the business isn't reliable or safe," Dennis said. "I've organised a new one for him, at a good rate of course." Dennis winked at Nick. "And the Audi dealership's got the green light. Your mum and I were celebrating before you arrived."

"Great." Nick nodded.

Margot sat up. "Did you know about Audi?"

"Yeah, well, kind of." He glanced at Dennis, whose grin still stretched from ear to ear. "Dad was telling us about it the night we had dinner at Em's…when we were looking at his new car."

"At least someone listens when I speak," Dennis joked.

"I do listen," Margot huffed. "But you talk about cars a lot and sometimes I—"

"Tune out." Dennis winked. "You'll pay more attention once we sell a few. It's a pity Audi don't make work vans, Nick, but I've got you a good deal on a Renault."

"Yeah," Nick croaked. He cleared his throat. "It was actually the van I wanted to talk to you about."

"Sorry it's taken a bit longer than planned," Dennis said. "Things still haven't gone back to normal with the supply of new vehicles. It took me an age to get the Audi."

Margot looked from her husband to her son. She hadn't known that the car was an Audi until the night of the town meeting and this was the first she was hearing about a new van for Nick.

"I wondered if you could waive the payments," Nick blurted.

Dennis lowered the glass that was halfway to his mouth. "For how long?"

Nick shrugged.

"You mean give it to you?"

"No…but…You were going to give Gunter's place to Emily."

"No, we weren't." Dennis looked at Margot. "Did you put him up to this?"

She wilted under his incredulous look. "I didn't even know he was getting a new van."

"I haven't mentioned it to Mum." Nick gripped his hands so tightly his knuckles went white. He stared into this father's sharp gaze. "You're the one who manages the money."

Margot opened her mouth to object but it suddenly hit her that Nick was right, to a degree. Everything they owned or owed with the dealership was in their joint names. Margot never worried about going into the finer details though. Dennis always managed that. He ran things past her when she needed to sign. She'd always trusted him to make the big decisions.

"And you're the one that manages yours," Dennis said.

"The cost of Gunter's place is way more than the van," Nick persisted.

"And we didn't buy Gunter's place so I don't see your point."

"Buying a house and the business has left me no wriggle room but I've come up with a pla—"

"You lived rent-free here for almost two years."

"Emily and Cameron did too when they were first married."

Margot and Dennis had hardly ever lived completely alone since they'd had children. Nick had moved into a rental property when he and Kayla first married but Em had lived with them while she'd been at uni and then for the first year or so after she and Cam were married while they did up the little house behind the shop where they lived now.

"I'm glad we were able to help you both get a good start," Margot said with a smile, still trying to smooth the waters.

"If you need more income Kayla needs to step up," Dennis said. "The boys are both at school now. She should get a real job instead of faffing about with those yoga classes."

Margot winced as the colour rose in Nick's cheeks. She and Dennis had often discussed Kayla's lack of input to the family finances. She'd been at uni when she and Nick met but she'd deferred before the arrival of their firstborn. She'd hardly ever left the boys when they were little and had breastfed them till they were at kindy; she grew her own vegetables, made their clothes. She was a wonderful mother but did little to contribute to the family income. Nick had been on a good wage while he'd worked for Otto but it was a very different thing now that he owned the business.

"It's not just a yoga class. She does all kinds of volunteer work at the Hills Community Hub and she does the paperwork for the business." Nick defended his wife. "That's a significant number of hours."

"Of course it is," Margot said brightly to ease the tension. "I used to work in the dealership before we had you and Em and for quite a few years after."

"Kayla wants to go back to uni and finish her degree so she can get a decent job."

"That's very good news."

"And costs money," Dennis grumbled.

"Which is why we've come up with a plan to—"

"She needs a paying job. Volunteering is all well and good but it doesn't bring in any money. What about the Providore, Margot? You're often short-staffed there."

"Only sometimes," Margot blustered. "It wouldn't be a regular paying job." Kayla had filled in a few times when she and Nick had been living with Margot and Dennis. She'd shown no adaptability or intuition for the work and Kath had suggested they not have her unless they were desperate.

"Kayla doesn't want to work in hospitality, Dad. She wants to finish her social work degree."

Dennis snorted. "It'll be a lot of years before that earns her any money."

"You're just being obstinate because you don't approve of university degrees," Nick snapped.

"Well, what good did it do your sister? She taught for five minutes then gave up to go into business with her husband. And your cousin, Jerome, all that time on a law degree and he's teaching English to Japanese."

"Japanese lawyers." Margot felt the need to defend her nephew, who was working for a Japanese law firm supporting lawyers even if he wasn't exactly practising as one. "Without his knowledge of the law he wouldn't have that job. And Em might go back to teaching. You never know."

Dennis dismissed her with a shake of his head. "Kayla won't be earning money anytime soon unless she takes on a part-time job."

"You could afford to help us, Dad." Nick's face was set rigid as a rock but he blinked several times. Margot's heart broke for him. She hadn't seen him this vulnerable since he was a teenager.

"We did help when you bought the business. Money towards the purchase." Dennis topped up his glass with the last of the bottle.

"You gave Em money for their business too," Nick snarled. "More, I suspect." Margot chewed her lip. He was right. "The business has ended up costing more than I thought."

"You should follow that business plan you prepared."

"It's not as simple as that. Otto wasn't exactly truthful with the state of some of the equipment. And I can't take on any of the big jobs on my own. I need an apprentice. But as I said, we—"

Dennis snorted into his glass. "You just have to pull your head in, not waste money."

Nick pushed to his feet. "I'm not spending it on gambling or buying expensive cars."

"Of course you're not." Margot rose too. Nick was having a dig at Dennis, who liked a night out at the casino from time to time.

Dennis twirled his wine but didn't get up. "I've earned the money I spend and I'll do it in whatever way I like."

Nick shook his head and stalked from the room.

Margot glanced at Dennis, who was studying his glass, and then followed her son to the door.

"Nick, wait," she said as he tugged it open.

He stopped but didn't turn back.

"You should have given me a heads-up about the van. I could have spoken to your dad first. He's in a funny mood tonight."

Nick spun back. The anger shone through his watery eyes. "It's not just tonight. You're blind to his miserable side."

Margot gasped. "Your father's not miserable. He's been very generous to you and Emily."

"When it suits him. It's not as if I'm asking him to give me his last five cents. He's got plenty of money. Kayla and I need some help, that's all. We've had to rejig our business plan. I don't expect to get it for nothing but—"

"Calm down, Nick." Margot lay a hand on his arm. "Your dad was probably taken by surprise, that's all. We didn't realise things were so tough for you. Let me talk to him. I'm sure there's something we can do to help."

He sighed. "Thanks, Mum, and thanks for dinner." He brushed a kiss over her cheek and let himself out.

Margot shut the door. Several things bothered her. The foremost was concern for her son, of course, and the disagreement with his father, but their argument had raised other issues. The house was in Margot's name – something her father had insisted for both her and Roslyn – but Margot had used her property to help Dennis set up the dealership, which was in both their names. She was more of a silent partner, it was true, but just as she enjoyed the profits she was also half-responsible for the losses they'd faced at different times. The dealership was doing well now but it hadn't always been smooth sailing.

The other thing that bothered her was Gunter's place, or at least their lack of success in securing it. She'd left it up to Dennis to put in a bid he thought would get it for them and be within their budget to achieve, even if they'd had to borrow some. The land had productive vines that would have covered the repayments. The Audi dealership announcement had surprised her. It sounded as if Dennis hadn't left it on the back burner for long after they'd initially looked into it. Surely they couldn't have afforded both the land and the addition to their business.

"Margot?"

She spun at the sound of his voice.

He flicked on the hall light. "What are you doing standing out here in the dark?"

"I was jus—"

"Sam rang." He waggled his phone at her. "He and a few of the other golf fellas have ended up at Fred's pub for a meal. I said we'd eaten but we might go down for a drink."

Margot blew out a breath of relief. She hadn't been quite sure how she was going to tackle the subject of their money situation. Now she'd have time to think about it. "You go," she said.

"C'mon, Margot, it's Friday night. A few of the other wives are there." Dennis smiled, a soft twist of his lips that radiated charm. "And I might need a driver." He pulled her into a hug. "Don't worry about Nick. He needs to know he can't just get a handout whenever a new idea takes his fancy. We'll work something out."

The relief she'd felt earlier deepened, expanded by his words and the warmth of his hug. She was worrying needlessly. "Okay," she said. "But we'll take my car."

eighteen

Amber hummed under her breath as she unpacked the clean glasses. It had been an extra busy Friday night so far but she was still rolling with the high that Roslyn's offer had given her. She'd almost floated to work after their talk, her steps springy as if she were suddenly weightless. Her excitement had been short-lived as she'd reminded herself it wasn't a long-term solution, but the thought of having a roof over her head for at least the foreseeable future had been such a relief she'd unpacked her box of food and stored it in the pantry cupboard before she'd left for work.

There was still the rent to sort out. Maybe it was foolish but she wanted to pay her way and she trusted Roslyn to be fair. Amber knew she couldn't expect anything for nothing. Even Fred's free meals meant no complaints when asked to do extra. Not that she objected to that. Amber took pride in a job well done. It was one of the few things she felt she had control over.

"Hey, love. A man could die of thirst here."

She glanced at the guy grinning at her from the end of the bar then looked around but the other barman was collecting glasses from tables.

"Chop chop," the guy called.

She moved steadily towards him, eyeballing the round-faced rosy-cheeked guy who looked barely old enough to drink. She should ask him for his ID, instead she plucked up his glass and beckoned him with her finger. His face creased in a goofy grin and he leaned in. He'd be lucky to be eighteen. He reminded her of her little brother. She grabbed his ear and tugged him closer.

"Oww."

She cut off his complaint with a glare. "You're no man and I'm not your love. My name's Amber. Remember that."

She let go of his ear and he rubbed it, glaring at her.

"You bi—"

"Shut up and listen." She leaned closer again, her voice low but menacing. "You call me by my proper name and mind your manners and I won't call the cops to check your fake ID."

His face went red and his eyes widened. She'd been guessing but she'd hit the mark.

"Everything all right here?" The other barman came up behind her.

"I think so," Amber said brightly, still eyeballing the young smart-arse.

He nodded. "Just getting a refill."

Amber poured his beer, he handed over cash – another sign he was younger than he pretended – and moved back to the group playing pool.

Fred appeared from the dining room and rested one large arm on the bar. "It's not too busy here at the moment and they're rushed off their feet still in the kitchen. Would you go and lend a hand delivering meals, please, Amber. I'll help keep an eye on the bar."

"Sure." She didn't mind changing roles. The pub had been busy the last few days and she'd hardly seen Tom. Her break and his hadn't coincided since they'd had the chef's pizza special. Tonight it had been a pasta dish. She'd wolfed down half before her shift started. The rest she'd take home for tomorrow.

The kitchen was busy – even the second chef was moving faster than usual. The waitress was heading to the main dining room, her arms loaded with plates piled high with fish and chips. Amber looked at the food pass lined with more plates and read the dockets beside them.

"That lot's all for the front room," Tom said as he passed her, lumping a huge bag of frozen chips.

Amber picked up the first two – she'd not mastered the art of balancing more on her arm – and set off for the front room. It was a smaller room off the main dining room and tonight the table was packed with a rowdy crowd. She moved to the head of the large table that dominated the room. It was mostly men and only a few women. They were all talking loudly, a few of the men half-plastered. She glanced at the plates.

"Beef schnitzel with mushroom gravy and chicken schnitzel parmie."

The man closest to her took the beef without even making eye contact and someone further down waggled a hand for the chicken. There wasn't a lot of space between the chair backs and the walls and most of this group were bigger men sprawled in their seats, leaving little room to manoeuvre.

"Come on, love, it'll be cold before I get it," the chicken schnittie man called.

The woman closest to her turned and lifted a hand to take the plate Amber offered and they both paused as they recognised each other. Roslyn's sister stared at Amber, her small pointy nose tilted up as if she'd stepped in dog poo.

"Margot, take the bloody plate and pass it along, will you," chicken schnittie man called again. "The girl's stuck."

"In more ways than one," another male voice called from across the table and a few chortles followed.

Amber could only assume they were referring to the slight bulge beneath her shirt. She shoved the plate at Margot who pushed away in surprise and the plate tilted between them. The chicken with its parmi topping stayed glued to the surface but a heap of chips slid onto Margot's lap.

She yelped and jumped up. Amber managed to level the plate and swing it out of her way.

"Sorry," she spluttered as the crowd erupted with laughter and unhelpful suggestions with one man offering to eat from Margot's crotch.

"Hey, settle down, fellas," the man beside Margot commanded. "Are you okay, Margot?" he asked and turned his glare on Amber. "Don't just stand there – go and get a cloth."

Amber saw red then. She wasn't going to be treated like a doormat by these entitled morons. She lifted the plate with the full intent of smashing it into the man's face. A large hand gripped her wrist and another took the plate.

"What's happened here?" Fred's voice boomed but with the hint of jollity Amber had heard him use with drunks. "You happy punters upsetting my staff?"

"You must be desperate to have staff like this one, Fred," a male voice chortled.

Amber swept her stormy gaze around the table searching for the owner of the remark. A pie-eyed man with ruddy red cheeks and nose hair winked at her.

"All okay, Margot?" Fred asked.

Margot was staring down at her pants and another woman was brushing a serviette over them. "No harm done," she said. "At least the salad missed me." The small bowl of greens and its sticky dressing had upended on the table and not her lap.

"Take that back to the kitchen and get a fresh one please, Amber." Fred let go of her arm and handed the plate back. "I'll help Margot."

Amber stuck to the spot as if her feet had grown roots. Several fluttering kicks poked from inside her and she blew out a breath. She turned in the small space between Fred's bulky frame and the door. The voices around the table grew loud again.

She strode back to the kitchen, her hands shaking as the anger trickled from her body like liquid through a sieve, leaving seeds of resentment and humiliation festering behind.

Chef paused long enough to take in her garbled story and Tom flicked her a sympathetic look from his position at the deep fryer.

"The schnittie's fine then," Chef declared. "Just a clean plate, a top-up with fresh chips and another salad, Tom." He passed the plate along and Amber was sent to deliver two bowls of pasta to the main dining room while the other waitress delivered the rest of the order to the front room. They were busy for a while, Amber fuelled by the aggravation of her mishap with Roslyn's sister and the arrogance of the people she was with.

When the orders on the pass began to slow Chef suggested she sit on a stool for five minutes and have a drink of water. She'd not been there long when Fred stuck his head into the kitchen.

Amber's stomach lurched when his gaze settled on her. She couldn't afford to lose this job.

"Bar's getting busy again, Amber. You up to it or do you need to go home?"

"I'm fine," she said as she leaped to her feet.

"We'll be right in here now," Chef said. "That's the last of the orders."

Amber glanced at the clock. It was almost nine. The late-Friday-nighters would be filling the bar. Usually they'd been a younger crowd she'd enjoyed interacting with and obviously Fred wasn't ready to sack her yet.

Margot settled into the couch with her glass of sparkling water. The other two wives had managed to get their husbands out the door already and it was just her and Dennis and a couple of his single cronies left. Their group had taken over a space in a corner of the front bar that had been set up with tub chairs and small couches.

Conversation between the men washed over her and from her spot tucked away in the poorly lit space, Margot studied Amber as she worked behind the bar. The girl was efficient and quick, engaging in banter with the customers, where she could only be described as animated. There was the odd "Hell yeah" or "That's awesome", and she waved off a young couple with an exuberant "Thanks guys". Only occasionally did Margot see a sign of the scowling face that had been the norm in her two interactions with Amber. She had what could be described as a hard face for her young years. And she was pregnant. Margot was appalled all over again that Roslyn had let the girl stay in her cottage. After all the grief of her last tenants Roslyn had sworn off renting. What on earth would happen once Amber had the baby? And what hurt most was that Roslyn hadn't mentioned it.

"You've got a handle on it, haven't you, Margot?"

She turned from her observations of the bar to see the men all looking at her expectantly.

"On what?" she asked, glancing at Dennis. They'd been talking about cars when she'd tuned out.

"I heard you're leading the charge against the hotel development." Grant was the man she liked least of Dennis's golf mates. He was brusque and self-assured, twice divorced and usually with a woman half his age on his arm. Margot found him intimidating.

"I wouldn't call it a charge exactly," she stammered.

"Organising petitions and protest meetings before you know all the facts is a bit presumptuous. I hope you're not going to burn your bra too."

Margot wilted under his pompous gaze.

"You've just been gauging interest, really, haven't you, Margot," Dennis said. "People are a bit concerned about the impact on Jesserton, that's all."

"Don't blame them," Sam slurred. He'd had way too many drinks and was sprawled across his chair in a state of disarray.

"But it's not just about Jesserton, is it?" Grant persisted. "A boutique hotel in this region would be an employment opportunity and be of benefit to a wide range of businesses."

Grant lived in a large home on acreage in nearby Glasforest surrounded by similar neatly set out sizable properties. There was little risk he'd ever have a hotel built next door. Instead of retreating as she usually would, her annoyance at his arrogance gave her courage. "I suppose it's fine as long as it's not next door to you."

"Nonsense." He dismissed her with a wave of his hand. "You'll hardly know it's there."

"What about all those extra people wanting to play on our golf course though?" Dennis joked.

"The sketch I saw looked rather savvy," Grant persisted. "Something for Jesserton to be proud of, I'd have thought."

"Just like the upgrade of the park would be in Glasforest," Margot said. She knew very well that Grant opposed the upgrade of the run-down park facilities to a modern play space and barbecue area.

"That's different. A hotel provides accommodation for people to stay longer and spend their money. Glasforest doesn't have the shops and facilities Jesserton does."

"Traffic on the roads, water supply, sewerage and rubbish disposal," Margot said. "It's something both projects have to consider. A hotel would have far more impact than a play space."

"Margot's a bit passionate about it." Dennis patted her leg.

She glared at him. He hadn't liked the idea of a hotel either.

"You should stand for mayor, Margot," Sam said. "There's a vacancy now that the crazy woman has finally been honest about her affair and run off with her boyfriend."

"I gather his wife was just as surprised as her husband," Margot said.

Dennis's eyes widened.

"It takes two to tango," she said, surprising herself.

"Surely it's time for a good man in that position," Grant said, as if she hadn't spoken at all. "That young accountant guy who's on council, Brett someone – he's got his head screwed on right. And he lives in one of the smaller towns, doesn't he? Probably understands the needs well." The three men began to toss about names of possible candidates.

Margot picked up her glass to take a swallow and had to grip it hard to halt the tremble in her fingers. The three of them had dismissed her. Sam was drunk and Grant had always been arrogant but it was Dennis's brush-off that had upset her the most.

nineteen

Roslyn let herself into her house, went straight to her bedroom and lay on her bed without even taking off her shoes. She'd been outwardly calm while she'd been with the specialist, hoping young Dr Joe had it all wrong and she was wasting everyone's time going to visit a rheumatologist. He hadn't been wrong. All the tests and scans had confirmed Joe's diagnosis of rheumatoid arthritis and, if she was totally honest, her own. It had been a punch to the gut. Deep down, she'd known but hadn't wanted to face it. Family history had been questioned. Roslyn's mother had been affected by rheumatoid arthritis from a young age. She'd had deformed and painful fingers for almost as long as Roslyn could remember. But Roslyn's symptoms were different and she'd hoped.

She held her hands out in front of her. She got the occasional swelling and pain in them but it never lasted and she could brush it off, but the pain that flared in her hips and knees and sometimes her feet had been far more restrictive. Still, she'd stuck her head in the sand and stayed in complete denial.

The specialist had said hip replacement was a last resort. Roslyn had come away with medication to try and a brochure that talked about being physically active, sticking to a healthy diet — "alcohol sometimes" had stuck in her mind — and learning to manage pain. That was a joke. Managing pain was what she'd devoted much of her working life to, and she'd been self-medicating to avoid the truth.

She stared at the ceiling, berating herself. It was as if her medical knowledge had been for nothing, which reminded her of Richard, which made her feel even more melancholy, which made her body ache. Roslyn closed her eyes. There'd been low times in her life — the tough years of proving herself as an anaesthetist, the death of her mother and later her father, Jerome declaring he was going to marry a local and live permanently in Japan, Richard's illness and death and more recently the loss of Gunter. This diagnosis was not in the same basket yet it had knocked her flat, taken the wind from her with the force of a thump to her solar plexus and left her gasping in its wake. For the first time in her life she felt vulnerable. She closed her eyes, gripping the quilt beneath her in her hands.

A soft knocking sound broke the silence. Roslyn's eyelids flickered. She wasn't sure how long she'd been lying on her bed but she felt cold and the afternoon light had lost its brightness.

It wouldn't be Margot — she'd just let herself in. And Roslyn had only seen her that morning. It had been a brief cool interchange to swap some vegetables. Margot had been distracted. She was obviously annoyed about something but Roslyn had been too focused on her upcoming appointment to be worried about Margot's latest drama.

The knock came again, louder this time. She eased herself up to a sitting position, her limbs stiff but not so painful.

"Yes, I'm coming," she barked.

Roslyn's bedroom opened straight into the family room and she stepped through the door and saw Amber, her hand cupped to the glass, peering in.

"It's open," she said and crossed to the kitchen where she stopped by the bottle of red wine she'd opened the night before then bypassed it and flicked on the kettle, while behind her Amber let herself in.

"Are you okay?" Amber's voice was tentative.

"Yes." Roslyn got out a cup and her hand hovered over another. "Would you like a cup of tea?"

"No...thanks." Amber moved closer. "Are you sure you're okay? You look a bit...pale."

Roslyn brushed her hands across her cheeks and dragged her fingers through her hair. "I lay down after I got back from the city and dozed off." She put a tea bag in her mug. "Why are you here?"

"Geez, you cut to the chase, don't you?" Amber snapped. "I was coming to organise the rent but then I saw water running down the drive and you're so fussy about wat—"

"Blast!" Roslyn spun then gasped and swore as she gripped her hip.

"What is it?" Amber came closer, a panicked look on her face.

"It's nothing." Roslyn batted her away. "Just my blasted hip." She hobbled towards the door. "The timer must've stuck."

"Let me go," Amber said.

Roslyn gave in and rested against the bench. "Just turn the tap off...thank you."

By the time Amber returned the pain had abated and Roslyn had poured her tea. She remained propped at the bench.

"It's stopped now," Amber said.

"It's bore water but I don't like to waste it."

Amber looked puzzled so Roslyn explained again about there being no mains water and that what she used on her garden and in her pool came via a bore from underground. The houses relied on the rainwater collected in the tanks. She reiterated her conditions for renting again – there was no point in dillydallying – and a figure she thought reasonable. She hadn't bothered to do the sums on paper. It was just a number she thought might be within the realms of Amber's budget and would leave the girl with money for other things.

Amber's face lit up. "I can manage that."

Roslyn had a brief moment of regret. She was a thief taking money from someone who was homeless but Amber wanted to pay and it had to be a realistic amount.

"I can give you my bank details," Roslyn said.

"Okay."

"I won't do it now…tomorrow. I'll drop it over."

Amber nodded and hung by the door, making no move to leave.

"Was there something else?" Roslyn asked.

"Yeah." She glanced around. "You said there was a TV."

"Oh yes, sorry, I'd forgotten again. But it's too big for you and me to carry. I'll ask Dennis or my nephew to help."

"Okay." Amber glanced towards the other room. The yearning in her face revealed her youth. "I'll see you later then." She turned slowly and let herself out. The small round ball that was her baby silhouetted by her t-shirt took Roslyn by surprise. Amber was so thin still – except for the small bulge it was easy to forget she was pregnant. A baby going to have a baby.

"They'll be here on Sunday," Roslyn called after her then waited as silence settled again. She understood how a TV helped fill a space in an empty house. She didn't actually watch a lot of TV herself but often had it on as background noise. Through the window Amber kept walking, giving no sign she'd heard. Roslyn picked up her phone.

※

Amber walked quickly back along the drive to her cottage. She wasn't sure what she'd been hoping for. She could have taken up the offer of a cup of tea so that she could have lingered, talked to Roslyn about her visit to the doctor, a woman this time. She'd been softly spoken and had gently quizzed Amber about her health and reminded her to eat well. Another one of those do-gooders. At least Amber's blood pressure was normal and the baby was fine and she didn't need another check-up for a month. Somehow she'd felt Roslyn's offer of the tea had been made out of politeness rather than a real desire for Amber to join her.

Amber was relieved she hadn't gone back on her offer of the cottage at least. Roslyn was nothing like the old bag at the caravan park but Amber had been let down too many times to have a lot of trust in what people said. The rent was doable though. She suspected on the open market the cottage could ask a lot more but she wasn't going to argue.

She let herself back inside. Fred had given her the night off. After her trip to the doctor she'd done a bit of shopping. She'd bought a family-sized pie that had been marked down and a few veggies. The doctor had gone on about eating properly but Amber had few skills in the kitchen. She planned to boil a potato and some carrot and maybe one of Roslyn's zucchini to go with the pie but she wasn't all that hungry yet.

She picked up the book she'd been reading and sunk back on the couch, but found herself staring instead at the cupboard that sat along the opposite wall. It was where she imagined the TV would go. Restless, she tossed the book aside and slid open the cupboard doors. She hadn't looked inside it before and was surprised to see a CD player flanked by large speakers and, on the shelf below it and stacked beside it, piles and piles of CDs. She sifted through them: classical music, opera, jazz, a few musicals she'd never heard of and then tucked at the back she found an odd assortment of albums from singers like John Farnham, Olivia Newton-John, Bob Dylan and Elton John.

She settled on the floor, her back against the cupboard and picked them up one at a time, turning them over to read the back. The songs made her think of Russ, one of her mum's boyfriends, the only decent one, who'd hung around for about a year when Amber turned ten. Russ made her a cake for her birthday and bought her a notebook and some coloured pens, one of the few gifts she'd ever received for her birthday. Of course he was far too good a bloke for her mum and he hadn't lasted till Amber's eleventh birthday. She'd spent that with her little brother in the cold, bare back room in the dump of a house belonging to the dropkick her mum had hooked up with next.

She gave a brief thought to her brother, the boy she'd tried to keep safe since the day he'd been born four years after her, but he'd learned to deal drugs from another of their mum's boyfriends and by the time he was thirteen Amber knew she'd lost the battle.

She flipped the Elton John cover in her hands. The songs were all so familiar. Russ always had the CD player going, at least until he'd come home one day and it wasn't there. Sold as a package with all the CDs he'd collected. It'd been his pride and joy and the last straw. Amber had cried when he'd left but her mum had been on a high from the drugs she'd bought with the cash from the sale and didn't even know Russ was gone until several days later when the food had run out and the electricity with it.

She put the CD in the player and settled back on the couch, focusing on that one good year of her life when there'd been food on the table, clean clothes, and a warm blanket on the mattress she shared with her brother.

Too restless to sit she stood, turned up the sound till it vibrated up through the floor. She stepped and twisted to the beat of "Crocodile Rock", belting out the chorus with Elton. The baby stirred in her belly. "You going to be an Elton John fan, Beetle?" She rested her hand over the movements but the baby wasn't enough to prevent the wave of despair that swept her as the next song rolled on. "Candle in the Wind" always made her feel sad.

Amber had been determined to make a better life for herself and it had been an epic fail. She'd done okay at school, she'd avoided the drugs and the creepy men her mother hung out with, and she'd even got a part-time job at a supermarket. She'd met Tyson at a music gig. He was older – she hadn't realised how much then. He'd been kind, understanding of her non-existent home life. He'd looked out for her, treated her as if she was special, and when he'd said he was moving to Penola in the south-east of the state she'd jumped at the chance to put the huge distance between herself and the downward spiral she was facing at home.

Up until she'd discovered she was pregnant life had been fairly good with Tyson. They'd found a place to live and both got jobs at the local pub. And when they weren't working they'd partied or just chilled out together. Tyson got testy sometimes if she didn't keep the place tidy. And sometimes he'd swear and carry on if his favourite shirt wasn't washed or she'd mucked up his dinner, but it had been a small price to pay. She loved that they had their own place and didn't mind doing her best around the house. After all, Tyson paid the rent and covered the cost of most of their daily needs. And he'd been protective of her if other blokes looked twice at her in the pub. She'd felt special, important to someone for the first time in her life.

She'd turned eighteen just as they'd arrived in Penola. Tyson had bought her a gold necklace threaded through a small glittering ball. She put her hand instinctively to the nape of her neck where it had sat until he'd ripped it from her the night he threw her out.

She lowered herself to the floor, resting her back against the couch. A shiver wriggled down her spine as she recalled how angry he'd been when she'd told him she was pregnant. He'd called her so many awful names, but "useless" had hurt the most. Somehow it echoed in her head and was far worse than his swearing at her. He'd told her to have an abortion and she nearly had. It had been booked, and then she'd seen him with another girl, feeling her up out the back of the pub. Amber had gone off at him when he'd got home and that was the night he'd been rough with her, hit her across the face so hard there'd been a mark for weeks after he'd thrown her out. She was only grateful that she hadn't gone ahead with the bird tattoo she'd been planning, entwining their two names.

She'd camped at her friend's place for a few days but Immi was out all day at work and off with her boyfriend most nights. Amber had felt miserable and alone. The loss of Tyson's affection had hurt more than the time she'd finally realised her mum didn't care if she lived or died. The day before the abortion she'd spent hours curled in a ball, crying, rocking herself in the depths of deep despair. Finally, when she had no tears left, it had come to her, like one of those bolts out of the blue that people talked about. The one person in the world who would love her when no-one else did was her baby and she couldn't get rid of it.

When Tyson had thrown her out she'd left with only a few clothes so she'd gone back to their old place when he was at work. She'd packed up the rest of her personal things, some of the household items, then she'd taken the bedding from the spare bed, put it all in the station wagon that had been parked in the shed and driven away.

She batted the heavy tear that rolled down her cheek and sniffed. She'd thought her life was set when she'd left home with Tyson. Trouble was, in trying to get away from her mum she'd ended up just like her, pregnant and alone at nineteen. Tyson had been right when he'd called her useless.

Roslyn was surprised to see Amber's car still parked at the cottage. No light shone from any of the windows but music thudded. She glanced back to Nick, who was making his way slowly along the path behind her pushing the trolley. He wouldn't let Roslyn help.

She slipped her spare key into her pocket and knocked on the door firmly to be heard over the music. After her second knock the sound lowered and Amber appeared at the door, her face red and blotchy.

"Sorry, have I disturbed you?" Roslyn said. "I thought you'd be at work, then I saw your car was still here."

"Night off," Amber said. "There's a big weekend coming up. Live music and stuff." She rubbed her face then and looked beyond Roslyn at the sound of wheels crunching on the gravel.

"My nephew's brought the TV."

"Okay...thanks."

Roslyn pushed the screen door wider as Nick came to a stop as close as he could get, one hand on top of the blanket-wrapped TV. Roslyn had given him a brief background about Amber and why his help was required. He'd come over almost immediately – turned out he'd needed Roslyn's help too but in a different way. They'd talked for quite a while before they'd loaded up the TV.

"Amber, this is Nick."

"Hello." He smiled.

"Can I help?" Amber said.

"I should be right." Nick tugged at the blanket and Roslyn lifted it away. Once the TV was uncovered, he manoeuvred it inside on his own, Roslyn and Amber holding doors open and clearing his path. He lowered it to the floor in the lounge and looked around.

"Where do you want it?"

"It goes on top of the buffet." Roslyn pointed to the large cupboard with its doors open. "The connections are behind there." Roslyn smiled at Amber. "Nick's an electrician. He's a big help to me with anything like this." Elton John was singing in the background. "I see you've discovered Richard's CD player."

"Elton John reminds me of Uncle Richard and his pool parties." Nick grinned at Roslyn then Amber. "We were allowed to invite our friends over to swim in the pool but Uncle Richard was in charge of the music."

"He didn't like anyone touching his player," Roslyn said.

"Oh, sorry...I—"

Roslyn batted a hand at Amber. "What's the point of them if they're not played? He's not here to do it."

Nick hefted the TV up and Amber took one end, helping him place it, then he reached around and started plugging in cables.

"It will only be free-to-air TV, I'm afraid," Roslyn said as Nick started tuning in the channels. "But I guess you'll find something to watch."

"Thanks."

Nick flicked through the channels leaving a current affairs program playing. "All sweet," he said and glanced around. "Anything else you need done?"

"No...I'm good."

She looked anything but good – she was bedraggled like a tired twelve-year-old. Roslyn wondered if something had happened since she'd stopped in at the house but she knew there'd be no point quizzing the girl, especially with Nick there. She simply nodded and guided him to the door. "Good night."

"The place looked clean enough," Nick said as they walked back to Roslyn's, the rattle of the trolley masking his voice.

"It did." The lounge had been neat and there'd been no sign of the plastic crates. From what Roslyn had been able to see of the kitchen it too had looked tidy. Amber wouldn't have been expecting her so it was a relief to see she was actually looking after the place.

"She looks so young."

"She is." Roslyn gave him a gentle poke. "You're not so old yourself."

"I feel it." They came to a stop by Nick's van. "I'm almost double her age and I've hardly got anything more to show for it."

"Enough of that maudlin talk. You've got a beautiful wife and children, a roof over your head—"

He snorted.

"And a good business."

"Not according to Dad's standards."

Roslyn gripped his arm. "I think perhaps your parents have given you the idea that things come easily, Nick. You might be struggling at the moment but you're way better off than that poor girl and don't you forget it."

He nodded. The dull yellow glow of the outside light highlighted the worry lines on his face. He did look older in that moment and so like Dennis. "How long will she stay?"

"I don't know." Worry returned to the pit of Roslyn's stomach. "I've done a bit of investigating myself. There doesn't seem to be anywhere she can go."

"Kayla's been sorting out the baby stuff we've stored. She was going to donate it to the Hub, where she volunteers. Maybe there're things Amber can use."

"That's kind of you." And it reminded Roslyn that he may look like Dennis but there was a temperate side to Nick that he got from Margot.

She startled as he gave her a quick hug. "Thanks, Roslyn. You don't know what a relief tonight's been."

"I'm glad I could help, but remember it's just between us."

"I'll have to tell Kayla."

"Of course. And thanks for your help with the TV."

"Anytime," he said as he climbed into the van.

"I'll see you Sunday."

He paused, one foot still on the ground. "I'm not sure."

"Why not?"

"Things are bit off with Dad and Mum at the moment."

"You know there have been times when I haven't wanted to attend our dinners either." And especially not host them but she kept that to herself. "But we're family and we stick together. Put the disagreement with your parents behind you. Besides, I've got the pool ready and it looks like the weather will be good. The boys can have a swim before we eat." Roslyn pointed a finger in the air as she thought of something else. "In fact, can you come a bit earlier? There're a couple of things I'd like to run past Kayla."

He gave a half-hearted shrug, waved and shut the door.

Roslyn watched as he drove off. She meant what she said about family and she was sad to be keeping her agreement with Nick quiet, but she knew it was for the best. Margot would only be upset but Dennis, well, Dennis would be Dennis, bombastic about Roslyn's involvement. Nothing good would come from them knowing, not for now anyway.

She pondered the family dynamic as she slowly made her way back inside where she made a cup of tea and switched on her own TV. As she made herself comfortable, Roslyn smiled. Perhaps it was the distraction of the company or the medication that the specialist had prescribed but at the moment she hardly felt a twinge from her dodgy hip.

twenty

The cups and a plate hit the cement floor with a loud shattering crash. Margot gasped and straightened the tray she was carrying before any more could slip off.

"What happened?" Kath appeared from the shop and, taking in the shattered crockery, she immediately grabbed a broom while Margot lowered the now half-loaded tray to the bench.

"I…there was too much on it," Margot blurted.

"We'll be buying more crockery at this rate," Kath said.

"It's only a couple of cups."

Kath paused to study her, a frown on her face. "I'm joking, Margot. We all break things from time to time."

Margot got the mop and went over the floor after Kath had finished sweeping.

"Are you okay, Margot?"

She stopped rubbing back and forth over the same patch. "Yes."

"You're not still bothered by the petition thing, are you? I really think we should—"

"No." Margot shook her head. Kath had popped in over the weekend and they'd cleared the air but the petition had been removed from the counter when Margot had come in to open up the previous Saturday. Here it was Friday again and she'd only discovered it buried under some food catalogues when she'd been tidying her desk earlier. "A few things on my mind, that's all."

"I hope searching for new workers is one of them."

Margot nodded. Kath had brought up needing extra staff several times before.

"I've got a few suggestions I want to run past you," Kath said. "There's been no time this week."

Lani poked her head in. "Can you do a couple of ham cheese toasties to go please, Margot? One with tomato." She glanced at Kath. "I've got a few customers lined up and some coffees to make."

"Coming."

Margot put away the mop and took some pre-prepared sandwiches from the fridge to toast. Truthfully, she'd not given much thought to any of Kath's suggestions. The business was running well and they were busy enough without adding more to their load. The Prov was already much bigger than either of them had planned when they'd begun. Kath also ran a part-time cleaning business and there'd been many days when Margot had done extra hours at the Prov to help her out. She'd resented the extra workload but recently Kath had cut back her cleaning hours so things were a bit more even again.

The proposed hotel had taken up all Margot's free time. She'd been on tenterhooks since her Monday meeting at the council office. Unfortunately the meeting had been cut short by a fire drill but she'd come away with a deal of information to process. And the council officer's parting words had given her some hope. There was a process to follow and council were still gathering information and, yes, she could certainly present her petition.

She'd put a post on the Jesserton Jabber asking those who were interested and able to attend a meeting next Tuesday. It'd been her phone buzzing that had distracted her with the tray of crockery earlier. She took it from her pocket now and glanced at the group page. There were several more members now and quite a few replies just in the last little while. Most were full of encouragement for her but also a lot of excuses for non-attendance. She read on.

Thelma: *I'LL BE THERE*

Sandy: *I've had a cancellation for tomoz am if anyone wants their nails done*

Margot frowned at the next response.

Kath: *It's good to gather info but we should make sure it's not biased one way. I suggest we meet with Xavier and ask him to answer any questions raised from the next meeting.*

Geraldine: *Good idea*

Sozz PO: *Yes very sensible*

Freds Hotel: *Don't let them think we're interested*

Sandy: *Who's Xavier?*

Kev: *Sounds like a plan*

Golds: *How can protecting Jesserton be biased? maybe it's you who needs to rethink Kath*

Thelma: *XAVIER IS THE HEAD HONCHO FOR THE DEVELOPER*

Greg: *No personal attacks here lets keep it nice*

Geraldine: *I'd love my nails done tomorrow Sandy*

The strong smell of toast snapped Margot's attention back to the kitchen. She dropped her phone on the bench and lifted the lid on the sandwich press. The toasties were deep golden brown and some of the cheese had oozed out. Margot tidied them up, slipped them into brown paper bags and took them out to the counter where there was still a short line of people waiting for coffee.

Lani looked at the two bags in Margot's hands. "Which one's got tomato?"

"Oh, damn, I forgot." She handed over one of the bags and went back to the kitchen. She didn't dare put the sandwich back in the press so she started again. By the time she took it out Lani was looking a little agitated.

"I told them it would be quick," she hissed as Margot handed over the bag.

"Sorry," Margot murmured. Sometimes she wondered who was the boss here, but while Lani could be brusque she was also reliable and efficient.

The afternoon continued in a series of near mishaps but somehow Margot got to the four pm closing without breaking anything else or mucking up any more orders. She was glad it was her weekend off. Since her trip to the council office she was too distracted for the shop. It hadn't just been the hotel development she'd been looking into. She took out her phone and read Esther's message again. She'd never responded to it but she'd re-read it several times in the last few days.

"Thanks for all your hard work, Lani," Kath said as she gathered her things.

"I'll see you tomorrow." Lani waved and hurried out the door.

Margot put away her phone and went back to unpacking the dishwasher, but instead of going out to close down the till, Kath hung in the kitchen.

"I'd like to talk before we finish up, Margot."

Warning tingles radiated in Margot's stomach. She'd been feeling them a lot lately.

She shut the door on the empty dishwasher and turned around. Kath had put a small bottle of lemonade and two glasses on the table they used for food prep. She drew up a stool and began to pour the lemonade.

"Coffee machine's off," she said. "Thought we'd have something cool. It's quite warm outside still but then it is almost mid-December so I guess it's to be expected."

Kath was flustered, which was so unlike her. She put a glass in front of Margot as she pulled up a stool opposite.

"I've heard from the installers. The blinds will be done early next week."

"Goodness, they have been quick."

"I didn't think we'd have much luck this close to Christmas. Even though they said they'd fit us in you can never be sure but they said they can come Monday or Tuesday. That's good for us. We're not open so we won't have to worry about customers being in the way."

Margot nodded and took a sip of her lemonade. The bubbles added to the turmoil in her stomach.

"I really think it will improve our street presence."

"I'm sure you're right." Margot smiled encouragingly. She was happy to go with it as long as it didn't mean more work for her, especially now.

"I'd like to advertise for two more casuals."

"Two!"

"And I think we should offer one of our long-term casuals permanent hours."

Margot nearly choked on her lemonade. "Why?"

"Lani's a great worker but if we had another full-timer, we could extend our hours and overlap for the busy times."

"Wait a minute. What do you mean 'extend our hours'?"

"There's nowhere close for people to get an early-morning coffee. I've been asking around – people would like to buy a coffee and maybe even a bite to go on their way to work. Instead of opening at nine and missing all that traffic, I think we should open at seven thirty."

This time Margot did splutter into her glass. "Which people?"

"Greg next door and his staff, some of our regular tradies, people travelling to the city for appointments or work. I've been talking to the bakery that supplies our bread. We can get our delivery early and sell some of their speciality loaves."

"This is getting out of hand, Kath. It was meant to be our little business, not the huge concern you're talking about."

"Opening a little earlier and selling bread is hardly a huge concern."

"But you want to take on extra staff." Margot shook her head. "I don't want to start earlier than I already do."

"A couple of casuals and one more permanent would mean more flexibility. You and I could stagger our hours too. That way there'd be four of us for the busy time and two for the mornings and afternoons."

Kath's face was alive with enthusiasm but Margot could also see the determination in her look.

"I'm worried we'd be taking on too much. We don't make a huge profit as it is."

"That's why I want to do more. I've been going over the figures and the projections look better than what we're doing now. There'd be some extra power and wages but what we sell should more than cover that. We'd need to talk to our accountant of course, get her opinion."

Margot shook her head. "This is all moving a bit fast – first the new blinds, now staff and extra hours."

Kath drew a deep breath and clasped her hands together on the table. "I know this is a hobby for you but—"

"Hardly a hobby," Margot said. "And I work just as hard as you do."

"I'm not saying you don't put in. Of course you do, but you've got Dennis's income. You don't rely solely on the Prov, whereas I do."

"You've got your cleaning business."

"Actually." Kath cleared her throat. "I've been thinking of giving it up altogether."

"But you always said you didn't want all your eggs in one basket when it came to your income."

"I did but life changes, doesn't it? I enjoy working here so much more and I'd prefer to put my energy into cleaning my own business rather than someone else's."

"That's certainly a surprise."

"I wanted to get it straight in my head before I put it to you. I know you don't want extra hours but if we could continue to alternate our weekends, I'd like to open Tuesday, maybe even Monday."

Margot shook her head, a small lump of dread forming in her chest. When would she fit in her volunteer work and time to help Dennis and her family, and still have time for some precious moments to herself, let alone a new direction that was starting to gain traction?

"When the new supermarket's open we're sure to get more custom. They're going to be open seven till seven."

"How do you know that?" There'd been tradies there for the last week or so and lots of rubbish carted away.

"There's a sign in the window. They reckon they'll open in January."

"In that case we wouldn't need to open early and sell bread."

"Specialty bread," Kath stressed. "And most of our sales would be coffee. The supermarket won't have local bread or a barista."

Once more Margot shook her head. "It's not what we agreed when we started, Kath. I can't manage extra days."

"I'd work them, with an employee or two but…" Kath flapped her hands. It was a skittish gesture, not like her at all. "I'm jumping ahead. Let's just see what the accountant thinks about extra staff and one more permanent."

She picked up their empty glasses and put them in the dishwasher and together they finished shutting up the shop. Kath chatted about a music gig her daughter had been to, the weather predicted for the weekend and the success of their latest vegan addition, the spinach, artichoke and zucchini bite recipe Margot had perfected. To Margot the conversation felt forced, as if they were dancing around the real topic, that their once-in-sync ideas about their business were on shaky ground.

The delicious smell of slow-cooked beef brisket met Margot as she let herself into her house. Thank goodness she'd had the forethought to put it on before she left for work. Preparing more than a salad for tonight's meal was the last thing she'd felt like doing but she really needed to talk to Dennis about her plans and he loved her Mexican-style beef. She gave a brief thought to a Friday-night wine with Roslyn but she still had to pickle the onions to go with the beef and make the dipping sauce.

Everything was well and truly ready when Dennis arrived home – luckily the dish was hard to spoil – but her spirits dropped when she saw his face. He was what her dad would have called well-oiled.

"How did you get home?" she asked as he brushed a boozy kiss across her cheek.

"One of the new mechanics lives this way. He dropped me off."

"I didn't know you had a new mechanic."

"We've got two." He lifted the lid on the meat to take a sniff.

"Two?"

"We've been understaffed since Bob retired. These two blokes are from India. Their English is good and they're Renault-trained, which is a bonus."

"I'd forgotten Bob had gone. I feel as if I'm out of touch with the car yard."

"We just had a few drinks after work for him, back in May. I told you about it at the time. You wanted to throw him a party but he didn't want a fuss, remember?"

Margot nodded. She did now that he'd said.

"Anyway, you manage the donation requests and keep up with the sponsorship stuff. That's an important part of our business."

"Hardly." Margot knew he got her to deal with the regular requests they received and to liaise with the clubs they sponsored because he didn't like doing it but knew it was important for their business to be seen to support the community. It wasn't the money he begrudged but the time, and Margot quite enjoyed it.

"And you provide the little cakes with the car badge for new vehicle purchases."

"I keep a stash in the freezer and ice them as needed. It's not a lot of effort."

He threw an arm around her shoulders and hugged her close. "It's a personal touch and customers like it."

She pulled away. "I suppose I'll have to design an Audi badge now."

"No rush. I don't want you worrying about the yard. I do that for both of us. Anyway, everything's fine now. A big improvement from when things were so tight last year, and the Audi dealership will add a real feather to our cap. I've already got a lot of interest."

"That's a positive."

"Sure is. I hope you haven't forgotten our work end-of-year drinks party the Friday before Christmas."

"Of course I haven't." Margot had been freezing food for weeks in readiness.

"Everyone loves your catering." He kissed her forehead. "And we can hopefully make it a celebration of the new dealership as well."

"I haven't been much help to you with that. I really have been distracted between the hotel and council and...there's...there's something I'd like to—"

"You've got plenty on your plate with your petition and the Providore and the kids, you don't have to worry about the car yard. I've got it humming." He plucked up the bottle of red she'd opened and poured himself a drink. "That meat smells damn good. Let's eat."

Margot waved him towards the dining room. "You go in – I'll bring the food."

"I thought we might eat in front of the telly tonight. There's a show I'd like to watch."

Margot's spirits dropped lower. She disliked eating on her lap, especially a messy meal like this one, but she nodded in agreement. The night was ruined anyway. There was no way she could talk things over with Dennis when he'd had several drinks already. He was a happy drunk but in no state for the serious conversation she'd planned.

twenty-one

Dinner at Roslyn's

Beetroot Hummus, Assorted Nuts, Potato Crisps

Rissoles, Crumbed Chicken, Green Salad, Pasta Salad, Roast Vegetable Salad, Garlic Bread

Fruit Salad & Ice Cream, Cheese Platter

Margot and Dennis walked through their yard towards Roslyn's. Margot had tried several times over the weekend to talk to him but something had always stopped her. He had to go in to work, he was watching TV, he'd gone off to golf. Surely her husband should be the one to discuss such an important decision with? But it was just that lately she didn't feel as if she'd have his support. That he might try to shut her down before she began. That's why she'd decided on a more public family announcement. Now her words were trapped inside her in a tight knot and she wasn't sure she'd get them out at all.

They were met with the sound of splashing and shrieks as they wound their way around Roslyn's fruit trees towards her house.

"The kids must be here already," Dennis said.

Margot glanced at her watch. It was only just five. She'd assumed she and Dennis would be the first to Roslyn's for dinner. She wanted to find out if Amber was going to be there. She hoped not. She needed a private talk with her family and she couldn't do it with a stranger there. And she wanted to suss out Roslyn's menu. She'd only brought a cheesecake but she had some other things prepared that she could always nip back for if necessary.

Roslyn, Nick and Kayla were sitting at the outdoor setting watching the boys in the pool. Roslyn caught sight of them crossing the drive and waved. Margot put down her basket and kissed each one on the cheek. She thought Nick and Kayla's responses a little cool whereas Roslyn was effusive – not like her at all. The knot in Margot's stomach tightened. She hadn't had a chance to talk to Dennis about Nick's van yet either.

"Sit down, sit down," Roslyn called. "Would you like a beer, Dennis, or straight to the red wine? You don't have to drive."

Dennis lifted one of the beers from the esky he'd carried over. "All good for now, but I'll take you up on the wine later."

"I think it will cool down by mealtime so I thought we'd move inside to eat." Roslyn was still exuberant. "I was hoping you two men might cook the meat for me. The barbecue's clean."

Dennis and Nick both acquiesced and Roslyn turned her attention to Margot. "Now, what have you made?"

Margot lifted her chin. "How do you know I made something?"

"Because you always do," Roslyn quipped and the other three laughed, a quick break in the wall of tension around them before it slammed up again.

"Raspberry cheesecake," Margot conceded. "I know you don't always make sweets so—"

"I've got fruit salad and ice cream," Roslyn said with no sign of annoyance. She glanced at Kayla. "No good for you though, I'm sorry."

"That's why I brought the cheesecake. It's vegan friendly." Margot smiled at Kayla but got barely a response.

"Does it need the fridge?" Roslyn asked. "I'll take it inside." She reached for the dish. "What are you drinking? Kayla has a riesling on the go and I've opened a chardonnay."

"Chardy, thanks." Margot moved closer to the crystal-blue water to watch her grandsons, who were having a wonderful time diving for toys in the bottom of the pool. Behind her Nick and Dennis were having a stilted conversation about golf.

Roslyn had just returned when Emily and family arrived with Geraldine. Margot's nerves frayed just a little more. She was relieved to have Emily and Cam here – she felt certain of their support – but she hadn't pictured Geraldine being a part of her reveal. She didn't usually come to family dinners when they were at Roslyn's.

"Emily kindly offered me a ride when I saw her during the week," Geraldine said. "My car's broken down again." She gripped Margot's arm in a tight squeeze. "I can't wait till I get your car."

"My car?" Margot gaped at Dennis, who flung his arm around Geraldine.

"Remember I said you'd have to wait just a little longer? Margot's new car isn't quite ready yet."

Margot felt as if her jaw was almost at her feet. She snapped it shut as Dennis winked at her.

"I hope one extra's okay, Roslyn?" Geraldine said as Dennis offered her a drink.

"The more the merrier."

Margot eyeballed her sister. She was still being very exuberant. So not like her.

Roslyn gave a quick clap of her hands. "I was speaking to Jerome earlier and he sends his love to you all."

Margot was distracted by a squeal from Isabella as she joined her cousins in the pool. The water looked inviting and the children were having so much fun. She watched them a moment, casting the odd look in the direction of the cottage. Only the roof was visible beyond the garden that ran along the back of the pool but she hadn't noticed a car there when they'd crossed the driveway. She hoped that meant Amber was at work or out somewhere, but she couldn't help moving a little further across the yard to get a better look.

"Amber's not coming, if that's what you're jittery about." Roslyn's voice came from behind her.

Margot brushed a hand across the low hedge of lavender that edged the lawn. "Just looking at your garden."

"Of course you are." Roslyn quirked an eyebrow. "Amber's at work but if she's still staying in the cottage at Christmas—"

"She'll be here that long!"

"She could be. It's only a week-and-a-half away. I thought I'd ask her to join our family for lunch."

Margot forgot about the knot in her stomach and pictured the sullen-faced girl Roslyn had taken in. "I don't mind being hospitable but that girl is most unpleasant."

"I don't think life's been easy for her."

"Please don't play the 'I've had a tough life so I can behave badly' card. She spilled food in my lap at the hotel and carried on as if it was my fault. She almost threw the remains at Dennis."

"Did she?"

Margot pursed her lips. Roslyn's tone was patronising, as if Margot couldn't be believed.

"She might not want to join us," Roslyn went on. "But I'd like to offer the invitation."

"Sounds like you're going to whether I agree or not."

Roslyn's face softened. "What's going on, Margot? You're jumpy and it's not like you to be uncharitable."

Margot drew in a deep breath. The knot was still there, tight in her stomach. "I may as well get this over and done with."

"What?"

Margot didn't answer her sister but headed back towards the rest of the family, who were chatting animatedly. She stopped at the end of the table and called for their attention as Roslyn joined her.

"Sorry to interrupt but I've an announcement to make."

"That sounds very official, Mum," Emily said. She lifted Henry from the edge of the pool, where she'd been dipping his feet in the water.

"It'll be about food," Dennis chuckled. "You've made more than you admitted, haven't you, Margot? I saw all sorts in the fridge before we left."

She gritted her teeth. Everything Dennis said lately annoyed her.

"You look so serious." Geraldine's eyes were wide with alarm. "You've got some nasty illness!"

"No, no." Margot waved a hand at Geraldine. "This is about me and council."

"You're not going to stand against me, are you?" Cam grimaced.

"Of course not." Margot managed a smile. "I think you'll make a great councillor." She took another deep breath as the knot threatened to twist her in half. "I am plan—"

"I know." Dennis put up a hand. "You're running for mayor." He laughed at his joke and there were several other chuckles and titters.

The knot in Margot's stomach unravelled and erupted in a fount of anger. She cleared her throat loudly. "You're right, Dennis, I am."

He laughed again but this time no-one else did. He sat up straight. "You can't be serious."

Margot swallowed, the barb of his words stabbing all the way down. "I am."

Everyone spoke at once then, asking why, when and how. "Give Mum a chance." Nick's voice was the loudest.

"I've been thinking about it for a while, actually." She'd decided to find out more and had got up the courage to ring Esther.

"But you're the least political person I know."

Dennis's astonishment undermined Margot. "It's not about politics," she stuttered.

The silence around her was only punctuated by the splashing and laughing in the pool.

"Quite right, Margot." Cam was the one to come to her defence. "The mayor's role is more about being an adviser and a figurehead – running the meetings, liaising with the CEO, performing ceremonial and civic duties and a whole lot of other stuff."

"You really want to do that, Mum?" Nick's question had a worried edge to it. "I know I suggested it the other day but I was only jok…" His voice trailed off as Margot pinned him with a glare.

"It's certainly something different," Geraldine said.

Roslyn looked down her nose at Margot. "It would be a challenging undertaking." Margot hated it when she put on the wiser-big-sister hat.

"You'd have to chair meetings, know the protocol," Dennis said.

"I have been on council before," Margot snapped.

"And she did lead the local Red Cross group very capably for years." Geraldine nodded sagely at him.

"And organised local businesses to donate leftover food to the Hills Community Hub's meals and cooking programs as well as running the odd cooking class."

Margot was relieved Kayla was on her side. She opened her mouth but Dennis cut her off.

"You hate the limelight, Margot. You avoid public speaking."

"I managed it at the town meeting."

"Asking a question isn't much of a big deal," Dennis scoffed. "Even Thelma asked a question."

The tight knot in Margot's stomach that had surged with anger sank back in a queasy slosh of unease. She looked at each of them, either worried or surprised expressions on their faces except for Dennis. He simply looked smug. The bravado she'd been building all week as she'd read through the requirements, explored the role, imagined what she could bring to it, deserted her now. "I thought at least my family would support me."

"Remember how relieved you were when your term was up last time?" Dennis said, more subdued now. "It's not that you're not capable, Margot, you're just not suited to it."

She stared at the bottom of her empty glass. Dennis was right. She couldn't even convince her own family of her potential – how could she convince the voters of the region? A wave of embarrassment swept her.

"Is there more wine?" She turned to her sister. "I'd like another glass."

Roslyn frowned. "That bottle's empty but there's plenty more inside."

Margot spun on her heel and strode off. Behind her, Dennis called her in a cajoling tone, other voices murmured. Roslyn spoke over them all. "I think it's time to get the meat on please, Dennis."

"Kids! Too much splashing," Nick called over squeals of excitement. "Keep the water in the pool."

Margot let herself into the house and shut the door on the lot of them.

Roslyn stared after her sister. They were close but there were still times Margot surprised her. It had never crossed Roslyn's mind that her little sister would be interested enough in the role of mayor to actually stand. Roslyn felt she should have handled it better. After all, she was the eldest.

"Oh dear. Margot's upset now," Geraldine said as she took a large handful of potato chips.

"Poor Mum." Emily pouted.

"She'll calm down," Dennis said. "You know how she hates confrontation." He waved a hand in the direction Margot had gone. "Case in point."

He'd been Margot's harshest critic and his placating tone annoyed Roslyn. She pinned him with a stern look. "We focused on the negatives rather than the positives."

"She did do a good job of rallying everyone over the hotel business." Bits of chip flew from Geraldine's mouth and she put a hand up to cover it. "Sorry."

Emily groaned. "We shouldn't have turned on her like that."

"Don't include me in your sweeping statement," Cam said. "I think she'd do a great job."

"We weren't very supportive, were we?" Nick pulled the ring top from his beer. "Should someone..." He cast a worried look towards the house.

"Let her cool down a minute then I'll go in," Dennis said.

"I'll go," Roslyn said. "If you get the barbecue started, I'll get the meat for you." She set off before Dennis could stop her.

Roslyn stepped inside to find Margot with her back to the door staring at the ducks on the wall in the sitting room, a full glass of wine in her hand.

"Are these new?" Margot said over her shoulder.

"Gunter gave them to me."

"I thought they were familiar."

"You found the wine."

"Yes, something I'm capable of, at least." Margot turned, her jaw jutting out just like it had when she was a child and didn't get her own way, which hadn't been often.

"It's not that I don't think you're capable, it's just not something I thought you'd..." Roslyn screwed up her nose. "Be interested in."

"Sometimes you can be wrong, you know."

Roslyn ignored the sarcasm. "If you're elected mayor, you won't be able to run off when people have different views to yours."

"I didn't run off. I walked away to get a glass of wine. I needed time to rethink. I had imagined my own family would be full of support instead of shooting me down in flames."

"We didn't all—"

"Too challenging for me, you said."

"I didn't—"

"Dennis I'll deal with later but you're my sister, Roslyn. I thought you'd be supportive in this."

"I am." Roslyn huffed. "You can't have a hissy fit over a disagreement. There'll be plenty of those with council."

"I know that."

"And if you think by being mayor you'll be able to have some influence on the hotel project, I think you'll be mistaken."

"Of course you would."

"You can't be prejudicial if you're mayor."

"That's you to a tee, isn't it, Roslyn. Assuming I'm not up to the job. Why don't you run for mayor? After all, you know everything, don't you."

Roslyn sighed and shook her head. "It's this kind of emotional outburst that won't do you any good. And you hate conflict."

Margot drew herself up, her wine threatening to slop over the rim of the overfilled glass. "I do but I've been working on that. I've sure been getting plenty of chances to practise." She glared at Roslyn. "And that doesn't mean I can't have a level head and engage in a sensible discussion."

"I never said you couldn't."

Margot snorted and took a slug from her glass.

Roslyn ignored her and lifted the trays of meat from the fridge. When she turned back, Margot was staring at her resolutely from the other end of the bench.

"Are you sure this is what you want to do?" Roslyn asked.

"I am."

"Then of course you have my support."

"Thank you." Margot picked up the trays of meat, juggling her glass of wine as she set off for the door. "You might want to check your garlic bread. Smells like it's burning to me."

Roslyn detected the strong scent of well-cooked bread as the back door shut with a thud. She flung open her oven and flapped at the cloud of smoke that swirled towards her.

"Damn and blast," she muttered as she pulled the tray from the oven.

twenty-two

Margot took another sip of the chardonnay Roslyn had produced from her cellar. The fruity flavour rolled smoothly over her tongue and left a toasty oak finish. She nestled back in the sagging director's chair and surveyed her family still gathered around the outdoor table.

When she'd returned after thumbing her nose at them for their lack of support they'd all been apologetic and offered in various ways to throw themselves behind her mayoral campaign. Dennis's apology had still held a hint of condescension but they could talk later. Margot hadn't wanted to interrupt the evening again since everyone had relaxed and moved on to chatting about other things.

The night had turned balmy and there'd been no need to go inside. When the meat was cooked they'd topped up their glasses and stayed put. After their swim, some food and a vigorous game of hide-and-seek in the garden, the three older children were sprawled on a rug on the lawn watching a movie on Roslyn's tablet. Henry had fallen asleep in his mother's arms and the adults were at various stages of relaxation.

"That was a delicious meal, thank you, Roslyn," Geraldine said.

"I must say I did enjoy those rissoles." Dennis smacked his lips. "You'll have to give Margot the recipe."

"You'll need to ask Kev if he'll part with it," Roslyn said. "I bought them from his butcher shop."

"The cheesecake was good, Mum," Emily said.

"So tasty," Kayla agreed, which was the most enthusiasm Margot had received from her all evening.

"I found the recipe online," Margot said. "I'll send you the link."

"I hate to break up the party but we should get these kids home to bed," Emily said and called Isabella, who wailed her annoyance at missing the end of the movie.

"It's great you're running for mayor, Mum."

Emily's words and hug warmed Margot, building her fragile confidence a little.

"Let's catch up one night and talk campaign strategies," Cam said as he brushed a kiss over her cheek.

Geraldine said her goodbyes. "I'm not sure I can make the meeting about the hotel this week. I'll let you know." She glanced at Dennis. "My car's not reliable."

"We'll be sorting that very soon," he said with a pat on her shoulder.

"Is the meeting something I should know about?" Roslyn asked.

"I wish you were on Facebook – you'd get all the messages then," Margot said.

"Or you could just tell me."

Margot sighed. "There's a meeting Tuesday night in the small dining room at the pub so that I can explain what I found out from my visit to council and to plan next steps."

"Busy time of year to be calling meetings," Roslyn said.

Margot hadn't thought of that. There was a lot on.

"I think we should head home too, Margot." Dennis picked up the esky. "I've got an early start tomorrow."

"All right." Margot glanced at Nick and Kayla, who hadn't moved. "I guess it is getting late."

"There's only fifteen minutes left on the movie," Nick said. "No school tomorrow."

"Of course." Margot tousled the damp hair on her grandsons' heads. "I'd forgotten the school holidays have started."

The boys gave her quick bleary-eyed smiles before locking their gazes back on the screen. Nick and Kayla both offered cheeks for her to kiss.

She squeezed Nick's shoulder. "Talk soon."

Dennis said a general goodnight and turned for home. "Come on, Margot."

"Thanks for a lovely night, Roslyn." Margot hugged her sister and set off after her husband. She was determined they'd be having a good talk tonight before anyone's head hit the pillow.

Roslyn sat back in her chair. "That wasn't so bad, was it?"

Kayla smiled but Nick shook his head with a frown.

"It's as if we never discussed them helping us out with finance for the business."

"They're not going to talk about it while everyone's here. Anyway, we've sorted that out between us. The paperwork's signed – I'll transfer the money on Monday."

Nick sighed. "Thanks, Roslyn."

"We really appreciate it." Kayla nodded. "It means I can go back to uni part time."

"I'm glad I was able to help." Roslyn batted a hand at them. She still felt guilty she was going behind Margot's back but what good was money if she couldn't help family? And the wider community, which was what she needed to investigate further. "Can you stay a little longer? I'd really like to finish the conversation we started before your parents arrived."

Nick looked to Kayla.

"The boys will be fine," she said. "They can sleep in tomorrow."

"Great." Roslyn leaned in. "I was hoping you could fill me in a bit more on the running of the Hills Community Hub."

"I only volunteer there."

"Which means you'll know far more than me about it. As I said, I've been investigating possible solutions for Amber. I'm not sure what will become of her once she can't work. She'll have a new baby to look after and she doesn't have a lot of basic cooking and home skills."

"She might like the young mums group. It's a morning tea and a chat session. It's run by volunteers. I'm one of them. We try to keep it informal but we discuss all sorts from caring for kids to basic healthy cooking and budgeting. There's also a community cafe. They run hospo training sessions from time to time: barista courses, table service, operating a till, that sort of thing."

"She's obviously got some skills if she's working for Fred," Nick said. "He runs a tight ship."

"I think she's a hard worker for sure," Roslyn agreed. "But I'm not sure how well she eats and parenting on her own won't be easy."

"We offer support with those things." Kayla took out her phone. "I'll send you a link to our website."

"Do you have many people come along?"

"Sometimes it feels like the need far outweighs our capacity."

"Who funds it?"

"Donations mostly. Some people are very generous. And we attract some government funding."

"Sounds like it's a bit precarious to maintain."

"It is. And the demand for our services grows each week, but we do our best."

"And who's actually in charge?"

"A committee from various churches oversees it and they get a grant to pay a social worker and a part-time office person. All the rest are volunteers." Kayla paused and studied Roslyn a moment. "Anyone can help out. There's just the usual paperwork, police checks et cetera, but nothing arduous."

"You should go, Roslyn," Nick said. "They need people with skills."

"What could I do?" Roslyn scoffed. "Put them to sleep?"

"Sometimes it's simply offering a cup of tea, a quiet space and the opportunity to chat." Kayla smiled.

Roslyn nodded. She'd never been hands-on with her philanthropy, always preferring to quietly offer money but trying to find help for Amber had made her wonder if there was something beyond money she could be doing.

"Amber would probably fit in quite well," Kayla said. "She might even be able to help with the hospitality training."

"She's fairly independent. I'm not sure she'd take kindly to me suggesting she go along."

"Why don't I call in when she's home?" Kayla said. "Those couple of bags of baby things I gave you are just the tip of the iceberg. I could tell her about the bigger items I've got – the pram, the bassinet, the high chair…there's so much gear." She groaned. "Anyway, we could chat and I might be able to let her know about what the Hub offers."

"Thanks, Kayla."

Nick kissed his wife and nodded towards their boys. "Time to go, I think."

Both of them were asleep, the music from the movie credits playing to thin air.

Margot had unpacked the esky, washed the few dishes, wiped down the sink and benches twice and was inspecting the fridge for any items that required throwing out when Dennis finally came inside. His phone had rung before they'd even made it to the back door.

Margot had rolled her eyes when he'd said, "Hello, Sam, what's up, mate?" She'd taken the esky and gone to the kitchen while Dennis had paced outside. Phone conversations with Sam could go on so she was glad to hear Dennis enter the kitchen behind her.

"What's happened this time?" she asked.

"Another date gone pear-shaped. Honestly, I don't know why he puts himself through it. Hardly any of his online matches have gone past the first date."

Margot winced. She'd known Sam nearly as long as she'd known her husband. Dennis had been best man at his wedding, they'd celebrated the births of his three sons and lots of birthdays, and had been by his side when his wife had died. Since the boys had left home he'd given himself a makeover – dyed his hair, updated his wardrobe, bought a sporty car – and started online dating. He got himself so worked up over the dates before he went that he drank a little too much to get up courage and then afterwards he'd drown his sorrows and ring Dennis or one of his other friends.

"He must get all the duds," Dennis said. "Even that sappy woman he brought to the golf wind-up didn't last."

"He thinks he's going to find someone like his wife."

"That's never going to happen. She was a gem."

"And he drinks too much."

"A bit of Dutch courage before he goes out. I don't blame him."

"I wish he didn't try so hard. Underneath he's a nice man who's lonely. Can't you tell him to just be himself?"

Dennis blinked and shook his head. "I can't tell him how to act with women. Hell, I'd hate to be in his situation." He pulled Margot into a hug and kissed her firmly on the lips. "Don't ever leave me."

Margot enjoyed the warmth of his arms, the faint lingering scent of his aftershave.

"We should go to bed," he murmured in her ear.

She would have gone in a heartbeat. For once she didn't feel tired and he hadn't drunk too much but she pulled back. "We need to talk about me running for mayor."

"Not now." He groaned.

"There's so rarely a chance."

He sighed. "I need to get into the office early tomorrow."

"See." Normally Margot would give in, let him go, but this was important and she needed her husband's support. "You've just spent twenty minutes on the phone with Sam, surely you can give me a few minutes of your time."

"Okay then, what about a nightcap?"

"No, Dennis, let's just have a water." He sighed, sat, leaned back in his chair and folded his arms. She put a glass of water in front of him and sat opposite. He ignored the glass.

The knot that had been binding her insides half the night tightened. She sipped some water, took a deep breath and looked up. "I really want to do this, Dennis."

"The hotel might be beyond your reach to control."

"Being mayor isn't just about developments that may or may not suit our area." Margot cleared her throat. "I've had a couple of talks with our mayor."

"Esther?"

"I have her support."

"Won't do you much good – she's gone," he scoffed.

"She's still got a lot of contacts. I spent some time with the deputy mayor last Monday. He was also aware of lots of things I've been involved in over the years. Sports clubs, Red Cross, the church community groups, the redevelopment of the park in Sheffield."

"You're a hard worker, Margot. No-one can doubt that."

"They both think I've got what it takes to be the spokesperson for council."

"Of course you have."

Margot studied him for signs that he was teasing.

Dennis slid his hands back and sat up straighter. "You'd be busy going to events, promoting the area." He drained the water and waved the empty glass as if it was a baton and he a conductor. "You'll be opening exhibitions, speaking at dinners, doing media interviews…"

Margot's mouth went dry. She took another sip of water. "If…" Her voice croaked, she sipped again. "If I'm mayor there'd have to be some changes, compromises, to our lifestyle."

Dennis leaped up. "We should get a cleaner. You've always wanted one."

"When the kids were at home. I probably don't need—"

"I can talk to our garden guy, get him to do more."

"He already does—"

"You'll have to cut back your hours at the Providore. You and Kath will need to think about taking on more staff."

Margot blinked. "Kath's been wanting to do that anyway."

"And it's just as well we're swapping your car, although I might need to rethink that." He paced. "You should drive the Audi. Can't have the mayor in an everyday car."

"It's not about which car I drive, Dennis."

He grabbed her and kissed her. "I know, I know, but it doesn't hurt to drive a top-of-the-range car when you're the mayor."

She pulled back a little and looked into his eyes. "So you're with me on this?"

"Of course."

"But all those things you said about me avoiding conflict and hating public speaking—"

"You'll get better at it. The previous mayor knew nothing about civic and ceremonial duties but she soon learned, and you're much smarter than her."

The knot in Margot's chest that had tightened before she'd sat Dennis down dissolved altogether. "Thank you."

"And you know I'll be right there with you whenever you need a plus one." He let her go and paced. "I should probably get a new suit. I haven't had one since Em's wedding."

"I've got to campaign and win the election first."

He stopped pacing and looked at her. "Is someone else standing?"

"A man called Colin North."

"Never heard of him."

"I gather he's lived in the region a long time. He's older, retired—"

Dennis grabbed her again. "I'll help with the campaign. I've had a bit of experience with Rotary and golf club elections. And I'm sure we can get lots of those people on board. You'll need a platform to stand on. Something that people will relate to."

"I'm doing this because I want to see transparent processes."

"I know what you mean but it sounds a little…dull. You need a slogan, something people can relate to – you're well known around here but not necessarily in the broader council area."

"Give Margot a Go!" She chuckled but Dennis ignored her, tapping his fingers to his forehead, contemplating.

"The last female mayor left us in the lurch. This Colin North might come across as older, wiser, more stable."

"That's hardly fair—"

"What about 'Give Margot a Chance' or…" Once more he tapped his cheek. "What's that ABBA song…the one about chance?"

"'Take a Chance on Me'?"

"That's it. 'Take a Chance on Margot'."

"Really?"

He nodded, reached for her and started dancing her round the kitchen singing the chorus of "Take a Chance on Me" over and over again. Margot had a sneaking suspicion his sudden exuberance was about her being an ad for the car yard but she tucked that away, simply happy to have his support.

twenty-three

Amber stepped around the end of the supermarket aisle and halted so suddenly the man behind her narrowly avoided hitting her with his trolley.

"Amber?" The woman in front of her beamed at her.

Amber pulled her face up into a forced smile. "Hi, Deb." Her lips dropped swiftly as a man joined Deb. Amber nodded at him. "Cory."

He gave a brief dip of his head, his sharp gaze sweeping over her.

"Fancy running into you. We're visiting rellies in the Hills," Deb said. "Are you living here now?" She looked around as if Amber's home might be right there in the supermarket.

"Just visiting," Amber lied. Deb and Cory had lived down the road from Tyson's place and Cory had done the odd shift at the pub. He and Tyson were mates.

Cory stared at her now, his eyes narrowed.

Amber's mouth went dry as she recalled Immi's warning that Tyson was looking for her. It wouldn't be about her or the baby, she could be sure of that.

"We're killing time waiting for Cory's cousin," Deb prattled on, oblivious. "Have you got time for a coffee?"

"I'm running late, Deb, sorry," Amber stammered. "I've got an appointment." She turned and made for the entrance, leaving her basket of goods and dashing out into the mall, weaving between other laden customers as Christmas music jingled merrily from the shopping centre speakers.

Her heart thumped hard in her chest. She pressed a hand against it, slowed her hurried steps and glanced over her shoulder. People sidestepped her but no-one paid her any special attention and there was no sign of Deb or Cory.

She blew out a steadying breath, ducked her head lower and strode out into the warm air of the undercover car park. She'd become so used to being invisible, to living somewhere no-one knew her, it had been a shock to come face to face with people she recognised. Mount Barker was huge, more like a city, and she'd almost believed herself invisible here after living in the much smaller town of Penola with Tyson.

Amber walked steadily to her car. She'd needed the things she'd left behind but she couldn't go back and risk seeing Deb and Cory again. There were plenty of other supermarkets she could go to but she turned her car for Jesserton and the seclusion of the little town where she felt safe. Maybe Deb and Cory would forget they'd seen her by the time they returned to Penola, not mention it to Tyson. Amber didn't want to have to move on. She needed to keep her job for as long as she could and while Roslyn let her stay in the cottage she had a roof over her head. There were a few shops in Sheffield. She'd have to go there for her supplies.

She gripped the steering wheel tighter and swore as the lights ahead turned red. She wanted to put as much distance between her and Mount Barker as she could. There was no way she'd come here again, just in case.

Margot was pleased to see Nick's van was in his driveway when she pulled up out the front. He sometimes stopped in at home for lunch if he was in the vicinity and hopefully she'd managed to catch him. She was eager to share the good news.

The previous night she'd taken advantage of Dennis's good humour after he'd finished dancing her around the floor and broached the subject of the new van. They'd come to an arrangement that would help their son out, something that wasn't exactly a handout but that he could manage.

She took a container of cake and another of biscuits from the back seat. She'd done some baking as soon as she'd returned home from her aqua aerobics. The cake wasn't vegan friendly but the biscuits were. Margot didn't want Kayla to feel excluded from the gift. She went down the side of the house, past the cracks in the wall that Nick had patched but not had time to paint.

The happy sounds of her grandsons playing in the backyard greeted her before she rounded the corner.

"Nanny!" they cried in unison and rushed to meet her with hugs. The youngest tried to tug the cake container from her hands.

"Have you eaten your lunch?" she asked.

"Yes," they chorused.

"They have."

Margot looked up to see her son standing in the doorway clutching a travel cup.

"Are you off?" Margot asked.

"About to be." Nick's face was stern. "Boys, leave Nan alone."

They stopped trying to see what she had in her containers. "There's cake and biscuits if it's okay with your parents," she said, suddenly feeling a bit awkward.

"Yay!"

Margot relinquished the containers and they raced inside with them.

She smiled at her son. "I was hoping to catch you before you went back to work."

"What about?"

"You and Kayla. The van. Your dad and I—"

"You don't need to worry, Mum. It's sorted."

"Hi, Margot." Kayla stuck her head out the door. "Thanks for the goodies." She looked from her husband to her mother-in-law. "Would you like a coffee?"

"I don't want to hold you up."

"Nick was just going back to work but the boys and I aren't going anywhere."

"Perhaps a quick one. I've got an appointment at the council office."

"You're definitely running for mayor?" Nick said.

"I am."

"Good on you, Mum. You'll be great." He brushed a kiss across her cheek. Margot basked in his encouragement. This husband–father person that she still thought of as her precious little boy. She was so proud of the man he'd become and she appreciated his support.

"Mum's come about the van," Nick said to Kayla. "But I told her we're sorted."

"I don't understand," Margot said. "You said you needed our help."

Nick glanced down and shifted from foot to foot.

"Oh, Nick," Margot said. "Please tell me you haven't organised another loan from the bank. Your dad and I can save you the extra costs."

"Of course not. We're in too much debt for that." There was a flash of despair in his eyes and Margot's heart ached for him.

"You haven't gone to one of those loan companies – they'll charge—"

"We haven't." Nick glanced back at Kayla, who was looking as if she'd been caught with her hand in the lolly jar.

"But you were so desperate the other day." Margot gasped. "You haven't done anything silly, have you? Dad and I can help. I told you he was just in a bit of an odd mood when you came round the other night."

"Yeah, he's like that a lot."

"Nick," Kayla murmured, putting a hand on his shoulder.

Margot stood a little taller. "I'm here because we want to help but—"

"I had a plan, Mum. I didn't expect to get the van for nothing."

"He can be a bit—"

"Bloody-minded!"

"Your dad loves you, Nick."

"He wouldn't even listen to my idea."

"I told you we'd had a chat and—"

"Too late. Roslyn listened and she didn't quibble."

"Roslyn!"

"Nick." Kayla's voice carried a hint of reproof.

"You took money from Roslyn?" Margot gaped at her son.

Nick sighed. "We didn't take her money. She liked our plan and with a few tweaks she's on board."

"I can't believe it. Why would you go to Roslyn?"

"Because she at least listened before making a decision."

The pain of rejection left Margot hollow inside. Roslyn always used money to get what she wanted. She'd kept her own husband and son at arm's length and now she was trying to win Margot's son over with her handouts.

"It's a business deal, Mum."

Margot snorted. "It's never that simple with my sister."

Nick's phone rang. He glanced at the screen, stepped away and answered.

Kayla gave an apologetic smile. "His phone rarely stops. There's plenty of work. It'll be helpful once the apprentice starts."

"Apprentice?"

Kayla winced this time. "Part of Nick's business plan was to take on an apprentice."

"Yes but..." Margot shook her head. "Roslyn's footing the bill."

"Not exact—"

"I have to go," Margot said. It was still half an hour before her appointment at the council office but she needed time to get her head around Nick's news and prepare herself for the meeting.

"Thanks for the food," Kayla called after her.

Margot didn't respond. She was too busy thinking about how smug Roslyn would be, helping out Margot's family. Margot paused at her car and took a deep breath. As mayor she'd have to deal with all kinds of clashes. This was good training in conflict resolution. She got into her car and gripped the wheel. Also in personnel management, which she'd practise on her husband. Dennis would not be pleased to learn of Roslyn's interference either.

twenty-four

Standing by her pool in a shaft of sunlight Roslyn lifted one leg and then the other, then slowly bent from side to side. She wasn't totally pain free but the medication was obviously making a difference and she'd attended her first aqua aerobics session. Mid-morning on a Tuesday was a much better time. The group had been all women around her age and no-one was bothered about being seen in their bathers. Roslyn wouldn't exactly say she'd enjoyed it but she'd go again next week. She hadn't had much faith in lifestyle changes to help with her condition but perhaps there could be something to be said for the exercise.

She stared into the crystal-blue water of her own pool and bent down to test the temperature. Richard had been the one to swim regularly and she'd join him sometimes but recently, without him urging her, she rarely bothered. Silly to maintain a pool that was only used by family and visitors. She should get back into the habit of swimming in it.

A car rolled slowly down the drive along the other side of her house. Roslyn hadn't seen Amber since the weekend and she still had the bags of baby items Kayla had left. She hurried towards the sound just as Amber's car appeared through a gap in the trees. Roslyn put up a hand.

The car stopped suddenly, the wheels grating in the gravel as Amber caught sight of her and lowered her window.

"What's wrong?"

"Nothing. I just—"

"You scared me."

"Sorry. You're not working today?"

"Keeping tabs on me?"

"No, I just—"

"I've had two days off. It was a huge weekend at the pub."

The purple was fading from Amber's hair but it was freshly washed and Roslyn realised there was actually colour in her cheeks.

"My nephew's wife was here on Sunday and left some baby things. She wondered if you might like them…or some of them…"

Amber's frown changed to a smile. "That was nice of her."

"Yes…well." Roslyn stopped. She was not a prevaricator and yet here she was stumbling over her words. "Would you like to come in, have a look, have a coffee?"

"Sure. I'll unload my shopping and come back."

Roslyn had put the coffees on the table by the time Amber knocked tentatively on the door and came in. She put a brown paper bag on the table.

Roslyn eyed the name on the bag. "You've been to Sheffield."

Amber shrugged. "Couldn't be bothered going all the way to Mount Barker and the bakery's good there. I got some muffins."

"Have a seat," Roslyn said. She waved at the three shopping bags hanging on the back of the chair. "Kayla said you're welcome to take the lot or just what you need."

"Thanks." Amber pulled back the edge of one bag and peered in. "I've got a few things but—" she shrugged. "How much stuff can one tiny person need?"

"I've no idea. My son's in his thirties and my only grandchild was born overseas but if my sister's grandchildren are anything to go by, a truckload." Amber's eyebrows raised. "Although I'm sure half of it isn't necessary."

Amber reached into a bag and lifted out a colourful blanket. Roslyn smiled. "My dad knitted those squares. He called it his hand and mind therapy. He hated sitting in front of the TV with nothing to do so he taught himself to knit. Got a friend to sew the squares together and put the backing on. He gave it to Nick and Kayla when their first son was born."

"If it's special shouldn't you keep it?"

"What am I going to do with it?" Roslyn glared at Amber. "And before you say a knee rug you can zip your lips."

The spark Roslyn had seen in Amber's eyes flashed brighter and she smiled.

"My grandson lives in Japan and Kayla said she offered it to my niece when she had her children but she declined. I suspect it's a bit rustic for Emily's taste but Kayla found it useful."

Amber put it to the side, then added milk to her coffee and took a sip. "That's good." She glanced around Roslyn's kitchen. "You've got a proper coffee machine."

"Another purchase of my husband's. I'm mostly a tea drinker but Richard was a coffee snob."

Amber glanced around again. "Have you been on your own for long?"

"Almost ten years."

Amber nodded and they sipped in silence for a while. Then she wiggled a finger towards the wall.

"Were the ducks his too?"

"Why would you think that?"

"You don't seem like a duck-on-the-wall kind of person."

Roslyn laughed and the conversation between them came more easily until Amber started to fidget.

"Sorry," she said. "I'd better go. I really need to pee."

"But you haven't finished your coffee. Use my bathroom." Roslyn waved to the door leading from the kitchen. She was pleased Amber had come in for coffee. She couldn't believe she was thinking it but she was actually enjoying the girl's company.

Margot could see Roslyn through the glass. She was sitting at her table staring into her coffee cup. Margot let herself in.

"Good morning." Roslyn stood abruptly. "Do come in."

"I could see you weren't busy." Margot huffed. "I just came over to let you know tonight's meeting's been postponed."

"Oh, right, okay then." Roslyn glanced towards the other end of the room.

Margot could tell from her response she'd forgotten all about the meeting.

"There's too much on at this time of year. I don't know what I was thinking, suggesting a meeting. I'm cooking every spare minute for the dealership Christmas party on Friday night. The Providore is busy as and we've got the school holiday gingerbread session and Christmas lunch..." Margot glanced at the table and reached her hand out to smooth the top of the baby blanket their dad had knitted, swallowing the sharp pang of loss seeing it evoked. "What's this doing here?"

"Kayla's been cleaning out her baby things." Roslyn glanced across her kitchen again, as if she was expecting Kayla to appear. "She thought Amber might find some of them useful."

"But she can't give this away." Margot hugged the rug to her and caught the sharp scent of mothballs. "Dad knitted it."

"And I'm sure he'd prefer it was used."

"But it should stay in the family."

"Emily didn't want it and Kayla and Nick aren't having more."

"How do you know?" Margot snapped. Was this something else they'd discussed with Roslyn and not with her?

"I'm only assuming because they said they wanted to clear out all their baby gear." Roslyn frowned at her. "What's going on, Margot?"

"I know we're sisters and we do lots for each other, but you really shouldn't have interfered, Roslyn. I don't know how Dennis will take the news."

Roslyn held up a hand. "Stop. What are we talking about now?"

Margot gritted her teeth. She hadn't meant to blurt it out like that but Roslyn's big-sister superior tone got up her nose. It also stirred the familiar creep of self-doubt. She put the rug down and began before she ran out of resolve.

"I called in on Nick and Kayla yesterday. I know you gave them money for their new van."

Roslyn frowned. "That's between them and me. I asked them to keep it to themselves."

"I've been working on Dennis and we'd come up with a solution, then when I called on Nick to tell him about it he said he didn't need our help. I didn't want him in more debt to the bank so I pushed him and—"

"Browbeat him till he told you, I assume."

"I did not—"

"There was no need to—" they barked at once.

"I know you've got money to burn but you don't need to use it to bribe my children," Margot snarled.

Roslyn reared back as if Margot had slapped her.

"It's our business," Margot said, pleased to see her normally unemotional sister react.

"Nick tried you first," Roslyn said. "But I gather you didn't hear him out."

"He sprung it on us."

"His plan was sound and he's family. I don't have money to burn but I am in a position to help. I was happy to be involved."

"Of course you were."

"What do you mean by that?"

"You failed your own family so you want to meddle with mine."

Roslyn's pale complexion faded further.

Margot knew she should stop but she'd worked herself up. Dennis had been out late at a meeting the previous night and she hadn't broached the subject of Roslyn helping Nick with him so it was still all bottled inside her.

"Work was always your priority. Jerome spent more time with me when he was growing up than with you."

"Not this old chestnut." Roslyn sighed.

"What do you mean?"

"Dad told me you worried I didn't spend enough time with Jerome."

Margot's mouth fell open. She'd never imagined her father discussing what she'd said to him with Roslyn even though the reverse had often happened.

"Jerome had two parents, grandparents and an aunty and uncle and cousins right next door. He's grown into a wonderful man and

I'm quite confident that's partly because he got plenty of love and nurturing."

"From others while you were off at work and never there for the important things."

They glared at each other and then Roslyn picked up the blanket and held it towards her.

"I don't know what's brought all this on but if the blanket is that important to you, keep it."

"Huh!" Margot ignored the rug her sister offered. "You're always so good at deflecting so you don't have to face reality. Jerome wanted a sibling, Richard wanted another child but not Doctor Roslyn Jesser. No time for family. Your head's always been too high for the rest of us. You were too busy to even realise your own husband was sick."

Roslyn blanched.

"And you hardly shed a tear for the poor man when he died." Margot knew she was in dangerous territory but she couldn't stop herself.

"We all deal with grief in different ways."

"And your way is to ignore it. To keep working as you've always done. Jerome needed you."

"And he had me, but he was twenty-two when his father died, not a child."

"Work was always your priority."

Roslyn dropped the rug back to the table. "That's enough, Margot," she hissed.

Margot's heart thudded loudly in her ears. There was a louder scuffling sound, then the door to Roslyn's bathroom opened. She gaped as Roslyn's tenant strode towards her, eyes ablaze.

"You're a piece of work, aren't you?" Amber snarled. "I always wanted a sister when I was a kid. Thought having a sister would be great. Glad I didn't." Amber turned to Roslyn. "Are you okay?"

"I'm fine," Roslyn said and Margot snorted.

"I'll go then." Amber took the bags that had been hooked on the back of one of the chairs. "Tell Kayla thanks for these. And thanks for the coffee."

It was only then that Margot noticed the two coffee cups on the table. She looked from the cups to Amber, who had her rock-hard face in place.

"You can keep your precious blanket," she snapped. "I wouldn't want my baby contaminated by it."

Margot gasped and she blinked back tears as the door shut with a bang behind Amber. Silence settled around them.

Roslyn was the one to break it. "There was no need for that, you know. Dad would have been happy for the blasted blanket to be used. You get far too sentimental."

"I'd rather have emotion than be as cold and hard as a rock."

A low hiss whistled over Roslyn's teeth. "I think you need to go home."

"Don't worry, I am." Margot plucked up the blanket. "And I will keep this. Kayla shouldn't have been giving it away." She slammed the door behind her and as soon as she was out of sight she barrelled off across the yard towards home full of righteous indignation, tainted just a little by the niggling feeling that she'd acted like the kid who'd taken their bat and left the cricket game.

twenty-five

Roslyn remained where she was, pondering how her great start to the day had gone so pear-shaped. Margot could be passionate, volatile, parochial, evasive, annoying, a whole gamut of things, but she was rarely unkind. It wasn't true that Roslyn was like stone, but she had never worn her heart on her sleeve as Margot did. She'd learned quickly to keep her emotions in check when she started her medical training in a predominantly male world.

She'd teared up once in the early days, when a senior doctor had badgered her over a diagnosis and then she'd doubted herself and he'd belittled her in front of the other interns, nurses and patients. He'd then gone on to rave about women not being suited to medicine unless they were nurses. Her diagnosis had been right – he'd just been a bully. She'd kept her emotions well hidden after that but she had learned empathy from an early age watching her mother suffer the effects of rheumatoid arthritis. While Roslyn may have shown a leathery exterior in her work, she never lost empathy for her patients. She earned the nickname Frosty from those who knew her well – cold as ice on the outside but soft like ice cream on the inside.

Richard had been the one to want a child and he'd offered to be the one to spend more time at home. Not that Roslyn hadn't wanted a child but it had taken her thirteen years to finally become an anaesthetist and then she'd had to keep working to build her credentials. She'd been in her mid-thirties by the time she had Jerome and she couldn't stay away from work for long. Not unusual these days but stay-at-home dads hadn't been as common back then.

Richard had thrown himself into parenthood and that had given her the scope to focus on her work. They'd been a good team. He'd have liked a second child but she kept putting it off. He'd been ten years older than her and by the time she turned forty and he fifty, she'd convinced him one child was enough. They had a wonderful holiday in the Greek Islands instead. She'd loved her husband and her son and she'd also loved her work. None of that was contradictory.

A sudden wave of pity swept her with such force she put her head to her hands. She'd been retired a few years now and while life had been busy when she first gave up the hectic world of medicine, it had almost ground to a halt these days. Now here she was, sixty-seven, alone, trying to manage a sometimes debilitating disease with no challenges to distract her.

There was a soft tap on the glass door. Roslyn's head shot up. Amber was peering in at her looking very worried. She opened the door and stuck her head in.

"Has she gone?"

Roslyn nodded.

Amber came inside. "Are you okay?"

"Of course."

"I know she's your sister, Roslyn, but that Margot is a piece of work."

It wasn't kind but Roslyn smiled. What a good feeling it was to have someone take her side, even if it was a nineteen-year-old who was, Roslyn glanced down, literally barefoot and pregnant.

"I see you've been swimming," Amber said.

Roslyn frowned. "Checking up on *me* now?"

"You've got towels and bathers on the line."

"I went to an aqua aerobics session this morning."

"Oh." Amber glanced behind her. "What about your pool?"

"Another of Richard's projects."

"Don't you use it?"

"Not much any more."

"But you had the pool man here."

"The family enjoy it."

"It's quite a warm day out," Amber said.

Roslyn paused and took in the towel over Amber's shoulder, the singlet top, shorts and bare feet, and realised she was being as thick as two planks. "Would you like to swim? You're welcome to."

"If you're sure it's okay."

"Of course."

"Why don't you come in too?"

"No, I've had my water exercise for today but I'll come out and sit while you swim." Roslyn followed Amber outside. In the aftermath of Margot's assault, which is what her sister's outburst had felt like, Roslyn had momentarily forgotten Gunter's legacy. She was surprised at herself, having thought of little else since she'd found out about it. She pulled back her shoulders. That's what self-pity did to you. Filled your mind with useless melancholic nonsense. Roslyn did have a job and a purpose, and she owed it to her good friend, Gunter, to follow it up and get it right.

Margot sat on the garden bench in the shade of the Japanese maple, clutching the blanket to her chest. She was still shaking from her run-in with Roslyn and that awful girl she'd taken in. She took some long slow deep breaths. It was a strategy she'd been working on to calm herself when she was anxious. Gradually her heart rate slowed and the tremble in her fingers eased.

She'd been stewing over Roslyn's interference since Nick had told her about the loan. She hadn't been able to let it go and now she was annoyed with herself for having it out with Roslyn. Her sister should never have got involved with Nick's problems – it was something Margot and Dennis needed to sort out, although Margot wasn't keen to discuss it with Dennis. He'd be cross at Nick when it was Roslyn who was the problem.

Her phone vibrated in her pocket and she took it out. There was a text from Cam. *Have you seen this?* and a link to an article, but before she looked at that she noticed there were notifications of a host of responses on the Jesserton Jabber. She opened the app and scrolled up to the first post for the day, which had been up at 7.30 that morning.

Kath: *We're trialling stocking fresh sourdough loaves in the Providore each morning this week.*

Margot blew out a breath. Kath was quick to act on things they'd barely discussed.

Sandy: *Keep a loaf for me Kath. BTW I've had a cancellation for a cut and colour this arvo. Ring me if you want the spot.*

There were then several replies about hair appointments and bread. Margot flicked over them until a post from the Threadgolds caught her eye.

Golds: *Did you read about our new supermarket?*
Larry: *Can't wait till it opens man. We need a supermarket.*

Geraldine: I hear its going to be gourmet.

Golds: We won't be able to afford to shop there.

Kev: I've been approached to supply meat

Geraldine: Can someone give me a ride to the meeting tonight

Thelma: WE WONT HAVE A BUTCHER ANY MORE

Tam: The pubs struggling to stay open

Tess: I heard the Prov is cutting back hours too

Sozz PO: OMG

Margot gasped. How on earth!

Golds: We can pick you up, Geraldine

Kev: My butcher shop IS NOT closing Thelma

Greg: I told you that, Thelma, and the meetings been cancelled for tonight. Margot posted a message yesterday.

Freds Hotel: The pubs going great guns at the moment but I'm short-staffed. If you know anyone looking for casual hospitality work send them my way.

Golds: Why is the meeting cancelled?

Thelma: HOW WILL OUR LITTLE TOWN SUPPORT TWO BUTCHERS

Kath: The Providore is going well too. Extending hours if we can get more staff. Contact me if you want some casual hours.

Freds Hotel: What Kath said

Kev: There won't be two butchers Thelma

Greg: Everyone's too busy for a meeting.

Thelma: BUT WE DONT KNOW WHATS GOING ON

Sandy: Calm the farm, Thelma – pop in for a hand massage

Larry: Does anyone know where I can buy laying hens

Margot sighed and scrolled back to Kath's post. They'd only talked about extending their hours on Friday and Kath had said she'd run it past the accountant. Surely she hadn't done that already. Although if Margot became mayor they'd certainly need an extra person from time to time in the Providore even without increasing their opening hours.

Margot's phone rang and, as if thinking about her had conjured her up, it was Kath.

"Have you got a few minutes to meet me at the Prov?" she asked.

Margot said she could. It was as good a time as any to have a discussion about the future. She hoped Kath wouldn't want too many more changes. They'd done so well with their business and it worked fine the way it was. Margot had already had one emotional confrontation today. She really didn't want to argue with her long-time friend as well as her sister. She took some deep calming breaths and set off.

A few minutes later she let herself in the back door of the Prov and made her way through the empty kitchen. It was cool inside with no cookers going and no action.

"I'm in the shop," Kath called.

Margot found her at the counter clearing the surface, a two-tiered basket stand at her feet.

"What are you doing?" Margot asked brightly.

"Just rearranging the countertop to make room for the bread basket."

"I did read on the Jesserton Jabber that we were starting that this week."

Kath flicked her a guilty look. "Sorry. It all happened quickly. I popped in to chat with them about the possibility of stocking their bread and they were keen. I was going to ring you then I got sidetracked. We did talk about it but…well, it might not be viable for long anyway."

"Why not?"

"Have you read the article about the supermarket?" Kath took out her phone.

"Cam sent me a link but I haven't looked at it yet."

"Here it is." Kath started reading. "'*Gourmet Supermarket for the Hills. Meyer and Brightman, the company behind the proposed Jesserton boutique hotel, have teamed up with one of South Australia's finest supermarket groups to create a mini-supermarket in Jesserton.*'"

"Meyer and Brightman will own everything before long," Margot said.

"There's more." Kath continued reading. "'*The group purchased the building in the main street of Jesserton, which was previously run as a supermarket, and it is currently being refurbished. The external facade has been kept but with a facelift, and the inside completely renovated with a modern interior. It will open early in the new year, a spokesperson for the group said.*'" She glanced towards the window.

"That part sounds okay," Margot ventured.

"It does but not the rest, listen." Kath read on. "'*Catering to residents and visitors, the store will offer local premium fresh produce, including meat, pre-prepared vegetables, salads and fruit. It is hoped some fish will also be provided and there will also be ready-made meals on offer, which the spokesperson said will be restaurant quality.*'" Kath waved her phone towards the shelves of gourmet products they stocked. "We already offer local produce and it sells well for us. It was different to anything Teakles used to stock and they didn't open Sundays. This supermarket's going to be open longer hours and seven days a week."

"Maybe we can adapt." Margot glanced at the shelves. They were stocked with all kinds of sauces, pickles, crackers and jams, and similarly the fridge was filled with dips and cheeses and cured meats. "A lot of these come from small businesses. They probably won't be able to supply enough to stock a supermarket."

"Not all of them, I suppose, but it's a bit of a downer." Kath lifted the bread display into the space she'd created. "If they don't open till after Christmas we've got time to suss it out, I guess."

"And just keep doing what we've been doing," Margot said brightly. "It's probably not the right time to try to expand."

"On the contrary, I think it's the best time. We should start straight after Christmas. We'll have a trade pattern established before the supermarket opens. And then if it is open seven days a week we will be too."

Margot pursed her lips.

"Don't make that face."

"I'm not making a face. I just can't see me doing more than I already am." Margot didn't think now the time to mention her run for mayor. "Speaking of doing more, you have remembered I'm finishing up straight after lunch on Friday? I've got the dealership Christmas party."

"Of course. All the extras you ordered will be with Friday morning's delivery and I'll make sure Lani and two of the casuals get away early so they'll be ready to help."

"Thanks." Margot glanced around the shop. It looked as fresh as it had when they'd started. Both of them had been determined never to let it look shabby and now there was the extra sparkle of Christmas decorations. "Everything looks great, doesn't it?" she said. "We've created a good business, Kath."

"But it could be better. The accountant thinks we could generate more income with some—"

"You've seen the accountant already?"

"Yesterday. She had an opening. I'd done my homework so I jumped at it."

"Without asking me?"

"We talked about putting our ideas to the accountant." Kath's shoulders drooped. "Honestly, Margot, I wanted to go on my own. I feel as if you've become a bit…" She winced. "A bit negative about the business."

"That's not true."

"Put it this way. You act more like an employee than an owner."

"What does that mean?"

"You're often running late and leave early."

"I've got a life outside this business."

Kath sighed. "And that's our big difference. You see the Providore as a hobby."

"You've said that before." It was hard not to be annoyed at the insinuation that the Prov wasn't just as important to her but she'd come determined not to get upset. "That's how we started, remember? It was fun."

"It still is fun, but for me it's also an exciting business with lots of potential. I'd like the opportunity to make it grow. Jesserton and surrounds have changed in the years since we opened. It's much busier, more things happen here seven days a week and our shop could be the hub of it. I'm definitely not going to continue with my cleaning business in the new year. I don't have kids relying on me financially any more. I want to put all my energy into the Prov."

Margot's legs felt heavy. Kath's decision made her dread sharing hers. She leaned against the counter. "Kath, I'm going in a bit of a different direction too."

"Running for mayor?"

"How did you…"

"Thelma," they both said at once and laughed. The tension between them eased.

"She's a worry," Kath said benevolently. "But at least she was right this time. And good on you, Margot. I think you'll do a fine job as mayor."

Margot straightened. Her friend's words lifted her spirits further. "Thanks, Kath. I've still got to win the election and if I do I'll have even less time for the Prov."

"All the more reason to organise more staff. I've had a bit of interest just from that Jesserton Jabber post. I've got two girls coming in before we open tomorrow."

"You really are moving on this."

"You snooze, you lose." Kath glanced towards the window. "You haven't even noticed the blinds."

"I'd forgotten they were going in." Margot rounded the counter and crossed the shop to the large front window.

"To be fair they're rolled up but they're great when they're down." Kath moved towards the front door. "Do you want to see?"

"Don't unlock now. I'll get to see them in the morning."

"Can you come in at nine tomorrow? That's when the first girl's coming for an interview."

"I'll do my best."

"They're both school age but they're on holidays and it might be handy to have a few extra casuals who can work weekends."

"As long as we can afford them."

"We can. The lead-up to Christmas has been extra busy this year and I'm sure it will continue into January." Kath nodded emphatically and turned back to gaze out the window. "The unknown will be that blasted supermarket when it opens."

"I like the sound of a gourmet supermarket in Jesserton."

"You would."

"What does that mean?"

"Only that they sound expensive and not everyone's got as deep pockets as you've got."

Margot ignored the dig. People always thought car dealerships were gold mines but they had no idea of the costs. Her friend should though, they'd discussed it often enough. She followed Kath back out to the kitchen. "It's a supermarket. They'll surely stock a range. And hopefully they'll employ a few locals and give people another drawcard to visit Jesserton." She raised her eyebrows at Kath. "Which should be better for the Prov."

"All good reasons for a boutique hotel."

"That's totally different."

"Why, because it's next door to your place?"

"I don't imagine you'd like a hotel going up next to your house either but that's not the only reason."

Kath batted a hand at her. "Get off your soapbox, Margot. Let's see how it all pans out."

Margot lifted her chin. "I'm not going to wait until there's a big ugly blight looming over the town taking business from us, from the pub and who knows where else. It would be a noise hazard and visible across a large area. It's not my only incentive for running for mayor but I'll certainly be opposing Meyer and Brightman's plans for a project so big."

"Perhaps you shouldn't use that little speech when you're campaigning then," Kath said.

Margot frowned.

"Not everyone who might vote for you is against the hotel."

The breath went from Margot's chest. "Including you?"

"Including me."

twenty-six

Roslyn left the Hills Community Hub, her head buzzing with concern and confusion and, if she was being honest, embarrassment. She'd been both overcome and appalled by her afternoon there. Here it was less than a week before Christmas, and all those volunteers were working flat out to try to make circumstances better for an overwhelming number of people. Kayla had warned her, which Roslyn had found strange but perhaps her niece understood her better than herself.

Roslyn and Richard had decided years ago that, as they were lucky enough to own their own home and have all their needs met, they should share some of their wealth. She'd left it to him to sort out how, although she'd made the odd extra donation when something came up like the new roof for the local church, or support for the outreach unit for pain management that travelled to remote areas.

Except for the outreach unit she'd also given service to, Roslyn had always been too busy to be physically involved but Richard had been hands-on. He and Gunter had helped get a men's group going and from that had come the men who'd spent time on

Gunter's property learning new skills and simply chewing the fat. That's what Richard had said they'd been doing when she'd asked him one day. She'd called in at Gunter's late one afternoon and he and Gunter had been settled on the verandah with three chaps from the Hub. They had the reliable coffee pot and the remains of some cake and slices she guessed may have come from Margot. The three men from the centre had clammed up when she'd arrived and Gunter had eventually offered to drive them back to the Hub.

The same discomfort she'd felt then had been with her today. After "hello", "welcome" or "can I make you a cup of tea?" she'd been speechless, so out of touch with the reality of the needs of the different people seeking help at the centre.

Kayla had kindly said it was like that for many volunteers when they start. "Not everyone's a trained counsellor or social worker," she'd said.

Roslyn crossed to her car, almost ashamed of the Mercedes EV and her pride in owning it. She climbed in and lowered the windows. The heat of the late afternoon pressed in on her. She felt awkward and gangly, like a newborn calf.

She twisted in her seat as someone called her name. Kayla was crossing the car park holding up a basket. Roslyn had taken it with her, full of fruit and vegetables from her garden.

"You left this behind," Kayla said as Roslyn opened her door. "I was going to drop it in but then I saw your car was still here." She peered a little closer as Roslyn took the empty basket. "Are you okay? I did warn you it might be a bit crazier than normal today. And added to that your first visit can feel a bit as if you've been ambushed."

"I'm fine," Roslyn lied. "But I am concerned for all those people doing it so tough."

Kayla reached in and put a hand on her shoulder. "Every little bit of kindness makes a difference. Speaking of which, Nick is collecting the new van tomorrow and our apprentice will start in the new year. We both really appreciate your support. It's taken a huge weight from Nick's shoulders."

"You're very welcome." Roslyn nodded. "Amber was thankful for the baby items you left. Have you managed to catch up with her yet?"

"No, but I must. I've got a stack more baby things. Whatever she doesn't take I'll bring in to the centre." Kayla smiled. "It really is very good of you to put her up, Roslyn. Young mums are the hardest to find permanent accommodation for. I just wish more people would be like you and open up their empty granny flats and holiday houses."

"It's not a long-term solution, I'm afraid."

"I know, but at least it buys her a bit more time. It truly is a helpful thing." Kayla's phone rang. She glanced at the screen. "One more job to do on the way home."

"I'll see you Christmas Day if not before."

Kayla laughed. "Not as early as we'll be up but, yes, we're all looking forward to it."

Roslyn started her car and sat a moment as the air began to cool the hot interior. She'd planned to go home and put her feet up but the chat with Kayla had set thoughts in motion that might be the beginnings of an idea for Gunter's legacy.

Ten minutes later she pulled up in front of the Threadgolds' house. It was in another pretty part of town with leafy tree canopies, variegated hedges and cottage gardens out the other side of Gunter's property. She was pleased to see Martin's car was in the driveway.

"Have you got a minute?" she asked when he opened the door to her knock.

"It's still hot out there. Come in," Martin said. "Anne won't be long. I'll make some tea."

Roslyn followed him along the passage of their old stone home. Every patch of wall had a cupboard or a painting or a shelf of knick-knacks, and photos filled every spare space. She shuddered at the thought of so much clutter. Martin waved her to a seat, and while he waited for the kettle to boil he stacked the books and papers that were spread over the kitchen table to make space.

"We've been doing a bit of holiday daydreaming," he said.

Roslyn noticed the booklet on top of the pile was a travel brochure.

"Anne and I were about to have a cuppa when we got a call from some guests." Martin put a plate of biscuits on the table. "She's gone to help them. They're having trouble getting their entry key to work." He shook his head. "Honestly, some people have no idea. I'll be glad when we're done with all that."

"Are you closing your holiday rentals?"

"We're hoping to sell them off. A buyer might still run them as rentals."

"Is it because of the proposed hotel?"

"Not because of it, but it made us revisit our business. To be honest, we have such a high occupancy rate that while a hotel might take a bit of our trade, most of the people we have stay in our houses are groups who are friends or family and want the flexibility and privacy of shared accommodation. A hotel can put them all up but if they want to relax together they'd have to use the communal lounge area of the hotel and evidently it's not going to have a dining space so they'd have to go out for meals.

We think the rentals will still offer a viable option even if the hotel goes ahead." He glanced warily in her direction. "In fact, Anne and I are starting to think the hotel might be a good thing for the area."

"You'll get no argument from me," Roslyn said. "You're not leaving Jesserton though, are you?"

"No, this is home. But we've decided to retire and the sale of the properties will fund that. I'll be seventy-five next birthday and we want to go visit the grandkids interstate a bit more. Maybe take an overseas holiday." He glanced around. "We'll spend some money on this place. We've got five rentals these days and they're a tie."

"Five!" Roslyn hadn't realised it was that many.

"We're putting the big place on the market in January."

"The one on the road to Sheffield?"

"Yes. It's the most work with five bedrooms and bathrooms. It was our first holiday rental and it's a long time since we spent any money on it. We've stopped taking bookings for it from the end of January. It's in urgent need of some paint and repairs."

"It's got good bones. Such a beautiful house." Roslyn's thoughts drifted to the home that stood on the main road to Sheffield. It was surrounded by a big yard and had a couple of sheds.

"So," Martin said as he set their cups of tea on the table. "It's good to see you but you're not usually one for social calls."

"I wanted to run some ideas past you about emergency accommodation."

"In our rentals?"

They were interrupted by Anne bustling through the back door. "Hello, Roslyn. What a nice surprise."

Martin poured her a cup of tea and explained Roslyn had come about using their rentals as emergency accommodation.

Anne looked startled.

"That's not quite what I meant," Roslyn said quickly. "But you've got a cottage at the back of your house here like I have."

"It's hardly what I'd call a cottage." Anne chuckled. "A one-room granny flat."

"It doesn't matter," Roslyn said. "I know a few other people in the area who have granny flats and I thought you may know of more. Or even houses that are hardly used."

Anne and Martin glanced at each other.

"I'd like to try to find a way to harness those empty rooms," Roslyn said.

"I see." Anne's tone had a disapproving edge to it.

"I've put a young woman up in my place. Just a short-term arrangement."

"I did hear about that." Martin scratched at his beard.

Roslyn nodded. Nothing in Jesserton ever stayed quiet for long.

"Didn't think you'd let the place again after last time. And you knew that chap."

"That was unfortunate circumstances," Roslyn said.

Martin snorted. "You can say that again. Anyway, it's even riskier taking people in off the street, isn't it? Especially young women who've got themselves knocked up."

Roslyn opened her mouth to defend Amber but Anne beat her to it.

"Martin! You know nothing about the girl and her getting 'knocked up', as you crudely put it, wasn't something she did on her own." Anne wagged a finger at him. "Shame on you."

Martin screwed up his lips and scratched harder.

"Amber's got a car and a job." Roslyn thought it best to focus on the positives. "But she's young and has no rental history or major bills in her name. And yes, she's expecting a baby. I'm reliably informed that all those things combined put her at the bottom of the almost non-existent rental market."

"How long will she stay with you?" Anne asked.

Roslyn sighed. "I really don't know. I offered on the spur of the moment. She wasn't well, it was hot and she was sleeping in her car. Her doctor asked me and…"

Anne tutted.

"And you want anyone with an empty flat to take in people and have them living in their backyards?" Martin said.

The buzz Roslyn had arrived with slowed to a fizzle. When he spelled it out like that it did seem a stretch. Her spark of an idea was being extinguished before she'd had a chance to explore it.

"I understand what you mean." Anne smiled sympathetically. "I do feel guilty sometimes that we have all these properties and people are homeless."

"Our properties are what earns us income," Martin huffed.

"We don't use the flat in our backyard any more. These days it's an overflow storage area."

"Anyway, we're talking about apples versus oranges here." Martin looked back at Roslyn. "Your cottage is on a separate title but places like ours out the back aren't. There's a law against renting them to anyone but family."

"There was," Roslyn acknowledged. "But the rules were changed a year or so ago."

"Oh?" Recall dawned on Martin's face. "You're right, I'd forgotten."

"It's those empty granny flats I'm thinking of," Roslyn said. "If there was some way we could coordinate—"

"We?" Martin shook his head. "I think you're biting off more than you can chew here, Roslyn."

Roslyn tapped her steepled fingers together. It was difficult trying to organise this by herself but she'd been sworn to secrecy. Kayla or someone else at the Hills Community Hub would no doubt be a help but she had to gather the facts, come up with a plan and present it to Gunter's sons and Elvin without letting anyone in Jesserton get wind of it. Elvin had been clear about that.

"Can you humour me, Martin? All I'm asking for is the name and address of anyone you know in the area who has a granny flat. I'm not going to suddenly collect up homeless people and knock on doors asking for them to be housed. It's something I'm working on for someone else and that's all I can tell you for the moment."

Anne nudged her husband then reached for a pad and pen from the pile of things Martin had stacked at the end of the table. "Not all of them are necessarily empty but I'm sure our collective brains trust can come up with a list."

Roslyn was pleased that Anne was right. By the time she left she had a page with several names and addresses all within a ten-kilometre radius and she was feeling a little better about her idea again.

twenty-seven

"Your food is delicious as always, Margot." Bob nodded at his laden plate. "Thank you."

"You're welcome. I'm glad you could come back for the party. How's retirement?"

"Busy," he said and glanced around the showroom space. "The new Audi colours look good."

"We've had the black and white of Renault for so long it's nice to add some colour." Margot smiled. "And they double as Christmas decorations." Red, white and black bunting crisscrossed overhead. She'd gone less on the black and more on the red-with-white-spots paper. In the corners she'd hung bunches of paper honeycomb balls. And then she'd organised for the large Christmas tree right in the centre of the showroom to be decorated with red, white and black baubles. Tiny lights blinked in between the balls to add the finishing festive touch.

"And you've made your trademark decorated cakes. The rep should be very impressed with it all."

"He seems to be." She'd met him earlier, a smartly styled man with smooth words and a too big smile, but as Dennis had said, he'd contributed to the drinks that people were enjoying and all they had to do was make sure he was happy.

Margot took a quick sip of her champagne. It was her third glass but she'd taken nothing more than a mouthful from each one before she'd put the glass down to do something or be introduced to someone and then the glass would be gone. Her casual staff were very efficient.

Bob's wife joined them and asked after family and then a couple of the other mechanics wandered over to chat to Bob and Margot excused herself to check on the food. She was paying Lani and two of their casuals to serve the food and drinks and they were doing an excellent job but she liked to keep an eye out, just in case there were issues.

"I'm glad I've caught you here." A woman with rosy cheeks and bright eyes stepped in front of Margot waving a glass of wine and slopping some over the brim of the glass. No doubt her alcohol consumption could account for her glowing complexion.

"Hello." Margot smiled brightly. The woman was vaguely familiar and as the guests were staff and locals connected with their business plus partners, Margot felt she should know who she was talking to.

"I'm not happy about all this hotel stuff." The last word hissed over her lips in a shushing sound.

The face suddenly registered. She was the partner of one of the chaps from the accounting firm Dennis used for the business. They lived in Jesserton and they were both members of Jesserton Jabber.

"It's certainly a worry, Tess." Margot was pleased the woman's name suddenly leaped to front of brain.

"The worry is you trying to stop it." Tess wobbled precariously on her high heels and once again the "s" in her words came out as a "shhh".

"Oh." Margot hadn't been expecting that.

"A boutique hotel would be marvellous for Jesserton."

"There's a lot to consider."

"What's to consider about more tourists, bigger turnovers for businesses, employment opportunities? We think it's very shortsighted of you to try to stop it. And we're not the only ones." The last *shh*ing came out with a small dribble of moisture over her lips.

"I guess we all have different thoughts on it," Margot said lamely. She knew there was absolutely no point in trying for a sensible conversation with someone who'd obviously over-imbibed but she couldn't help but wonder who besides Tess and her husband she was referring to. Most people who actually lived in Jesserton that Margot had spoken to didn't like the idea of a hotel. She tapped a nervous finger to her lips. That brought her friend Kath to mind. She wasn't on board. How many others could there be?

"We certainly do. There are some who won't even come into your shop if they know you're going to be there."

The sensation of a rock dropping to the bottom of Margot's stomach felt so real she pressed a hand to it.

"And now we hear you're running for mayor. I'd like to see a woman in the position again but you won't get our vote if you keep trying to block the hotel development. We've got a far more level-headed chap in mind."

"Well…I…Oh look, here's Lani." Margot beckoned madly as she caught sight of Lani leaving the kitchen with an armload of nibbles. "Have you tried the honey chicken sticks? They're very tasty."

"I suppose if they're yours they'll be good. That's one thing you do well, Margot. You should stick to your shop and not try to hold back progress in Jesserton." She was still hissing out her "s" and "sh" sounds but Tess's dark look was focused enough for Margot to feel as skewered as the honey chicken.

Lani arrived with serviettes at the ready and across the room Margot saw another familiar figure. Geraldine was offering around another platter of food.

"Excuse me, Tess." Margot smiled and edged away. "I just have to check on something."

Geraldine was heading towards the kitchen with an empty platter as Margot intercepted her. "What are you doing here?"

Geraldine stopped, a small frown crossed her brow. "Dennis invited me."

"I'm sorry. I didn't mean that how it sounded." Margot reached for the plate. "You're welcome, of course, but you don't need to be working. I've got some of the girls from the Prov to do that."

"I don't mind helping." Geraldine wrestled the empty platter back. "I never know what to say to people but you can have quite a conversation over a plate of food, can't you?"

Perhaps it was the fluoro lights but there was a pastiness to Geraldine's complexion.

"Are you feeling okay?" Margot asked.

"I had a bit of a tummy upset during the week but I'm fine again now." Geraldine leaned in closer to Margot. "Did you know the Threadgolds are selling up their holiday rentals?"

"No." Margot glanced around, checking the crowd, seeing if food or drink was needed.

"I thought Emily and Cameron might be interested."

Margot brought her gaze back to Geraldine. "The holiday rentals are hardly any bigger than where Em and Cam live now."

"Except for the one on the Sheffield road."

Margot had been turning away but she stopped, her eyes wide. "I'd forgotten about that place. It's almost a bit too big but I suppose some of the bedrooms could be multipurpose."

"And it's got that lovely yard and the one huge shed as well as some smaller ones. Perfect overflow storage space for their shop."

Margot's thoughts raced with the possibilities then she heard her name. A couple she'd met at church were waving to her. She acknowledged them with a smile and a nod.

Geraldine patted Margot's arm. "You should be with your guests. And don't worry about the catering."

"I'm not worr—"

"Lani and I have got it covered. She's a lovely young woman, isn't she?" Geraldine beamed. "I'm off to get a plate of those smoked salmon tarts next. I know they're not gluten free but it's such a small amount of pastry, isn't it." She bustled off to the kitchen, leaving a surprised Margot in her wake.

An arm slipped around her waist and as she turned Dennis's attempted kiss on her cheek became a peck on her nose. "It's going well, Margot." He lifted a glass of beer to his lips. "That's the first I've had all night. Been too busy to have anything yet."

His smile was wide and his eyes ablaze. She was pleased to note it was with excitement rather than too much alcohol.

"I didn't realise you were having so many extras beyond the staff," Margot said. "I hope there's enough food."

"Things moved fast with Audi in the end. The rep only confirmed he'd be here a few days ago and we decided it was a good opportunity for a soft opening. I didn't want you worrying any more over food. They're not here for that anyway." He gave her hand a squeeze. "And this is a good opportunity for you to schmooze a few people too, you know. Don't go back to the kitchen. Lani and the girls have it covered."

"And Geraldine."

Dennis nodded. "I did see her offering food. I asked her to give you some support but I didn't mean she had to work in the kitchen."

"I think she's quite happy." Margot glanced around. "I've just been bailed up by Tess Brown."

"She's had far too much of our champagne."

"Well, it's loosened her tongue. She took me to task over blocking the hotel development. Said she...they wouldn't be voting for me if I continued."

"You know not everyone's going to agree with you."

"Of course, but she said some people weren't coming into the Providore when I was there because of it."

"I told you you'd need to be tough skinned if you wanted to run for mayor."

"It's not the running for mayor that bothers me. I can't understand how anyone in Jesserton would want a hotel development looming over our town."

"Forget about it for tonight and concentrate on the run for mayor." He waved a hand towards a man in a plaid jacket with a bowtie at his neck. "Have you met our new magistrate? He'd be a good one to have on side."

Margot swallowed her concern over Tess's words and put on a smile as Dennis placed a hand at her back and urged her forward. There was a clattering sound from the kitchen. She glanced towards the door but Geraldine was there, beaming and waving her away.

"You sure are eating for two, as they say," Tom teased. "You used to always save some to take home."

Amber looked down at her empty bowl and screwed up her face. She'd been starving by the end of her shift. She and Tom had both agreed to do doubles. It was the Friday before Christmas and the pub was heaving. They'd both ended up on their break between shifts at the same time. Chef had given them a bowl each of the night's special and they'd taken it to the small courtyard at the back of the kitchen. Amber hadn't eaten anything since breakfast and she'd all but inhaled the chicken and veg risotto.

"You couldn't have helped make it," she threw back at him. "It tasted too good."

"I did help and you want to know what's in it?" His grin widened. "Anything we found in the fridge that was at its use-by date."

"You can't scare me," she retorted. "I'm used to eating food no-one else wants."

He laughed and reached for her bowl. "I could probably get you a bit more."

"Nah." She patted her belly. "I'm good."

"How's it going at the place you're renting?"

"Pretty cool actually. You should come over for a visit one day."

"I don't know. I got you kicked out of your last place."

"Roslyn's not like that old bag. She did say I could invite a friend over. Bring your bathers, there's a pool." Amber lurched forward and the upturned crate creaked beneath her. "You're on your own like me for Christmas. You could come over when we finish our shift. There's a spare bed."

Tom scratched at the patchy beard on his chin.

"It'd be fun. We could have Christmas together."

"I'll see how I go. Some of the guys from the hostel were talking about a party."

"No worries." Amber thought that's what she'd choose if she was in Tom's shoes. "You don't want to hang out with a knocked-up dummy like me."

"Don't put yourself down." Tom frowned at her. "You're a good person, Amber."

"What're you two doing slacking off out here?"

Even though they were entitled to the break, they both jumped at Fred's booming voice.

"At ease. Just came to check you're both okay." He held out two cans, a beer for Tom and a Coke for Amber then took another beer from his shirt pocket. "And I thought I'd take five myself." He tapped their cans. "Thanks for agreeing to a double shift."

Amber took a sip of the Coke then belched as the bubbles came up again faster than they'd gone down.

"You're both coming for Christmas lunch, aren't you?"

"Sure."

"Yes." They answered together.

"Good." Fred nodded. "And you're both okay? Working here?"

"It's tops," Tom said. "Wish I could stay longer but I'm heading to Western Australia in the new year."

Amber nodded. In her short working history Fred's pub was the best she'd had it. Fred worked them hard but he was fair.

"I'll be sorry to lose you, Tom. You know where we are if you're ever back this way," Fred said and took a long draught from his can. "I'm glad you're both happy here for now though. I've got a good team together."

"Hey, slacker, Chef wants you." The voice of the second chef bellowed from the door.

"Mostly." Fred blew out a breath then muttered into his can. "Beggars can't be choosers."

"Ivan's bark's worse than his bite," Tom said and gathered their empty plates. "Thanks for the beer."

The second chef was an a-hole. The few words they'd exchanged had been gruff and brief but Amber kept her thoughts to herself. Her back was aching and she lifted one butt cheek and then the other before settling again on the rough surface of the crate.

"You're sure you're okay to do a second shift tonight?" Fred asked. "I don't want to be accused of running my staff into the ground."

"Just good to be off my feet for a while. I'll be ready to get back to it soon."

"Right, that's my break over." Fred drained the last of his can and tossed it into a crate, the hollow clank harsh in the quiet outside the pub. "You make sure you're the first to leave tonight, young lady, once things quieten down."

"I'm good." Amber straightened so her shirt didn't cling so firmly around her belly. She didn't want any special favours.

Fred reached the door then turned back. "I forgot, there was a fella here the other day asking after you. Didn't tell me his name though."

The risotto in Amber's stomach set like a rock while her legs went wobbly, like jelly. She was glad she was sitting.

"When was that?" She tried to keep the worry from her voice.

"Tuesday." Fred frowned. "No, Wednesday. I reckon it was about four 'cause we had a lull and I sent the other two out for a break. You started later that day. You just missed him."

"What'd he look like?"

"Big bloke. Tall like me but not as wide around the girth." Fred chuckled and patted his rounded belly. "Dark hair, tats up both arms, bit of a scar here." Fred scratched a finger at the side of his mouth.

Amber struggled to keep the lump of risotto from rising up her throat.

"What'd he want?"

"I don't know but I didn't get a good vibe from him so I said I'd never heard of you." He fixed her with a sharp look. "Hope that was the right thing to do."

Amber shrugged noncommittally. "I don't know many people around here."

"I've never seen him before. He wasn't a local."

"Maybe I served him in the bar one night."

"You let me know if anyone hassles you. I won't have my staff being bothered by blow-ins."

"Thanks, Fred." Amber pulled a smile. It felt good to have someone look out for her.

Once he'd gone her fear returned. Tyson had said he'd look after her too and that had ended badly. She couldn't rely on anyone to take care of her but herself. The worry was the guy Fred had described had sounded like Tyson. He'd almost tracked her down.

She took out her phone and texted Immi, asking her if she knew where Tyson was. She didn't have to wait long for the reply. Immi was at the pub where he worked and she sent a photo. It was taken from a distance but it was definitely Tyson behind the bar. So he was four-and-a-half hours away in the south-east of South Australia, but from Fred's description she was sure he'd been in the bar of this pub only an hour before she'd started work the previous Wednesday.

She thought of Deb and Cory. They must have mentioned seeing her but that'd been kilometres away in Mount Barker. How had Tyson tracked her to the pub in Jesserton?

twenty-eight

Amber relaxed, arms and legs outstretched, head back with her ears just below the water, staring up at the cloudless blue sky through the clear roof of the pool shelter. The water was warm enough not to shock and the sensation of floating weightlessly the best thing for her body.

The lead-up to Christmas had been crazy at the pub. There'd been big groups in every night for dinners and parties as well as the usual crowds enjoying the good weather and celebrations of the Christmas season. Amber dropped into bed each night so tired she barely got her head to the pillow before she was asleep and then she woke each morning feeling as if she'd been run over by a truck. The bribe she used to get herself out of bed by mid-morning was a swim. Roslyn had said she could use the pool whenever she liked and she'd taken her up on it, swimming nearly every day since.

A movement beside the pool caught her eye. She moved her head slightly. Roslyn peered at her, a worried look on her face. Amber pushed her feet down and her head up and shook the water from her ears.

"I said hello but you didn't hear me," Roslyn said.

"It's peaceful...just floating."

Roslyn waved a hand towards the small table setting beside the pool. "I brought out some iced lemonade if you'd like some."

"Thanks."

"I could see you from the kitchen window. You'd been floating for a while."

Amber glanced towards the house. She hadn't thought about Roslyn being able to spy on her. She dried herself with her towel and noticed the wrinkled skin on her hands. She'd lost track of how long she'd been in the water. "Did you think I was dead?"

"Don't joke."

A small wriggle of something in her belly that wasn't the baby made Amber pause. It was a sensation she'd rarely felt, so it took her a moment to recognise the lift that came when someone actually cared if she lived or died. She chased the warmth of it away with a sip of the icy lemonade. Her stay here was short term. She couldn't allow herself to get too settled or to think Roslyn cared for her any more than she had when she'd been a stranger in the doctors' car park.

"Has Kayla called in?" Roslyn asked.

"Yeah, yesterday morning."

"I must have been out."

Amber shrugged. She'd liked Kayla but it was all a set-up. She'd talked about a place called the Hills Community Hub where she volunteered and the support they could offer. Amber was sure Roslyn was looking for a way to get rid of her and she'd sent Kayla with her suggestions for meeting other mums-to-be, relaxation sessions, cooking classes – all very well but none of it put a roof over her head.

"I wondered if you'd like to have Christmas with us."

The lemonade Amber had just sipped fizzed back up her nose. She lurched forward, spluttering.

Roslyn gave her some tentative pats on the back then withdrew. "It's not that terrible a suggestion, surely."

Amber cleared the burn from her throat with another quick sip of lemonade.

"No...sorry...thanks. Not what I expected."

"It's only three more sleeps, you know," Roslyn said with a sparkle in her eye. The previous week when Amber had had her first swim Roslyn had given her a small Christmas tree for the cottage. There had been a sparkle in Roslyn's eye then too. She said everyone needed a little Christmas in their life. The tree was fibre optic and when Amber had plugged it in she'd been mesmerised by its constantly changing colours.

"We have lunch at Margot's," Roslyn went on. "You already know Kayla and Nick. They have two boys and then Margot's daughter Emily and her—"

"Thanks, Roslyn, but I'll be at the pub."

"Oh, I hadn't thought you'd be working. I suppose they are open for Christmas these days."

"Tom, the English backpacker, doesn't have family here. I don't think the second chef has any. He never talks about them. A few of the other staff have family interstate. Chef offered to work 'cause they're doing meals so Fred's putting on an early 'pub family' lunch."

"That's good of Fred."

"He's a much better boss than my last one, that's for sure."

"It's going to be warm on Christmas Day so we'll probably spend the afternoon here by the pool and eat the lunch leftovers for a late dinner. You're welcome to join us when you get back."

"Thanks." Amber forced her lips up in a smile. "Don't think your sister will want me here though."

Roslyn huffed out a breath. "I honestly don't know what's got into Margot lately. She's one of the kindest people I know and usually as soft as butter."

"That's not how I'd describe her."

"By the time you get back from the pub she'll have mellowed. She'll be half asleep from the exhaustion of organising all the food and fanfare she does for Christmas lunch and too much wine. She probably won't even notice you're here."

This time Amber didn't have to force the smile. They both sat staring into the pool. Amber couldn't get Margot out of her head nor the things she'd said to Roslyn the day they'd argued over the baby blanket.

"I'm sorry you got caught up in our little spat the other day," Roslyn said. Obviously she was thinking about it too.

"I thought if I just stayed quiet in the bathroom there'd be a break or she'd leave but…she said some terrible things to you."

"All of which she regrets now, I'm sure. She'll apologise eventually." Roslyn shifted in her chair, stretched one leg out and settled again.

"You still having trouble with your hip?"

"It's not so bad now. I've seen a specialist." Roslyn stared down at her legs and the silence stretched out a moment longer. "Evidently I have rheumatoid arthritis."

Amber screwed up her nose. "Sounds nasty."

"It can be. The doctor seems to think it can be managed with the treatment regime she's given me."

"Must be weird being a doctor and having to go to the doctor."

"I have to admit doctors can be the worst at looking after their own health."

"Some aren't good with patients either. That guy in the car park the other week wasn't very…what's that word…em…empe…"

"Empathetic? I'm sure Dr Wu's a fine doctor. He wouldn't have had a lot of experience yet but he was worried about you. I've never practised as a GP. It's a very different role to specialising in anaesthetics."

"You knocked people out?"

Roslyn smiled. "I sure did. Most patients don't remember me because I did my job well, caring for them through their operation and managing their pain afterwards. That was something I got very involved in beyond my surgical work. Pain management is a very interesting field and…" Roslyn's smile turned into a frown. "I haven't practised for a few years now." She put down her glass and brushed the front of her shirt with her hands.

"Is that why you only had one child?"

Roslyn stared down at something in the direction of her feet, as if the answer to Amber's question would come from there.

"Sorry, I'm being nosy. Tyson…my ex used to say I asked too many questions."

"There were many reasons that we only had one child. My work life was much more demanding than my husband's. He worked at the university, a professor, and could do some of his work at home. He took some leave while Jerome was small. But Richard was also ten years older than me. By the time we thought of the possibility of a second child I was turning forty and back then the risks were more of a focus than the successes." Once more Roslyn stared down then she let out a short laugh. "Richard was turning fifty and wasn't so keen on going back to nappies and sleepless nights. Margot's children were right next door and only a little older than Jerome so almost like siblings." She paused to take a mouthful of lemonade and this time she gazed off across the yard. "Margot also stayed at home with her children so she would have Jerome over but Richard often had all three at our place too, so it wasn't as one-sided as she described."

"She gets upset easily, doesn't she?"

"Yes, but not usually so angry with it."

"So what did Richard die of?"

Roslyn studied the glass in her hand. The silence stretched out and Amber chewed her lip, wishing she hadn't asked.

"You are nosy, aren't you?" Roslyn put the glass on the table with a purposeful thud. "Richard had cancer. Diagnosed too late, my fault according to my sister, and he went downhill very quickly."

"Sorry." Amber wasn't sure if she was sorry because she'd asked the question or sorry for Roslyn's loss.

"This Tyson you mentioned…your ex?"

The warmth drained from Amber's body as if the sun had gone behind a cloud. "Did I?"

"You said he accused you of being nosy."

Amber stared at Roslyn and shrugged.

Roslyn shifted awkwardly in her seat. "I guess it's me who's being nosy now, but is he the father of your baby?"

"Why does it matter?"

"Well, I…I don't suppose it does…"

"Biologically, yes." Amber's hand went to her belly. "He didn't want it though. It was a mistake. I'd been taking the pill but…we'd had a few big nights out, I…well, I wasn't well for a few days, forgot to take it and…" She shrugged. "Tyson's not a fan of condoms."

"I see. So when you discovered you were pregnant you did consider all your options?"

"I was all lined up to have an abortion." Amber whispered the words as if it would somehow protect her baby from discovering she'd almost got rid of it. "I changed my mind."

"There's always adoption."

Amber pressed her hand tighter. "If I just had somewhere to live I could manage on my own. I've got a job, I'm putting money aside."

"But once the baby comes…you've got no family you can call on?"

Amber snorted. "My mum and brother are useless. They've probably forgotten I even exist."

"Someone else who could help you?"

"A few friends but they're either back in Penola or in worse situations than me."

Roslyn shook her head. "It can be a huge job raising a child."

Amber stiffened. "Yeah, well, you hand-balled it, didn't you?" she snapped. Margot had been right about one thing. Roslyn was pretty high and mighty. "I'll be looking after my baby."

Roslyn stood and picked up the glasses. "I'd best get going, things to do."

Amber stood too, aware she'd ruined something but not sure what.

"Yeah," she stammered. "I'd… I'd better get ready. Takes me a bit longer to walk to the pub."

Roslyn turned back, her serious mask in place. "Is there something wrong with your car?"

"No." Amber shook her head. "I decided walking was better for me."

"In this heat? And what about late at night, walking home in the dark?"

"I don't believe in the bogeyman any more." Which wasn't entirely true. The smallest chance that Tyson might find her lurked in the back of her mind. Since Fred had told her he'd been at the pub she'd been leaving her car out of sight at the cottage as much as she could.

Roslyn's eyebrows raised. "I was thinking more of the poor condition of the path, the lack of lighting and how tired you must be at the end of your shift."

"It's fine."

"Are you sure there's nothing wrong with your car? I could give you a lift if—"

"The car's good, really. I might take it today since it's getting so hot." There was a spot down from the pub she'd earmarked to park in back when she'd still been sleeping in her car. It was tucked away, not easily seen from the road.

"All right." Roslyn nodded brusquely. "Well…I…don't forget the invitation for Christmas Day if I don't see you before."

"Thanks," Amber mumbled but she was talking to Roslyn's back as she walked away.

Roslyn put the glasses in the sink. She couldn't help flicking a glance at the pool, but it was empty. A few wet sploshes on the pavers were the only sign anyone had been in it.

The conversation she'd had with Amber had been so easy in places and downright awkward in others but she'd done her best. It just confirmed her feelings of being out of her depth when dealing with the more personal details of people's lives, so different to her own. She didn't know what to talk about. In Amber's case Roslyn had tried to answer her questions honestly in the hope the girl might share more about herself. She'd been passionate about her baby, dismissed the idea of help from family or friends and that was it. Roslyn felt as if she knew little more about her than when she'd first taken up the offer of the cottage.

She drifted from the kitchen to the sitting room. There would be no video call from Japan today. They would do that on Christmas morning, opening gifts that had been sent and received several weeks earlier. Her only plans for the day were to continue to work on her ideas for Gunter's legacy.

She paused to look at the ducks flying across her wall. Gunter had hung them on his kitchen wall in a line from largest to smallest but Roslyn had opted for a triangular cluster. Their beaks were wide open and their wings askew as if they'd just lifted startled from the water. Something about them amused her. Gunter had rightly assumed they'd be a humorous memory of him. She was glad he'd thought to leave them for her, although she'd have preferred his lovely cuckoo clock but evidently his oldest son had been bequeathed that.

She stared at the open beak of the lead duck. "If only you could tell me what's best," she murmured then spun at a tap on the glass behind her.

Dennis had his head in the door. "Talking to the furniture, Roslyn." He grinned.

"They don't answer back," she retorted then noticed his smile slipped away as he stepped inside. She supposed he was here to have a go at her over helping Nick. She'd been expecting it ever since Margot had found out and blown her stack.

"Was that your tenant I just saw drive out?"

"I assume it was Amber. She'd be off to work."

"Fancy car for someone who's supposedly homeless."

Roslyn frowned. "An old station wagon?"

"Not just any station wagon. That's a Holden Commodore SS V." He said it with such reverence that Roslyn assumed that was something special.

"Looks in good condition too," he said. "Wonder how many k's it's done?"

"No idea but she seems to look after it well."

"So she should." He glanced back over his shoulder and flapped the front of his shirt against his chest. "Warm out there today," he said.

"It is." Roslyn waited, quite sure Dennis hadn't come over to discuss Amber's car or the weather.

"I've come to ask for your help."

"Oh? What with?"

"A surprise for Margot. I've got her a new car for Christmas."

Roslyn quirked an eyebrow. It was not what she'd expected him to say. "Does she know she's getting a new car for Christmas?"

"Yes and no. She knows she's getting a car but not when. I'd like her to have it Christmas morning."

"Do you want me to house it here? She might see it."

"Yes, I thought of that. I wondered if I could park it out of sight down the side of Gunter's house on Christmas Eve."

"I assume that would be all right."

"Aren't you overseeing his place?"

"I'm not doing much. It belongs to Meyer and Brightman now. I wander over every so often, have a look around in case of vandalism, check the garden and his watering system. Hillvale Winery are managing the vines."

"I guess I could ask Xavier."

"The project manager?"

"Yes. He's called in at the dealership a few times."

"Has he?"

"After a good deal on a car," Dennis added quickly. "I'll call him. That might be best but at least you'll know what's going on if you do go over and see it there."

Roslyn nodded.

"I'd better be off." He reached the door then turned back quickly.

Roslyn had been two steps behind him. She pulled up abruptly and felt the ache in her hip, which must have shown on her face.

"That hip still bothering you?"

"Not as bad. I've got some medication and exercises, which are all helping."

"Good." He nodded but she could tell from his look his mind was elsewhere. "The other thing I meant to say was thanks for your support for Nick."

Roslyn opened her mouth, closed it again, her surprise leaving her unsure how to respond.

"I spoke to him this morning and he filled me in. It was good of you to come up with a proper deal that holds him accountable."

Roslyn wanted to say Nick had been the one who'd come up with a decent business plan but Dennis went on.

"Margot's always been too soft on the kids. He needs to learn he can't just have handouts." Something Roslyn had always known but she hadn't realised Dennis thought the same.

"His business plan was good and I had the money to invest. He's still got to pay it back but at least he can avoid bank fees."

Dennis snorted. "I don't know that they'd have extended him any more credit. He probably would have had to go elsewhere at a much higher cost."

"I think a new van and an apprentice will build his business up and I get free call-outs." Roslyn smiled. "Win-win."

He nodded. "See you Wednesday."

He strode off leaving Roslyn a little bamboozled in his wake. His reaction to her funding Nick's business improvements had been the total opposite to Margot's. Such a surprise.

twenty-nine

"Here you are." Margot stepped outside as her husband walked up the back garden path. "I wondered where you'd got to."

"Checking if the garden needs water. It's been quite warm today."

"It's all on automatic timers." Margot looked over his shoulder. She was sure she'd heard the gate between their place and Roslyn's shut.

"I know. Stretching my legs. No golf today and you've been holed up in the study."

"I've been writing my campaign profile to go with my application. I want you to read it for me."

"Have you shown it to Roslyn? She's good with words."

Margot glanced in the direction of her sister's home again. "She'll probably make it sound too clinical."

She handed him the page and they both sat in the shade while Dennis read. The minutes ticked by and finally he looked up.

"This is good, Margot, but it might need a bit of tweaking."

She handed him her pen. "Tweak away."

"Don't use 'encourage'. That's too wishy-washy. 'Commit' is a stronger word. Say you'll commit to transparency et cetera."

He wrote on the page then tapped the pen to his lips.

"You haven't mentioned your experience. You should add you've done four years as a councillor and that experience, along with the skills and expertise you've gained running a business and your long history of community service, qualifies you to step into the role of mayor." He wrote on the page again then his lips twisted in a grimace. "I know I suggested the 'take a chance' idea but now I think it makes you sound risky. Maybe something like 'Let's work together'."

By the time he gave her back the page it was covered in blue lines and scribbles and Margot's earlier jubilance at the result of her hours of pondering and rewriting had dwindled away.

"Don't look so glum," Dennis said. "They're only suggestions that should help make it better. I saw your opposition's profile and it's a bit too rant-like for me."

"I haven't seen it yet."

"He talks about building big-ticket items as being his platform. He's a retired professor and thinks we should have a university here, of all things. He said the arts have been neglected and he also mentioned changing the negative attitude of council. That won't go down too well with most. There was nothing about what experience he'd bring to the role other than his being an academic and that he lives alone with three cats."

"We don't have pets." Margot looked at her page. "Should I have put more detail about our family?"

"It's not necessary. Voters want to know what your strengths are, what you can bring to the role and what you believe in. They don't need to know whether you've got pets or not."

She sank back and looked at the page. He hadn't changed everything – quite.

"Did I tell you we'll need your car tomorrow?"

She looked up from reading the changes he'd made. "No."

"You'll have to bring it in first thing."

"Why?"

"Time to get it ready for Geraldine."

"But I've got aqua aerobics at eight and what will I drive?"

"You can take the courtesy car until yours is ready." He pecked her on the cheek and stood. "After aqua will be fine."

"In my wet bathers," she wailed.

"Drive it in the back way to the workshop and give me a ring when you're there. It'll only take a minute to swap. And won't it be a lovely surprise for Geraldine. Her current car's had it."

"I suppose it would be a nice Christmas gift."

"Not exactly a gift but she's getting it for a good price." He winked. "Don't tell our son or he'll be complaining he's hard done by again."

Margot chewed the corner of her nail. She hadn't told Dennis about Roslyn's interference with Nick yet and right now she had enough on her plate. She didn't want to rock the boat.

Dennis glanced at his watch. "I think I'll go in and watch the golf, seeing I can't play." He waved a hand at her sheet of paper. "You should show that to Roslyn. She might have a few better suggestions."

Margot slumped back against the chair. Normally she'd have shown it to her sister first but since their harsh words, well, at least, her harsh words, they hadn't spoken. A wave of embarrassment swept Margot as she recalled her visit to Roslyn and then the shock of Amber appearing. It was bad enough what she had said to her sister but that girl hearing it all was mortifying. Then Amber had added her bit. It was hard to imagine a way to come back from that awful scene.

She looked down at the jumble of words on her page, took her pen and paper and went back to the computer. She needed the distraction but the zing had gone from her step after showing it to Dennis. She doubted her ability to campaign for mayor let alone take on the role if she won.

Determined to refocus, she retyped the profile with Dennis's suggestions and by the time she got to "Your future matters. Let's work together" her confidence had returned. She was doing this for all the right reasons. She did care deeply for her community and its future. Margot tidied the pens and restacked the books and pamphlets she'd been looking through, filed some paperwork that had been stacked for a while, and emptied her water glass and set it to the side ready to take back to the kitchen, but still she was reluctant to leave the office.

She picked up her phone and opened the Jesserton Jabber, scrolling through posts about tree lopping and furniture to give away, an ad for a local fence builder, a lost bird notice. No wonder updates about the hotel development got missed. It had been the reason the page had been created in the first place but seemed to have been overshadowed. She stopped as she noticed Roslyn's name. The post was from someone Margot didn't recall.

Ted345: *Does anyone here have Roslyn Jesser's contact details? I hear she's looking for a granny flat.*

Thelma: *WHY WOULD ROSLYN WANT A GRANNY FLAT SHES GOT A LOVELY HOME WITH ITS OWN GRANNY FLAT*

Greg: *Might be looking for a place for the young woman she has staying*

Golds: *She's making a list of granny flats for someone*

Sandy: *Who?*

Larry: *Big brothers watching*

Golds: *Don't know*

Freds Hotel: *Did anyone get a visit from the company man yesterday*

Thelma: *WHAT DO YOU MEAN BIG BROTHERS WATCHING*

Ted345: *Can someone let her know ive got one. Kevs got my details*

Sandy: *It's a joke, Thelma*

Greg: *Margot checks this page she can pass on the message*

Sozz PO: *Do you mean Xavier when you say company man? I saw him going into a few shops yesterday. What was he up to? @Kev?*

Larry: *Im not joking*

Kath: *Xavier didn't call in at the Prov. BTW we're open this Mon and Tue morning for coffee and bread. Call in between eight and ten.*

Margot sighed at that. She and Kath had had another discussion, more heated between them this time, about being open the two days before Christmas, which were days when they'd normally have been shut. They weren't going to trial Monday and Tuesday opening until the new year but Kath had wanted to keep going with the bread, which had been popular. Margot had refused to go in and Kath had said she'd do it with the casuals.

Margot continued on with her scrolling through the replies and Nick's name jumped out at her.

Nick: *I can pass on the message to Roslyn if mum misses it*

Sozz PO: *Did you see the shoes Xavier was wearing? They were worth a bit*

Thelma: *IVE GOT A GRANNY FLAT*

Nick: *Your granny flat's not safe to live in, Thelma*

Freds Hotel: *Anyone know what Xavier was up to*

Thelma: *ROSLYNS MAKING A LIST NICK AND IVE GOT A GRANNY FLAT*

There were no more additions to the post after Thelma's. No further mention of Xavier Zamon. Margot shook her head and dropped her phone back to the desk. It could give you a headache just trying to keep up with each tangent of conversation. She was curious about Roslyn though. Why on earth was she making a list of granny flats and who for?

Margot glanced at her watch. It was almost time for a wine. She took the page off the printer and went to the lounge where Dennis was sprawled across the couch, snoring softly, an open beer can on the table beside him, the TV playing to itself.

She drew herself up straight, knowing there was only one other person who could help her. She had to eat humble pie and apologise to her sister. It was a bit early but Roslyn was bound to have a bottle of wine on the go.

Roslyn put down the book she'd been reading. It was very quiet in her yard, not a breath of wind, and she thought she'd heard the gate. Still in her bathers with an old shirt of Richard's over the top, she adjusted the towel she'd draped over her bare legs. Footsteps sounded and then Margot appeared carrying a small platter.

"Have you been swimming?" she said with a little too much incredulity in her voice.

"I have."

"Good heavens, when was the last time you swam in your own pool?"

"About an hour ago."

Margot pursed her lips and put the platter on the table. "I brought some cheese and crackers. I thought you might be having a wine."

"Not yet."

Margot nibbled at the corner of her nail then tugged out the chair opposite Roslyn and sat. "What are you reading?"

"Getting a head start on the next one for book club."

"That's not till February. If I get time to read over Christmas it'll be something light and enjoyable."

Roslyn shrugged. February would come and her sister would be doing her usual lamenting she hadn't had time to read the book club book.

Margot pressed her hands to her legs, drew up her shoulders and took a deep breath. "I'm sorry for what I said the other day," she blurted. "I shouldn't have gone off at you like that."

"It's been a while. I can't remember what you said." Roslyn remembered very well but she didn't want to hang on to the hurt her only sister had caused.

"Well, I said those things about…" Margot faltered under Roslyn's piercing stare. "Oh. You're teasing me."

"Let's forget it. Water under the bridge, as Dad would have said."

Margot relaxed back in the chair. "Dear Dad. Sometimes I miss him as acutely as if he'd only just gone."

Roslyn remained silent. She'd had enough retrospection lately. It was too easy to be maudlin when you lived alone.

"I've written a profile…" Margot slid some pages out from under her platter. "For my mayoral campaign."

Roslyn nodded, glad to take their discussion in a different direction.

"I wondered if you'd read it…see what you think."

"Are you sure?"

"Yes."

"What if I suggest changes?"

"Dennis has already pulled it apart."

"I see." Roslyn stood. "I've got a rosé chilling. I'll bring it out and we can look the profile over together."

By the time she returned with the wine bottle in an ice bucket and two glasses, Margot had taken the wrap off her cheese platter, which also had olives, cornichons and some kind of paste, and she'd set out two sheets of paper on the table with a pen.

They tapped their glasses and took a sip of the rosé.

"Perfect for this weather," Roslyn said. "Now, what's happening here?" She waved at one of the pages, which was covered in writing and cross outs.

"That was my first attempt and the other one's with Dennis's suggestions taken in."

Roslyn gave only a cursory glance to the first then picked up the second and read it through twice before she lifted her gaze to Margot, who was watching her intently.

"It sounds good."

"Really?"

Roslyn took a breath, still not convinced Margot was ready for constructive criticism. "I do have one suggestion."

"One is good. Dennis had lots."

"I don't think you should mention the hotel."

"But that's why I'm standing for mayor, to try to stop it."

"What will you do with the rest of your time once the hotel goes ahead—" Roslyn held up her hand as Margot opened her mouth. "Or is stopped. Either way it's only one thing in all that council has on its plate. I think you should keep it more generic. You could say the future belongs to our children and we should be mindful with our planning, decision-making and actions so that any change doesn't jeopardise that future."

Margot looked defeated for a moment then the resolve returned to her face. She picked up the pen. "Tell me again what you said."

Roslyn repeated her suggestion, looking over Margot's shoulder as she wrote.

"Then you could cross out that bit about rigorous application." Roslyn tapped the page. "And I think you should insert 'I believe' here near the end where you're talking about your experience."

Margot crossed out and scribbled in the gaps.

"Now read it back to me."

"'I am running for mayor because my heart and soul are—'"

"Doesn't sound like it."

Margot cleared her throat. She felt like she was back in school. She always got nervous when asked to read out loud. "'*My heart and soul are in this community. I am a lifetime Hills resident and I believe I have a strong—*'"

"That 'I believe' isn't needed."

"Oh, for goodness sake."

"You asked for my opinion. You don't have to say you believe there. Save it for that final summary. Where I suggested you put it."

Margot pursed her lips, crossed it out and continued. "'*I am a lifetime Hills resident and I have a strong appreciation and understanding of our region.*'"

"Much better." Roslyn nodded.

Margot drew in a breath and went on. "'*It is both a unique and remarkable environment that we must protect for everyone. The future belongs to our children and we should be mindful with our planning, decision-making and actions that any change doesn't jeopardise that future. There should be a much more rigorous application process for any development that could impact our region.*'"

"Cut the last sentence, it's a repeat of the previous one, just different words."

Margot applied her pen again and read on. "'*It is important to me to ensure councillors and ratepayers are kept well informed and I will commit to transparency and responsible economic management. I have previously held the position of councillor for a term and I believe...*'" She glanced up. Roslyn nodded again so she continued. "'*I believe that experience, along with the skills and expertise I've gained while running a business, as well as my long history of community service, qualifies me to step into the role of mayor. Your future matters. Let's work together.*'"

"Impressive." Roslyn clapped her hands. "I'd vote for you. I just wonder if it should be 'our' future matters rather than 'your'. Our sounds a bit more like we're all in this together."

Margot tossed down her pen and picked up her glass. "I'm over it."

Roslyn snorted. "This is just the beginning."

"I know, and some days I'm chomping at the bit ready to tackle it and others I question my sanity."

"No doubt most in leadership do that."

They both sipped their rosé. Roslyn felt the most relaxed she had in a long while. The swim had been refreshing, then sitting in the warm air under the shade and reading, now sharing a glass of wine with her sister, and she felt pain free. She closed her eyes, revelling in the moment.

"Thanks, Roslyn."

She flicked her eyes open again. "I didn't do much."

"For believing in me."

Roslyn reached for a cracker to avoid her sister's gaze. She did believe in her, but unfortunately her belief was that Margot didn't have the stamina it would take to be mayor. "What have you brought here?"

"You should try the quince paste. It's a new brand we've been stocking in the Prov and it's been very popular."

Roslyn added some cheese to her cracker with a smear of the paste.

"Kath's worried the new supermarket's going to cut into our business."

"Why?"

"Sounds like it's going to be more upmarket and gourmet than Teakles' was."

"And you're not bothered?"

Margot sighed. "Kath's trying to build an empire. I liked The General Providore the way it was when we started."

"It's a wonderful asset to Jesserton, you know. Hopefully you can coexist with the supermarket."

"There's been a lot of chat about it on the Jesserton Jabber." Margot paused, a slice of cheese part way to her mouth. "Which reminds me, there was mention of you making a list of granny flats. What's that about?"

Roslyn clenched her teeth. She had known once she started contacting people about their properties it would be difficult to keep it quiet. "What on earth's the Jesserton Jabber?"

"A Facebook group Fred set up when we started planning meetings about the hotel. I told you about it. Anyway, what's this about a list of granny flats?" Margot wasn't to be deflected.

"Just a project I'm working on for someone."

"Who?"

Roslyn was used to keeping things close to her chest but the burden of working on Gunter's legacy alone was wearying. "I called in at the Hills Community Hub the other day and there's a need for housing. I said I'd investigate."

"Really?"

"You don't think I'm capable?"

Margot studied her a moment, the surprise on her face changing to acceptance. "Of course you're capable – it's just that you've never been hands-on with charity work. That was more Richard's thing."

"Richard was certainly the visible side of our philanthropy." Roslyn knew she should bite her tongue as she always had but sometimes she tired of her husband being seen as the saint. She'd worked hard for the money they donated as much as he had, but he enjoyed being practical, like he'd been with the men who worked in Gunter's vineyard.

"He was such a good man." Margot's face crumpled. "I miss him. Of course it would be far worse for you," she added quickly.

"Of course I miss him but that doesn't change that he's gone." Roslyn topped up their glasses, wanting to steer the conversation away from Richard before she got blamed again for letting him die. "Why were the granny flats being discussed?"

"A chap wanted to let you know he had one?"

"Who?"

Margot frowned. "Ted someone. He said Kev had his details."

"I think that's the man who does deliveries for Kev and a few others. Drives that blue van."

"Oh yes, he lives down that lane off the main street. What would be the plan for these granny flats?"

"I think it's just an idea at the moment. They didn't say exactly. I offered to ask around our area."

"It's good of you, Roslyn." Margot brushed her fingers along the edge of the table. "How's your lodger going?"

"Amber's well. She works too hard but she seems to thrive on it."

"But how much longer will you house her? She can't stay forever."

"She has tried to find something else. I gather it's not easy."

"I suppose not." Margot's response lacked belief.

"Amber's one of the reasons I went to the Hub. Kayla told me about the programs they run there and I wanted to know more about assistance for housing. Young women on their own are often at the bottom of the list. They've usually lived at home or with a fella and they've no bill or rental history."

"Surely they're not thinking of putting young women up in people's granny flats?"

"No. At least, I'm not really sure. I'm just helping with the info gathering." She kept her responses vague but it would be so much easier if she could explain Gunter's legacy and get Margot on side to help.

"Well, as I said, it's good of you to help out, but the practicalities of charity work aren't really your thing, are they?"

Roslyn pursed her lips as if she'd just had lemon juice smeared on them, glad she hadn't weakened and taken her sister into her confidence. She would wait and see where tomorrow's meeting took her.

thirty

On the busy Monday before Christmas Roslyn had picked a cafe in Stirling, several towns away from Jesserton, for her meeting with Elvin, the lawyer managing Gunter's estate, and Xavier, representing Meyer and Brightman. The timing wasn't the best, given it was only two days till Christmas, so she'd been pleased when they'd agreed to meet with her. She had the bare bones of a plan for Gunter's legacy and if Meyer and Brightman came to the party they'd be involved. She'd thought she might have to wait until the new year to present her proposal. And Roslyn didn't like waiting.

Outside the mid-morning sun was doing its best to penetrate the leafy shade protecting the street, while inside in the cool air of the cafe Roslyn and the two men occupied a booth at the back, giving some privacy. She gave them each a copy of her plan as soon as the coffees arrived and then ran through it. The two men listened, asked some questions, and then the conversation went back and forth for some time. In the end neither seemed daunted by her proposal, although Xavier had made it clear it wasn't his decision to make and Elvin had cautioned the money wouldn't stretch without fundraising or some kind of outside funding but he could follow up on some things for her.

"It's a big plan," he said as they stood and shook hands. He locked his serious gaze on hers. "Ambitious."

"I know," Roslyn said firmly. There was a lot of work ahead and some of it depended on Meyer and Brightman coming to the party. She turned to Xavier.

"Quite a wide scope." He shook her hand. "But I'm happy to look into it further."

Roslyn had thought him simply a yes-man for the company when she'd first met him but underneath the suave charm was an astute businessman who knew what was what. He reminded her a little of Dennis in that respect.

"There's a lot to organise and I'm not sure it will all be possible," Elvin said. "But I think Gunter would have liked it."

Roslyn nodded. Elvin had known Gunter well. She was happy with that. There was a lot more to map out but she had the two big players on board. Xavier and Elvin had a little tussle over who'd pay the coffee bill and then they made their way out of the cafe.

"Are you happy for me to run the idea past his sons?" Elvin asked. "Make sure they're happy with the direction we're going in before we proceed."

"Of course."

The temperature outside was pleasantly warm and Roslyn was digging in her bag for her sunglasses so she didn't notice the woman approaching until she almost collided with them.

"Watch out, Elvin," Xavier called.

"Careful." Elvin gripped the woman's arm to avoid her running straight into him.

"Oh, I'm sorry." The woman blustered and Roslyn's sunny mood evaporated as she recognised Geraldine – well, her voice at least. Roslyn had to look twice. Perhaps it was the beige dress but her complexion was pale and her cheeks hollow, not at all like the formerly rosy-cheeked Geraldine. And her usually neatly styled hair was damp and plastered to her face.

"I was in such a hurry and not watching…" Geraldine flapped her hands. "Sorry, sorry." She glanced sideways then gasped as she recognised Roslyn. "Oh…Roslyn…fancy meeting you here." Her eyes widened with curiosity and she looked back at the men.

"We're both a fair way from home," Roslyn said, cursing that of all people it would be Geraldine they'd run into. She was just thinking she'd take Geraldine aside when the other woman stepped away.

"Oooh," she groaned. "I have to go." With a pained look she set off along the footpath almost at a gallop. Roslyn had never seen her move so fast.

The men said their farewells and more Christmas wishes were exchanged. Roslyn waved them off then went in the opposite direction along the street. As soon as she got home she'd ring Martin Threadgold and ask if he'd not rush into putting his big old house on the market for a little while. But before she left Stirling she wanted to visit the bookshop for a last-minute Christmas gift she'd been thinking about. She set off across the road, distracted by the chance encounter she'd just had. It was unfortunate to have run into Geraldine. She hoped the woman's haste and bluster might mean she'd forget about seeing them but knowing Geraldine it was doubtful.

Margot kept glancing at the footpath as she edged her car along the busy main street of Stirling. There were people everywhere but no sign of Geraldine. She'd already been along the street once and going slow had earned her a toot from a car behind. She'd startled and tried to pull into a park, flicked the windscreen wipers instead of the indicator, realised it was a no-standing zone and then driven on, earning another blast from a horn.

Adding to her confusion was the unfamiliar car. She'd dropped hers off that morning after her aqua class and taken the courtesy car. She'd only been home a short time, just showered and dressed when Geraldine had called and asked Margot to collect her. She'd sounded distressed so Margot hadn't quibbled but when she'd reached the corner where Geraldine said she'd be waiting there were people everywhere and no space to pull in.

It was such a nuisance to have to be here at all. Margot still had a zillion things to prepare for Christmas Day as well as for the gingerbread-making workshop later that afternoon at the Providore. It was a school holiday class she and Kath ran every year but would mean her afternoon would be gone. Margot hadn't been able to ignore the distress in Geraldine's voice. Evidently she'd caught the bus and now she wasn't feeling well and wanted to get home quickly.

Margot scanned the footpath. She was just about to try to call when a small group shaking hands outside the cafe caught her eye. Margot twisted back to look again as she passed. It was definitely Roslyn with two men in suits, one of whom had looked like that Xavier Zamon from Meyer and Brightman, and the other also seemed familiar. What on earth was Roslyn up to now?

Her phone rang but of course it wasn't connected to the courtesy car's bluetooth. She searched frantically for somewhere to pull in. Luckily she spied a supermarket ahead but by the time she'd found a park her phone had stopped.

The missed call was from Geraldine. She called straight back.

"Are you all right?" Margot asked as soon as Geraldine answered.

"Upset tummy," Geraldine puffed into the phone. "I moved away from the corner because I could tell you'd never get a park."

"Are you anywhere near Foodland? I'm in their car park."

"Just across the road."

"Good. I'm in a white Renault." Margot got out of her car and watched the street.

Geraldine appeared, moving quickly, and Margot waved to catch her attention.

"What's happened to your car?" Geraldine's face was creased in concern.

"Dennis has it at the yard getting it ready for you."

"Oh, that's wonderful. I caught the bus here this morning because my car's so unreliable and now with this tummy of mine—"

"Let's get you home."

"This is good of you, Margot," Geraldine said as soon as they were underway. "I've been in the public toilets for twenty minutes and it wasn't very pleasant."

Margot gave her a quick sideways glance. "You do look a bit pale. Perhaps you've got a tummy bug."

Geraldine shook her head. "It's happened a few times lately. A sudden bout of diarrhoea takes me by surprise. I had to leave Sandy's salon straight after my haircut the other day. No time for a blow-dry. And did you know she's doing up the rooms out the back of her salon as a day spa?"

"No. That's a huge change."

"She's going to employ a full-time masseuse. It'll be lovely for us though, won't it— ooh." Geraldine gripped her stomach.

Margot gave her a wary look. "Are you all right?"

"I'll be fine once I get home. I need to be near the toilet for—"

"I don't suppose you happened to see Roslyn while you were in the street?" Margot changed the subject or she'd get far too much detail of Geraldine's every symptom. Best to keep her mind off whatever was bothering her.

"I did actually. I was in such a hurry I nearly ran her over, or at least one of the men she was with. I'd just come from the toilet and I knew you'd be trying to find me and there were no parks so I was—"

"Did you see who she was with?"

"Oh, yes."

Margot negotiated the roundabout with a quick look at her passenger. Geraldine had one hand pressed to her stomach and the other gripped the door handle.

"Gosh, we're close to that car in front, aren't we?" she said.

Margot looked back to the road and braked. The car ahead had slowed for someone crossing the road.

"Who were they?" she said once they were underway again.

Geraldine twisted to look back over her shoulder. "I didn't recognise the car."

"No, I mean, did you know the men Roslyn was with?"

"Oh, yes." Geraldine nodded then she shook her head. "At least one of them."

"Which one?" Margot wanted to reach out and slap the woman, she was being so slow.

"That company man, Xavier someone."

"Zamon. And the other?" Margot had only got a quick glance at the tall, smartly dressed man but there'd been something familiar about him.

"No, well, at least, not before but I might if I saw him again. Poor man, I nearly bowled him over I was in such a hurry. I was looking ahead to a clear space so I could wait for you and—"

"You didn't know him?"

"No, but that Mr Zamon called out to him because I was going to collide with him and he grabbed my arm and—"

"What did he call out?"

"Who?"

"Xavier Zamon. Did he call out a name?"

"Oh, yes. It was…" Geraldine pressed a hand to her forehead. "Edward…no, Elvin, I think. Struck me as an old-fashioned name."

Margot slapped a hand on the steering wheel. "I knew I'd seen him somewhere before. He's Gunter's solicitor." And now she recalled why the man in the car that had dropped Roslyn off after her so-called lunch with friends had seemed familiar. It was the same man.

"I suppose Roslyn's got to—"

"Bloody Roslyn." Margot slapped the steering wheel again and the car lurched slightly. "I knew she was up to something. She's never been opposed to the hotel development like the rest of us. She's probably been in cahoots with them from the start. She always said she didn't know much about Gunter's estate but I think she's up to her neck with the goings-on. Well, she's not going to sneak anything past me."

Margot gripped the wheel tighter and put her foot down as they zoomed onto the freeway. Beside her Geraldine remained silent.

Amber had just arrived for her shift at the pub. The bar was quiet. Most of the customers were dining in the other room. Fred had asked her to start a bit earlier but then she could leave as soon as dinner service was finished. He wanted her for two shifts the next day. He was banking on Christmas Eve being a big one for the pub.

The bloke behind the bar had the phone to his ear and beckoned her over as he caught sight of her.

He held out the phone. "Call for you."

Before she had time to object he pressed the phone into her hand and walked off.

Amber stared at the phone as if it were a spider on her palm. Who would be ringing her at work? Then she thought of her phone, which had gone flat as she'd arrived. Maybe Roslyn was calling her but why?

She lifted the phone to her ear. "Hello?"

"Amber, you little bitch. I knew you—" She stabbed at the off button and tossed the phone back under the counter.

The sour taste of the cheese-and-pickle sandwich she'd eaten for lunch rose up into her throat. Tyson had found her.

The phone started ringing again. She snatched it up, blocked the number and stared at the screen, terrified it would ring again.

"Who was that?" Fred was watching her from the other side of the bar.

"Nuisance call. I blocked it."

He quirked his big bushy eyebrows. "Okay. You all right on your own out here for a while?" He beckoned the barman. "I need some help out the back."

Amber glanced around. There were a couple of men at the other end of the bar and two small groups set up around the high tables. "Sure, I can manage."

As Fred and the barman left a customer stepped up to be served. The phone started ringing again.

"You want to get that?" The bloke nodded in the direction of the phone.

She shook her head. "What can I get for you?"

He gave his order and the phone stopped. Amber had just finished serving when it started again. She left the bar to collect empty glasses. There was no way she'd be answering the phone again.

She turned back to the bar with hands full of glasses as Fred reached over and picked up the phone.

After the initial pleasantries his gaze lifted to hers, his bushy eyebrows raised.

She gave a slight shake of her head.

"Not here, mate, sorry," Fred said and disconnected.

Amber went behind the bar and stacked the glasses into the crate for washing.

"That call was for you," Fred said.

"Sorry."

"Sounded a bit like that bloke that was asking for you the other day."

Amber gripped the handles of the crate as Fred came around the bar and stopped beside her.

"Want to tell me what's going on?"

Amber's hands fell to her sides. Tyson could ring anytime from another phone. Anyone who worked at Fred's pub could take the call and hand the phone to her, or even worse, give more details about her life here. She turned to Fred.

"It's Tyson. My ex."

"Giving you a hard time?"

Amber nodded.

"Well, he won't be welcome in my pub and I'll let the rest of the staff know not to take any calls for you…okay?"

Fred's look was so earnest Amber almost wanted to hug him but she stayed where she was. "Thanks, Fred." From the corner of her eye she saw a woman approach the bar. She moved off to serve her.

Amber chatted while she poured the drinks, the easy banter releasing her angst over Tyson. There was nothing to stop him from turning up here again looking for her but she felt safe for now. This was an extra busy period for pubs and he was unlikely to leave Penola to chase her while he was earning good money. The holiday season had bought her some time.

Margot pulled up outside the butcher shop, ignoring the harsh sound of her tyre rim grating along the kerb. After dashing out to collect Geraldine earlier in the day, she'd forgotten all about picking up her Christmas meat. She just had time to collect it and get it home before she had to return for the gingerbread-making session at the Prov.

There were two women in the shop and only Kev behind the counter. The sound of their urgent discussion ceased as Margot stepped inside. One of the women was Sandy. All three stared at her in surprise as if they'd been caught doing something they shouldn't.

Sandy was the first to move. "Hello, Margot." She took a wrapped parcel from the counter. "Thanks, Kev. Merry Christmas. Have a good break and I'll see you in the new year."

"I'd better be off too," the other woman said. Margot smiled and nodded as she passed. She recognised the woman as a local but not someone she knew well.

Margot watched them leave, the air around her heavy with words unsaid.

"Come for your Christmas meat?" Kev went to the fridge and came back with a cardboard box full of white paper packages. "There you are." He gave her a nod then looked away.

"Did you remember a kilo of those rissoles Dennis liked?"

"In the box." Kev patted one of the parcels.

Margot took out her purse and paid, still feeling the weight of something in the air that she'd disturbed with her entrance. Kev normally chatted ten to the dozen but not today.

"Is everything okay, Kev?" she asked.

"Just the usual weariness for this time of year."

Margot glanced along the counter but it was clear of anything that resembled the petition.

As if he sensed what she was looking for, Kev ducked under the counter and bobbed back up, flapping it in his hand.

"I won't be having this here any longer," he said as he pushed it towards her. His gaze didn't meet hers but was low as if he was checking the array of meat on display in his cabinet. He'd spoken softly, almost apologetically, so she thought she'd misheard.

"Is it full? I can print more." Margot lifted the first page, which was filled with signatures, but the second had only a few.

"I know I was against the hotel development originally but now that I've found out a bit more about it I—"

"From who?" Margot recalled the sudden silence when she'd walked in and Sandy's hurried departure. "People gossiping in your shop probably don't have all the facts."

"I've thought about it a lot, Margot, and I think a boutique hotel will be good for business."

"How?" Margot was so shocked by Kev's turnabout her question came out as a scoff.

Kev's face went a deeper red than his usual ruddy complexion. "Xavier Zamon paid me a visit to explain how the hotel might be of benefit to the community and to my business in particular."

"I'm not sure how much you can trust what that man says."

"Why not? It made good sense to me."

"What did he say?"

"That the supermarket would be looking to me first to supply their meat."

"What's he got to do with the supermarket?"

"He's the one who got the company on board to purchase Teakles' place. The boutique hotel won't have a restaurant but each room will have basic kitchen facilities and—"

"The *proposed* hotel."

Kev shook his head. "You know, Margot, the only thing holding it up is some of the local community and I think it's very selfish."

"Selfish!" The shock of such a suggestion fizzed and bubbled inside her. "How can you say that? Jesserton is dear to my heart, dear to many people's hearts. A hotel like they're proposing would change everything."

"Not all change is bad you know, Margot." His words fell softly.

"Of course I know that." She picked up the box of meat and Kev placed the petition pages on top.

"The new hotel would be a boost for your business too." He nodded towards his window and The General Providore just over the road.

"The Prov doesn't need a boost."

He looked surprised at that. "Kath's been talking up a few changes and plenty of people have appreciated the longer opening hours."

"That's as may be but we might not be able to sustain them."

"The hotel might mean you could. If even half of what Xavier's been talking to me about goes ahead it will mean I can keep my shop open."

"You were thinking of closing?"

"I didn't want to. My dad started this business. These last few years I thought I'd be the one closing it."

"You sell such good quality meat."

"I get a lot of local support and a bit from Sheffield but not many from further afield make regular trips here for their weekly meat shop. Jesserton's out of the way."

"Which is what makes it special."

Kev shook his head. "Teakles' was run-down, my business was struggling, I know even Greg was talking about cutting back his hours. The local community alone isn't enough to keep our businesses afloat any more." He looked Margot fully in the eye for the first time since she'd entered his shop. "I think we need this new hotel."

thirty-one

The General Providore was abuzz with the chatter of children and the conversations of their parents gathered for the annual gingerbread biscuit–making session. Numbers were down from previous years but those who were around the table icing and decorating their biscuits were having a wonderful time.

Kayla was there with her two boys and she'd kindly offered to help oversee Isabella as Emily couldn't stay. Margot was just setting out some extra bowls of icing when the waif-like child next to her granddaughter waved a spatula in the air smearing icing in all directions, including Isabella's hair. Margot was able to gently relieve him of his colourful weapon and distract him with lollies to put on the gingerbread star he'd been decorating. His baby sister was toddling around, spreading spilled icing and shoving dropped lollies in her mouth. Margot glanced around for their mother but she was on the other side of the table deep in conversation with Kayla, oblivious to the antics of her unruly children.

Margot was just wondering how she could tactfully redirect the woman to come and supervise them when the boy called out to her and she headed over.

She admired her son's handiwork and plucked the toddler to her hip. Ignoring the sticky hands and the colourful dribble running from her child's lips she turned to Margot, who was subtly trying to edge Isabella's biscuits out of reach of the waif-child.

"You're Kayla's mother-in-law, Margot, aren't you?"

"That's right."

"Thanks for organising this. My son loves being creative."

Margot glanced back at the boy. If spreading icing and lollies from one end of the table to the other was being creative he was certainly that. She pulled her lips into a smile.

"I'm glad they're enjoying themselves. I don't think I've seen you in here before."

"I'm Summer, Larry's partner. You've probably seen him in here. Loves his chai. We've just moved into that property on the edge of town. The rambling stone house with the green roof and various sheds. With working on the house and all the animals to look after I don't get out much."

"Oh yes, Larry was the one who was after some laying hens. Did he get some?"

"Yes. We're planning to sell free-range eggs and Kayla was saying you might stock them here."

"We have a supplier at the moment but we've lost our back-up and we like to have another provider in case supply drops off." Margot winced as the little boy splattered more icing everywhere, green this time.

Summer continued, oblivious to her son's wild behaviour. "Kayla also said you had a petition about stopping the hotel development."

"I do."

"I'd like to sign it and I'm sure Larry would too. We moved here to get away from the rat-race. Jesserton appealed because it seemed like a nice community with not so many tourists clogging up the street. A boutique hotel would bring a lot of extra people. We're worried it will change the lovely close-knit community vibe here in Jesserton."

"My husband and I feel that way too," Margot said. She was still jittery after her conversation with Kev earlier. It was reassuring to talk with someone who thought like she did, even if they were new to town. "We think there should be more attention paid to meeting the needs of the permanent residents rather than those who are here for a day or two."

"Whereas I'm the opposite." Kath had moved up beside them with a tray ready to collect the empty lolly and icing containers. "Those day and overnight trippers bring extra money to the town that helps it to thrive." She nodded to the table of busy children and parents. "So we can keep doing things like this that end up costing us money rather than making it."

Margot was surprised by Kath's snappish comment. "This is more about providing a fun local activity than making money."

"I know." Kath sighed. "I guess I'm just disappointed we didn't get the usual numbers. We normally have two tables going. There's lots of gingerbread dough left."

"We can make it into biscuits to sell," Margot said chirpily, wondering when she'd get the time to do that.

"I might sell a few with coffees tomorrow morning." Kath sniffed. "I heard some of the families didn't come because they wouldn't support a business that was against progress." She looked at Margot as if it was her fault.

"I'm not against progress," Margot blustered. "And I wasn't going to mention it but I heard the opposite."

Kath's jaw dropped. "What?"

"It's true." Summer set her squirming toddler back on the floor. "There was a lot of discussion about that at the mums' group

Christmas party. There are others like Larry and I who don't want some fancy hotel full of entitled rich people cluttering up the town. Our kids won't be safe. Some of the mums were pretty fired up and saying they were shopping elsewhere because someone here in your shop was all for the hotel." She stared at Kath whose cheeks flushed a deep pink.

The toddler reached up and took one of her brother's biscuits and he began to yell. Summer ducked down to deal with her children.

Margot nibbled at the corner of her fingernail.

"Well, I was busy this morning." Kath said it as if it were a competition. "I sold out of bread and we made a stack of coffees and food to go. They were mostly locals." And with a "so there" air she hoisted the tray of crockery she'd collected and set off for the kitchen.

The Prov had been busy over the weekend too, but when Margot thought about it some of their regulars hadn't come in. Of course they could be away but she couldn't help but replay Tess's comment from Friday night about people not coming into the shop if she was here and Kath had just suggested the same. She collected up some more of the detritus from the decorating table and followed Kath.

"What was all that yelling about?" Kath asked.

"Summer's little girl took one of her brother's biscuits."

"I hope she dealt with it."

Margot glanced back. Summer was holding the toddler and leaning over the table to help her son. "She is."

"We'll have to wash the chairs and the wall where he was sitting. I don't mind exuberance but that mother doesn't seem to care what her kids do."

"She was saying they were planning to have free-range eggs to sell."

"Eggs! It's her kids who are free-range." Kath nodded towards the shop. "Those two have made more mess than all the others combined."

"You seem a bit uptight, Kath. Are you sure you should be opening the extra hours?"

"I'm fine. It's just people like that one out there that get up my nose. New to town and already telling us how we should do things. Opposing the hotel."

"She was telling me they moved here for the alternate life, away from the rat-race."

"One hotel's hardly going to create a rat-race."

"It's not just the hotel, it's you wanting the Prov open seven days, a fancy supermarket—"

"I thought you liked the idea of a gourmet supermarket."

Margot groaned. "I did…do. We're a big enough community to warrant a small supermarket but as you say it's the extras they'll do, catering for tourists. Did you know Sandy's doing up her back room and advertising for a masseuse?"

"I did hear about that. It's something she always wanted to do."

"I wonder why now?"

"Why not now? You seem to be concerned about the smallest of changes, Margot. Since when have you become so set in your ways?"

Margot frowned. "I like change as much as anyone but not to the detriment of others."

Kath huffed out a breath, her usual vibrance nowhere to be seen.

"It's such a busy time of year," Margot said. "Everyone's a little strung out. Perhaps we should take an extra few days' break. Close between Christmas and New Year."

Kath drew herself up. "I'm fine and I don't want to lose the momentum I've started. We'll be closed Christmas and Boxing days. I told you I'm happy to do the hours and it's my weekend to work before New Year anyway. You can take the whole week off if you want. The casuals we've taken on are both very good and I've decided to stay open all day on the Monday and Tuesday."

"You've decided."

"You made it clear it was up to me."

"Yes, but it's clear to me you're overdoing it."

Kath shook her head. "We've got the staff and they want the hours. As I said, we were quite busy this morning and we turned a few away this afternoon when they thought we were open."

"It's getting out of hand."

Kath frowned. "What is?"

"Everything." Margot swept an arm in the air.

"You know I'm keen to expand but you don't have to be involved. In fact, you can take more of a back seat if you want."

"What do you mean?"

"You're moving in other directions these days. If you can't do the days you're committed to you'll need to pay for staff to cover."

"I can do the days I'm rostered as we originally decided when we set up the business." Margot's insides swirled with a mix of anger and unease. "Anyway, you just suggested I have time off. What's going on, Kath?"

"Nothing's going on, other than I want to run The General Providore as a full-time business and you don't. I thought if you took some time over the Christmas break to think about that, we could come up with a new business arrangement in the new year. Either fifty-fifty like we are now but with the extra hours or, say, seventy-thirty if you want to do less."

Margot could only gape at her friend as the swirling sensation inside her became an overwhelming wave of anxiety. The shop, Dennis taking on the new brand at the dealership, the hotel and the community unrest, as well as her decision to run for mayor – there was so much happening. She was being pulled in every direction when all she wanted to do was think about the delicious lunch she was planning for her family for Christmas.

"Nanny!" Isabella's wail startled her. The little girl was standing in the doorway, her eyes wide with alarm.

"What is it, darling?" Margot bobbed down and as she did big tears began to roll down Isabella's cheeks.

"That boy took one of my biscuits." She threw herself into Margot's arms as another yelp and a cry came from the shop.

"Bloody hell!" Kath snarled and strode off to investigate.

Margot wiped Isabella's cheeks and assured her there were plenty more biscuits, wishing that her own troubles could be so easily fixed.

thirty-two

Christmas Lunch at Margot and Dennis's

Festive Dip with Corn Chips

Coconut Prawns with Mango, Cucumber & Mint Salad; Sweet Potato & Avocado Bites

Baked Salmon, Roast Turkey with Cranberry & Pecan Stuffing, Glazed Tofu Roast, Honey Hasselback Potatoes, Glazed Heirloom Carrots, Roasted Garlic Green Beans & Red Capsicum

Fig & Custard Tart, Individual Christmas Puddings, Mini Pavlovas

Margot inspected her perfectly set Christmas table. She liked to have Christmas lunch in their dining room because they nearly always used the outdoor entertaining area for the rest of the year. The golden teak table was bare of cloth except for a white linen runner down the centre and lying along that was a gold foil branch with clusters of red berries. Two simple gold candlesticks nestled among the berries, supporting long white candles. Each person's setting had a rolled red napkin circled by a gold band set across the centre of a white plate and their name written on a dark green leaf attached to a red bauble. The only other hint of colour was the gold on the rim of the water glasses.

She'd gone for a minimalist, rustic look and was pleased with the result but instead of the uplift of spirits her decorating usually brought, she felt flat. She'd not talked further with Kath after the ruckus with the gingerbread biscuit group. After everyone had left they'd cleaned up and Kath had gone home, leaving Margot to bake the remaining dough. Alone at the Providore she'd had plenty of time to mull over Kath's suggestion they revisit their business arrangement. It hurt to think her friend was moving on in a direction Margot hadn't foreseen or wanted.

Added to that was the general unrest in town. When she'd gone out to roll up the blinds, another job added to their end-of-day pack-up list, Greg from the plant shop had caught her. He said Xavier had been to see him too, talked about how they might be able to work together, but Greg hadn't been keen.

"I just don't like the guy," he'd said.

"Kath seems taken with him but I haven't formally met him," Margot had replied.

They'd been standing on the edge of the footpath when Greg nodded across the street. "It feels a bit like them and us."

"What do you mean?"

"Kev, Sandy and the new supermarket all keen for the boutique hotel, and us on this side not so."

"Kath thinks it's a good idea."

"People are taking sides, you know. Whatever happens won't be good for this community." His words had had an ominous ring, then he'd moved back inside as a customer entered his shop.

Margot had slept fitfully that night then the next day had pushed everything else from her mind as she'd worked her way through her Christmas preparations. She'd stayed up very late making sure she had as much prepared in advance for today as she could. Then this morning Dennis had dragged her out of bed early to look at the new car that waited in their driveway, complete with huge black-and-white ribbon.

"I had it hidden over at Gunter's so I could surprise you," he'd said.

She'd loved it, of course, and the colour. It was a deep electric blue, a little more demure than the vivid green car she'd had to say goodbye to. That car had also been parked in their drive with a black-and-white ribbon on it awaiting Geraldine's arrival.

They'd met the family at church for the Christmas service and adjourned back to Margot and Dennis's for presents, picking up Geraldine on the way. She'd been beside herself with excitement over her new car and thankfully seemed to have gotten over whatever had troubled her on Monday. Roslyn had joined them late morning. Margot had done her best to be polite to her sister but it was difficult when the sight of her sent Margot's annoyance meter sky high.

The cheerful chatter of adult voices, punctuated with the more excited tones and the odd squeal of delight from the children, echoed from outside. Margot was just about to head out when her phone rang from somewhere else in the house. She searched for it, finally tracking it down underneath a potholder on the kitchen bench.

"Hello?" she answered quickly before the call ended.

"Hi, Margot." Kath sounded tired.

"Merry Christmas. Aren't you down in town with family?"

"Just about to head off...I thought you should know though. There's been a bit of trouble in the street."

"At your house?"

"No, the main drag. Some of the shops have been splattered with what looked like red paint."

"Oh, how awful." Margot clapped a hand to her forehead. "Who'd do that? What about the Prov?"

"The Prov's fine. It's all on the other side of the street – the supermarket, the hairdresser and the butcher shop. Their doors were painted with big red Xs but it turns out it's not paint…well, not proper paint. The kind kids use, they think. It's washing off okay."

"Who would do that?" Margot said again. "And why? Jesserton's usually such a quiet place."

"My guess would be something to do with the hotel."

"Really?"

"I don't know but I can't think of any other explanation."

"Surely it's not someone we know. It must be kids from somewhere else."

"There was a big chat about it on Jesserton Jabber – didn't you see it?"

"I've hardly had time to scratch myself today let alone look at my phone."

There was silence for a moment. Margot checked her phone to make sure it was still connected.

"Perhaps you should." Once again Kath paused. "I've got to head off. Just wanted to let you know everything's okay at the Prov. Give my love to your family."

"And mine to yours."

Margot stared at her phone, her finger hovering over it. Kath had sounded…exactly what Margot couldn't put her finger on. It could have just been concern over the paint attacks but—

"Here you are." Emily stepped into the kitchen. "Do you need help with anything?"

"Not yet." Margot glanced at her watch. They'd eaten sweet treats while they'd opened presents so she was holding off on lunch for a little longer. "The turkey will be at least another hour."

"Perfect. The coconut prawns won't take long to cook and Kayla's bites won't either. We'll get on to them soon. Time to come out and sit for a while." Emily slipped an arm through hers. "We're opening the champagne."

Margot left her phone on the bench. The community chat could wait.

"Here she is." Dennis put a glass of champagne in her hand. "Not only the best wife, mother, sister, friend, but soon to be mayor."

Everyone raised their glasses as Margot tried to play down the praise.

"Let's not get ahead of ourselves."

"I've met your opposition," Nick said. "He's trapped in last century. You're a shoo-in for the job."

"We'll have two family members on council." Emily beamed from her husband to her mother.

Cam quirked his eyebrows. "We'll see. I've got some serious contenders and I'm afraid you do too, Margot. There's a third nomination for mayor."

"Who?" they all chorused.

"One of the councillors has thrown his hat in the ring, Brett Moss – he has a local accountancy practice."

"He was at the meeting Meyer and Brightman held," Margot said.

Dennis nodded. "His main office is in Mount Barker, not far from the dealership. He's only a young whippersnapper. Not experienced like you, Margot."

"He's my age," Cam said.

"And Cameron's very knowledgeable, Dad." Emily pulled a face at her father.

"I think the role of mayor needs some experience and seniority, that's all."

"'Cause younger people can't possibly know what they're doing," Nick said with a hint of sarcasm.

"No need to get antsy," Dennis snapped.

"Doesn't he have to resign from council to run for mayor?" Margot cut in quickly, determined there'd be no harsh words today.

"Yep." Cam nodded. "That means another councillor vacancy to fill."

There was a moment's silence while everyone took in the news and Margot pondered the difference a third runner might make.

"You've both got my vote," Nick said.

"You'll be wonderful as councillor and as mayor." Geraldine beamed from Cameron to Margot.

"Surely Brett has left it a bit late," Dennis said.

"Nominations don't close until early January." Cameron shrugged. "We could still get more contenders."

Margot sipped her champagne and let the conversation flow around her.

"Can you help me make this, Nanny?" Isabella held a coloured cord to which she'd added several wooden beads but was struggling to slip the next one on.

"Of course." She took the purple cord and poked the end through the bead Isabella held then watched as she pushed it along and selected more beads.

Margot wasn't distracted by the activity – it gave her thinking time. Standing for mayor was once more back in her thoughts. She hadn't met her first opponent yet but she'd heard a few disparaging remarks. No doubt she had her own detractors but she found it hard to believe there'd be many. Brett Moss might be a bigger challenge though. She'd have to find out more about him.

Roslyn kept out of the discussion about council. She was concerned her sister may have bitten off more than she could chew but she'd never say it, especially after their pleasant Sunday afternoon when the discord between them had been calmed. And thankfully Geraldine hadn't mentioned running into her outside the cafe with the two men so hopefully she hadn't mentioned it to Margot either.

Margot had been distracted when Roslyn had arrived. They'd exchanged brief pleasantries and gifts then Margot had disappeared off to the kitchen alone, insisting she didn't need any help for the moment. Now she'd returned and since the discussion about council nominations she'd been sitting at the other side of the room making necklaces with Isabella.

"More champagne, Roslyn?"

She looked from Nick to her glass in surprise. "No, thank you. I'll wait for our meal before I have another."

"Sparkling water then?" Nick held up the bottle in his other hand.

"Thanks." She held out her glass.

"How's Jerome and the family?"

"All well." Roslyn smiled. "We had a lovely video catch-up this morning." Roslyn looked around the room and spoke more loudly. "Jerome sends his best to you all."

"We'll move into the dining room soon." Margot had extricated herself from the necklace-making and was heading back from the kitchen. "Kayla and Emily will have the entrees nearly ready."

Roslyn offered a smile but her sister had already moved on to organise the wine for lunch. Perhaps it was her imagination but she was beginning to feel as if Margot was avoiding her.

She'd also noticed Geraldine, who'd stuck to sparkling water and hadn't eaten any of the savoury nibbles on offer, wasn't saying much. Roslyn wasn't sure if it was the mauve-and-blue floral dress she was wearing that made her look washed out or if she really was.

"Time to move inside, everyone," Margot announced. "Entrees are ready."

Nick's boys groaned. They'd got some kind of construction kit for Christmas and had been engrossed building a structure then racing marbles along tracks and up towers and down valleys.

It took a while but finally they were all seated at Margot's dining table, including Henry in a high chair. There were no crackers to pop but Margot had provided everyone with a Christmas joke to read out, and then the coconut prawn dish Emily had made and Kayla's sweet potato and avocado bites were served.

Roslyn was seated between Nick on one side and Geraldine on the other. Before they began to eat Geraldine excused herself for the bathroom, Nick's youngest shoved away his plate and declared he wasn't eating "corns", which knocked over the glass of very nice wine Roslyn had brought with her. There was a lot of dabbing, cleaning and fussing before everyone finally settled at the table for the entrees.

The dishes had barely been cleared when Isabella's necklace came undone and beads went everywhere, her cousins laughed and she had a meltdown. Cameron took her outside to calm down. Roslyn offered to help Margot with serving the turkey and was rejected, Dennis cranked up the aircon because the air in the dining room was getting very stuffy and Geraldine excused herself again.

"More wine?" Kayla asked. Her offer of help had been refused too. Only Emily and Dennis, whose job it was to carve the turkey, went with Margot to the kitchen.

"Thanks."

"Sorry about my boys. They've eaten more sugar today than they'd normally eat in a month."

"We all overindulge at Christmas."

"What's Amber doing today?"

"Working, but Fred's putting on a lunch for the staff at least. She might join us this evening."

"She's a smart young woman."

"Who's that?" Emily asked as she set bowls of vegetables on the table.

"Roslyn's tenant, Amber."

"Can't be too smart," Emily scoffed. "Pregnant, on her own and nowhere to live."

Roslyn had to bite her tongue. Emily really could be clueless sometimes.

"Life doesn't always go the way we expect," Kayla said.

"No, it doesn't." Emily turned to Roslyn. "You were the last person I expected to give Nick a loan."

"Emily," Margot chided as she carried in the baked salmon followed by Dennis with the roast turkey. "I told you to keep that to yourself."

Nick snorted. "There are no secrets in this family."

"Why does it have to be a secret?" Emily snapped. "Unless you've got some reason to hide it."

"I asked Nick to keep it in confidence." Roslyn eyeballed her snooty niece. "It's really not anyone else's business."

"Emily, can you help me bring out the rest of the food," Margot said. "Please start serving, we won't be long."

Cameron returned with a calmer Isabella and Dennis and Nick topped up drinks as Emily came back with the potatoes and Margot with the roasted tofu and the gravy.

She looked around the table. "Where's Geraldine?"

"I'm here." Geraldine settled in her seat with colour on her cheeks and lips as if she'd just reapplied make-up.

Roslyn glanced sideways. She didn't want to ask how she was or she'd get inundated with her every symptom. Perhaps she had some kind of bug. Roslyn edged away a little and began to serve herself some food.

The atmosphere around the table relaxed again as Nick's boys read out more silly jokes and everyone tucked into the delicious food, including Geraldine. Roslyn still got the impression that Margot was avoiding her, but perhaps it was just the pressure her sister had put herself under with all the preparation for today. No matter what else was going on in that crazy head of hers, Margot wouldn't let anything spoil her well-oiled Christmas celebrations.

thirty-three

Amber re-read the message on her phone, hoping she'd misunderstood. It was a text from her friend Immi wishing her Merry Christmas. That bit was fine but it was what followed that sent a shiver down her spine in spite of the fact that she was out the back of the pub where the hot afternoon sun beat down on the flimsy verandah over her head. Immi had messaged that she and her partner had gone to the pub where Tyson worked for Christmas arvo drinks and he wasn't there. Evidently he'd worked the lunch shift and then taken two days off.

Amber jumped as a shadow fell across her legs.

"Sorry, didn't mean to startle you."

She looked up into Tom's cheeky grin, which was quickly replaced by a frown as he pulled up an upturned crate next to hers.

"Are you okay?"

"Yeah." Amber's phone beeped as the screen died and she swore under her breath.

"You sure?" Tom nudged her gently with his shoulder.

"A friend with some bad news, that's all. Nothing I can do now."

"So it's still okay for me to come to yours later?"

"Of course." Amber shoved her useless phone in her pocket.

"I'm looking forward to a swim."

"The pool's in Roslyn's backyard. She invited me…us for dinner and a swim. There's a catch though."

"She's a fire-breathing dragon?"

Amber laughed and the knot in her chest loosened. Tom usually managed to brighten her day.

"She'll probably have family there. Some of them are nice but some of them are a bit…" She wrinkled her nose. "Snobby."

"Do we care?" He nudged her again.

"We don't."

Tom stood. "I'd better get back to it. Just took a few minutes' break before I start on the pots. I should be done in an hour or so."

"I'll probably still be in the bar. Come and find me once you're done."

He gave her a mock salute and went back inside. Amber stood too, stretched her back and took a step towards the door as Fred came out. He glanced over his shoulder then back at Amber.

"You drive your car today or walk?"

"My car. Why—"

"Good. You can head off. I've got enough help in the bar." He pushed her bag at her as well as the Christmas gift he'd handed out to each of his staff earlier, still in its carry bag.

"But my shift—"

"Your man's here."

"My man?"

"That guy that's been looking for you. Your ex."

Once more Amber felt a chill run through her body in spite of the heat. "Tyson?" she hissed.

"I told him you weren't working today. He doesn't know where you live, does he?"

Amber shook her head, unable to form any cohesive words.

"Go home and stay put. I don't need you tomorrow. He can't hang around forever."

She clutched her bag to her chest and turned to the side gate.

"Hang on. I'll just make sure he's still at the bar."

Amber paced like a trapped tiger while he was gone. Bloody Tyson. He was a shithead and she'd underestimated him. She thought he'd give up looking for her but he was also stubborn. She swung around at footsteps behind her.

Fred waved her off. "Get going. He's nursing a beer at the bar."

"Thanks, Fred. Can you tell Tom I've left early? He's coming my way when he's done."

"Will do." He shooed her towards the gate.

She didn't need any further encouragement. She headed along the path round the back of the pub and up the road to the empty block where she'd parked her car out of sight. Every step she took she cursed. Tyson wasn't going to give up easily but she wasn't going to give in without a fight either.

Margot lay on her bed and stared up at the ceiling while beside her Dennis snored softly. The younger ones were relaxing in the outdoor room playing games with the children and the senior adults had all retired for a short rest, Geraldine and Roslyn both to their respective homes. Margot was very pleased with herself.

It had been a lovely Christmas so far and her lunch had been delicious, even if she did say so herself. Everyone had helped, of course, but Margot had made sure their contributions would suit her plan, and they had. Dennis had even tried and enjoyed the roasted tofu.

There'd been several times when the conversation had drifted to dangerous territory but Margot had managed to deflect or change the subject. Nick and Dennis had been snippy with each other for a moment, Emily had had a dig at Nick about the loan from Roslyn and Geraldine had mentioned almost running into Roslyn the other morning. Roslyn had been quick to change the subject then and Margot had let it go. She was not allowing anything to sour her special Christmas Day. There were things she'd deal with later, like her sister and her obviously secret meetings with Elvin and Xavier, but Christmas lunch was not the place for ironing out differences.

Margot sighed and reached for her phone. She was tired but not sleepy.

Kath had mentioned Jesserton Jabber so Margot opened it up. There was a string of replies to the post about the vandalism.

Sozz PO: *What an awful mess in the street. Is everyone all right?*

Golds: *What's happened?*

Thelma: *DID SOMEBODY CALL THE POLICE?*

Sandy: *Someone's painted red Xs on our shop fronts*

Kev: *Not bothering the police with this today. It washes off. No real damage done.*

Sozz PO: *I took lots of photos*

Greg: *Nothing done to shops on my side of the street*

Thelma: *THAT'S A GOOD IDEA THE POLICE LIKE CRIME SCENE PHOTOS*

Golds: *Why would someone do that in our quiet town?*

Thelma: GOOD THING NOT ALL SHOPS BUT AWFUL ON CHRISTMAS DAY

Golds: Does anyone need help?

Freds Hotel: No damage here

Sandy: Makes you wonder

Greg: Who should we contact about the supermarket?

Kath: The Prov's secure and no damage. If you see this, Margot, no need to come down.

Kev: Sandy and I will clean off the supermarket

Tess: If Margot's running for mayor she'd better get on top of this.

Margot huffed at that. She was fast beginning to dislike Tess. What on earth did any of it have to do with running for mayor? She scrolled on to the next comment.

Thelma: WONDER WHAT

Greg: The supermarket looks the worst hit from here. I'll come and help.

Sandy: Makes you wonder why only the places in favour of the hotel development have been painted

Kath: I'll come and help too

Tess: If it's to do with having a hotel or not it needs to be settled quickly. Brett Moss is a good operator and he's running for mayor. He'll have my vote.

Sozz PO: Maybe they were disturbed before they got to the other side of the street

Freds Hotel: We're not that kind of town, Sandy. Don't stir up trouble. And we don't need to be told who to vote for on this platform, Tess

Golds: You'd hope not. We're off to check our holiday rentals.

Thelma: JESSERTON IS A PERFECTLY HARMONIOUS COMMUNITY

Greg: Are you in favour of a hotel now, Martin?

Kath: Lots of people are, Greg

Freds Hotel: More against than for if the talk at the bars anything to go by

Tess: This is a community forum and we live in a free country – we should be able to state our opinion here, Fred.

Thelma: BUT IT SHOULDNT MATTER IF YOURE FOR OR AGAINST WERE ALL FRIENDS

Larry: If anyone sees a brown and white billy goat can you let us know

Margot tried to scroll on but Larry's had been the last reply. Then she noticed the row of small round head shots of group members was much shorter than it had been last time she'd checked. She clicked on the member list and scrolled. There were fewer people in the group now, and of the names that were missing she noted there was no Sandy, Kath or Kev.

thirty-four

Christmas Dinner at Roslyn's

Festive Dip with Corn Chips

Sticky Orange Soy-glazed Ham, Coleslaw, Spinach Apple Salad, Zesty Citrus Avocado Salad

Leftovers from Margot's

Roslyn was thankful the day was still warm and they could stay outside. Her kitchen dining area was small and she couldn't be bothered setting the formal dining table. Much nicer to keep it casual at the large outdoor setting in the shade by the pool.

When she'd arrived back from Margot's she'd sat on the couch with her feet up rather than lie on her bed. She'd been dozing but she was sure she'd heard a car going down the drive. It would be Amber back from the pub. No doubt she'd be needing a rest too. Roslyn hoped she'd come and join them for a swim and dinner.

Funny how she'd been so reluctant to have Amber stay in the cottage and now she was glad of it. Not that they saw a lot of each other, but to Roslyn's surprise she found she was enjoying knowing Amber was around. The young woman had helped her to narrow down the ideas for Gunter's legacy that she'd presented to Elvin and Xavier earlier in the week. Amber didn't realise her role of course but by finding out about her needs Roslyn had decided on a plan. While Gunter's bequest was generous there wasn't enough money to help with every worthy cause. Elvin had been right to caution her to keep it to herself.

Voices outside brought her to her feet with only a slight twinge. Life had certainly become easier since she'd started on the medication and, who knows, perhaps the swimming and losing a tiny bit of weight had helped too.

Kayla tapped on the glass door and Roslyn waved her in.

"The kids are all keen for a swim," she said.

"And some of the adults," Nick called.

"Go for it. I'll finish the salads and carve the ham so I don't have to worry about it later. Help yourself to the drinks in the bar fridge."

"Thanks."

Roslyn watched them through the window as she worked. The four parents were laughing and playing with the excited children. It was lovely to see their enjoyment and even though she was only separated from them by the glass of the window melancholy tugged at her heart. If only her actual flesh-and-blood son Jerome, his wife and child were here it would be perfect. Even though they video-called regularly she missed them and it would be months before their next visit.

Christmas dining had been Richard's passion. When he'd been alive they'd taken turns with Margot to host lunch. Roslyn wondered if deep down that's why she didn't want to hold lunch at her house any more – it reminded her too much of him and his joy in preparing the food. Richard had done most of the cooking, delighting in trying new recipes while she'd been his rudimentary sous chef.

Nick tapped on the window. She pushed it open.

"There's a drink with your name on it out here," he called.

"Coming," she replied and reminded herself how lucky she was to have her sister's family so close.

She picked up the colourful dip she'd put together surrounded by corn chips, the second time she'd made it for the day, and carried it outside just as Margot and Dennis arrived carrying eskies and armloads of food.

"The party rolls on," she said as they set their things down.

"The weather's perfect." Dennis popped a beer while Margot gave her a half smile and wandered to the edge of the pool.

Roslyn gave a brief thought to what she might have done to upset her sister this time but then Geraldine arrived, with a bottle of soft drink and a box of chocolates no less. Roslyn was speechless as she took the offerings but then she spied Amber and a young chap heading across the lawn.

"Hello!" She waved. "I'm so glad you could come."

"This is Tom, my English backpacker mate from the pub. He's on his own too so…"

"Thanks for having me," Tom said and produced a six pack of beer and a bottle of wine.

Roslyn didn't say she hadn't invited him – she was glad Amber felt she could bring a friend. "Come and meet everyone." Roslyn ushered them towards the pool and introductions were conducted under extremely rowdy conditions.

In the end it was Geraldine, Dennis, Roslyn and Margot nursing Henry who were the only ones out of the water. Roslyn laughed. It truly was good to see such a happy crowd using the pool. Richard would have loved it.

"We need some of Uncle Richard's music." Nick dripped his way to where he'd left his things on the lawn. "I made a playlist."

He took a bluetooth speaker and his phone from his bag and soon the happy beat of "Crocodile Rock" filled the air.

"Isn't this fun?" Geraldine said and with more energy than she'd shown all day she started chair-dancing to the music.

The heat from the late afternoon sun lingered as the day ebbed into a pleasantly warm evening. After the swimming the younger generation had worked up an appetite again so the food was brought out. Amber had stepped up as Roslyn's main helper, her actions bringing an unexpected lift to Roslyn's earlier low spirits.

No sooner had the last mouthfuls been eaten when the children wanted to go back in the pool. Roslyn shooed away the younger adults' offers of help so that they could be by the pool. Nick set another playlist going, something more modern this time, Roslyn suspected, as she didn't recognise the song, but it was pleasant enough in the background.

Dennis took Henry to the steps of the pool where they both put their feet in, leaving the three women, then Geraldine asked to use the bathroom and just Roslyn and Margot remained. Roslyn glanced across at her sister, whose gaze was set steadfastly in the direction of the pool. Margot had hardly said more than a few words to her all day.

"Can I get you another drink?"

"Not at the moment, thank you." Margot spoke politely and precisely as if she were a stranger.

Roslyn sighed. It had been a good day and an even better evening. It would be easiest to ignore Margot's mood. It may not even have anything to do with Roslyn, although deep down she suspected it did.

Laughter from the pool drew her attention. Amber had gone back in the water closely followed by Tom and they were playing some kind of ball game with the children.

"Looks like your boarder has picked up another man," Margot said. "It'll end up like the last situation you had in the cottage if you're not careful."

Her haughty tone chipped at Roslyn's resolve. "I believe Tom works with Amber at the pub. They're friends, that's all."

"For now. But who knows? It could turn out to be like the last man you had there. The friends ended up staying."

Roslyn was tired of having the debacle of their last tenant laid at her door. "The 'man' was a university colleague of Richard's, not mine. Richard was the one keen to let him stay but neither of us could have foreseen him taking in lodgers of his own and then being so difficult to evict."

Margot sniffed. "Poor Richard was terribly unwell. Lucky you had Dennis and I to help."

Roslyn gritted her teeth. "Wasn't I, though."

Margot glared at her. "Are you being sarcastic? Because if you are, that's quite unfair."

"What's unfair?" Emily asked. She and Dennis had returned from the pool. Henry was asleep in her arms.

Roslyn got to her feet, happy to change the subject. "Would you like to put him down on a spare bed?"

"Thanks, Roslyn," Emily said. "But you stay put. I can manage."

"You two aren't arguing again, are you?" Dennis said as Emily walked away. "It's Christmas." He patted his wife's leg but she brushed his hand away.

"I was just warning Roslyn she needed to be careful with her tenant. We don't want a repeat of last time."

Roslyn glanced towards the pool. There was plenty of noise and music to cover Margot's words.

"She seems harmless enough," Dennis said. "I've had a chat to her about her car. Told her if she's in need of money I could get her a good deal on it."

"Why would you do that?" Margot asked.

"It's worth a bit. I thought she could do with the money." Dennis poured himself a red wine and settled in a chair. "You're not planning on moving, are you, Roslyn?"

"No."

"I heard a little rumour you were looking at one of the Threadgold houses."

"Where did you hear that?" Roslyn snapped, at the same time as Margot said, "Which one?"

"I was at the post office yesterday and I heard Anne Threadgold talking to Sally."

Roslyn pressed her lips together, berating herself for not leaving it till after Christmas. Anne had answered the landline when she'd rung and Martin had been off somewhere. Roslyn should have left it but she'd forged on, excited by her ideas, and she'd asked Anne if they'd be prepared to put the sale of the big house on hold for a few weeks.

Martin had rung her back later full of questions so she'd explained as briefly as possible her idea that it would be good accommodation and shared space for people on a program she was working on. She'd had to give him a brief outline but hadn't mentioned Gunter's money would be buying it. Martin had a few reservations but he'd been prepared to hold off putting it on the market until she could give him more details.

"Roslyn!" Margot's bark startled her. "Which house are you talking about?"

"It's not for sure, just an idea."

"Which one?"

"Their big old place on the Sheffield road."

"Why would you want that?" Margot hissed.

"It's not for me."

Margot sat back, a puzzled expression on her face then she lurched forward. "You're not buying it for Em and Cameron, are you?"

This time it was Roslyn who was puzzled. "No, why would I do that?"

"You bought the van for Nick."

"I didn't exactly buy it—"

"That was a business loan, Margot," Dennis said. "Why would Roslyn just up and buy a house for Emily?"

"Because she knows I wanted that house for Emily."

Roslyn's eyebrows shot up.

"Since when?" Dennis said.

"I only heard the Threadgolds were selling the other day. I haven't even spoken to Em and Cam but it would be perfect for them."

"So how could I have possibly known?" Roslyn asked.

Margot pursed her lips and lifted her nose a little higher.

"It's a huge old place." Dennis shook his head. "It would need a ton of money spent on it."

"In which case what good would it be to Roslyn?" Margot's gaze narrowed as she leaned in a little closer. "You're being very odd, you know, Roslyn. You're tossing your money about lately."

"I told you I was helping out, finding some local information for the Hub."

"Where would the Hub get the money to buy that place and to spend on doing it up?"

"Sometimes they get bequests," Dennis said and as he did Roslyn saw the looks on both their faces change.

"Did Gunter leave money for the Hub?"

Roslyn gritted her teeth. She didn't like to lie directly. "In a way."

"In what way?" Dennis asked.

Margot's eyes grew wider. "It's got something to do with that meeting you had with Elvin and Xavier, hasn't it?"

"Why were you meeting with them?" Dennis said.

Between both their sharp gazes Roslyn felt like a butterfly pinned to a board. She couldn't make an excuse to go home – she was already there.

"You've been up to your neck in this business with Gunter's property from the start, haven't you?" Margot snarled. "Sneaking around, keeping secrets." She gasped. "How much did they pay you?"

"That's none of your business."

"You seemed to know a lot about the sale of the property," Dennis said. "Did you get a cut from it?"

Roslyn thought she was maintaining a straight face but Margot gasped and grabbed her arm. "You did! I can't believe it. You probably sat in on the decision on who won the expression of interest."

"I did not. That was between the agent and the executors, who were following Gunter's wishes."

"But you were in on it somehow," Margot persisted.

"They asked my advice on a few things."

Dennis's shrewd eyes pinned her again. "Such as?"

Roslyn glanced towards the pool but all the young ones were still having fun there and neither Emily nor Geraldine had returned from the house. There was no escape.

"Look," she said. "I was asked to keep things to myself until Gunter's legacy was locked in."

"What legacy?"

"Locked in how?"

"You must keep this to yourselves." Roslyn glanced towards the house again. "Gunter wanted someone to purchase his place who might build some kind of business that would include supporting the local community in some way, particularly marginalised people—"

"How would a boutique hotel do that!" Margot snapped.

Roslyn ignored her. "It wasn't just about the highest bidder. Each of the prospective purchasers was asked to show how they might do this in any plan they had for the property."

"We weren't asked, were we, Dennis?" Margot glanced at her husband.

"No." He took a large gulp of his wine.

Roslyn was trapped. Dennis wasn't lying when he said they hadn't been asked to submit a proposal because they'd never put in an offer. She'd seen the list even though she shouldn't have. For whatever reason Dennis had let Margot believe they'd put in a bid and Roslyn wasn't going to be the one to open that can of worms.

"As I said, I wasn't part of that process but once the sale went through my job's been to investigate how Gunter's money can be best spent in our community to support those in need."

"Why you?" Margot asked.

Roslyn shook her head. "We were friends." She hadn't asked for the burden Gunter had placed on her but she had to admit it had given her a purpose she'd been lacking in her life since her retirement.

"We were Gunter's friends too," Margot said. "We often caught up with him. I cooked him the odd meal or treat. Dennis helped him out when he needed an extra pair of hands sometimes."

"It's not a competition, Margot," Roslyn snapped. "I didn't ask for this job."

"But I'd be thinking you've been paid well for it," Dennis said. "A cut of the profits perhaps?"

"Yes. Why can't you tell us?" Margot leaned closer. "We're family, after all."

"Because it's not about the money, it's about the good that can be done with it."

"Dennis is right, isn't he?" Margot went on as if Roslyn hadn't spoken. "That place sold for a ridiculously high price and you got a percentage of the sale."

Roslyn sucked in a breath through pursed lips. Margot was getting worked up and it was hard to deflect her when she got like this.

"Allowing this awful development to go ahead so you could line your own pock—"

"Hey, hey." Nick's placating call cut across Margot's tirade. "What's going on here?" He studied them from the end of the table, the hand he'd been using to rub at his wet hair with a towel still as he looked from one to the other.

"Your aunt's proving yet again how sneaky she is," Margot said. "She's been in cahoots with the developer of the hotel. My own sister!" She glared at Roslyn. "You don't care that a hotel will ruin our community – it's all about the money!"

There was a brief moment when no words were spoken, when the chatting and splashing sounds of those still at the pool filled the hurtful space left by Margot's words. Roslyn knew from experience there was no point trying to reason with her sister when she got this worked up.

"Mum." Emily's worried call drew their attention to the house. "I don't think Geraldine's very well but she won't let me do anything."

Margot sighed and rose to her feet. "Where is she?"

"Inside. She's okay but she's very pale. Amber's sitting with her."

Margot strode off and reluctantly Roslyn followed her. It was her house, after all.

Inside, Margot shooed Amber from her position beside Geraldine. Amber made a face and stepped out of the way.

"I brought some dishes inside and found her bent over your island bench," Amber murmured. "Then Emily came out and we got her to sit here and have a glass of water."

"Thanks." Roslyn stood in front of the two women on the couch. Margot was patting Geraldine's hand soothingly.

"You really don't seem to have been well for a while, Geraldine," Roslyn said. "Have you seen a doctor?"

"Not lately. I've been to the counsellor though."

"She's always had an irritable tummy and with the Christmas food…" Margot's voice trailed away.

"You appear to have lost quite a bit of weight in the last week or so," Roslyn said.

Geraldine nodded. Her wan face turned to Roslyn full of trust.

"Any pain?"

She waved vaguely over her stomach area.

"Other symptoms?"

"Nausea sometimes and I feel bloated. And lately the diarrhoea." Geraldine shook her head. "But there's no blood."

"It could be a persistent bug." Margot patted Geraldine's hand again.

"It could," Roslyn said. Dammit, it could be any one of a million things but it did need investigation. "You should see your GP again and get some tests."

Geraldine's hand went to her mouth. "You think I've got what your husband had, don't you?"

"I'm not thinking anything other than you've been feeling unwell for a while, you have a variety of symptoms and you've lost weight, so you need to see your doctor again."

"But I could have bowel cancer." Geraldine's eyes were wide in her pale face, full of alarm.

"I'm sure it's not that." Margot tutted then looked up at Roslyn. "Now you've upset her. You don't like giving medical advice, Roslyn, remember."

"I'm only doing what any concerned person would do."

"For goodness sake, you didn't intervene when your own husband was sick – why would you stick your bib in now?"

Roslyn's breath whistled over her teeth and her fingers clenched so tightly to her palms that her nails dug into her skin.

Margot patted Geraldine's shoulder. "You might just have one of those irritable tummy sessions you get sometimes."

Geraldine drew herself up. "I think I'll go home."

"Should she be on her own?" Emily asked.

Roslyn glanced around. She'd forgotten Emily and Amber were there. They both looked uncertainly between the three older women.

"Why don't you stay the night with us?" Margot soothed.

"I'm feeling a bit better now." Geraldine rose to her feet and Margot stood too.

"Would you like me to drive you?" she asked.

"No, it's not far."

Roslyn stepped back as the two made for the door. If she was within arm's length of her sister she'd be tempted to strike her.

They stopped at the door and Geraldine turned back. "Thank you, Roslyn. It's been lovely." Then she looked to Margot. "I'm fine now. I'll just say goodnight to the others and be on my way."

"I'll ring you in the morning," Margot said.

"You're off, Geraldine?" Dennis met his sister-in-law in the doorway, hugged her goodnight and came inside. He looked to his wife. "She seems okay?"

"No thanks to Roslyn," Margot snapped.

"Mum," Emily cautioned.

"It's been a big day," Dennis added quickly. "Might be time to head home."

He was probably being wise but Roslyn was past being wise with her irritating sister. "Geraldine has been unwell for a while. Suggesting she see a doctor is common sense."

"Don't speak to me as if I'm silly. Of course it is but you didn't have to grill her. Now she thinks she's got cancer."

"She's what?" Dennis said.

"We don't know what's wrong so there's no point jumping to conclusions," Roslyn snapped.

"That's not your usual style, is it? Poor Richard would attest to that if he was here."

Behind Roslyn Emily gasped. "Mum," she whispered.

"Oh my sainted aunt, will you let it go?" Roslyn shook her head. "Richard kept his symptoms to himself for too long." Roslyn's breath faltered and the heaviness of regret settled in her chest. "It wasn't until after he'd died I found all the unused screening tests scattered amongst his things."

"You were his wife and a doctor."

"And he was an adult responsible for his own health. I didn't check up on him nor did he me. Do I wish I had? Of course. But it never crossed my mind that he wouldn't do the simple test that might have saved his life." Her words hung in the air, heavy with regret, sorrow and loss. It had truly surprised her when after his diagnosis Richard had admitted to overlooking the bowel screening. He'd been such a sensible man in every other way.

An arm came round Roslyn's shoulder. She expected it to be Emily and was surprised when she glanced around and the concerned eyes staring back at her were Amber's.

"I think you lot should clear out," Amber said. "Roslyn's entitled to some peace in her own bloody house."

"You'd defend her, of course, with your cosy accommodation deal," Margot spat. "Don't come to us for help when it all goes pear-shaped again, Roslyn."

"Mum, let it go," Emily murmured from behind.

"We should go home." Dennis put an arm around his wife's shoulders and began to steer her to the door. "We all need a good sleep and we'll clear the air tomorrow."

"Don't bother," Roslyn and Margot snapped in unison then Roslyn pulled a wry smile. "At least we can agree on that."

thirty-five

Amber carried a tray outside with all the things for tea laid on it. After Margot's meltdown she'd left and so had Emily and her family. Nick and Kayla and their boys were still there, and Tom, of course, although he'd headed back to the cottage to shower. He'd been oblivious to the family blow-up that had taken place inside. Kayla had been the one to suggest tea and to Amber's surprise Roslyn had let the two of them organise it in her kitchen while she sat outside with Nick and the boys.

Only the women had tea. Amber suspected Nick might have if Tom hadn't promised to have another beer with him on his return. The two young boys were lying on their towels stretched out on the lawn, the little one asleep and the other listening to music on his dad's phone.

"Sounds like Mum went off her tree again," Nick said once the tea was poured.

"Why does she keep going on about the last tenants?" Amber asked. "What's that got to do with me?"

"Absolutely nothing." Roslyn sighed. "The last chap we had in there paid his rent on time and the bills for the cottage but it was only meant to be temporary and there was no formal agreement. Then unbeknown to us he let the second bedroom to two other men. We didn't see the extra money, of course, and they didn't look after the cottage very well."

Nick snorted. "That's an understatement. They almost trashed the place."

"Hmmm." Roslyn nodded. "It came to a head when they had a big party that went all night and into the next day. My husband was quite ill by then. Margot and Dennis had to take charge, the police were involved, it was awful and dragged out for ages. I had to refurnish the place once they finally left."

"I'm looking after the cottage," Amber said quickly.

"Of course you are. Anyway, that's all in the past." Roslyn shrugged. "I'd rather not talk about it any more. I don't want to add more fuel to Margot's fire." She glanced at Nick. "She already thinks I'm trying to steal you away from her."

"What?" he spluttered.

"Exactly my response," Roslyn said. "Now let's change the topic. I hope everyone's had a good day in spite of the last little upset."

"It's been a great Christmas," Kayla said.

"Better than last year, that's for sure." Nick grinned. "Remember one of the boys got a bee sting and his foot swelled like a balloon and the other broke that stupid plane thing—"

"It was a helicopter." Kayla chuckled. "And Isabella was coming down with that nasty flu so she was miserable. Poor Em was feeding Henry and she had a cracked nipple…"

"And Dad had done something to his knee. He was in a lot of pain."

"It was a tantrums-and-painkillers Christmas," Kayla said.

"I'd forgotten all that." Roslyn laughed.

Amber watched them over the rim of her cup. She was happy to see Roslyn relaxing again. She wasn't a bad old duck beneath the tough shell she usually put on. When Margot had been attacking her and Roslyn had talked about her husband she'd oozed heartbreak. Showing emotion wasn't something Amber associated with Roslyn and it had stirred something inside her too. That bloody Margot was a piece of work. Amber had thought her own family was dysfunctional but even though these people had money and nice houses they had their own set of problems.

"What about you, Amber?" Roslyn said. "I know you had to work but I hope you've had a good day."

"I have. And thanks for the books, Roslyn."

"You're welcome."

Amber suddenly remembered the present she'd wrapped for Roslyn. "How stupid. I forgot all about the gift I got you."

"You didn't have to get me anything."

"It's not much but…" She shrugged awkwardly. "I thought you might like it. I had a chocolate each for the kids too." She glanced at the boys then back to Kayla. "You can take it home for them for another day. I'll be right back."

Amber set off towards the cottage, cross with herself for forgetting. She'd been anxious when she'd got home from the pub. Knowing Tyson was nearby had set every nerve on edge. She'd been glad when Tom had arrived and they'd gone straight to the pool where it had been good to be in a group. She'd been keenly aware of Margot's snooty looks but everyone else had been welcoming. Even when Roslyn had quietly given her the books Amber had still not thought of the odd little gift she'd found in an op shop.

She let herself into the cottage where there was music playing from the bathroom and the sound of the shower still running. She winced. She hadn't told Tom about the issue with water and short showers. She'd skip one herself to make up for it.

The lights were off in the rest of the cottage except for the spare room off the lounge where Tom was going to camp the night. A small amount of light filtered around the partly open door. Amber felt along the wall for the lounge switch.

A hand came from behind and went over her mouth. She jumped and the contents of her stomach threatened to rise up as she heard a familiar voice in her ear.

"Found you, bitch."

She struggled but Tyson had pulled her arm up behind her back and the pain of it took her breath away. She tried to twist her mouth from his grasp to suck in some air.

"Stop fighting me or that baby of yours will get a punch."

She stilled immediately, putting her free hand to her belly.

"I'm going to let you go now but if you yell or try anything silly, I'll fuck you up before you know it." He yanked her arm harder. "Okay?"

She nodded through the pain.

He let her go and she sagged to a chair, cradling her arm. She glanced towards the bathroom, hoping Tom would stay in there. He was a small guy and no match for the muscly shitface towering over her.

Tyson squatted down in front of her. "It'd be a shame to break your new boyfriend's pretty nose so keep your trap shut. I won't be here long."

"He's not my boyfriend," Amber hissed.

"Yeah, whatever." He reached forward and traced his fingers down her neck to the top of her shirt. She shrunk away from him and he dropped his hand back to his side, disgust on his face.

"Kids change women. I told you to get rid of that baby."

"How did you even find me?"

"Did you think I wouldn't?" He grinned. "Cory's a good mate. Told me he'd run into you and that you were still preggers. He followed you that day but he lost you on the edge of town. Small place like this, if you buy enough beers at the local pub you can find out whatever you need. It wasn't a surprise to find out you worked there." His grin turned to a sneer. "What else are you good for now you're preggers? Then I found some guy at the bar today who was happy to tell me where you were living."

Amber sank lower into the chair. She'd been stupid to think she could hide in such a small place.

"So now I'll just collect my property and I'll be off."

"What property?" The voice from the door accompanied by the light flicking on startled them both.

Tyson leaped to his feet and swung around, his fists clenched. Amber blinked in the sudden brightness then felt sick all over again at the sight of Roslyn alone in the doorway.

"Who the hell are you?" Tyson snarled.

"My landlord."

"A friend."

Amber and Roslyn spoke at once.

"You'd better get back to where you came from. This is between me and Amber." Tyson spoke dismissively, rightly deducing, in Amber's opinion, that Roslyn was no threat.

Roslyn brought her arm forward and lifted some kind of bat-club thingy to her shoulder. "No-one needs to get hurt," she said calmly. "Kindly explain what you're doing here."

Tyson looked from Amber to Roslyn then he laughed. "Kindly explain? Are you one of those English ladies, head of the castle or something? And what do you reckon you're gunna do with that?" He jerked a hand towards the thing in Roslyn's hand.

The water stopped in the bathroom but not the music. Once more Amber glanced towards the bathroom and this time she hoped Tom would come out. One or two people wouldn't bother Tyson but three of them together might be more of a threat. And Roslyn had that club thing but would she use it?

"This is my property and you're trespassing."

"Is that right." Tyson took a step towards Roslyn then as quick as a striking snake he grabbed for the handle she held.

Amber was surprised at just how fast Roslyn snatched it away from his grasp and even more so when Nick appeared behind her at the same time as the bathroom door opened.

"What are you all doing?" Tom asked brightly then his face fell as he noticed Tyson. "You're the bloke that's been stalking Amber."

"I have not." Tyson looked back at Amber. "What crap have you been telling people? Just give me the keys to the car and you can all go to hell – or not, I don't care. I won't bother you again."

"Why are you bothering her now?" Roslyn took a step into the room with Nick and Tom on either side of her as if they were all joined at the hip.

Tyson ignored the question and turned back to Amber. "Give me the bloody keys."

Amber's glance darted from him to the other three. Tom was waving a hand at her to move back.

"Why should she do that?" Tom said loudly.

Tyson swung back to him. Amber rose carefully and edged around so the chair was between her and Tyson.

"It's my bloody car," he roared.

"It's registered in my name." Amber's chin jutted forward. She was more confident now that she was out of his reach and had three friends in the room.

"Only 'cause you tricked me."

"I didn't," she shouted back.

"If the car is registered in Amber's name, why do you think it's yours?" Roslyn asked.

"If the car's registered," Tyson mimicked Roslyn in a silly voice. "I paid for the bloody car so it's mine."

"I paid a thousand towards it and it's registered to me." Amber glanced at Roslyn. "I've got the paperwork."

"Good," Tyson snarled. "You can transfer it to me and I'll be on my way."

Nick pulled out his phone. "I'm calling the police. They can sort it."

Amber's heart skipped a beat and the baby prodded from within. She didn't want the police involved. They might take Tyson's side.

"Okay, okay." Tyson patted the air. "If Amber pays me back the money it cost me I'll let it go."

Amber snorted. "As if."

"How much?" Roslyn asked.

Tyson folded his arms across his chest and looked Roslyn up and down. "Forty thousand."

"You paid under seven thousand for it," Amber said. "And a thousand of that was mine."

"Yeah! But the old lady who was selling it had no idea of its worth."

He wasn't lying about that. Amber had wondered why he'd spent his last savings and conned some from her to buy a second car. So when Immi had said he was looking for her she'd known it had been the car he'd wanted. What she hadn't realised was exactly how much more it was worth until Dennis had brought it up and she'd googled it.

"So you ripped off an old lady," Amber sneered at him. "Geez, Tyson, you're a really good bloke."

He swung his hand at her but she ducked away.

"Right! Calling the police now." The authority in Nick's voice pulled Tyson to an abrupt halt as he was careering around the chair to Amber.

He turned back and held up his hands. "Okay. I'll go."

Roslyn put a restraining hand on her nephew's arm. "If he leaves now and doesn't show his face here again we've no need to call the police." She stepped to one side of the door, guiding Nick with her, and Tom moved to the other, leaving a wide path for Tyson.

He flicked one last hateful glare at Amber and strode past them.

"And you won't ever be coming back here or bothering Amber again," Roslyn said.

Tyson stopped in the hall where the lines on his face were illuminated by the light from the bathroom, giving him an evil look. "She owes me."

"I think you owe her far more."

"Whadda ya mean?"

"Child support."

Tyson's mouth fell open. "That little bastard she's carrying isn't mine."

Amber put a protective hand over her belly. "It is," she hissed. "But don't worry, you'll never see it."

"You don't need to be present in your child's life but you do have to pay for its care." Roslyn spoke calmly, patting the club still resting lightly on her shoulder. "If the car is worth as much as you say, that should cover it."

"No-one can prove it's mine," Tyson spat.

"Oh, yes, we can."

All eyes were on Roslyn as she held up the bat. "Your DNA is on this and on several things I've seen you touch in this room."

Tyson focused on Roslyn. His eyes narrowed. "Bitch."

"Just one of the many names I've been called in my time." She lifted her chin. "Now are we clear? The car is child support so you will never come near Amber again. If you do, the police will be called."

Tyson glared at them all one last time then with a growl of rage he spun and strode out the front door.

Amber sank slowly to the floor as the jelly in her legs turned liquid providing no strength to hold her up.

"I'll follow him," Nick said. "Kayla's in the house with the boys. I want to be sure he leaves."

"I'll come with you." Tom followed him out the door.

Roslyn sat in the chair beside Amber and rested the bat beside her. "Are you all right?" she asked.

Amber nodded. Her voice had deserted her as well. She noticed a tremble in Roslyn's fingers as she wiped them on her skirt. "What about you?" she croaked.

"I'm fine."

"What made you come?"

"Nick's oldest said he'd seen someone in the shadows going down the drive. I thought he meant Tom but he said he thought it was after Tom left. Then he wasn't sure what he'd seen. You'd been gone a while and Nick and Kayla were inside doing dishes so I sent him in to tell his parents and I decided to investigate."

"With a...what is that thing?" Amber pointed to the long-handled object with its cylindrical base that was propped between them.

"A croquet mallet. I got them out earlier this afternoon in case anyone wanted to play but you were all in the pool so I didn't bother suggesting it. It was the nearest handy thing."

"He drove off in a hot-sounding ute." Nick was back with Tom.

"That'd be his," Amber said.

"There was someone else with him," Tom said. "Just caught a glimpse of her before he shut the door."

"Probably brought his new girlfriend to drive the car back for him." Amber's blood still boiled at the thought of him taking the car.

Nick shook his head at Roslyn. "I'm not sure I should have let you stop me calling the police."

"Imagine how busy they'd be tonight," she said. "We'd have had to keep him here somehow and short of actually hitting him on the head with the mallet, I'm not sure we'd have been able to restrain him. I thought it better to try to scare him away."

"Is it true you've got his DNA and you can prove the baby is his?" Amber asked.

"I've no idea but I was betting he didn't either." Roslyn chuckled then they were all laughing as the tension of the night's events overflowed.

Tom flopped to the floor beside Amber and put a gentle hand on her shoulder. "He didn't hurt you, did he?"

"No, thanks to you lot." Amber looked at each of her helpers in turn.

"I'm glad you weren't on your own," Tom said.

"How did you know who he was?" Amber asked.

"After you left the pub today Fred asked each of us to quietly take a good geek at him so we'd know what he looked like. Your friend the sous chef even had a drink with him."

"That creep Ivan. He was probably the one who told Tyson where I was living."

"What's to stop him coming back?" Tom looked up at the others.

"Is the car really registered in your name?" Nick asked.

"Yes," Amber snapped.

"Chill." Nick put up a hand. "I was just checking."

"Tyson bought the car over the phone. Sent me to collect it. That's why it's got my name on the papers."

"What if you sold it?"

Amber shrugged. When she'd found out the car was possibly worth a lot more than Tyson had paid for it she'd thought of it as her investment for the future.

"I'm guessing it's probably not insured," Nick said.

Once again Amber shrugged. She'd never thought about insurance.

"Why would you say that?" Roslyn asked.

"A V8 like that registered to a…" he glanced at Amber, "under twenty-year-old. It'd cost an absolute fortune."

"Oh dear," Roslyn said.

"How would I get around if I sold it?"

"In a different car," Nick said. "One that's cheaper to run and not so big."

"If there's no car to chase he might be more likely to stay away," Roslyn said.

They all pondered that a moment then Nick's phone buzzed.

"It's Kayla," he said. "She's wondering what's going on. I told her to stay inside with the boys and lock the doors."

Roslyn nodded. "You go and take them home, we'll be fine."

"I will, on one condition."

Roslyn's eyebrows quirked up. Amber recognised it as the look she gave when she was challenged.

"You turn on the security cameras I installed for you a few years back that you never use."

"They're a nuisance. I get a phone alert if someone sneezes."

Nick tipped his head to one side. "They're not that sensitive but they do show you anyone coming up the drive or approaching your front and back doors."

Roslyn glanced at Amber then back to Nick. "All right."

"Good." He nodded at Tom and gave Amber a quick smile.

"I'll come back to the house with you," Roslyn said. "Say goodnight to Kayla." She turned to Amber. "I'll leave you the mallet." They both looked at the weapon still propped against the chair. A smile twitched on Roslyn's lips. "And make sure you lock up."

"I'll look out for her." Tom flopped an arm over Amber's shoulders after she'd locked the door behind Roslyn.

Amber smiled. Tom was a lightweight. Tyson could have flattened him with a shove but it was Tom's kindness and that of Roslyn and Nick that spread a warmth through her chest, a cosy feeling she wasn't used to. Even with Tyson's visit it was still the best Christmas she'd ever had.

thirty-six

The morning after Christmas Margot woke with the most terrible headache and did something very rare for her – she stayed in bed. Dennis had tried to talk to her but she'd taken pain tablets, stuck her head under the pillows and sent him away. She'd dozed for a while but all the things she'd said and Roslyn had said kept replaying in her mind. By mid-morning when Dennis came in with a cup of tea and some toast she sat up to accept it.

"I'm off," he said with a peck on her cheek.

Margot focused on him and realised he was in his golf clothes. He played a round with a group of his mates every Boxing Day.

"Enjoy," she said.

Dennis lingered by the bed, concern on his face. "Once you're feeling better, perhaps you should go over to see Roslyn, clear the air."

Margot almost choked on the toast she'd bitten off. "Me? If anyone should be apologising, it's Roslyn. She's always looked down her nose at us, Dennis, a car salesman and a secretary. She's flaunted the money she made and now she's using it to buy our children's affection, make herself look good in the community.

I've put up with her overbearing, condescending ways all my life." Margot slapped her hands on the bedcovers and made the tea slop wildly. "Why should I be the one to apologise?"

He put his hands in the air. "Okay, take it easy then. I'll see you this afternoon."

"We're eating leftovers for dinner," she called after him.

There was no response. In the distance a door closed. Margot settled back against the pillows and slowly sipped her tea. Perhaps she'd stay in bed all day.

Emily and Cam were off visiting his family and Nick and Kayla hers so Margot wouldn't be seeing any of them today. She'd also decided she'd take Kath's suggestion of a holiday from the Providore, which meant she wouldn't be back there for over a week. She'd have all that time to think about the Prov and her future there, although it did make her sad when she pondered the changes Kath was making.

And of course there was her mayoral campaign to work on and her "stop the hotel" crusade. With the petitions she'd already collected they were well on their way to having the numbers to submit that to council in the new year. She planned to collect the rest in her time off. There was also the town meeting to reorganise. It seemed so long ago she'd visited the council office about the proposed hotel. She needed to revisit her jotted notes and set a new date for a meeting so she could share the details with the others.

Margot reached for her phone. Her finger hovered over the Jesserton Jabber icon then she lowered her phone to the bed. She wasn't feeling strong enough to deal with any negativity today. Although if those who wanted the hotel were leaving the group perhaps there wouldn't be any. It saddened her to think the hotel was dividing the usually supportive community so dear to her heart. The people of Jesserton had always pulled together for major projects in the past.

It didn't really surprise her that someone like Tess Brown would think a fancy hotel was a good idea but that sensible people like Kev and Sandy had obviously changed their minds? That had been a shock.

The phone beneath her fingers began to ring and when she lifted it up it was Geraldine's name on the screen. Margot pressed her fingers to her lips. She hadn't even given her sister-in-law a thought this morning.

"Hello, how are you?" Margot spoke brightly, hoping to deflect Geraldine from giving too many details. She didn't have the strength for it today.

"I'm feeling a bit flat but not too bad," Geraldine said. "I think Roslyn's right though, I should go back to the doctor so I'll make an appointment as soon as they open again."

"Well, of course you should go to the doctor," Margot gushed to cover her annoyance at the mention of Roslyn. "I'm sure I suggested that too. I've got some time off so I could come with you if you like."

"That's very kind of you, Margot, but Roslyn's going to come with me."

"Roslyn!" Margot nearly choked again and this time there was no toast in her mouth, nothing but a bitter taste.

"She rang this morning to see how I was and—"

"Roslyn did?"

"Yes. It was kind of her to check on me. I said I was going to get an appointment as soon as possible and I asked if she'd come with me."

"Roslyn!" Margot was stuck on repeat like a cracked record. "Why not me?" she squeaked.

"Roslyn's a doctor."

"Roslyn's retired and she was an anaesthetist, not a GP."

"She understands medical-speak," Geraldine soothed. "You know how doctors rattle on with all those complicated words and you forget half of what they said before you've left the surgery. I thought Roslyn would be able to take it in better and decipher it for me."

"If that's what you want." Margot sniffed. "As long as you're all right for now I won't hold you up."

"I was just going to say—"

"I'm glad you're okay. Talk later." Margot cut Geraldine off and jabbed at her phone to end the call. She tossed it aside along with the breakfast tray, got up and paced the room. Roslyn didn't even like Geraldine. Was there no end to her infiltration of Margot's family? Roslyn was family, of course, but she'd never interfered with Margot's. Now she was giving Nick money, chumming up with Geraldine – even Emily and Dennis had seemed to be taking Roslyn's side last night.

Roslyn was seven years older than Margot and all their lives she'd played the big-sister card. She'd been first to do everything, naturally, because she was older in many instances, and Margot had always looked up to her, but there were times when age didn't matter but Roslyn would always say *you're too young to do that yet* in a superior tone.

Like when their dad took Roslyn to work with him. It would sometimes happen on the days when their mum was suffering with her arthritis and Margot usually got sent to the family next door who had kids her age. Their dad worked in hospital administration and his office was a much more interesting place with forms and folders, all kinds of papers and pens, and adding machines and typewriters that Margot had thought were fancy machines back then. She'd loved playing in his office but it was usually Roslyn who went with him. She'd tell how she'd file papers, stamp letters, run errands, even do some basic letter typing. All he let Margot do was put the address on the back of envelopes with a rubber stamp.

When Roslyn was fourteen she'd had her hair cut to shoulder length. At seven Margot had wanted to have hers shorter as well, arguing it was nothing to do with age, but their mother had said her auburn curls were too pretty to cut off. Of course Margot had taken to the hair herself with the scissors and then she'd been miserable for weeks when her mother had marched her off to the hairdresser to fix it and she'd ended up with a boy haircut. Roslyn had shaken her head and queried her sanity.

And when Margot was twelve she'd wanted to be an air hostess. She'd turned the lounge room into a plane using the armchairs plus the kitchen chairs to create an aisle and delivered pretend food and drinks, cushions and magazines to fictitious passengers. At nineteen Roslyn had started university and had ridiculed Margot's ambitions as being nothing but a glorified waitress. It had spoiled Margot's fun to think her adored big sister didn't believe her ambition a good one.

In spite of that and the many other times Margot had been second fiddle to Roslyn, they were sisters and living next door to each other and they'd maintained a closeness others envied. Margot stopped pacing and hit her fist into her palm. She had better things to do than be thinking about bloody Roslyn. She marched to the tallboy and tugged open the drawer that contained her underwear. The photo propped on top wobbled with the force. She reached out a hand to steady it then paused to take it in. A photo of Margot and Roslyn with their parents taken a year or so before their mum had died. Margot had been sixteen and Roslyn in her early twenties and studying hard. Margot smiled and trailed a finger over their happy faces. They'd been at a church luncheon.

She stiffened, straightened the photo and gathered some fresh underwear. There was no time for reminiscing – she had a lot to do. Top of her list had to be planning the next meeting about the hotel. She turned her back on the photo and strode to the shower, a plan of action already forming.

"Oh yum, that's divine." Amber spoke through a mouthful of strawberry that Roslyn had plucked straight from the bush.

Roslyn smiled as a trickle of red dribbled over Amber's lip and down her chin. Tom and Amber had joined Roslyn for brunch by the pool. The two younger people had had another swim and then Tom had gone off to work. Amber had eaten a few strawberries from the platter of fruit and had been amazed when Roslyn said she'd grown them so Roslyn had taken her on a tour of her vegetable garden.

"Surely you've eaten strawberries before."

"Not as good as this," Amber said, popping another in her mouth.

"I think they taste better straight off the bush. They're warm and juicy."

"I didn't realise they grew like this."

"Did you think they grew in punnets in the supermarket?" Roslyn teased.

"No, but I didn't realise you could have a patch in your backyard like this."

"My friend, Gunter, who used to live the other side of Margot, helped me set this up. He was a much better gardener than me but somehow I've learned a few things from him."

They'd wound their way through the vegetable patch and were now close to Roslyn's side fence.

"Your sister has a fancy garden." Amber was looking along the path to where the wire gate through to Margot's yard was visible.

"Hers is much more formal than mine. I like the more natural look; native trees and plants, a small patch of lawn by the pool and a few flowers. And my fruit trees and vegetables, of course."

"She was pretty fired up last night."

"Margot can overdramatise things." Roslyn turned her back on the gate and strolled along the path towards the house. Her sister had always been good at tantrums to get her own way. When they were kids it'd often worked in Margot's favour, much to Roslyn's disgust. Margot had grown out of that behaviour but sometimes she'd still flare up about something that she felt was wrong or unfair.

Still, Roslyn had been shocked by last night's outburst. She'd forgiven her sister many small slights over the years but the venom she'd poured out had been hurtful. Lately Margot's tantrums had become more frequent and Roslyn was finding it harder to turn her big-sisterly cheek. It was only the other day Margot had apologised for her previous hurtful outburst and then last night she was right back at it again as if no reparatory words had been exchanged between them. There was certainly no way Roslyn would be visiting her sister any time soon to get another dose of that.

They were crossing the driveway and Amber paused to look towards the road. Roslyn had noticed her give several furtive glances in that direction during the morning.

"Are you worried Tyson will come back?" she asked.

Amber shrugged. "I don't know."

"Perhaps we should see the police. Apply for a restraining order."

Amber shrugged again. "You telling him you had his DNA might keep him away. He'll probably believe that. Back when we first met he'd lost his licence for a while. I don't know why but I think there may have been someone hurt. The police called on him a few times. He was happy to have me drive him around. Then earlier this year he was involved in a punch-up at the pub. Tyson was full of himself, flexing his muscles, acting like he was the bouncer. He got pinged for excessive force. He's not keen to see the police."

"The DNA thing was a bluff but he should be paying something for his child's care."

They continued walking along the drive towards the cottage and came to a stop beside Amber's car.

"If this is worth as much as Dennis seems to think, it might be worth trading it like Nick said."

"Maybe." Amber ran a hand almost reverently along the shining duco.

"You could accept Dennis's offer to take a look. He'd give you a fair appraisal."

"Are we talking to Dennis?"

Roslyn smiled at the question. "It was lovely of you to stick up for me last night but my sister picked a fight with me, not you. And Dennis tries to keep out of any…" Roslyn quirked an eyebrow, "disagreement we have. I'm sure he'd come over if I asked."

"Can I think about it?"

"Of course you can. It's completely your decision." Roslyn checked her watch. "Time's getting on and I've a bit to do so I'll leave you with it. Enjoy the rest of your day off."

"Thanks."

Roslyn set off back along the drive. Now that word had got out that she was asking about the Threadgolds' house and people already knew she was making a list of granny flats, it wouldn't be long until someone like Thelma put two and two together and came up with six. She really needed to nut out the finer points of her plan so that Elvin could make a start in the new year and any rumours could be nipped in the bud.

"Roslyn?"

She turned back at Amber's call.

The girl was coming towards her, holding out a small shape wrapped in Christmas paper. "I keep forgetting to give you this."

Roslyn took the gift without argument this time. She'd discovered Amber could be as stubborn as she was.

"What is it?"

Amber gave her a look that left Roslyn in no doubt as to the foolishness of the question. She peeled back the paper and then the bubble wrap. She looked at the strange object and then to Amber and then she began to laugh.

Amber grimaced. "Do you like it?"

"I love it." Roslyn held up the mug to look at it more closely. The ceramic bowl had been sculpted on the outside to give the impression of feathers and the handle was shaped and painted as the neck and head of a duck that looked very similar to the flying ducks on her wall. She laughed again. "I think it's truly one of the most thoughtful gifts I've had in a long time."

She flung out one arm and gathered Amber in a quick hug. The girl was stiff in her embrace but then gave her some pats before they stepped apart, nodded at each other and went their separate ways.

By late afternoon Roslyn was done. She shut down her laptop and stacked her various papers and booklets into one neat pile. Finally the scribbles and notes she'd been making for weeks had been collated into one concise document ready to send to Elvin once he was back at work. No longer just ideas and suggestions, but a detailed plan on how Gunter's Legacy could work.

Now that she had laid out her ideas in concise language, she was hopeful the group that ran the Hills Community Hub would also accept it. The whole thing relied on them adopting her ideas for Gunter's money as part of their program. Elvin had agreed with her that it was better to do that than begin a whole new charity, which was beyond their scope. Gunter's Legacy would add to the existing work and programs at the Hub in several ways – staffing, extra housing and a training-for-work program.

She sat back and glanced at her clock. It was almost five and she had another bottle of that nice rosé in her fridge. It was a shame that Margot had gone completely off the rails the previous evening. Now that the plan was almost ready to launch and the cat was partly out of the bag anyway, Roslyn would have enjoyed her sister's opinion on the workings of Gunter's Legacy. She was more hands-on with charitable work than Roslyn – she might notice where tweaks should be made.

Roslyn drew in a deep breath then slowly blew it out. Sadly there was no way she was crossing the yard to receive another dose of her sister's vitriol. Kayla would help, and of course the people who ran the Hub, but it would have been nice to have Margot's support. She took the wine from the fridge, and instead of pouring some into a glass she used the duck mug and raised it in the air towards the set on the wall.

"Here's to you, Gunter. Your kindness and generosity continues. I hope you'd like the plan."

Roslyn sipped her wine. She still wasn't totally comfortable with the task he'd put upon her but she'd given it her best shot. The sad thing was she was celebrating alone.

Margot stuck her head into the lounge. Dennis was still sprawled on the couch watching the TV through the backs of his eyelids where he'd been since he came home from golf. She continued on to the kitchen and looked in the fridge. There was a half-drunk bottle of chardonnay left from the previous day. She took it out and poured a glass. Considering her slow start to the day it had ended up being very productive. She'd run her campaign ideas past Dennis later, maybe over dinner, along with the outline for the town meeting she'd organise after new year and her thoughts on the Prov.

That had been the most difficult and sad task, but in her head Margot had pulled every aspect of the business apart and reassembled it. She had to make Kath see their business was working well the way it was. Margot didn't want to change it nor did she want to give it up. There was as much of her blood, sweat and tears in the success of The General Providore as Kath's but Margot had no room in her life for extras.

While she'd eaten her simple lunch for one, Margot had got quite worked up as she'd jotted down the changes Kath was making and the impact that was having on Margot. Then she'd remembered to take the emotion out of her response, and, as hard as that had been, she'd crossed out and rewritten what she thought was a decent plan for them to move forward and both be happy.

The town meeting had taken her more time, although "town meeting" might be too broad a title now. It depended if there'd be a cross-section of people or only those still against the hotel. She'd gone through all the notes she'd taken from her meeting at the council, her research on the internet and what she'd found out about Meyer and Brightman's hotel proposal and put it all into a cohesive list.

One thing that had become obvious to her was that no matter how much she tried to keep her mayoral campaign neutral and with a broad platform – she'd remembered Kath's words that some who might vote for her might also want the hotel, and Roslyn saying Margot needed more than the hotel issue to build her campaign on – she'd discovered that it was almost impossible to keep the campaigns for stopping the hotel and for running for mayor separate. In her mind the two things were too firmly entwined. She'd got to the point where she needed to run it past someone else. She hoped that would be Dennis when he finally returned to the land of the living.

Every so often through the afternoon she'd thought of Roslyn when she wanted to test an idea and then she'd remembered how deceitful her sister had been and had continued on alone. Her list of negatives about the hotel proposal had grown and now she wondered if there was something rigged about the whole expression-of-interest thing for Gunter's property. She and Dennis hadn't been offered the same information as the other bidders. Roslyn had said that was nothing to do with her but Margot's trust in her word had been blown away. Perhaps Dennis should investigate it further. If something underhand had happened the whole sale process could be in doubt and that could add weight to stopping the hotel.

Margot glanced from her kitchen window in the direction of her sister's place. From this position she couldn't see it for the trees, of course, and that was just as well. If she saw Roslyn or even anything to do with her, in the next week, the next month… Margot took a sip of wine…the next year! it would be too soon.

thirty-seven

Amber drove into Mount Barker with a mix of anticipation and weariness. She was tired and had slept late. This was her first full day off since Boxing Day. The lead-up to New Year and then the event itself had been even bigger than Christmas at the pub. And the anticipation she felt was due to Dennis's visit the previous evening and the news he'd given her.

Roslyn had arranged for him to come over when he'd got home from work and before Amber did her evening shift at the pub. He'd been impressed with the good condition of her car and its low kilometres, and the ballpark figure he'd said she could possibly get for it had left her speechless. She'd done her own google search but not really knowing the exact model had kept the results broad, and then there were badges and series. She understood none of it.

Now as she pulled up in front of his dealership and took in the fancy cars on display she wondered if she'd really trade it for something more suitable, as Dennis and Nick and Roslyn had all suggested. She ran her hands around the steering wheel. This car had been her means of escape from Tyson – to a degree. She hadn't counted on him chasing after her, but then she hadn't known its full value then. It had also been a roof over her head, her portable home on and off, until she'd moved into the cottage. Trading it was as if she were betraying a good friend. On the other hand, Dennis had assured her she'd get another good car and the amount of money he'd suggested could be left over was more than she'd imagined she'd ever see in her bank.

She'd have to be careful but she'd be able to stay home with the baby for a bit longer before she went back to work. She could buy a new phone. Hers barely held charge at all any longer. And she'd be able to get decent childcare, maybe even a permanent place to live. She hadn't looked at rentals for a while and Roslyn hadn't mentioned it but the cottage wasn't a long-term solution.

Roslyn had offered to come with her to the car yard but Amber knew how busy she was with her work on the Hills Community Hub expansion. Besides, she needed to do this for herself, for the future, for her baby. She pressed a hand to her stomach. "For us, Beetle," she whispered. "I'm doing it for us."

An hour later she was driving home again in a smart Renault. She'd wanted to go to the supermarket but didn't dare take this car. It wasn't hers yet and the thought of an accidental knock or bump was too scary.

Dennis had asked her to leave the Holden with him. He'd made a few calls before she'd arrived and said he'd had some genuine responses, one from interstate. It might take several days but he was optimistic he could make a good sale for her and then she could buy a more suitable car. He'd shown her a couple of the second-hand cars he had in the yard that he thought would suit her better than the Holden, and when she'd shown interest in this one he'd suggested she drive it while he had her car. If she liked it and he sold the Holden he'd do a good deal for her and give her the difference.

Roslyn had looked strangely at him when he'd suggested the idea the previous night, as if he'd done something unexpected.

"Won't you take a cut?" Amber had asked.

"It's not necessary," he'd said. "I'm happy to do a favour."

"No catches?" she'd asked.

He'd held out his palms. "Car salesmen get a bad rap sometimes and maybe some of them deserve it, but I think you could do with a break and I'm happy to help."

Roslyn had beamed at him then and offered him a glass of wine.

Now she'd driven the car successfully through the busy traffic in town and onto the open road Amber felt just a little more relaxed as she cruised back to Jesserton. It was a hot January day but instead of putting on the aircon she lowered the window and let the wind rush across her face and toss her hair. Music played on the radio and she turned it up and belted out the chorus of "Cover Me In Sunshine" along with Pink, her baby tapping the odd beat from inside. Even though she noticed it more often, it was still a strange sensation she hadn't got used to. She drummed her fingers on the wheel in time to the music. The car was a breeze to drive. It didn't have the same power as the Holden but Dennis had said she'd get better fuel economy and it would be easier to park. And the fuel gauge actually worked. There'd be no more guessing about that.

Life was definitely on the up. Just one thing would bother her about selling the Holden for such a good price. Not about Tyson, it was karma where he was concerned, but she felt bad for the lady he'd ripped off. She'd been so kind to Amber when she'd picked up the car. She'd taken her inside to do the changeover at her kitchen table, made Amber a cup of tea and produced a delicious home-made cake. Then she'd talked about the car being her son's pride and joy but he'd been killed in an accident, and she'd got a bit teary. She'd said she didn't have money for his funeral and that's why she was in a hurry to sell the car. Like Amber, the lady hadn't known the true value of the car and Amber didn't like it when bad things happened to nice people.

Margot waited for Lani and the other casual girl to leave before she went in search of Kath. They'd not said much to each other since Margot had returned to work, other than polite banter about Christmas and any back and forth necessary to the running of their shop.

Kath was checking the till and looked up when Margot entered.

"Do you have time to chat?" Margot asked politely as if she were speaking to a stranger rather than her long-time friend and business partner.

"Of course," Kath said. "You just missed Thelma. She was bursting to tell everyone the culprit for the red paint incident's been found."

"Who was it? Can we believe Thelma?" Margot didn't know which question to ask first.

"Bloody free-range guy's young brother."

"Free-range? Oh, you mean Larry."

"Yes. His teenage brother was staying and heard the discussion about who liked the hotel idea and who didn't. He decided it'd be funny to pinpoint the businesses in favour."

"If it's true, I'm relieved. I'd hate to think someone we know here in town would do such an awful thing."

"Thelma says next time the kid's here Larry's sending him to apologise and to offer to do some jobs for those he made extra work for. He'd better not come my way or I'll put a flea in his ear."

"Doing some cleaning would be a good way for him to learn his lesson but I can't believe he'd take it upon himself to have done such a thing in the first place. Larry must have been very vocal about the hotel."

"Some people are getting quite worked up about it. I had two women nearly throw the coffees I'd just made them at each other this morning. They came in all friendly and both left in a huff and went their separate ways. I'm afraid it's going to be difficult to sit on the fence. People are either all for the hotel or all against it."

Margot nibbled at her fingernail. "But they don't have to fight about it, surely?"

Kath shrugged. "Anyway, I assume you wanted to chat about the business? I hope you've had time to think things over. We were very busy while you were away."

"Are you saying that's because I wasn't here?" Margot was still thinking about the hotel and the people who were supposedly boycotting places because of their owner's stance.

"Of course not – don't be so sensitive. We were busy, that's all. The weather's been great. There were lots of extra people about. Being open more hours has worked well."

"I wonder if the new supermarket will make any difference."

They both looked to their window and the huge sign adorning the front of the supermarket declaring a grand opening party for the next day.

"It's one of the things I need to talk to you about," Kath said. "The head honcho guy came to see me last week. He's wondering if we're interested in making a few salads and ready-to-eat meals they can put in their deli section. They'll stock a few of the things that are popular in their other shops but they're keen to have some local food as well. Meals people can take home and eat or heat and serve."

"Another thing." Margot groaned. "Who's going to do this extra work?"

"I knew you'd take a negative stance," Kath snapped.

"Don't get cross, Kath," Margot said placatingly. "Surely we can talk about this."

"We did. I told you what the supermarket guy told me and you immediately canned it. Good discussion, Margot." She snatched up the money bag and pushed past to the kitchen.

Margot followed. "Give me a break, Kath. It's the first I've heard about the extra cooking."

"You had a break," Kath snapped. "And I really had hoped it might have made a difference, that you'd come back smiling, refreshed and enthusiastic, but instead you've dragged yourself around the last three days as if you were about to have your head chopped off."

"I have not," Margot huffed.

"Lani asked me if you were unwell."

Margot opened her mouth then closed it again. She'd had lots on her mind and perhaps she hadn't been paying as close attention to the others as she should.

"We had such a good week here last week." Kath's eyes shone as she threw out an arm to take in the kitchen. "The new casuals are doing a great job – have you said more than a few words to them? And the others plus our permanent staff have really stepped up. It's as if the longer hours have given everyone some continuity, some incentive or something, I don't know." She shrugged. "Like it's been a new start as well as the new year."

"It's early days. With Christmas and New Year you haven't even had a full week yet."

"We have, you know. We've been open every day since taking the two days off over Christmas. Lani has really stepped up in the kitchen. She loves the cooking and she's good at it. Thank goodness, 'cause it's my least favourite thing."

Margot felt a little stab of something, hurt, jealousy maybe – the kitchen was generally her domain. Right from the start Margot had done most of the cooking while Kath had run front of house unless it was the weekend, of course, but then they always had Lani and one or two casuals to help. "I'm glad she's taking an interest," Margot said with just a touch of snippiness.

"She'll need some more training, of course."

"Well, I suppose I—"

"I was thinking TAFE part time."

"Oh."

"If the hotel goes ahead, the supermarket guy seemed to think they'd want to have a small menu of ready-made meals guests could access. The hotel won't have a restaurant so if people want to eat in they could order some kind of picnic hamper perhaps."

"From us?"

"I've no idea how it'll work yet. It all depends if the hotel goes ahead and then what they'll want exactly."

"Good grief, it just gets worse. You'll have us opening at night soon."

Kath pursed her lips.

"Don't tell me that's on your list of new things," Margot snapped.

"Of course it's not. We'll keep the earlier opening but we'll still be closing at the usual time."

"We!"

"I really had hoped you'd be with me on this."

"How can I be? It's too much!" Margot slapped a hand against her thigh.

Kath's shoulders drooped. "I don't think your heart's here any more, Margot."

"What are you saying?"

Kath pulled her shoulders back and looked Margot squarely in the eye. "Maybe it's time for you to let it go altogether."

Margot gaped at her friend, her head a whorl of thoughts, none of them kind. "That's what you've wanted all along, isn't it? You wanted my money and my help to get the Providore going and now that it's humming along you want me gone so you can build Kath's empire."

"Don't be ridiculous."

"That's a nice thing to say. You're the one being ridiculous, overextending us."

"If you're worried, I'll buy you out."

"With what!"

Kath shook her head. "I know I was on the bones of my bum after my divorce but I am capable of saving, investing, working hard."

"I work hard too," Margot shouted.

"When it suits you," Kath shouted back.

"You can be a real…bitch, Kath." Margot spat the words and a wave of rage, fuelled by the unfairness of Kath's claims, shuddered through her. She tossed off her apron and snatched up her bag. "Well, you've got your wish. I hope it doesn't choke you." She strode out of the back door, pulling it hard behind her. It had warped last winter and she had to tug it a second time to shut it. Over the thud she thought she heard Kath call but she didn't stop.

She made it to her car before tears began to roll down her cheeks. She managed to wrestle the door open, slide into the seat and rest her head against the steering wheel. How had she and Kath got to this? She wiped the tears from her cheeks with her hand then searched for a tissue to blow her nose. She needed a friend and she'd just walked out on one. Dennis wouldn't be home and she wouldn't darken Roslyn's door under any circumstance. She took a deep breath and pressed her fingers to her eyes. Geraldine had been going to the doctor earlier today but she'd no doubt be home now. Margot would go there for some TLC.

"Thanks for the tea, Geraldine." Roslyn sat the partly drunk cup back on Geraldine's coffee table. The tea had been too weak with too much milk but she'd sipped some of it to be polite. "It's time for me to be off home."

"Thank you for coming with me today. I found that locum doctor quite difficult to understand."

"He did have a strong accent but he was on the ball. I agree totally with his leaning towards coeliac disease, but the blood tests and the biopsy will give a better indication."

"I did try to tell him I've avoided gluten for years."

Roslyn gritted her teeth. "You're not strict with that, Geraldine."

"I let my hair down sometimes. It was worrying when the symptoms accelerated."

"As he said, you may have been a bit intolerant to gluten but something may have triggered this more serious condition."

"Serious?"

Roslyn held up her hands. "I mean, you'll have to be strict in avoiding gluten in your diet. No letting your hair down sometimes."

Geraldine's breath puffed over her lips and she sagged to her chair like a deflating balloon.

"As the doctor said, go on eating as normal for now and try not to worry."

"Will you come with me when I have the surgery?"

"It's not surgery, just a simple biopsy and yes, I can accompany you."

"Thank you." Geraldine managed a wan smile. "You've been so kind."

"Hello, Geraldine, are you home?"

They both sat up at the sound of Margot's voice and the rattle of the screen door as she came in.

"I'm glad to see you," Margot said as she burst into the kitchen then stopped in her tracks as she saw Roslyn.

"I assume your enthusiasm is for Geraldine, not me." Roslyn stood. "I'll leave you to it."

"It's not cancer, Margot. Isn't that a relief? I've got coeliac disease."

"You've still got to have that confirmed," Roslyn said with a sigh.

"Which isn't all that wonderful," Geraldine continued as if Roslyn hadn't spoken. "But I suspected and Roslyn says if I stick to the right diet I'll be fine."

"Well," Margot said. "That's good, isn't it?"

Her face was blotchy as if she'd been crying but Roslyn knew it would only cause trouble if she asked.

"I'll put the kettle on." Geraldine bustled to the bench. "Will you stay for another cup, Roslyn? It's lovely to have you both here. Have you seen the new supermarket's opening over the weekend? Won't that be great." Geraldine prattled on, oblivious to the wall of tension that was building in her kitchen.

Margot glanced towards the door.

"No!" Roslyn barked.

Margot winced and looked as if she were about to cry.

That had come out a bit sharper than Roslyn had intended. She cleared her throat. "Thank you, Geraldine, for the offer, but I really do need to get going."

Geraldine turned back from the sink and smiled. "All right then. I'll see you bright and early Tuesday morning. Roslyn's going to come with me when I have my operation."

"What operation?" Margot squeaked.

Roslyn let herself out with a sigh. Goodness knows what embellishments Geraldine would add to her story but Roslyn wasn't going to hang around and correct her.

thirty-eight

Amber pulled up in the street outside the Hills Community Hub. Instead of turning off the motor she left it running to keep the aircon on and took a moment to gather her thoughts. The Renault had been hers for a week now and the largest amount of money she'd ever seen had been deposited in her bank account. She still found it hard to believe.

A warm sensation enveloped her that had nothing to do with the heat of the January day or that she'd just finished a tiring lunch shift at the pub. As she'd been doing for days, she searched for the source of the almost carefree feeling that accompanied the warmth and finally, sitting here in her new car on this hot summer's day, it came to her. The money gave her some security, a state she'd rarely been in.

Even though she'd said goodbye to the Holden and she still didn't have a permanent place to live, she was buoyed by a sense of safety for her and her baby. Amber grinned in the rear-view mirror, poked out her tongue at her reflection then glanced around in case someone had seen her acting weird. The often busy street was empty at this late hour of the afternoon.

She looked along the road towards the Hub. She'd been attending weekly basic cooking sessions in the community kitchen and had found herself enjoying it. Roslyn had encouraged her to pick any vegetables she wanted from her garden. There were things she didn't recognise and others she had no idea what to do with but, between Roslyn and the woman at the Hub who made the most delicious stuff, Amber was expanding her usual two-minute noodles and canned meals to include more fresh food. Fred still encouraged her to have a meal at the pub but she was quite amazed when she made something tasty that Roslyn assured her was much better for her. She'd never thought of cooking as fun before.

Amber wasn't here for the cooking this time. Kayla had asked her to call in for a chat about how she might be able to help some of the other attendees start learning some bar skills. Amber wasn't sure what help she'd be. She'd never done any formal training but had learned on the job. No-one at the Hub had been judgey though, and Amber had been surprised at how quickly she'd felt comfortable there. The people she'd originally thought of as do-gooders might well be, but they seemed legit.

Amber took out her new phone and checked her bank balance as she'd been doing regularly ever since the money dropped into her account. The baby made a small jab-jab-jab inside her and her earlier buoyancy ebbed a little. No matter how much she pushed it to the back of her mind the niggle of regret returned every so often, sapping her contentment with its insistence. It was her other reason for coming to the Hub today and something she hoped Kayla might be able to help her with.

Helen from book club drew Roslyn aside at the end of the Hub meeting. "This project will be an amazing boost for our community," she said. Helen was one of the members of the Hub committee and she'd been particularly supportive of Roslyn's presentation.

"All thanks to Gunter," Roslyn said. She was extremely happy with the response she'd just had from her meeting with the committee who ran the Hub and the staff who worked there. Gunter's Legacy truly did appear to be taking shape and becoming a reality. The committee had agreed in principle to their part, which would involve an expansion of their already established program assisting people to learn new work skills.

"God bless him," Helen said. "I wish more people were as generous in life and in death as he was."

"He was a good friend to many."

"And well done for bringing a few more local businesses on board to add to our work-skills program. Hillvale Winery was a special coup. How did you convince the old tightwad that owns that place to be involved?"

"He likes the very delectable and very expensive pinot noir and chardonnay he makes from Gunter's hand-tended grapes. I reminded him of that long partnership, of how Gunter upskilled many people over the years who've ended up working in local vineyards and how happy Gunter would have been to see Hillvale involved. And if all goes to plan, Meyer and Brightman want to contract his winery to continue to manage and harvest Gunter's grapes." Another thing Gunter would have been happy about and Roslyn herself was pleased the vines weren't going to be ripped out.

"Well done you, I say, and I especially like the idea of the pre-employment program for mothers."

Roslyn nodded. "And even better we'll be able to offer them a place to live while they do the program now that the Threadgolds have agreed to sell their big place on the Sheffield road."

"And at such a reasonable price."

"I think Martin liked the idea of being seen as a bit of a philanthropist."

"Whatever it takes." Helen chuckled. "That program will fill a gap we've had. Our shelter is only a temporary solution but the house—"

"Goldie's Place, we're calling it." Roslyn quirked her eyebrows. "It was Martin's request."

Helen laughed again.

"The one sticking point is my granny flat idea. I can't get many on board with that." Roslyn had done her best to convince people that they could be on a roster system, offering a week to a month's accommodation to someone in need. To her disappointment only a few owners had shown any interest.

"It could still happen," Helen said. "It's been marvellous the way you've put the plan for it all together. No doubt Margot would have been a big help to you with that."

Roslyn wasn't sure whether to be annoyed that Helen thought she couldn't manage on her own or sad – she'd have loved Margot's help once Elvin had given the go-ahead, but since Christmas she'd only had glimpses of her sister. Roslyn had forged on alone. "She's very busy with her campaign for mayor."

"I bet she is. I hope she doesn't push the 'stop the hotel' barrow too hard though. She's got some stiff opposition and it might cost her some votes." Helen flapped a hand as if she was brushing away a fly. "Anyway, it's wonderful to see Gunter's Legacy coming to fruition under your steerage. It will be a bit to maintain but I'm sure you're more than capable."

"Oh, no." Roslyn pulled a face. "Once it's all set up I won't be involved any longer."

"But someone will have to represent your program on the committee."

"I'm not—"

"Hello, Roslyn, Helen." Kayla came from the kitchen followed by Amber.

"Nice to see you," Helen said. "I'd better get going. The pizzeria is busy tonight and we're short-staffed again. We love skilling people up but the last few have got jobs in the city and moved away. Good for them, but it means our list of casuals has dwindled."

"Helen looks happy," Kayla said. "Did the meeting go well?"

"It did."

"Why are you frowning then?" Kayla asked.

Roslyn lifted her chin. "I was just thinking on something else Helen said. Nothing bad though. The committee were all in favour so I can report back to Elvin and we can get things started."

"Fantastic," Kayla said.

"What are you two up to?" Roslyn smiled at Amber, who'd been so happy lately but was looking now as if she carried the weight of the world on her shoulders.

Amber opened her mouth then looked down at her feet.

"Amber's offered to give some tips to anyone looking for bar work," Kayla said quickly. "She's feeling a bit nervous about it so we're just going to map out a few suggestions on how to go about it."

"Great idea."

Amber looked up and nodded.

"You're quite capable, you know," Roslyn said.

Amber nodded again but the ready smile and the sparkle she'd had in her eyes since getting her new car had disappeared.

"I'll leave you to it." Roslyn set off for her car, sure that Kayla would be able to help Amber with whatever was bothering her.

Margot settled back in the passenger seat of Dennis's Audi and blew out a sigh as he manoeuvred the car out of the residential care centre car park.

"That went well." He reached over and patted her leg. "How are you holding up?"

"All right." She sighed again. They'd been at an afternoon tea talking to residents and Dennis had offered to go with her, which she'd been happy about.

"You don't sound pleased."

"I am."

"You're not worried about that chap who said a man should hold the esteemed position of mayor, are you? He's obviously a friend of Colin North's, the way he was sprouting on about needing a university in the Hills."

"No."

"You were quite sharp with him."

Margot frowned. "Was I?"

"I was impressed. You normally back down when someone confronts you like he did."

Margot had listened politely to the man's diatribe for a minute or two and then had spoken about equal rights in twenty-first century Australia and the financial implications of trying to build a university in the Hills. "I thought I rebutted quite well."

"You did, but with more force than you usually do."

Margot shrugged. "You've all told me I'm too much of a shrinking violet so I've been practising various techniques." She glanced at her husband. "In the mirror."

He laughed.

"Anyway, I'm not bothered by old-fashioned thinkers like that man. Hopefully they're a dying breed. It was something else that came up just before we left. I was chatting to a woman who'd been a friend of Gunter's wife and we were reminiscing about the great picnics we had at the Brosts'." Outside her window tall gums flashed past along the winding road and between the gaps in the bush she caught glimpses of the rolling valleys, dotted with cattle or vines and the odd dam. "It was such a beautiful property. It truly breaks my heart to think the cottage could be replaced by a hotel and the garden by driveways and parking bays. If only we could have bought the place."

"You really have to let that go, Margot."

"It's odd that we didn't get a chance to put forward our vision for the property though. Roslyn said all bidders were given the opportunity."

Margot turned back from the view and looked at her husband. He had sunglasses on and he was focused on the road so she couldn't see his eyes but she saw the twitch in his jawline. He was clenching his teeth.

"We discussed ballpark figures," she said. "But you never told me what our final offer was."

Dennis remained silent.

"There would have been a lot of money tied up in the Audi bid. What did we offer for Gunter's?"

"Doesn't matter now anyway," he snapped. "You know we could never match the offers that were being made."

Usually when Dennis was gruff she backed down but she was learning not to do that.

"What was our offer, Dennis?"

He was gripping the steering wheel so hard his knuckles were turning white.

"Dennis?"

"Oh, for goodness sake, Margot." He slapped one hand on the wheel so suddenly it startled her. "We didn't put in a bid."

Her mouth fell open as her brain tried to make sense of what he'd just said. Outside the midday sun belted down with such ferocity the landscape shimmered but inside the chill that ran through Margot had nothing to do with the perfectly tuned air conditioning.

Dennis glanced her way. "Money was tight trying to lock in the dealership and I knew we'd never get Gunter's place so there was no point."

"You lied to me?" Margot stared at the man she'd been married to for almost thirty years. She'd never doubted him and now she wondered how often he'd done it before.

"I didn't lie but you assumed our bid had gone in and I let you continue to think that."

"That's deception, Dennis. You lied by omission." The pain of his betrayal carved through her so sharply she gasped. "You know how badly I wanted that property."

"And that wasn't realistic, Margot. We've got enough on our plate without it."

"It was for Emily," she snapped.

"Why would we go into so much debt for Emily? She's got her own place and she and Cam are doing okay."

"We are living on a property I inherited. We got a good start from my parents."

"The block wasn't worth very much back then and we borrowed a lot to build the house and the additions you've wanted since."

"You wanted them too."

They pulled into their garage. Dennis stopped the car and turned to her. "Look, Margot. Taking on the Audi dealership was a much better business proposition. One of us has to think with our brain instead of our heart. If we'd bought Gunter's place the house would have needed a lot of work and it would be years before Em and Cam could pay us back."

"The vines would have been income."

"Yes, but it would have all been too messy. And did you even ask Em and Cam if it was what they wanted?"

"We talked about it the first time Gunter was thinking of selling."

"Things change. I'm fairly sure Cam wants a place closer to their business. They're open six days a week. If they move he doesn't want it to be far."

Margot shook her head. "I still can't believe you lied to me."

He swore under his breath, something she disliked.

"You've got to move on, Margot. The campaign for mayor is more important."

"Now I'm beginning to wonder how much you're truly supporting me with that."

"I'm here, aren't I?" He threw up his hands. "I should be at work."

"Go to bloody work then, Dennis!" she shouted and fuelled by incandescent rage she stormed into the house.

She filled a glass with water but her hands shook so much she had to use both to guide it to her mouth. She drained the glass, thumped it down on the bench and began to pace. What was happening with the people in her life? Her sister, her good friend and now her husband. People she'd trusted and relied on and they'd all been deceitful in their own way. Geraldine had become chummy with Roslyn and she even wondered about the loyalties of her own children.

She stopped pacing and drew herself up. It was midday and she had time for a quick bite to eat before her planned meeting with a group concerned about a bypass road that had been proposed to run through their properties and after that she was catching up with some parents of young ones who wanted an upgrade of their nearby playground.

She'd continue by herself if she had to, focusing on the needs of the community without those she'd thought would be by her side.

thirty-nine

Dinner at Roslyn's

Roast Chicken, Tossed Green Salad, Hot Chips

Strawberries & Ice Cream

Roslyn sat on the pool steps with her feet in the water and a glass of wine in hand while Amber and Tom swam. The day had been pleasantly warm and while the two younger ones had worked the day shift they both had the evening off so Roslyn had invited them for dinner. She'd bought a cooked chook from the new supermarket, thrown a bag of frozen chips in the oven and tossed some ingredients from her garden together for a salad.

It was Sunday and should have been their first family dinner for the year but Nick and Kayla were with her family for a special anniversary and Emily and Cameron had the weekend off and had headed to the beach with friends. Geraldine had decided to take things a bit quieter for a while since her diagnosis and from Margot there'd not been a word.

Roslyn had had a quick chat with Dennis over the side fence a few days prior. She'd given him some of the abundance of zucchinis and tomatoes she was still harvesting. He'd said Margot was being kept busy with her campaign and had things on all weekend. Roslyn wasn't sure if it was an excuse or not. Dennis hadn't dallied for further conversation and Roslyn had decided to have her own small gathering for dinner.

"You should come in, Roslyn," Amber called. "It's great in here."

"I've already had a swim today."

Amber floated closer to Roslyn while Tom made an attempt to swim laps.

"Thanks for inviting us."

"You know you're welcome anytime."

Amber sat on the step beside Roslyn, the wet tank top clinging to her body accentuating her growing bulge.

"I'd tell you not to work so hard but I'm sure I'd be wasting my breath."

"I saw the doctor this week. She says I'm all good. I've got to keep working while I can. Get some money behind us."

"Surely you've got some breathing space now with the money from the car."

"She's giving it back." Tom had stopped swimming and was trying, not very successfully, to float.

"Shut up, Tom. I told you not to say anything about that." Amber kicked out with her foot, splashing him.

He sank, scrabbled away and bobbed up further down the pool. "I told her she was stupid."

"Why are you giving it back?" Roslyn asked gently.

Amber's face was screwed up in a tight frown as she continued to glare at Tom, who'd gone back to swimming laps.

"I didn't think it was fair. That poor lady had to sell her son's car to pay for his funeral. Neither of us knew it was worth so much. I've got a good car and a new phone – I think she should have the rest."

"It's very generous of you." Roslyn pondered just how generous and how decent Amber was being.

"Kayla helped me write the letter. I didn't want to ring and trip over my words and I wasn't sure quite how to say all that I had to say. We put her place as the return address."

"You could have used my PO Box."

Amber glared in Tom's direction. He was trying to float again. "I wanted to keep it quiet."

Roslyn nodded. "Fair enough." She completely understood wanting to keep charitable acts to yourself. "How about I put the chips in the oven now? Tom looks like he's working up an appetite."

"Not sure he deserves food now."

Roslyn chuckled. "Let's forgive him."

"Have you forgiven Margot yet?"

Roslyn was halfway to her feet. She glanced in the direction of her sister's house and straightened. "Sisters can be complicated."

"Some of the girls at the Hub have said how nice she is. They really like it when she does the cooking classes. When I said I lived out the back of Margot's sister's place they didn't know who you were but I said you were the better sister."

"That's very kind of you."

"Not kind. It's the truth. I reckon she's got a split personality or something."

"She seems to be under a lot of pressure. Sometimes that can affect the way people behave."

"There you go letting her off the hook again."

Roslyn smiled. "I'll put the chips in the oven. There are drinks in the bar fridge. You and Tom help yourself."

She glanced in the direction of Margot's place again as she went inside. Split personality was one way to describe her sister's current state but Roslyn didn't think that Margot's cantankerous behaviour was due to any medical condition. Now that Roslyn had had some time and space from her sister, the hurtfulness of their last encounter had abated. Unkindness was not normal behaviour for Margot.

Roslyn was quite sure taking the lead on opposing the hotel and also campaigning for mayor had a lot to do with Margot's Jekyll-and-Hyde conduct and she felt a twinge of guilt over it. Rightly or wrongly, Margot felt Roslyn had betrayed her and as the older and perhaps less melodramatic sister, she needed to do something about that.

Amber stretched out on the sun lounge and closed her eyes. She enjoyed her job at the pub and living at Roslyn's was so easy and comfortable she wished she could stay. If only her life was a fairytale and wishes came true.

A drip of water splashed her leg. She opened her eyes and Tom was there, rubbing himself dry with a towel. He shook his head and his shaggy hair splattered drips over her again.

"Hey," she growled.

He grinned and did it again.

She sat up, brushing at the drips on her legs. "Piss off!"

"Haven't heard that in a while," Tom teased.

"You haven't been this annoying for a while."

He sat on one of the other poolside chairs. "You looked too content lying there."

"I was."

Tom shrugged and looked back at the pool. "You're lucky, being here."

"I know. Wish I could stay."

"You moving out? Maybe Roslyn would let me live here for my last month."

"Geez, jump in my grave, why don't ya."

"Looking out for number one."

The pool gate clanged and Roslyn approached carrying a tray with glasses of iced water. "You two need to keep your fluids up," she said as she handed them one each.

"Thanks, Roslyn," Tom said. "I totally get why Amber's going to hate leaving here."

"No rush to do that." Roslyn's steady gaze was almost a physical force holding Amber to her seat.

"Can't stay forever." Amber sipped the icy water. "When I was at the Hub the other day the woman who helps people find accommodation said there was a flat that would soon be vacant and my name was at the top of the list for it."

"I see." Roslyn's face was stiff beneath her sunglasses.

"Sounds like a dump compared to the cottage," Amber joked. "But it's in Mount Barker, close to the Hub and not too far from shops and a small park."

"Not far from Jesserton either then."

"No. I can keep my job at the pub and at least the flat's mine for as long as I need it."

"It's a good start," Roslyn said. "I'm pleased for you."

"You gave me my first start." Amber swallowed some water to try to shift the lump that had formed in her throat.

"We didn't exactly begin as friends though, did we?" Roslyn chuckled.

Amber shook her head, smiling as she recalled the first time they met. "But we are now."

"Indeed we are. And you know you're always welcome here, even if it's just for a swim."

Roslyn tapped her glass against Amber's and they held each other's gaze a moment. Amber was pretty sure the determination she saw in Roslyn's look mirrored her own.

"So when Amber moves out…what will you do with the cottage?"

"Shut up, Tom!" Amber held out her glass, threatening to tip the icy contents on his head.

forty

It was a warm January night when Margot was finally able to convene the town meeting to update everyone on her hotel research. She'd chosen the small hall across the road from The General Providore for the meeting, hoping that at seven pm on a Tuesday evening there'd be enough in attendance to make Fred's front dining room too small but not so many that they needed the larger hall at the Lutheran church.

She didn't know whether to be pleased or concerned when the hall began to fill with not only locals but a few people from surrounding towns. The butterflies in her stomach flapped a little harder when she saw the various contenders for council were among the crowd, even Cameron who'd thought he wouldn't be able to make it – although at least he was a supportive contender; she wasn't sure about the others. And then the butterflies threatened to rise up her throat when she noticed the two men who were running for mayor, Brett Moss and Colin North, were also taking a seat. Not together – they were on opposite sides of the small hall, but she did wonder whether they'd colluded and decided to divide and conquer.

They were both nice enough men, although she found Colin rather fond of the sound of his own voice and Brett a little too smooth-talking for her liking. She'd met them at a council presentation earlier in the month and then run into them at various times as they'd been attending functions and events, getting out and about to meet as many people in the short time before the election as they could.

She scanned those gathered again. Dennis wasn't here, of course. She was still angry with him so she'd rather he wasn't in the audience to add to her unrest. She'd seen two of his golf mates come in though. Sam she didn't mind, but Grant she could have done without. Geraldine had planned to come but she'd had an upset tummy. She still ate the odd sneaky treat, and that meant she'd have a bad day or so. Margot wanted to take her in hand and help her prepare delicious food that was gluten free but she just hadn't had the time.

She noted Thelma, Fred, Greg and Sarah from the post office were there and so were Kev and Sandy, along with the man who was managing the new supermarket. Lots of familiar faces but no Roslyn. Margot hadn't expected her sister to come. They'd hardly spoken since the day they'd run into each other at Geraldine's, although Margot had heard plenty of praise for her sister and Gunter's Legacy from several different people. Roslyn had tried to make contact twice this week but Margot had shut her down.

As she took in the crowd, the butterflies were flapping so hard in her stomach she'd have almost welcomed Roslyn's steadying presence. Instead of chatting to fifteen or so people about her findings, as she'd thought would be here, there were more like forty, and when Tess Brown walked in with a couple of her cronies Margot truly thought she would vomit. She took the calming deep breaths she'd been practising then moved to the front of those gathered, straightening her shoulders and lifting her chin. If she was to be mayor she had to get used to this.

Roslyn slipped quietly into the back of the hall and edged along the wall to a space in the corner. She'd heard from Nick that Dennis wouldn't be at tonight's meeting. He'd muttered something about his dad having a prior commitment. Nick himself couldn't be there and Henry was unwell so Emily wasn't coming either, and Roslyn had been surprised to see Cam walk in ahead of her. She'd thought he was working late. Geraldine wouldn't be here. She'd been feeling poorly for a couple of days. Roslyn suspected it was probably to do with the pasty she'd bought from the Sheffield bakery. Geraldine was still coming to terms with what totally gluten free meant.

The mood was high in the community and Jesserton was divided on the topic of yes hotel or no hotel so the meeting could become fiery. Roslyn thought someone from the family should be here for Margot, although whether her sister would think she was a support or a detractor would be another matter. They'd still barely spoken two words to each other since Christmas.

Roslyn had tried on a couple of occasions since determining to mend the relationship the previous Sunday. She'd rung Margot but it had been a brief, stilted exchange. Margot had said she was in the middle of cooking and couldn't chat. Then two days ago Roslyn had called in at The General Providore and discovered Margot was no longer working there. Kath had seemed rather troubled by it but they hadn't been able to talk for long as the place had been busy. The Providore had been a special venture for both women and Roslyn had driven straight to Margot's house to find out what was going on. Margot had met her at the door, bag and keys in hand – she'd been on her way to a meeting and had no time to talk. Roslyn was very concerned her sister was boxing herself into a position that was untenable.

Someone moved into the space beside her. Roslyn glanced around and met Xavier Zamon's smile. He nodded and they both looked to the front as Margot began to speak.

"Thanks for coming, everyone." The rumble of voices quickly died away. "It's good to see so many here on such a warm evening. I promise not to keep you long."

Roslyn glanced up at the two ceiling fans, which were doing little to move the warm air. Several people were fanning themselves with hands or papers. She hoped they were all well hydrated.

Margot continued. "This meeting is to fill you in on my findings in regard to a hotel being built on the edge of Jesserton and…" She faltered as her gaze swept Roslyn and then moved on to Xavier. Margot cleared her throat. "I do understand there are differing views. My purpose here is to present the reasons why a hotel is not a good idea for our town."

There were a few mutters and mumbles but they went quiet as she continued. "When I went to the council to find out more, I did so on behalf of many in our community who were concerned about a hotel development on our doorstep. There are several reasons why I believe the hotel would be a detriment to our community."

"Mainly because it would be overlooking your place," a man interjected. Roslyn couldn't see his face but he was sitting next to Dennis's mate Sam.

"Actually, Grant, I'd like to clear the air on that right now," Margot replied with calm authority. "Earlier today I met with Meyer and Brightman's representative, Mr Zamon, who's here tonight." She nodded in their direction. A few people turned and muttering broke out. "Mr Zamon showed me the amended plans for the hotel, which were done after the initial feedback from the community. The hotel will now only be four storeys. The top floor will not be visible above the existing hill line and all rooms will have a view out across the valley rather than in the direction of my home or those across the Sheffield road on its other side. I'm no longer concerned about being spied on." She said it in a jokey voice and a few people chuckled. Roslyn quietly cheered her sister.

"I have other concerns, however, which I don't think have been adequately addressed and that I believe impact the whole community, not just me. The first is that the scope of this development is outside of anything built in the small communities of this region. It has a well-designed but extremely large footprint and will permanently scar the natural landscape of our region."

Margot continued, speaking clearly and listing each of the concerns: water, sewerage, traffic, noise and the impact on Jesserton. "We're a small community," she said. "We're used to some tourism, of course, and we welcome that, but we're not big enough to cope with the impact something of this scale would have. With a hotel of this size on our doorstep our little town would get no rest from outsiders who are only here on holiday. It might mean some additional jobs, but do we want the constant crowding of our streets and inundation of visitors and traffic that it would bring? I don't believe a hotel like the one proposed truly reflects the culture of our town."

"Neither do I." Sarah from the post office leaped to her feet and began clapping, which drew a larger response from the crowd.

"Excuse me." The man sitting next to Cameron rose to his feet. "There are a group of us here tonight representing the traders of the region outside Jesserton, which includes Hahndorf and other nearby towns." He waved his arm to take in the row beside him.

Roslyn could only see the back of Cam. He had his head down, shifting in his seat.

Their spokesman continued. "We're here to show support for the several businesses in Jesserton who think a hotel would be good for this region. As do we."

"It's not your town though, is it?" Thelma huffed.

"This is a Jesserton meeting," someone else called out and then lots of voices spoke at once.

Margot had to tap her foot loudly on the wooden floorboards to gain attention and when the noise died down she spoke again. "This meeting was simply so I could pass on what I've found out so far. Hopefully there will be other opportunities for individuals to debate the pros and cons. The final thing I want to say is a deal-breaker as far as I'm concerned." The last shuffles and mutters ceased as everyone in the hall focused on Margot again. "It comes back to the basic function of the land, which in the case of Gunter's place is primary production. His vines are some of the oldest in the Hills. They've been carefully hand tended and produce top quality grapes – something we should be proud of and not want to spoil. His property hasn't been rezoned and could not have a hotel built on it."

Roslyn sucked in a sharp breath as a loud burst of clapping ensued. Beside her, Zavier straightened and then Brett Moss rose to his feet and Roslyn's buoyancy over her sister's presentation trickled down to her shoes.

"Excuse me, Margot," Brett said. "I need to correct something you said. May I come forward?"

Margot nodded, and even from the back of the hall Roslyn could tell her composure had slipped.

Brett stood beside Margot, facing the crowd. "Good evening, everyone. My name's Brett Moss. I was a councillor until the by-election was called and I resigned to run for mayor. Like my friend Margot here." He smiled at Margot, and Roslyn got the clear impression of a cat sizing up a mouse. "I just want to read from the Plan SA fact sheet about rural value-adding developments." He waved a piece of paper in the air. "It's a while since you've been on council, Margot, but mayoral candidates were given this fact sheet in our packs at a recent council presentation that the three of us attended. We've all been very busy, of course, so perhaps you haven't had a chance to read it yet." He fixed Margot with a smug smile.

"I...I'm sure I did." Margot paled and Roslyn's heart sank.

"It's a few pages long so perhaps you didn't get to the end," Brett continued and Roslyn wanted to leap up and wipe the smile from his face. "It's only a small paragraph under the heading, Productive Rural Landscape Zone, which says, '*This zone promotes agriculture, horticulture, value adding opportunities, farm gate businesses, the sale and consumption of agricultural based products, tourist development and accommodation that expands the economic base and promotes its regional identity.*'" He looked up. "So there's no zoning reason as to why the hotel shouldn't go ahead."

Roslyn closed her eyes and blew out a breath as everyone began talking at once. She opened them again as Brett clapped his hands to call for attention. "Gunter Brost's land would be the perfect example for meeting the criteria for this new zoning regulation."

Rumbles and mutters swept the hall. Roslyn shifted the weight from her aching leg, her angst for her sister adding to the pain.

Brett held up his hands and the crowd settled.

"There's something else I thought you might like to know – I heard it just before I arrived here today. After gathering information and taking into account responses to the hotel development, including the petition you so capably organised, Margot, council will form an assessment panel to decide whether to back the proposal or not."

Fred leaped to his feet. "What does that mean?"

"A neutral panel made up of planners, architects, engineers and one representative from the local area, a councillor elected by council, will weigh up all the information and make a decision on the development which will then be sent to the developer." He looked out across the hall and Roslyn sensed his gaze fall upon Xavier beside her. Brett's smile widened and Rosyln glanced sideways to see the quick nod of Xavier's head.

"Gunter caused this mess," someone shouted.

Thelma leaped to her feet. "He did not. Gunter was a good man. He'd never have wanted a hotel on his property."

"He's not here to object," Sandy growled.

A chair was shoved aside.

More people stood, words were muttered then shouted between those who agreed a panel was a fair way to go and those who didn't, between those who wanted a hotel and those who objected.

Fred put his hands on Kev's shoulders, who had Greg by his shirt collar. As Fred tugged Kev back the shirt ripped. A scuffle began.

Roslyn ducked past and moved through the agitated crowd looking for Margot. She ran into Kath, who was doing the same thing. They both ducked as an empty paper cup flew over their heads.

"What a mess this has become," Roslyn said, keeping a wary eye out for any more missiles.

"That was pretty awful for Margot," Kath said.

"Hijacked at her own meeting," Roslyn said. "I think she must have slipped out the back and gone home. We should head there."

Kath looked down at her feet. "We've had a bit of a bust-up."

"Join the club." Roslyn put a hand on Kath's shoulder. "Let's get out of here. She needs her friends."

forty-one

Margot sat at the small table in the kitchen of The General Providore and put her head in her hands. Her life was over. Or at least the past sixty years of it. She wasn't going to die, not today, even if a small part of her imagined that the easier option. She pictured Roslyn's indignant snort at the idea. Right now Margot would be glad to hear her sister's censure but that was as likely as water turning to wine. She'd seen Roslyn at the back of the room beside Xavier, of all people, but then they had been in cahoots all along.

    She looked around the tidy kitchen, lit by the glow from the desk lamp. This was her escape room. She'd parked out the back of the Prov and walked to the hall. When she'd slipped away from the seething crowd she'd let herself in to the Prov instead of driving home. No-one was there so she might as well sit here alone as anywhere.

    She trailed her fingers across the stark white tabletop. It sparkled from the vigorous clean she'd just given it. Full of pent-up energy after the meeting, she'd gone over the kitchen from top to bottom. Every surface gleamed. There had been plenty said of her in recent times – doubts about her sanity, her loyalty, her love – but no-one could accuse her of leaving the place unclean.

Now she had no energy left and there was no avoiding her moment of reckoning. She had to go home and face her family. That sounded dramatic – something her detractors would say she was good at – but in truth it was how she felt, as if her world had imploded. The past few months had held drama and emotional pain building to tonight's debacle. The nausea quivering in the pit of her stomach and the lump lodged in her throat were constants now. Whatever the verdict with the bloody hotel, it hardly mattered any more, not to Margot. Everything else that mattered to her was in shreds; she didn't know who to trust or where to turn. Her husband, her sister, Kath, even Geraldine had betrayed her in some way. And tonight Cameron had added his knife to her back. He hadn't said anything, in fact he'd squirmed in his seat as the other chap had spoken, but he'd been part of the group of traders supporting the hotel. Margot could only assume Emily would be too.

She cast a final gaze around the room. It wouldn't have her name on it soon – one more heartbreak to come from her fork-in-the-road decision months earlier. She thought back on it. Opposing the hotel had been a community decision at first and somehow she'd taken the lead with it. Then the idea of being mayor had been seeded – by who? She'd been encouraged by Esther, Thelma and several others – even Kath and eventually Dennis and the rest of her family had thought it a good idea. She hadn't been alone then but she was now.

"I thought you might be here."

Margot's breath hitched. For a brief second she'd thought it had been her sister's voice. But of course it wouldn't be Roslyn.

"Geraldine?"

"Yes, it's me." Geraldine tugged the door further and came right in, her face flushed as if she'd been rushing. She blew out a breath, or was it a sigh? "We've been looking for you for ages."

"We?"

"Your family. Dennis, the children."

Margot drew in a deep, ragged breath. Not Roslyn though. There was no coming back from the damage caused by their last words. Words Margot regretted now but they'd been the final straw, not the whole kit and kaboodle. The demise of their relationship had been a slow burn that had begun years earlier, if the truth be known.

"Let's go home, Margot."

Geraldine smiled so kindly that Margot felt her already cracked heart would break right open. She dragged herself upright.

"Let me drive you," Geraldine said. "We can collect your car in the morning."

Margot glanced around the empty shop once more, drew back her shoulders and followed Geraldine out the door. She snibbed the lock and pulled it securely shut behind her. There was a bow in the wood and if you didn't tug it firmly sometimes it didn't latch. She'd been meaning to get a carpenter in to look at it. Still, it wasn't her problem any more. Kath would have to deal with it.

Geraldine's car was at a slight angle parked beside hers in the small space of the staff car park. They drove out onto the main street, which was empty of cars. Everyone had gone home. Another wave of embarrassment swept her as she replayed the end of the meeting and Brett's revelation making her look a fool. There'd been so much paperwork to take in and she had cast her eye over the document he'd referred to but he'd been right. She'd read the first part, which had seemed to support her stance of no hotel, and she hadn't read on. No-one would want to vote for a mayor who didn't have their facts straight.

"Are you okay, Margot?" Geraldine's question brought her focus back to her surroundings. They were turning into Roslyn's driveway.

"What are we going in here for?"

"Roslyn didn't want you to worry about anything but relaxing with a glass of wine, I think were her words."

"Roslyn?"

"This was all her idea."

"What was?"

Geraldine pulled into a space behind Nick's van and in front of that was Emily's car.

"What's going on?" The anxiety that had faded as they'd driven towards home surged through her again.

"Your family are waiting for you." Geraldine got out of the car, and when Margot didn't move she came round and opened the door. "Come on, enough self-pity for one day. Get out of the car."

Margot pressed her fingers to her lips and complied. She'd never heard Geraldine speak with such authority before. Margot trailed behind her through Roslyn's carport and out to the back garden where music played and people were sitting around the outdoor table.

"Here she is," Geraldine announced.

"Mum!" Emily hurried over and wrapped her in a big hug. "We heard it was a tricky meeting. I'm so sorry I wasn't there."

Margot glanced around. "How's Henry?"

"Sleeping. His temp's come down and Cam's home with the two of them." Emily winced. "He said he was sorry the meeting went how it did."

"You both want the hotel but you've never said."

Emily winced again. "We didn't at first but running a business isn't easy. You know that. The traders think a hotel will be good for all our businesses and Cam and I have come to agree."

"I see."

"We don't want this to divide us though, Mum." Emily's lips pulled into a beseeching smile. "Cam sends his best. He really didn't think the meeting would go like it did. Oh, and he said to tell…well, remind you, because you probably already know. A council assessment panel means anyone who's put in a response for or against the hotel is entitled to make a presentation to council."

Emily slipped an arm through hers and Margot sagged against her daughter. "I'm not sure it will make any difference." She was all out of fight.

Nick was on her other side, planting a kiss on her cheek. "Kayla's home with the boys but she wanted you to know she's thinking of you. We heard you had a rough night but don't give up, Mum. All that work you've done can still be presented to the panel."

"We'll see."

Dennis stepped up in front of her. The kids moved aside and he took her gently by the shoulders and pulled her in close. "I'm sorry, Margot. About everything," he murmured in her ear. They clung together for a moment and the comfort she found in her husband's arms eased the last of the tension from her body.

"Time for a glass of wine." Roslyn had moved up beside them. She held a glass of red towards Margot. "I've opened a bottle of 2010 shiraz. You know what a good year that was."

"Why?" Margot took the glass.

"Why not?" Roslyn tapped her glass against Margot's. "To you, my dear sister."

Tears brimmed in Margot's eyes. "I'm sorry, Roslyn."

"So am I. Let's put it behind us. You've had some troublesome times and I sincerely hope tonight's ambush by Brett Moss has lost him more votes than he gained."

"Roslyn's told us all about that," Dennis said. "I'm sorry I wasn't there. I would have punched that smart-arse Brett Moss right on the nose."

"That would have been a big help," Roslyn said. "Come and have something to eat. I haven't been cooking but Kath kindly brought some things." She stepped aside and it was then that Margot noticed her friend sitting at the table.

Kath rose warily to her feet. "Roslyn and I both looked for you after the meeting. It really wasn't very kind of Brett to shoot you down at your own gathering." She gave Margot a quick hug. "Where were you?"

"I found her in the kitchen at the Providore," Geraldine announced as if she'd discovered a pot of gold at the end of the rainbow. "I know that's her special place."

Kath huffed out a breath and shrugged. "Of course. You and I have to do some more talking about that."

"But not tonight,' Roslyn said. "No deep and meaningfuls – let's just relax. Nick, can you put on some music that's not quite so jagging on the nerves, please?"

Emily laughed. "We need Uncle Richard's playlist."

Nick pulled out his phone. "On it."

Margot sat at her sister's table and settled back into the comfy cushions on the chair. Around her the conversation went on.

"Not that song, Nick, it's too dreary," Emily chided her brother.

"You pick then," he snipped back.

"That's not gluten free, Geraldine," Kath said as Geraldine reached for a savoury tart. "These two plates are both GF."

"A little doesn't hurt," Geraldine said, gazing wistfully at the tarts.

"Surely you learned your lesson this week," Roslyn said. "Remember how bad you were feeling earlier today? That's a much better song thanks, Nick."

"Thanks to me," Emily said.

Kath laughed. "Bloody kids. They don't stop bickering even when they're adults."

Margot caught Roslyn's eye across the table. Roslyn quirked an eyebrow at her and grinned.

Beside her Dennis slipped his hand into hers and gave it a squeeze. And for the first time in a long time Margot felt like part of her family again.

forty-two

Amber cast her gaze over Roslyn's outdoor setting. Everything looked to be in place. No doubt she'd be told if it wasn't. Roslyn had been barking orders all afternoon. It was autumn and while today had been quite warm, the evenings had started to get chilly so first they'd set up inside in Roslyn's larger living area. Then, when the day looked to be holding its warmth and they'd realised Cameron's family and friends were coming too, Roslyn had decided it would be nicer out by the pool where there was more room.

She was hosting Cameron's and Margot's election party – or non-election party, depending on how the count went. Amber wasn't registered to vote but even if she had been she still wasn't sure if she'd have voted for Margot. Evidently the two sisters had forgiven each other and once again Amber thought if she'd been in Roslyn's shoes she wasn't sure she'd have been so kind, but Roslyn had said there'd been fault on both sides.

She moved around the table and placed a hand over her belly as it brushed the back of a chair. Sometimes she still forgot there was a baby in there but the way her belly was growing she was worried about how much longer she'd be able to work in the confined space behind Fred's bar.

"People are arriving." Roslyn bustled towards her carrying a cheese platter in each hand. Amber took them and placed them on the table as Roslyn went to greet the first guests arriving in her backyard. They weren't people Amber knew but Roslyn was guiding them towards her and Amber found herself tugging at her shirt and straightening her shoulders.

"Come and meet Amber." Roslyn rattled off their names. "She's one of the family these days and she's been a wonderful help to me today."

Amber immediately took drink orders — something she knew she was good at — and hurried off to organise them with an extra spring in her step and a warm glow in her belly that had nothing to do with the baby stirring inside her. She'd got used to being around Roslyn, she was happy in the older woman's company. Roslyn was almost like the grandmother Amber had never known. And she'd introduced Amber as one of the family. That had meant so much to Amber she'd had to bite her lip to stop the tears brimming.

She returned with the drinks as Isabella burst into the yard squealing, "My daddy's a councillor, my daddy's a councillor."

She was closely followed by her parents and baby brother and another crowd of people Amber didn't know. The party cranked up, along with whatever the hell the music was Emily had playing. Amber was flat out keeping drinks up to everyone. Nick arrived with his boys as Amber and Roslyn were topping up the fancy glass bowl with the punch concoction people were enjoying.

"Where's Mum?" he asked.

"Not here yet." Roslyn checked her watch. "She sent me a text earlier saying it's close and they were still counting but I would have thought they'd be here by now."

A particularly loud screech came from the speaker. Roslyn winced. "Do you think you could put on a more suitable playlist?"

"With pleasure." Nick grinned. "Kayla will be here soon. She's just waiting for something to finish baking. Can't get her out of the kitchen now that we've finished doing it up."

Amber set off to take drink orders and was just pouring more champagne when the music suddenly changed to ABBA's "Take a Chance on Me". Cheers and clapping erupted as Margot and Dennis made their way along the path from the carport.

They stopped by Roslyn's back door and both held up their hands for quiet. Nick cut the music and a hush fell over those gathered.

Margot drew herself up. "Thank you, everyone, for your support for me in this campaign."

There were cheers and wolf whistles and Emily and Nick and their children joined their parents then Margot held up her hands again.

"Colin North didn't attract many votes but it was tight in the end between Brett and me..." She glanced at Dennis. "However, the numbers weren't in my favour."

Soft murmurs and groans rippled through the crowd.

"I lost by less than twenty votes. Brett Moss is your new mayor."

The groans built to a crescendo and Margot held up her hands once more.

"Had I won I would have thrown my heart and soul into the role but a small part of me is relieved. Now I'll have time to put into several other projects that are also very important to me." Margot spread out her arms to pull her three older grandies in close. "My family, of course." Then she looked at Dennis. "Our dealership is getting busier and I've neglected that for some time." She nodded at Kath who was standing to the side. "My dear friend and business partner and I have expanded our business and I'm taking a slightly different role there, focusing on staff training and function catering. And then there's my sister Roslyn, who needs my help managing the most generous legacy left by our big-hearted neighbour Gunter."

People clapped and cheered and the sombre mood that had followed Margot's first announcement lifted a little.

"What about the hotel development?" someone called.

"Oh, yes." Margot nodded emphatically. "I won't be giving up on that until the final decision is made." There were cheers, perhaps not quite as loud as they had been for Margot's other announcements but then Amber assumed not all of the people in Roslyn's backyard were against the hotel.

When it was quiet again Margot called Cameron to join them. "We will have one member of the family on council. Congratulations, Cameron! We know you'll be wonderful in the role and we're all here to support you."

Once again people clapped and cheered. The music started up again, this time John Farnham belting out "Playing to Win", and Amber got back to pouring drinks.

Roslyn waited until people had finished offering Margot a mix of commiserations and best wishes. Finally the two of them stood alone. She pressed a glass into Margot's hand. "You must be thirsty. Try some of my punch."

Margot took the glass, eyeing its contents suspiciously.

"You spoke very well," Roslyn said. "How are you feeling?"

"A little bit annoyed. I hate being beaten by that smug-faced Brett." Margot took a small sip from the glass, swallowed and took a bigger gulp. "However, I do believe he'll be a good mayor. Better than I would have been, probably."

"Well, we won't know that now, will we?"

"The biggest feeling I have is relief. Until that final result was announced I'd been living under the weight of worry about how I was going to manage, and in the blink of an eye the weight lifted." Margot shook her head and lifted her arms as if she were a priest offering a blessing. "I feel so much lighter, so much better. People told me I should run for mayor and I listened to them instead of myself. Even you said I could do it."

"I still do but only if it's what you want. I don't think I ever said 'Margot, you should run for mayor'."

"You told me to stand up for what I believe in."

"Yes, but—"

"To take the emotion out of my speeches and presentations and make my point succinctly."

"There's a difference between being assertive and being aggressive."

Margot's shoulders slumped. "I turned into a bully."

"Not exactly." Roslyn's heart ached for her sister. "Public office is demanding and it's not for everyone. I think back when you first proposed to run for mayor I said something like it can be a difficult path and you needed to weigh up the pros and cons and decide if it was worth the angst."

Margot sighed. "It wasn't."

"You do so much for your family and your community. You're going to be far too busy to worry about being mayor." Roslyn hesitated. "And what you said about helping me with Gunter's Legacy?"

"I'd be happy to represent Gunter's Legacy on the Hub committee."

"That would be such a relief. I really don't enjoy meetings any more."

"You said it was all going well except your idea of using granny flats as emergency accommodation."

"I've spoken to people with flats in their yards but only a couple thought they might be involved."

"When you say spoken to people…I bet you told them with the sparsest detail and just expected them to go along with your plan."

"Well, I—"

"What you need is some kind of guarantee that they won't get stuck with a tenant like you were. The whole town knows that story. If I was going to let strangers use my granny flat I'd want reassurance that they had support, that wear and tear or even damage would be covered. And—"

"Margot, Roslyn," Dennis called. "Come and join the party. You can chinwag later."

"You go," Roslyn said. "I've got some more food to bring out."

"Let me help."

"I've got plenty of helpers." Roslyn shooed her away and went inside.

She paused in front of the flying ducks.

"Wish you were here, Gunter, but then I suppose we wouldn't be able to do all this work without your generous legacy. Between Elvin, Margot and me it's in good hands, my friend."

"Do you think he can hear you?"

Roslyn pressed a hand to her chest as she spun to meet Amber's steady gaze. "Where did you come from?"

"Getting more glasses from your lounge cabinet."

Roslyn took in the stemmed glasses threaded between Amber's fingers and blew out a breath. "You scared me."

"Sorry, but I was worried." Amber grinned. "First I thought you were talking to yourself and you know what that's a sign of."

"Cheeky," Roslyn said and slipped an arm around Amber's shoulders. "I wish you could have met Gunter. He would have liked you."

"So do you think he can?"

"Can what?"

"Hear you."

Roslyn looked back at the ducks and smiled. "I do."

forty-three

"Thanks, Margot." Lani's serious expression softened. "I really like my cooking sessions with you."

Margot nodded as a small ripple of pride swept her. She enjoyed cooking with Lani. "You're doing so well. That sauce is a tricky one to master but you've got it down pat."

Margot glanced around the tidy kitchen they'd just cleaned. "I think we've earned a coffee."

The two of them had come in early to use the kitchen while Kath and one of the casual girls managed the shop. Most customers in the first few hours of the day only wanted coffee or bread or a quick snack to take with them. Margot had to admit the new take-away breakfast menu was popular.

"I'll make them," Lani said.

Margot sat at the small table they used as a desk and tidied the papers on it. Kev's account was on the top. It reminded her of the awful night of the meeting. People were still divided about the hotel but most, like Cameron and Emily, were at least civil about it. Some, however, had cemented their differences with harsh words and physical violence. Since the meeting and their scuffle, Greg from the plant shop and Kev from the butcher didn't speak and their wives supported them, causing further division. Neither shopped in each other's business and Margot had heard Greg's wife no longer had her hair done by Sandy either, changing to a hairdresser in Mount Barker after almost twenty years of patronage.

"Coffee for you." Kath placed a mug in front of her and sat opposite with one for herself. "Lani's chatting to some friends who've come in so I'm taking a quick break. We'll have a small lull before the mid-morning rush." She raised her mug. "We're doing well, team Providore," she said and met Margot's gaze.

Margot nodded. "You were right about the early trade."

"And you were right that it's a lot extra but I think we're starting to get the balance sorted. The new casual's going well." Kath nodded towards the shop.

"I'm glad we're training people from the Hub," Margot said. "It seemed too hard before but now with more of us it's easy to have a trainee as well."

"And with Lani cooking you'll be able to concentrate on the catering jobs." Kath suddenly lurched back. "I forgot to tell you. You'll never believe what snippet of gossip Thelma had this morning."

Margot shook her head.

"She reckons Fred's changing his mind about the boutique hotel now."

Margot nodded. "He is."

Kath tipped her head to the side. "I'm sorry, Margot. He was one of your staunch supporters."

"It makes sense for his business. If the new hotel doesn't have a restaurant he could get a lot of extra trade. He's been wanting to do up his kitchen for years. Maybe it will mean he'll have the money to do it."

"You're being very magnanimous."

Margot sighed. "Pragmatic, I think. I can see both sides these days. I still believe the hotel, if it goes ahead," Margot still sincerely hoped it wouldn't but it was looking more and more likely, "will make changes to our community that people may regret further down the track, but I don't want to end up like Kev and Greg."

"And others. Summer and Larry have a huge sign on their front gate saying 'Ban the hotel'. The young mums' group has split into two."

"That's such a shame."

"We're good though, aren't we?"

Margot smiled at her friend. "Of course."

"If the hotel does go ahead we'll probably need more staff and I've been wondering about using our backyard as an alfresco area."

Margot gripped her coffee cup and took a sip.

"Sorry. I'm getting carried away, aren't I." Kath made a grimacey smile and held out her cup. "To the Prov."

Margot held hers up. "And to friends."

Amber pushed the last box into the spare room of the two-bedroom flat. She'd been on the go all day shifting from Roslyn's cottage. She stopped, put her hands to her back and stretched to get some relief from the ache.

The flat had come with basic furniture but little else. It had looked a bit glum after the cottage, but the people at the Hub had told her to take her pick from the donated household items they received and she'd managed to find a few extra bits and pieces to give the flat a cosy feel.

Kayla had helped her organise stuff for the baby. She looked at the bassinette set up beside her bed in readiness. It was two weeks till the baby was due and she still couldn't imagine actually holding it in her arms. She put a hand to her stomach. It was quiet now but it had been almost as busy as her earlier, stretching and poking her tight tummy as if she'd swallowed an alien.

Beside the bassinet was a modern chest of drawers with a change table on top. Amber had been surprised when Emily had asked if she'd like it. Evidently she and Cam weren't having any more kids and they'd put in an offer on a house near their shop they hoped to get. Emily said she wasn't taking anything there she didn't need.

Amber had been grateful for the furniture but still not sure how to take Emily. She was like Margot in so many ways. Amber often got the feeling she wasn't good enough for them but as she ran her hand over the top of the drawers and adjusted the container of wipes and creams Emily had bought for her, she thought she should give them the benefit of the doubt.

She stretched again, groaned and wished she could soak in Roslyn's bath. She took one of the new towels from the cupboard – another gift but from Margot this time – and decided to test out the shower.

Half an hour later she was dry and dressed again but instead of easing the pain had become unbearable. She moved around the flat unable to settle and feeling just a little scared. Had she overdone it with all the moving? Roslyn had warned her to take it easy but she hadn't listened.

She stopped her pacing and gripped the back of a chair as a warm sensation trickled down her legs. She looked down at the wet patches on her pants then grabbed her phone.

"Roslyn," she gasped as soon as the call went through.

"What's wrong?"

"I think it's the baby."

"I'm on my way."

forty-three

Dinner at Margot's

Vegetable Pâté on Crusty Bread, Spinach Artichoke Zucchini Bites

Pork & Apple Rissoles, Black Bean Burgers, Grilled Vegetable Salad with Beluga Lentils & Sesame Dressing, (Fillet Steak)

Blueberry Cheesecake Pie

Margot swept her gaze around her tidy kitchen, glanced at her watch and went out to the entertainment area where the table was set and all was in readiness for her first family dinner since Christmas. The rest of the family had taken turns while she'd been caught up with the election campaign but now that was all behind her and she'd put up her hand to host tonight's meal. She was ready with some time to spare so she sat in one of the comfortable recliners by the window.

It had taken longer than she'd expected to prepare the food. She'd had no trouble with the pâté and bites for starters or the rissoles, but the wheels had all but fallen off after that. She'd come across the black bean burger recipe while desperately looking for something a bit different to the usual that was both vegetarian and able to be barbecued. Not only did the recipe tick those boxes but it was also vegan, which meant no egg and then Isabella could eat them too. With a few gluten-free buns it also suited Emily and Geraldine.

The first hiccup had been when Dennis had seen the list of ingredients and had stormed off to buy some fillet steak, muttering about those who wanted some decent meat on the barbecue. Margot had thought her delicious pork-and-apple rissoles fitted that bill. The next hiccup had been when her first attempt at the black bean burger recipe had resulted in a black sludge at the bottom of her food processor. And then it had happened again. Thank goodness she'd bought extra ingredients. On her third try she'd ended up with a patty that shaped well and didn't fall apart. At least she'd made the blueberry cheesecake the previous night.

Dennis came from the house with an armload of bottles. "Here you are," he said. "Just topping up the drinks fridge."

"Then we're ready. Come and sit down." She patted the chair next to her and once he'd put the drinks in the fridge he joined her.

"How was golf?" she asked.

"Don't want to talk about it. I had a shocker of a round."

"Bad luck."

"How did your day go?"

"Fine except I had a terrible time making the black bean burgers." She put her hand up as soon as Dennis opened his mouth. "I don't want to talk about it."

They both grinned.

"We're okay, aren't we, Margot?"

"Of course."

"I'm sorry about the thing with Gunter's land and—"

"It was my dream, not anyone else's. I get that now. The house Em and Cam are buying is close to their shop and much better suited to their needs. Turns out they prefer a more modern home. One without draughts and creaky floorboards, I think Em said."

"The kids don't need handouts. They have to stand on their own feet."

"I know." Margot stared at her beautifully set table. She and Dennis would probably never agree on what that meant but she wasn't going to spoil the moment with an argument.

"Friday-night drinks after work went well." He smiled. "Thanks to you and your catering. The staff love it."

"I'm glad we'll be doing that once a month again."

"I saw you getting your ear bashed by the admin staff at one stage."

"Not bashed, we were just discussing the layout of the office. We've spent a lot of money in other areas of the business and that office really needs a makeover."

"They haven't said anything to me."

"I think they have but they didn't feel as if they were listened to."

Dennis winced. "That's why I like having you involved again. You're much better at all that…" He waved a hand. "Aesthetics and organisational stuff."

"Nanny!"

Isabella's face pressed to the glass door and Dennis leaped to his feet. "Here they are. Let's get the party started."

Amber followed Roslyn across the yard, her baby hugged to her chest and her feet dragging. Even though she'd been attending family dinners and Margot had been present, this would be her first at Margot's house and the first since the early arrival of Amber's son two weeks prior.

Roslyn stopped at the door and turned back to wait for her. "Come on. Anyone would think I was taking you to have your head chopped off. You're part of this family now so you have to endure Margot's dinner just like I do."

Whether it was the mention of being part of the family or Roslyn's teasing dig at her sister, Amber wasn't sure but her steps sped up anyway.

They paused at the door and Roslyn gently lifted the wrap. "He's just perfect, you know."

"Thanks to you."

"Rubbish!"

"I panicked."

"But you were fine once you got to hospital and you've taken to being a mother like a duck to water."

"Once again, thanks to you. It's been good staying at your place and having your help."

"I've enjoyed it." Roslyn looked away quickly. "They've seen us – we'd better go in."

They were met by a clamour of greetings. Everyone wanted to look at the baby, even though they'd all called in at various times in the last two weeks while Amber had been staying at Roslyn's.

"Can I hold him?" Emily asked.

Amber handed over her son and was offered a drink. She chose beer, earning a raised-eyebrow look from Margot and a grin from Roslyn. She hadn't had a beer since Tom's farewell drinks a few weeks before the baby had been born and she fancied one today.

Amber stood to one side a moment, taking in Margot's outdoor room. It was huge, nearly as big as half the cottage, and styled like one of those fancy house magazines.

Nick arrived with her beer. "Enjoy," he said.

"I'm glad you've come, Amber." Kayla joined them. "I've got something for you." She held out a letter. "It came Friday but I haven't had a chance to bring it over."

Amber stared at the envelope Kayla held as if it had the power to bite her. In truth it did. It had to be from the lady she'd bought the car from. When there'd been no reply in the first few weeks after she'd sent the letter Amber had almost forgotten about it. Only when she checked her bank balance, which she did less often these days, did she ponder the dent it would make to give the money back.

"Would you like me to open it?" Kayla asked gently.

Amber nodded. She felt sick. She wanted to return the money but a tiny part of her had hoped she wouldn't have to, especially now that she had her baby.

Kayla took out the page, glanced over it then offered it to Amber. "You should read it."

Amber shook her head.

"Perhaps you should have some water." Nick swapped her beer for a glass of water. "You look a bit pale."

Amber sipped, her gaze not leaving the letter in Kayla's hands.

"She apologises for taking so long to reply but she's been away." Kayla reached out and squeezed Amber's hand. "She thanks you for your honesty but it turns out her son owned his flat and he had a life insurance policy. She wants you to keep the money."

Nick grabbed the glass as it slipped through Amber's fingers. "Come and sit down." He directed her to a chair.

"What's happened?" Roslyn's concerned face appeared in front of Amber.

"The lady...the lady..." Amber gave Kayla a pleading look.

"The lady who sold Amber the car wants her to keep the money," Kayla said.

"That's good news." Roslyn frowned at Amber. "From the look of you I was worried it was something bad."

Nick pushed the glass into Amber's hand. "Drink more water."

She did as he asked and as she did the news sank in. "That's so kind of her." Amber managed to get the words out.

"Good things happen to good people." Kayla smiled at her.

"It's karma," Roslyn said.

"Do come and help yourselves, everyone," Margot called. "We're starting without Geraldine. She's just rung to say she's running late. It's finger food so you don't have to sit."

"Let's get some food into you," Nick said and offered Amber a hand.

She stared at it a moment.

"He's being chivalrous," Roslyn said. "It's okay to accept if you want."

Amber frowned. She had no idea what that word was that Roslyn had just said but she took Nick's hand and let him help her up. She'd recovered quickly after the birth but she was constantly tired and grateful she'd been able to stay with Roslyn.

Margot offered a plate of assorted food. "The pâté's vegetable. I think you'll like it."

Amber eyed the green paste. It looked like something that came out of her baby's bum. She chose one of the bites and then sat again, next to Emily this time, who was cuddling the baby and trailing one finger down his cheek. His lips tugged in and out in a sucking motion.

"He's just perfect. I could take him home," Emily said then laughed. "Here I am getting clucky and Cam and I have definitely decided no more babies."

"It'll be cool by the time you head back. I thought you might use this." Amber stiffened at the sight of the knitted blanket being thrust at her by Margot.

"She might not want that, Mum." Emily nudged Amber. "Grandpa knitted it. It's a bit fusty."

"I remember that rug," Nick said. "Grandpa was so proud to give it to us and it's a good warm one if you live in the Hills." He looked down at his sister. "Kayla and I were pleased to have it."

Emily blew out a small huff.

Amber lifted her gaze to Margot's. The older woman tugged her bottom lip over her teeth, a hesitant look on her face. Just beyond her Roslyn appeared, her eyes wide with concern, her face set as if she were holding her breath. Amber had never thought the two at all alike and yet in that moment, almost side by side, waiting for Amber's response, the sisterly resemblance was strong.

"Are you sure?" Amber asked.

"It seems I'm not getting any more grandchildren," Margot said. "I'd like you to have it."

"Thanks." Amber reached up and took the blanket, draping it over her baby, and it was as if the air around them shifted and settled with it. "I'd love him to have such a special keepsake."

"Good." Margot spun away but not before Amber caught the glint of tears in her eyes.

Isabella adjusted the blanket then looked up at Amber. "Does your baby have a name?"

"He's called Ross."

"That's a good name." The little girl gave an emphatic nod.

"It's a kind of mix of names of two people who've been very good to me. Your great-aunty Roslyn and a man I used to know called Russ."

Amber met Roslyn's gaze. They exchanged a brief smile then Roslyn turned away.

"I like that name," Isabella said.

"It is so hard trying to decide, isn't it?" Emily said. "A name is with them for life."

"It needs to suit the child," Nick said. "And you don't want a name every second kid's got." He looked pointedly at his sister.

"Well, at least my kids have names that are easy to spell." She looked in the direction of her nephews. "Azariah and Nahaliel will forever have to spell their names for people."

"Come on, folks, eat up." Dennis stepped in between his children and began filling his plate. "You know Margot has lots more food coming. Amber, you too." He passed her the plate he'd just loaded with bites. "No need to hang back. We're all family."

There was that word again. It settled around Amber like a warm blanket.

Roslyn and Kayla hadn't moved to the table yet.

"I'm so pleased the car and the money worked out for Amber," Roslyn said.

"She's got a good head on her shoulders and she's been going to the 'balance your budget' sessions at the Hub. I think she'll be fine as long as that awful ex of hers doesn't turn up again."

"I was worried about that too but Amber heard from her friend. Evidently he and his new girlfriend have done a runner interstate. The police had been asking questions about some fight that happened outside the pub and there were questions about the girlfriend. She's younger than Amber."

"Probably jumped from the frying pan into the fire like Amber. Guys like Tyson pick up young girls doing it tough and promise them a better life, then ditch them when they're done with them. Amber was lucky to run into you when she did. It's so good she has you to offer support."

Roslyn glanced at Amber chatting with the others. "She's got all of us. She's family now."

"What are you two doing over here?" Margot chided. "Eat, eat."

Kayla dutifully headed to the table.

"Is Geraldine okay?" Roslyn asked.

"Yes. She said she'd tried to cook something to bring and it didn't work out. She should be here soon."

"Thanks for making Amber so welcome. She was a bit nervous about coming here."

"To my place?" Margot winced. "I suppose we didn't get off to a good start. You were right though—"

"Of course."

Margot wrinkled her nose. "She's a nice young woman and she deserves a chance."

"I'm glad you get on. I hope she'll feel comfortable to visit us regularly. And I'd like to be a kind of surrogate grandmother to her baby."

"When does she leave your place?"

"Tomorrow. It'll be quiet without them."

"Not for long. I can add you to the emergency housing list. I'm sure we'll have someone else living in the cottage soon enough. I've got four other granny flats and each one is occupied at the moment."

"That's two more than I had."

"I think my approach may have been different to yours."

"I'm sure you're right."

"I think the scheme will grow once people see it working." Margot fixed her sharp gaze on Roslyn. "It's got a good bank balance behind it."

"Mmm. Gunter's Legacy was large."

"I've seen the books, Roslyn. Gunter's money for the various projects is allocated. The granny flat scheme is being funded by you, isn't it?"

Roslyn scratched at her neck. "It's the cut Gunter left me for looking after the place and coming up with the plan for his legacy."

"That's very generous."

Roslyn shrugged. "I'm well looked after. I didn't need it and so many people can benefit from it. After I had Amber come and stay in the cottage it made me think about all those hardly used flats in people's yards and how many people out there are doing it tough like she was. Sometimes people just need a place to stay for a while and a bit of a helping hand."

"Just like Gunter would have wanted."

"Yes."

Dennis laughed loudly at something Cameron said. Roslyn and Margot both stared in their direction.

"You knew Dennis hadn't put in an offer for Gunter's place, didn't you?" Margot said softly.

Roslyn pursed her lips and nodded. "I shouldn't have. Elvin asked me to sit in on the meeting they held to discuss the proposals put forward with each bid. It was meant to be anonymous so that I focused on the ideas. The outlines for the proposals didn't have the name of the bidder or how much they bid. I was early for the meeting and when the agent left the room for a minute the actual list of bidders was sitting on her desk."

"And you had a look?"

This time Roslyn winced when she nodded. "It was only a quick glance but they were all names I recognised, developers of one ilk or another and wineries."

"You didn't tell me."

"I truly was sworn to secrecy, Margot."

Margot put up her hands. "I know, I know."

"I'm sure Gunter would hate to think that his legacy had caused angst between us. That wouldn't have been his intention."

"I bet he wouldn't have liked the idea of a hotel on his property."

"The right kind of hotel maybe. After all, the money raised is doing so much good."

"I'll continue to fight it. I've got a lot of detailed objections to present to the council panel and I'm not alone."

"I know." Roslyn nodded. "But we won't let that come between us, will we?"

"No."

"Hello, everyone," Geraldine's sing-song voice called out as she stepped through the door carrying a shopping bag.

"Don't you look lovely?" Margot said.

Geraldine looked down at the vibrant floral dress that actually had some shape to it. "I bought it at that new boutique that's opened in the old shop beside the supermarket."

"I haven't had a chance to get in there yet."

"They've got some lovely things." Geraldine lifted a small box from her bag. "My cake was a failure so I picked these up at the supermarket. They're a mini dessert selection and they're gluten free."

"That's thoughtful of you," Margot said as she accepted the box.

"And while I was there I discovered they have a wine section." Geraldine pulled a bottle from the bag.

"In the supermarket?" Margot asked.

"Yes. I thought you might like to try this, Roslyn." She handed over a bottle.

Roslyn peered at the label in surprise. Supermarkets in South Australia weren't licensed to sell wine. She pursed her lips. It was non-alcoholic. She was prepared to give up many things but there was no way she was going to give up wine with alcohol in it.

"That's so nice of you, Geraldine," Margot said.

"How have you been?" Roslyn asked and immediately regretted it as Geraldine put a hand to her hip and leaned in.

"I've had a bit of an ache in my hip this last week. I hope I'm not getting that arthritissy thing that you have."

"Probably, Geraldine," Roslyn snapped. "At least half the population over sixty has some kind of arthritis."

"Oh, but I'm only fifty-seven."

Margot put an arm around Geraldine and drew her away. "Let's get you some of these nibbles before they're all gone." Margot threw a dagger look over her shoulder at Roslyn.

"That was a bit naughty," Amber muttered softly in her ear.

"Perhaps," Roslyn said and she smiled.

acknowledgements

The Adelaide Hills is a picturesque region of South Australia, only a short drive from Adelaide and a wonderful setting for this story. If you visit you will find the towns of Mount Barker, Hahndorf and Stirling but the others mentioned, including Jesserton, are fictional. Many small towns dot the region, which is the traditional land of the Peramangk people. Each town has their own uniqueness, and little bits of them were cobbled together to create Jesserton which exists only in my imagination and in this book.

I had chats with councillors, mayors and council employees to gather background for this story. And I want to send huge thanks to Ros Talbot, Rebecca Hewett and Andy Humphries who spent a lot of extra time answering my questions. What I gathered is that each council and each project has variations and nothing is straightforward when it comes to planning so I've taken the proverbial poetic licence and the various fictitious deviations are my own.

Thanks also to Cathy Obst for some insight into the workings of community support networks, to John Vasey for some background on car dealerships, and fellow author and GP Katie McMahon for medical advice, which, like Geraldine I may or may not have fully embraced. I'm very grateful to these three for their input and once again the diversions from reality are mine.

In the business corner thanks to my brilliant publisher, Jo Mackay, and my very talented editor, Annabel Blay, for loving this story and helping me make it the best it can be. You two are a dynamic duo. I'm so lucky to be working with you on this book, number seventeen, and hopefully there will be many more. And I'm very grateful for the keen eye of proofreader Annabel Adair. So many talented people make up the crew at HQ who bring this book to you – publishing director Sue Brockhoff; Jo Munroe, Eloise Plant, Stuart Henshall and the marketing team; Karen-Maree Griffiths and the sales team; and a shout-out to the design team headed up by Mark Campbell and with special thanks to Louisa Maggio and Darren Holt for another truly spectacular cover. You're the best!

In my home corner, as ever I am very grateful to my wonderful friends and family who help in so many ways. Thanks to you all and in particular to my husband, Daryl, for being my rock and making sure we're fed. Our children, their partners and our grandchildren are always encouraging and helpful in so many ways, from untangling plot points, to chauffeuring, to delivering kisses and hugs – Kelly, Steven, Harry, Archie, Dylan, Sian, Jared, Alexandra and Lawrence, thank you. This book is dedicated to the last three on the list. The Stringattas helped me with background and tweaks and I had many short writing retreats on their Adelaide Hills property to soak up the atmosphere and give reality to my setting. Family are also my first readers and this time Daryl, Kelly and Jared all gave me useful feedback in those early drafts. It really takes the whole family to write a book and I'm so grateful for mine.

The support of my writing colleagues is invaluable and for this book special thanks to Victoria Purman for our regular catch-ups and chats to keep both of us adding words to the page, and for an early brainstorming session where we went over the initial concept and the various ways it might pan out. Whenever I went down another research rabbit hole concerning council procedures, I may have cursed that session but I am grateful to you, Vic, truly.

Thank you to book reps, booksellers, librarians, reviewers, bloggers, and to you dear reader, wherever you are. I appreciate your support. You can keep in touch via Facebook and Insta and hear what I've been up to by subscribing to my quarterly newsletter. My website has the latest news about books and events and also has an email link where you can drop me a line. I love to hear from you.

Once more I've created a playlist on Spotify to follow this story. I couldn't resist coming up with an assortment of music for Richard's pool party list and I added in a few extras, some mentioned in the book and some just because. You'll find the playlist under my name and it's called "Head for the Hills".

I had so much fun, or was it procrastination, searching for the recipes that are listed at the start of each dinner chapter. I can't say I've made them all myself although some of them have gone on my 'recipes to try' list. I thought you might like to check them out and as most of them are available on the internet I've created a Pinterest page. Once again search my name and "Head for the Hills".

And finally a gentle reminder to do those early detection screenings, they might just save your life. www.cancer.org.au/cancer-information/causes-and-prevention/early-detection-and-screening

book club questions

- Roslyn and Margot both relied on each other to have their back through all of life's ups and downs. Why did that change during the story?
- If you have a sister, how did reading this book make you feel about your own relationship with her?
- If you don't have a sister or don't get along with your sister, how did you feel reading this book?
- What ideas did you have about homelessness and homeless people before you read the book? Have your ideas changed after reading about Amber's experiences? How so?
- Amber had a lot of odds stacked against her throughout her life. What qualities in her allowed her to be particularly resilient?
- If you lived in Jesserton would you be for or against the development? Why?
- Which character did you find the most complex or intriguing and why?
- What were some of your favourite scenes from the book? Why did they stand out for you?

talk about it

Let's talk about books.

Join the conversation:

@harlequinaustralia

@hqanz

@harlequinaus

harpercollins.com.au/hq

If you love reading and want to know about our authors and titles, then let's talk about it.